It's amazing what you can use for a ramp, given the right motivation.

Someone's collapsed fence was blocking half the road, jutting up at an angle, and I hit it at about fifty miles an hour. The handlebars shuddered in my hands like the horns of a mechanical bull, and the shocks weren't doing much better. I didn't even have to check the road in front of us because the moaning started as soon as we came into view. They'd blocked our exit fairly well while Shaun played with his little friend, and mindless plague carriers or not, they had a better grasp of the local geography than we did. We still had one advantage: Zombies aren't good at predicting suicide charges. And if there's a better term for driving up the side of a hill at fifty miles an hour with the goal of actually achieving flight when you run out of "up," I don't think I want to hear it.

The front wheel rose smoothly and the back followed, sending us into the air with a jerk that looked effortless and was actually scarier than hell. I was screaming. Shaun was whooping with gleeful understanding. And then everything was in the hands of gravity, which has never had much love for the terminally stupid. We hung in the air for a heart-stopping momen̲t̲ ̲.̲.̲.̲ ̲a̲t̲ ̲l̲e̲a̲st I was fairly sure the

FEED

MIRA GRANT

www.orbitbooks.net

Copyright © 2010 by Seanan McGuire

Excerpt from *Deadline* copyright © 2010 by Seanan McGuire

All rights reserved. In accordance with the U.S. Copyright Act of 1976, the scanning, uploading, and electronic sharing of any part of this book without the permission of the publisher is unlawful piracy and theft of the author's intellectual property. If you would like to use material from the book (other than for review purposes), prior written permission must be obtained by contacting the publisher at permissions@hbgusa.com. Thank you for your support of the author's rights.

Book design by Giorgetta Bell McRee
Cover design by Lauren Panepinto

Orbit
Hachette Book Group
1290 Avenue of the Americas
New York, NY 10104
www.orbitbooks.net

Orbit is an imprint of Hachette Book Group. The Orbit name and logo are trademarks of Little, Brown Book Group Limited.

The Hachette Speakers Bureau provides a wide range of authors for speaking events. To find out more, go to www.hachettespeakersbureau.com or call (866) 376-6591.

The publisher is not responsible for websites (or their content) that are not owned by the publisher.

Printed in the United States of America

First edition: May 2010

25   24   23   22   21   20   19   18   17   .16

This book is gratefully dedicated to
Gian-Paolo Musumeci
and
Michael Ellis.

They each asked me a question.
This is my answer.

FEED

BOOK I

The Rising

You can't kill the truth.

—GEORGIA MASON

Nothing is impossible to kill. It's just that sometimes after you kill something, you have to keep shooting it until it stops moving. And that's really sort of neat when you stop to think about it.

—SHAUN MASON

Everyone has someone on the Wall.

No matter how remote you may think you are from the events that changed the world during the brutal summer of 2014, you have someone on the Wall. Maybe they're a cousin, maybe they're an old family friend, or maybe they're just somebody you saw on TV once, but they're yours. They belong to you. They died to make sure that you could sit in your safe little house behind your safe little walls, watching the words of one jaded twenty-two-year-old journalist go scrolling across your computer screen. Think about that for a moment. They *died* for you.

Now take a good look at the life you're living and tell me: Did they do the right thing?

**—From *Images May Disturb You*,
the blog of Georgia Mason, May 16, 2039**

One

Our story opens where countless stories have ended in the last twenty-six years: with an idiot—in this case, my brother Shaun—deciding it would be a good idea to go out and poke a zombie with a stick to see what happens. As if we didn't already know what happens when you mess with a zombie: The zombie turns around and bites you, and you become the thing you poked. This isn't a surprise. It hasn't been a surprise for more than twenty years, and if you want to get technical, it wasn't a surprise *then*.

When the infected first appeared—heralded by screams that the dead were rising and judgment day was at hand—they behaved just like the horror movies had been telling us for decades that they would behave. The only surprise was that this time, it was really happening.

There was no warning before the outbreaks began. One day, things were normal; the next, people who were supposedly dead were getting up and attacking anything that came into range. This was upsetting for everyone involved, except for the infected, who were past being upset about that sort of thing. The initial shock was followed by running and screaming, which eventually devolved into more infection and attacking, that being the way of things. So what do we have now, in this enlightened age twenty-six years after the Rising? We have idiots prodding zombies with sticks, which brings us full circle to my brother and why he probably won't live a long and fulfilling life.

"Hey, George, check this out!" he shouted, giving the zombie another poke in the chest with his hockey stick. The zombie gave a low moan, swiping at him ineffectually. It had obviously been in a state of full viral amplification for some time and didn't have the strength or physical dexterity left to knock the stick out of Shaun's hands. I'll give Shaun this much: He knows not to bother the fresh ones at close range. "We're playing patty-cake!"

"Stop antagonizing the locals and get back on the bike," I said, glaring from behind my sunglasses. His current buddy might be sick enough to be nearing its second, final death, but that didn't mean there wasn't a healthier pack roaming the area. Santa Cruz is zombie territory. You don't go there unless you're suicidal, stupid, or both. There are times when even I can't guess which of those options applies to Shaun.

"Can't talk right now! I'm busy making friends with the locals!"

"Shaun Phillip Mason, you get back on this bike *right now*, or I swear to God, I am going to drive away and leave you here."

Shaun looked around, eyes bright with sudden

interest as he planted the end of his hockey stick at the center of the zombie's chest to keep it at a safe distance. "Really? You'd do that for me? Because 'My Sister Abandoned Me in Zombie Country Without a Vehicle' would make a great article."

"A posthumous one, maybe," I snapped. "Get back on the goddamn *bike*!"

"In a minute!" he said, laughing, and turned back toward his moaning friend.

In retrospect, that's when everything started going wrong.

The pack had probably been stalking us since before we hit the city limits, gathering reinforcements from all over the county as they approached. Packs of infected get smarter and more dangerous the larger they become. Groups of four or less are barely a threat unless they can corner you, but a pack of twenty or more stands a good chance of breaching any barrier the uninfected try to put up. You get enough of the infected together and they'll start displaying pack hunting techniques; they'll start using actual tactics. It's like the virus that's taken them over starts to reason when it gets enough hosts in the same place. It's scary as hell, and it's just about the worst nightmare of anyone who regularly goes into zombie territory—getting cornered by a large group that knows the land better than you do.

These zombies knew the land better than we did, and even the most malnourished and virus-ridden pack knows how to lay an ambush. A low moan echoed from all sides, and then they were shambling into the open, some moving with the slow lurch of the long infected, others moving at something close to a run. The runners led the pack, cutting off three of the remaining methods of escape before there was time to do more than stare. I looked at them and shuddered.

Fresh infected—really fresh ones—still look almost like the people that they used to be. Their faces show emotion, and they move with a jerkiness that could just mean they slept wrong the night before. It's harder to kill something that still looks like a person, and worst of all, the bastards are fast. The only thing more dangerous than a fresh zombie is a pack of them, and I counted at least eighteen before I realized that it didn't matter, and stopped bothering.

I grabbed my helmet and shoved it on without fastening the strap. If the bike went down, dying because my helmet didn't stay on would be one of the better options. I'd reanimate, but at least I wouldn't be aware of it. "Shaun!"

Shaun whipped around, staring at the emerging zombies. "Whoa."

Unfortunately for Shaun, the addition of that many zombies had turned his buddy from a stupid solo into part of a thinking mob. The zombie grabbed the hockey stick as soon as Shaun's attention was focused elsewhere, yanking it out of his hands. Shaun staggered forward and the zombie latched onto his cardigan, withered fingers locking down with deceptive strength. It hissed. I screamed, images of my inevitable future as an only child filling my mind.

"*Shaun!*" One bite and things would get a lot worse. There's not much worse than being cornered by a pack of zombies in downtown Santa Cruz. Losing Shaun would qualify.

The fact that my brother convinced me to take a dirt bike into zombie territory doesn't make me an idiot. I was wearing full off-road body armor, including a leather jacket with steel armor joints attached at the elbows and shoulders, a Kevlar vest, motorcycling pants with hip and knee protectors, and calf-high riding boots. It's bulky as hell, and I don't care, because once you factor in my gloves, my throat's the only target I present in the field.

Shaun, on the other hand, is a moron and had gone zombie baiting in nothing more defensive than a cardigan, a Kevlar vest, and cargo pants. He won't even wear goggles—he says they "spoil the effect." Unprotected mucous membranes can spoil a hell of a lot more than that, but I practically have to blackmail him to get him into the Kevlar. Goggles are a nonstarter.

There's one advantage to wearing a sweater in the field, no matter how idiotic I think it is: wool tears. Shaun ripped himself free and turned, running for the motorcycle with great speed, which is really the only effective weapon we have against the infected. Not even the fresh ones can keep up with an uninfected human over a short sprint. We have speed, and we have bullets. Everything else about this fight is in their favor.

"Shit, George, we've got company!" There was a perverse mixture of horror and delight in his tone. "Look at 'em all!"

"I'm *looking*! Now get on!"

I kicked us free as soon as he had his leg over the back of the bike and his arm around my waist. The bike leapt forward, tires bouncing and shuddering across the broken ground as I steered us into a wide curve. We needed to get out of there, or all the protective gear in the world wouldn't do us a damn bit of good. I might live if the zombies caught up with us, but my brother would be dragged into the mob. I gunned the throttle, praying that God had time to preserve the life of the clinically suicidal.

We hit the last open route out of the square at twenty miles an hour, still gathering speed. Whooping, Shaun locked one arm around my waist and twisted to face the zombies, waving and blowing kisses in their direction. If it were possible to enrage a mob of the infected, he'd have managed it. As it was, they just moaned and kept following, arms extended toward the promise of fresh meat.

The road was pitted from years of weather damage without maintenance. I fought to keep control as we bounced from pothole to pothole. *"Hold on, you idiot!"*

"I'm holding on!" Shaun called back, seeming happy as a clam and oblivious to the fact that people who don't follow proper safety procedures around zombies—like not winding up around zombies in the first place—tend to wind up in the obituaries.

"Hold on with both arms!" The moaning was only coming from three sides now, but it didn't mean anything; a pack this size was almost certainly smart enough to establish an ambush. I could be driving straight to the site of greatest concentration. They'd moan in the end, once we were right on top of them. No zombie can resist a good moan when dinner's at hand. The fact that I could hear them over the engine meant that there were too many, too close. If we were lucky, it wasn't already too late to get away.

Of course, if we were lucky, we wouldn't be getting chased by an army of zombies through the quarantine area that used to be downtown Santa Cruz. We'd be somewhere safer, like Bikini Atoll just before the bomb testing kicked off. Once you decide to ignore the hazard rating and the signs saying *Danger: Infection,* you're on your own.

Shaun grudgingly slid his other arm around my waist and linked his hands at the pit of my stomach, shouting, "Spoilsport," as he settled.

I snorted and hit the gas again, aiming for a nearby hill. When you're being chased by zombies, hills are either your best friends or your burial ground. The slope slows them down, which is great, unless you hit the peak and find out that you're surrounded, with nowhere left to run to.

Idiot or not, Shaun knows the rules about zombies and hills. He's not as dumb as he pretends to be, and he knows more about surviving zombie encounters than I do. His grip on my waist tightened, and for the first time, there was actual concern in his voice as he shouted, "George? What do you think you're doing?"

"Hold, on," I said. Then we were rolling up the hill, bringing more zombies stumbling out of their hiding places behind trash cans and in the spaces between the once-elegant beachfront houses that were now settling into a state of neglected decay.

Most of California was reclaimed after the Rising, but no one has ever managed to take back Santa Cruz. The geographical isolation that once made the town so desirable as a vacation spot pretty much damned it when the virus hit. Kellis-Amberlee may be unique in the way it interacts with the human body, but it behaves just like every other communicable disease known to man in at least one way: Put it on a school campus and it spreads like wildfire. U.C. Santa Cruz was a perfect breeding ground, and once all those perky co-eds became the shuffling infected, it was all over but the evacuation notices.

"Georgia, this is a hill!" he said with increasing urgency as the locals lunged toward the speeding bike. He was using my proper name; that was how I could tell he was worried. I'm only "Georgia" when he's unhappy.

"I got that." I hunched over to decrease wind resistance a few more precious degrees. Shaun mimicked the motion automatically, hunching down behind me.

"Why are we going *up* a hill?" he demanded. There was no way he'd be able to hear my answer over the combined roaring of the engine and the wind, but that's my brother, always willing to question that which won't talk back.

"Ever wonder how the Wright brothers felt?" I asked. The crest of the hill was in view. From the way the street vanished on the other side, it was probably a pretty steep drop. The moaning was coming from all sides now, so distorted by the wind that I had no real idea what we were driving into. Maybe it was a trap; maybe it wasn't. Either way, it was too late to find another path. We were committed, and for once, Shaun was the one sweating.

"Georgia!"

"Hold on!" Ten yards. The zombies kept closing, single-minded in their pursuit of what might be the first fresh meat some had seen in years. From the looks of most of them, the zombie problem in Santa Cruz was decaying faster than it was rebuilding itself. Sure, there were plenty of fresh ones—there are always fresh ones because there are always idiots who wander into quarantined zones, either willingly or by mistake, and the average hitchhiker doesn't get lucky where zombies are concerned—but we'll take the city back in another three generations. Just not today.

Five yards.

Zombies hunt by moving toward the sound of other zombies hunting. It's recursive, and that meant our friends at the base of the hill started for the peak when they heard the commotion. I was hoping so many of the locals had been cutting us off at ground level that they wouldn't have many bodies left to mount an offensive on the hill's far side. We weren't supposed to make it that far, after all; the only thing keeping us alive was the fact that we had a motorcycle and the zombies didn't.

I glimpsed the mob waiting for us as we reached the top. They were standing no more than three deep. Fifteen feet would see us clear.

Liftoff.

It's amazing what you can use for a ramp, given the right motivation. Someone's collapsed fence was blocking half the road, jutting up at an angle, and I hit it at about fifty miles an hour. The handlebars shuddered in my hands like the horns of a mechanical bull, and the shocks weren't doing much better. I didn't even have to check the road in front of us because the moaning started as soon as we came into view. They'd blocked our exit fairly well while Shaun played with his little friend, and mindless plague carriers or not, they had a better grasp of the local geography than we did. We still had one advantage: Zombies aren't good at predicting suicide charges. And if there's a better term for driving up the side of a hill at fifty miles an hour with the goal of actually achieving flight when you run out of "up," I don't think I want to hear it.

The front wheel rose smoothly and the back followed, sending us into the air with a jerk that looked effortless and was actually scarier than hell. I was screaming. Shaun was whooping with gleeful understanding. And then everything was in the hands of gravity, which has never had much love for the terminally stupid. We hung in the air for a heart-stopping moment, still shooting forward. At least I was fairly sure the impact would kill us.

The laws of physics and the hours of work I've put into constructing and maintaining my bike combined to let the universe, for once, show mercy. We soared over the zombies, coming down on one of the few remaining stretches of smooth road with a bone-bruising jerk that nearly ripped the handlebars out of my grip. The front wheel went light on impact, trying to rise up, and I screamed, half terrified, half furious with Shaun for getting us into this situation in the first place. The handlebars shuddered harder, almost wrenching my arms out of their sockets before I hit the gas and forced the wheel back down. I'd pay for this in the morning, and not just with the repair bills.

Not that it mattered. We were on level ground,

we were upright, and there was no moaning ahead. I hit the gas harder as we sped toward the outskirts of town, with Shaun whooping and cheering behind me like a big suicidal freak.

"Asshole," I muttered, and drove on.

News is news and spin is spin, and when you introduce the second to the first, what you have isn't news anymore. Hey, presto, you've created opinion.

Don't get me wrong, opinion is powerful. Being able to be presented with differing opinions on the same issue is one of the glories of a free media, and it should make people stop and think. But a lot of people don't *want* to. They don't want to admit that whatever line being touted by their idol of the moment might not be unbiased and without ulterior motive. We've got people who claim Kellis-Amberlee was a plot by the Jews, the gays, the Middle East, even a branch of the Aryan Nation trying to achieve racial purity by killing the rest of us. Whoever orchestrated the creation and release of the virus masked their involvement with a conspiracy of Machiavellian proportions, and now they and their followers are sitting it out, peacefully immunized, waiting for the end of the world.

Pardon the expression, but I can smell the bullshit from here. Conspiracy? Cover up? I'm sure there are groups out there crazy enough to think killing thirty-two percent of the world's population in a single summer is a good idea—and remember, that's a conservative estimate, since we've never gotten accurate death tolls out of Africa, Asia, or parts of South America—but are any of them nuts enough to do it by turning what used to be Grandma loose to chew on people at random? Zombies don't respect conspiracy. Conspiracy is for the living.

This piece is opinion. Take it as you will. But get your opinions the hell away from my news.

—From *Images May Disturb You*,
the blog of Georgia Mason, September 3, 2039

———

Zombies are pretty harmless as long as you treat them with respect. Some people say you should pity the zombie, empathize with the zombie, but I think they? Are likely to *become* the zombie, if you get my meaning. Don't feel sorry for the zombie. The zombie's not going to feel sorry for you when he starts gnawing on your head. Sorry, dude, but not even my sister gets to know me that well.

If you want to deal with zombies, stay away from the teeth, don't let them scratch you, keep your hair short, and don't wear loose clothes. It's that simple. Making it more complicated would be boring, and who wants that? We have what basically amounts to walking corpses, dude.

Don't suck all the fun out of it.

—From *Hail to the King*,
the blog of Shaun Mason, January 2, 2039

Two

Neither of us spoke as we drove through the remains of Santa Cruz. There were no signs of movement, and the buildings were getting widely spaced enough that visual tracking was at least partially reliable. I started to relax as I took the first exit onto Highway 1, heading south. From there, we could cut over to Highway 152, which would take us into Watsonville, where we'd left the van.

Watsonville is another of Northern California's "lost towns." It was surrendered to the infected after the summer of 2014, but it's safer than Santa Cruz, largely due to its geographical proximity to Gilroy, which is still a protected farming community. This means that while no one's willing to live in Watsonville for fear that the zombies will shamble down from Santa Cruz in the middle of the night, the good people of Gilroy aren't willing to let the infected have it either. They go in three times a year with flamethrowers and machine guns and clean the place out. That keeps Watsonville deserted, and lets the California farmers continue to feed the population.

I pulled off to the side of the road outside the ruins of a small town called Aptos, near the Highway 1 onramp. There was flat ground in all directions, giving us an adequate line of sight on anything that might be looking for a snack. My bike was running rough enough that I wanted to get a good look at it, and adding more gas probably wouldn't hurt. Dirt bikes have small tanks, and we'd covered a lot of miles already.

Shaun turned toward me as he dismounted, grinning from ear to ear. The wind had raked his hair into a series of irregular spikes and snarls, making him look like he'd been possessed. "That," he said, with almost religious fervor, "was the coolest thing you have ever done. In fact, that may have been the coolest thing you ever *will* do. Your entire existence has been moving toward one shining moment, George, and that was the moment when you thought, 'Hey, why don't I just go *over* the zombies?'" He paused for effect. "You are possibly cooler than God."

"Yet another chance to be free of you, down the drain." I hopped off the bike and pulled off my helmet, starting to assess the most obvious problems. They looked minor, but I still intended to get them looked at as soon as possible. Some damage was beyond my admittedly limited mechanical capabilities, and I was sure I'd managed to cause most of it.

"You'll get another one."

"That's the hope that keeps me going." I balanced my helmet against the windscreen before unzipping the right saddlebag and removing the gas can.

Setting the can on the ground, I pulled out the first-aid kit. "Blood test time."

"George—"

"You know the rules. We've been in the field, and we don't go back to base until we've checked our virus levels." I extracted two small handheld testing units, holding one out to him. "No levels, no van. No van, no coffee. No coffee, no joy. Do you want the joy, Shaun, or would you rather stand out here and argue with me about whether you're going to let me test your blood?"

"You're burning cool by the minute here," he grumbled, and took the unit.

"I'm okay with that," I said. "Now let's see if I'll live."

Moving with synchronicity born of long practice, we broke the biohazard seals and popped the plastic lids off our testing units, exposing the sterile metal pressure pads. Basic field test units only work once, but they're cheap and necessary. You need to know if someone's gone into viral amplification—preferably before they start chewing on your tasty flesh.

I unsnapped my right glove and peeled it off, shoving it into my pocket. "On three?"

"On three," Shaun agreed.

"One."

"Two."

We both reached out and slid our index fingers into the unit in the other's hand. Call it a quirk. Also call it an early-warning system. If either of us ever waits for "three," something's very wrong.

The metal was cool against my finger as I depressed the pressure pad, a soothing sensation followed by the sting of the test's embedded needle breaking my skin. Diabetes tests don't hurt; they want you to keep using them, and comfort makes a difference. Kellis-Amberlee blood testing units hurt on purpose. Lack of sensitivity to pain is an early sign of viral amplification.

The LEDs on top of the box turned on, one red, one green, beginning to flash in an alternating pattern. The flashing slowed and finally stopped as the red light went out, leaving the green. Still clean. I glanced at the test I was holding and let out a slow breath as I saw that Shaun's unit had also stabilized on green.

"Guess I don't get to clean your room out just yet," I said.

"Maybe next time," he said. I passed him back his test, letting him handle the storage while I refilled the gas tank. He did so with admirable efficiency, snapping the plastic covers back onto the testing units and triggering the internal bleach dispensers before pulling a biohazard bag out of the first-aid kit and dropping the units in. The top of the bag turned red when he sealed it, the plastic melting itself closed. That bag was triple-reinforced, and it would take a Herculean effort to open it now that it was shut. Even so, he checked the seal and the seams of the bag before securing it in the saddlebag's biohazardous materials compartment.

While he was busy with containment, I tipped the contents of the gas can into the tank. I'd been running close enough to empty that the can drained completely, which was scary. If we'd run out of gas during the chase . . .

Best not to think about it. I put the gas cap back on and shoved the empty can into the saddlebag. Shaun was starting to climb onto the back of the bike. I turned toward him, raising a warning finger. "What are we forgetting?"

He paused. "Uh . . . to go back to Santa Cruz for postcards?"

"Helmet."

"We're on a flat stretch of road in the middle of nowhere. We're not going to have an accident."

"Helmet."

"You didn't make me wear a helmet before."

"We were being chased by zombies before. Since there are no zombies now, you'll wear a helmet. Or you'll walk the rest of the way to Watsonville."

Rolling his eyes, Shaun unstrapped his helmet from the left-hand saddlebag and crammed it over his head. "Happy now?" he asked, voice muffled by the face shield.

"Ecstatic." I put my own helmet back on. "Let's go."

The roads were clean the rest of the way to Watsonville. We didn't see any other vehicles, which wasn't surprising. More important, we didn't see any of the infected. Call me dull, but I'd seen enough zombies for one day.

Our van was parked at the edge of town, a good twenty yards from any standing structures. Standard safety precautions; lack of cover makes it harder for things to sneak up on you. I pulled up in front of it and cut the engine. Shaun didn't wait for the bike to come to a complete stop before he was leaping down and bounding for the door, yanking his helmet off as he shouted, "Buffy! How's the footage?"

Ah, the enthusiasm of the young. Not that I'm much older than he is—neither of us came with an original birth certificate when we were adopted, but the doctors estimated me as being at least three weeks ahead of him. From the way he acts sometimes, you'd think it was a matter of years, not just an accident of birth order. I removed my helmet and gloves and slung them over the handlebars, before following at a more sedate pace.

The inside of our van is a testament to what you can do with a lot of time, a reasonable amount of money, and three years of night classes in electronics. And help from the Internet, of course; we'd never have figured out the wiring without people chiming in from places ranging from Oregon to Australia. Mom did the structural reinforcements and security upgrades, supposedly as a favor, but really to give her an excuse to try building back doors into our systems. Buffy disabled them all as quickly as they were installed. That hasn't stopped Mom from trying.

After five years of work, we've managed to convert a mostly gutted Channel 7 news van into a state-of-the-art traveling blog center, with camera feeds, its own wireless tower, a self-sustaining homing device, and so many backup storage arrays that it makes my head hurt when I think about them too hard. So I don't think about them at all. That's Buffy's job, along with being the perkiest, blondest, outwardly flakiest member of the team. And she does all four parts of her job very, very well.

Buffy herself was cross-legged in one of the three chairs crammed into the van's remaining floor space, looking thoughtful as she held a headset up to one ear. Shaun was standing behind her, nearly jigging up and down in his excitement.

She didn't seem to register my presence as I stepped into the van, but spoke as soon as the door was closed, saying, "Hey, Georgia," in a dreamy, detached tone.

"Hey, Buffy," I said, heading for the minifridge and pulling out a can of Coke. Shaun takes his caffeine hot, and I take mine cold. Call it our way of rebelling against similarity. "How're we looking?"

Buffy flashed a quick thumbs-up, actually animated for a moment. "We're looking good."

"That's what I like to hear," I said.

Buffy's real name is Georgette Meissonier. Like Shaun and me, she was born after the zombies became a fact of life, during the period when Georgia, Georgette, and Barbara were the three most common girl's names in America. We are the Jennifers of our generation. Most of us just rolled over and took it. After all, George Romero *is* considered one of the accidental saviors of the human race, and it's not like being named after him is uncool. It's just, well, common. And Buffy has never been willing to be common when she can help it.

She was all cool professionalism when Shaun and I found her at an online job fair. That lasted about five minutes after we met in person. She introduced herself, then grinned and said, "I'm cute, blonde, and living in a world full of zombies. What do *you* think I should call myself?"

We looked at her blankly. She muttered something about a pre-Rising TV show and let it drop. Not that it matters, since as far as I'm concerned, as long as she keeps our equipment in working order, she can call herself whatever she damn well wants. Plus, having her on the team grants us an air of the exotic: She was born in Alaska, the last, lost frontier. Her family moved after the government declared the state impossible to secure and ceded it to the infected.

"Got it," she announced, disconnecting the headset and leaning over to flick on the nearest video feedback screen. The image of Shaun holding back his decaying pal with the hockey stick flickered into view. No sound came from the van's main speakers. A single moan can attract zombies from a mile away if you're unlucky with your acoustics, and it's not safe to soundproof in the field. Soundproofing works both ways, and zombies tend to surround structures on the off chance they might contain things to eat or infect. Opening the van doors to find ourselves surrounded by a pack we didn't hear coming didn't particularly appeal to any of us.

"The image is a little fuzzy, but I've filtered out most of the visual artifacts, and I can clean it further once I've had the chance to hit the source files. Georgia, thanks for remembering to put your helmet on before you started driving. The front-mount camera worked like a charm."

To be honest, I hadn't remembered that the camera was there. I'd been too focused on not cracking my skull open. Still, I nodded agreeably, taking a long drink of Coke before saying, "No problem. How many of the cameras kept feeding through the chase?"

"Three of the four. Shaun's helmet didn't come on until you were almost here."

"Shaun didn't have time to put on his helmet, or he would have ceased to have a head," Shaun protested.

"Shaun needs to stop talking about himself in the third person," Buffy said, and hit a button on her keyboard. The image was replaced by a close-up shot of the flickering lights on our blood tests. "I want to screenshot this for the main site. What do you think?"

"Whatever you say," I said. The screen broadcasting our main external security camera was showing an abandoned, undisturbed landscape. Nothing moved in Watsonville. "You know I don't care about the graphics."

"And that's why your ratings aren't higher, George," said Shaun. "I like the lights. Use them as a slow fade in tonight's teaser, too—tack on something about, I don't know, how close is too close, that whole old saw."

"'Close Encounters on the Edge of the Grave,'" I murmured, moving toward the screen. It was a little too unmoving out there. Maybe I was being paranoid, but I've learned to pay attention to my instincts. God knows Shaun and Buffy weren't paying attention to anything but tomorrow's headlines.

Shaun grinned. "I like it. Grayscale the image except for the lights and use that."

"On it." Buffy typed a quick note before shutting down the screen. "Have we got any more big plans for the afternoon, folks?"

"Getting out of here," I said, turning back to the others. "I'm on the bike. I'll take point, but we need to get back to civilization."

Buffy blinked at me, looking baffled. She's a

Fictional; her style of blogging is totally self-contained, and she only sees the field when Shaun and I haul her out to work our equipment. Even then, she pretty much never leaves the van. It's not her job to pay attention to anything that doesn't live on a computer screen.

Shaun, on the other hand, sobered immediately. "Why?"

"There's nothing moving out there." I opened the back door, scanning the land more closely. It had taken me a few minutes—maybe too long—to realize what was wrong, but now that I'd seen it, it was obvious.

There should always be something moving in a town the size of Watsonville. Feral cats, rabbits, even herds of wild deer looking for the overgrown remains of what used to be gardens. We've seen everything from goats to somebody's abandoned Shetland pony wandering through the remains of the old towns, living off the land. So where were they? There wasn't as much as a squirrel in sight.

Shaun grimaced. "Crap."

"Crap," I agreed. "Buffy, grab your gear."

"I'll drive," Shaun said, and started for the front of the van.

Buffy was looking between us with wide-eyed bafflement. "Okay, does somebody want to tell me what's causing the evacuation?" she demanded.

"There aren't any animals," Shaun said, dropping into the driver's seat.

I paused while yanking my gloves back on, taking pity, and replied, "Nothing clears the wildlife like the infected. We need to get out of here before we have—"

As if on cue, a low, distant moan came through the van's back door, carried by the prevailing winds. I grimaced.

"—company," Shaun and I finished, in unison.

"Race you home," I called, and ducked out the door. Buffy slammed it behind me, and I heard all three bolts click home. Even if I screamed, they'd never let me back inside. That's the protocol when you're in the field. No matter how loudly you yell, they never let you in.

Not if they want to live, anyway.

There were no zombies in sight, but the moaning from the north and east was getting louder. I tightened the straps on my gloves, grabbed my helmet, and slung my leg over the bike's still-warm seat. Inside the van, I knew Buffy would be checking her cameras, fastening her seatbelt, and trying to figure out why we were reacting so badly to zombies that probably weren't even in range. If there's really a God, she's never going to know the answer to that one.

The van pulled out, bumping and shaking as it made its way onto the freeway. I gunned the bike's engine and followed, pulling up alongside the van before moving out about ten feet ahead, where Shaun could see me and we could both watch the road for obstructions. It's a simple safety formation, but it's saved a lot of asses in the last twenty years. We rode like that, separated by a thin ribbon of broken road, all the way out of the valley, through the South Bay, and into the cool, welcoming air of Berkeley, California.

Home sweet zombie-free home.

———————

. . . as he pressed his hand to her cheek, Marie could feel his flesh burning up from within, changing as the virus that slept in all of us awoke in her lover. She blinked back tears, licking suddenly dry lips before she managed to whisper, "I'm so sorry, Vincent. I never thought that it would end this way."

"It doesn't have to end this way for you," he replied, and smiled, sorrow written in his still-bright eyes. "Get the hell out of here, Marie. There's nothing in this wasteland but the dead. Go home. Live, and be happy."

"It's too late for that. It's too late for me." She held up the blood testing kit and watched his eyes widen as he took in the meaning of the single red light burning at the top. "It's been too late since the attack." Her own smile was as weak as his. "You called me the hyacinth girl. I guess I belong in the wasteland."

"At least we're damned together," he said, and kissed her.

—From *Love as a Metaphor*,
originally published in *By the Sounding Sea*,
the blog of Buffy Meissonier, August 3, 2039

———————

Shaun and I never met our parents' biological son. He was a kindergarten student during the Rising, and he survived the initial wave thanks to our parents, who pulled him out of class as soon as the data started pointing to public schools as amplification flash points. They did everything they could to protect him from the threat of infection. Everyone assumed he'd be one of the lucky ones.

The people next door had two golden retrievers, each weighing well over forty pounds, putting them in the range where amplification becomes possible. One of them was bitten—it was never determined by what— and began conversion. No one saw it coming because it had never happened before. Phillip Anthony Mason was the first confirmed case of human Kellis-Amberlee conversion initiated by an animal.

This honor does not help my parents sleep at night.

I am aware that my stance on pet ownership legislation is not popular. People love dogs, people love horses, and they want to continue to keep them in private homes. I understand this. I also understand that animals want to be free, and that sick animals are twice as likely to slip their restraints and go looking for comfort. Eventually, "comfort" becomes "something to bite." I support the Biological Mass Pet Ownership Restrictions, as do my parents. Were my brother alive today, he might feel different. But he's not.

—From *Images May Disturb You*,
the blog of Georgia Mason, November 3, 2039

Three

Buffy's neighborhood doesn't allow nonresident vehicles to enter without running blood tests on all passengers, so we dropped her at the gate where she could get tested and head inside on foot. I don't like pricking my fingers, and we were already looking at a second blood test when we reached the house. We live in an open neighborhood—one of the last in Alameda County—but our parents have to meet certain requirements if they want to keep their homeowner's insurance, and until we can afford to move out on our own, we have to play along.

"I'll upload the footage as soon as I finish cleaning it up," Buffy promised. "Drop me a text when you hit the house, let me know you made it okay?"

"Sure, Buff," I said. "Whatever you say."

Buffy's a great techie and a decent friend, but her ideas about safety are a little skewed, probably thanks to growing up in a high-security zone. She's less worried in the field than she is in supposedly protected urban environments. While there *are* more attacks on an annual basis in cities than in rural areas, there are also a lot more large men with guns once you get away from the creeks and the cornfields. Given a choice between the two, I'm going to take the city every time.

"See you tomorrow!" she said, and waved to Shaun through the van's front window before she turned to head for the guard station where she'd spend the next five minutes being checked for contamination. Shaun waved back and restarted the engine, backing the van away from the gate. That was my cue. I flashed a thumbs-up to show that I was good to go as I kicked my bike into a turn, leading the way back to Telegraph Avenue and into the tangled warren of suburban streets surrounding our house.

Like Santa Cruz, Berkeley is a college town, and we got swarmed during the Rising. Kellis-Amberlee hit the dorms, incubated, and exploded outward in an epidemic pattern that took practically everyone by surprise. "Practically" is the important word there. By the time the infection hit Berkeley, the first posts about activity in schools across the country were starting to show up online, and we had an advantage most college towns didn't: We started with more than our fair share of crazy people.

See, Berkeley has always drawn the nuts and flakes of the academic world. That's what happens when you have a university that offers degrees in both computer science and parapsychology. It was a city primed to believe any weird thing that came across the wire, and when all those arguably crazy people started hearing rumors about the dead rising from their graves, they didn't dismiss them. They began gathering weapons, watching the streets for strange behavior and signs of sickness, and generally behaving like folks who'd actually seen a George Romero movie. Not everyone believed what they heard . . . but some did, and that turned out to be enough.

That doesn't mean we didn't suffer when the first major waves of infection hit. More than half the population of Berkeley died over the course of six long days and nights, including the biological son of our adoptive parents, Phillip Mason, who was barely six years old. The things that happened here weren't nice, and they weren't pretty, but unlike many towns that started out with similar conditions—a large homeless population, a major school, a lot of dark, narrow, one-way streets—Berkeley survived.

Shaun and I grew up in a house that used to belong to the university. It's located in an area that was judged "impossible to secure" when the government inspectors started getting their act together, and as a result, it was sold off to help fund the rebuilding of the main campus. The Masons didn't want to live in the house where their son had died, and the security rating of the neighborhood meant they were able to get the property for a song. They finalized the adoptions for the two of us the day before they moved in, an "everything is normal" ratings stunt that eventually left them with a big house in the scary suburbs, two kids, and no idea what to do. So they did what came naturally: They gave more interviews, they wrote more articles, and they chased the numbers.

From the outside, they looked devoted to giving us the sort of "normal" childhood they remembered having. They never moved us to a gated neighborhood, they let us have pets that lacked sufficient mass for reanimation, and when public schools started requiring mandatory blood tests three times a day, they had us enrolled in a private school before the end of the week. There's a semifamous interview Dad gave right after that transfer, where he said they were doing their best to make us "citizens of the world instead of citizens of fear." Pretty words, especially coming from a man who regarded his kids as a convenient way to stay on top of the news feeds. Numbers start slipping? Go for a field trip to a zoo. That'll get you right back to the top.

There were a few changes they couldn't avoid, thanks to the government's anti-infection legislation—blood tests and psych tests and all that fun stuff—but they did their best, and I'll give them this much: A lot of the things they did for us weren't cheap. They paid for the right to raise us the way that they did. Entertainment equipment, internal security, even home medical centers can be bought for practically nothing. Anything that lets you outside, from vehicles to gasoline to gear that doesn't cut you off completely from the natural world . . . that's where things get expensive. The Masons paid in everything but blood to keep us in a place where there were blue skies and open spaces, and I'm thankful, even if it was always about ratings and a boy we never knew.

The garage door slid open as we pulled into the driveway, registering the sensors Shaun and I wear around our neck. In case of viral amplification, the garage becomes the zombie equivalent of a roach motel: Our sensors get us in, but only a clean blood test and a successful voice check gets us out. If we ever fail those tests, we'll be incinerated by the house defense system before we can do any further damage.

Mom's armored minivan and the old Jeep Dad insists on driving to his job on campus were parked in their normal spots. I pulled over and killed the bike's engine, removing my helmet as I started a basic postfield check of the machinery. I needed to see a mechanic; the ride through Santa Cruz had seriously damaged my shocks. Buffy's cameras were still attached to the helmet and back of the bike. I pulled them off and shoved them into my left saddlebag, unsnapping it and slinging it over my shoulder as Shaun pulled in behind me.

Shaun got out of the van and reached the back door three steps before I did. "We made good time," he said, positioning himself in front of the right-hand sensors.

"Sure did," I said, and positioned myself on the left.

"Please identify yourselves," said the bland voice of the house security system.

Most of the newer systems sound more like people than ours does. They'll even make jokes with their owners, to keep them at ease. Psychological studies have shown that closing the gap between man and machine increases comfort and acceptance and prevents nervous breakdowns stemming from isolation anxiety—in short, people don't get cabin fever as much when they think they have more people they can safely talk to. I think that's bullshit. If you want to avoid cabin fever, *go outside*. Our machines have stayed mechanical, at least so far.

"Georgia Carolyn Mason," said Shaun.

I smirked. "Shaun Phillip Mason."

The light above the door blinked as the house checked our vocal intonations. We must have passed muster, because it spoke again: "Voice prints confirmed. Please read the phrase appearing on your display screen."

Words appeared on my screen. I squinted to make them out through my sunglasses, and read, "Mares eat oats, and does eat oats, and little lambs eat ivy. A kid will eat ivy, too. Wouldn't you?"

The words blinked out. I glanced at Shaun, but couldn't quite see the words appearing on his screen before he was reciting them: "Oranges and lemons, say the bells of St. Clemens. You owe me five farthings, say the bells of St. Martins. When will you pay me, say the bells of Old Bailey."

The light over the door changed from red to yellow.

"Place your right hands on the testing pads," commanded the security system. Shaun and I did as requested, pressing our hands against the metal panels set into the wall. The metal chilled beneath my palm a split second before there was a stinging sensation in my index finger. The light above the door began to flash, alternating red and yellow.

"Think we're clean?" Shaun asked.

"If not, it's been nice knowing you," I said. Coming in together means that if one of us ever tests positive, that's all she wrote; they won't let anybody out of the garage until a cleanup crew arrives, and the chances of whoever comes up clean making it to the van before something happens aren't good. Our next-door neighbor used to call Child Protective Services every six months because our folks wouldn't stop us from coming in together. But what's the point of life if you can't take risks now and then, like coming into the damn house with your brother?

The light started flashing green instead of red, continuing to alternate with yellow for a few more seconds before yellow bowed out, leaving green to flash alone. The door unlocked, and the bland voice of the house said, "Welcome, Shaun and Georgia."

"S'up, the house?" Shaun replied, removing his shoes and tossing them into the outdoor cleaning unit before he walked inside, hollering, "Hey, 'rents! We're home!" Our parents hate being called "'rents." I'm pretty sure that's why he does it.

"And we survived!" I added, copying the gesture and following him through the garage door. It swung closed and locked itself behind me. The kitchen smelled like spaghetti sauce and garlic bread.

"Failure to die is always appreciated," Mom said, entering the kitchen and putting an empty laundry basket on the counter. "You know the drill. Both of you, upstairs, and strip for sterilization."

"Yes, Mom," I said, picking up the basket. "Come, Shaun. The insurance bill calls us."

"Yes, master," he drawled. Ignoring Mom entirely, he turned and followed me up the stairs.

The house was a duplex before Mom and Dad had it converted back into a single-family home. Our bedrooms literally adjoin; there's an inside door between them. It makes life easier when it's time for editing and prep work, and it's been like that all our lives. On the few occasions when I've had to try sleeping without Shaun in the next room, well, let's just say I can go a long way on a six-pack of Coke.

I dropped the laundry basket in the hallway

between our doors before going into my room and flicking the switch to turn on the overheads. We use low-wattage bulbs in the entire house, but I've abandoned white light entirely in my private space, preferring to live by the gleam of computer monitors and the comforting nonlight of black-light UV lamps. They can cause premature wrinkling if used extensively; what they can't do is cause corneal damage, and I appreciate that.

"Shaun! Inside door!"

"Got it," Shaun called. The connecting door slammed shut, and the band of light beneath it was cut off a second later as he slid the damper into place. Sighing with relief, I removed my sunglasses, forcing my eyes to open all the way. I'd been out in the sun for too long; even the UV lamps stung for a few seconds before my eyes adjusted and the room snapped into the sort of detailed focus most people only get in direct light.

"Retinal Kellis-Amberlee," as it's popularly called, is more properly referred to as "Acquired Kellis-Amberlee Optic Neuropathic Reservoir Condition." I've never heard anyone call it that outside a hospital, and even there, it's usually just "retinal KA." Those good old reservoir conditions: One more way for the virus to make life more interesting for everybody. My pupils are permanently dilated and don't contract in response to light, retinal scans are impossible, testing my vitreous and aqueous humors will always register a live infection, and best of all, my condition is advanced enough that my eyes don't even water. The virus produces a protective film and keeps the eyes from drying out. My tear ducts are atrophied. The only upside? Absolutely stellar low-light vision.

I tossed my sunglasses into the biohazard disposal canister and started across the room. My living space shares a lot of features with the van, including the part where Buffy maintains about ninety percent of the equipment and I understand less than half of it. Flat-screen monitors take up most of the walls, and we moved the group servers into my wardrobe last year when Shaun decided he needed more space for his weapons. Whatever. It's not like I was using it; I don't wear anything that actually needs to be hung up. I belong to the Hunter S. Thompson School of Journalistic Fashion: If I have to think about it, I have no business wearing it.

When you get right down to it, about the only similarity between my room and the room of your stereotypical twentysomething woman is the full-length mirror next to the bed. There's a wall dispenser mounted next to the mirror. I ripped loose a sheet of tear-away plastic and spread it on the floor, stepping onto it as I turned to face my reflection.

Hello, Georgia. Nice to see you're not dead yet.

Slicking my sweat-soaked hair back from my face, I started studying my clothes for the telltale fluorescence that under the black lights would indicate traces of blood.

Shaun and I operate under Class A-15 blogging licenses: We're cleared to report on events both inside and outside city limits, although we're still not permitted to enter any zones with a hazard rating at or above Level 3. The zones start at Level 10, the code for any area with resident mammals of sufficient

body mass to undergo Kellis-Amberlee amplific
tion and reanimation. Humans count. Level 9 means
those mammals are not entirely kept in confinement.
Buffy's neighborhood is considered a Level 10 hazard zone, which means it's safe to let your children
play outside, except for the part where it would instantly convert the zone to a Level 9. Our house is
classified as a Level 7 hazard, possessing free-range
mammals of sufficient body mass for full viral amplification, local wildlife capable of carrying blood or
other bodily wastes onto the property, insufficiently
secured borders, and windows more than a foot and a
half in diameter. There's legislation currently under
review that would make it a federal offense to raise
any child in a hazard zone above Level 8. I don't expect it to pass. It frightens me that it exists at all.

It requires an A-10 blogging license to enter a
Level 3 hazard zone with any prayer of being allowed
to exit it. We can't get those licenses or anything
above until we turn twenty-five and pass a series of
government-mandated tests, most of which center
on the ability to make accurate headshots with a variety of firearms. That means no Yosemite for at least
another two years. I'm fine with that. There's plenty
of news to be found in more populated areas.

Shaun feels different, but he's an Irwin, and they
thrive on wandering blindly into danger. All I've ever
wanted to be is what I am—a Newsie. I'm happy
this way. Danger is a side effect of what I do, not the
reason behind it. That doesn't mean danger throws
up its hands and says "oh, sorry, Georgia, I won't
mess with you." Contamination is always a risk when
dealing with zombies, especially when you have the

involved. The older infected are
concerned with keeping themselves from
worry about smearing you with their
precious bodily fluids, but new ones are fresh enough
to have fluid to spare. They'll splatter you if they can
manage it, and then count on the viral bricks filling their bloodstream to do the hard part for them.
It's not great as a hunting strategy, but as a way of
spreading the infection it works better than any uninfected person wants it to.

Not that anyone left in the world is actually
uninfected—that's part of the problem. We call people who have succumbed to viral amplification "the
infected," like it changes the fact that the virus is inside every one of us, patiently waiting for the day it
gets invited to take over. The Kellis-Amberlee virus
can remain in its dormant state for decades, if not
forever; unlike the people it infects, it can wait. One
day you're fine. The next day, your personal stockpile
of virus wakes up, and you're on the road to amplification, the death of the part of you that's a thinking,
feeling human being, and the birth of your zombie
future. Calling zombies "the infected" creates an artificial feeling of security, like we can somehow avoid
joining them. Well, guess what? We can't.

Viral amplification primarily occurs under one of
two conditions: the initial death of the host causing
a disruption of the body's nervous system and activating the virus already there, or contact with virus
that has already switched over from "dormant" to
"live." Hence the real risk of engaging the zombies,
because any hand-to-hand conflict is going to result
in a minimum casualty rate of sixty percent. Maybe

thirty percent of those casualties are going to occur in the actual combat, if you're talking about people who know what they're doing. I've seen videos of martial arts clubs and idiots with swords going up against the zombies in the Rising, and I'll be among the first to admit that they're damned impressive to watch. There's this amazing contrast between the grace and speed of a healthy person and the shambling slowness of the zombie that just . . . It's like seeing poetry come alive. It's heartbreaking, and it's sad, and it's beautiful as hell.

And then the survivors go home, laughing and elated and mourning for their dead. They take off their armor, and they clean their weapons, and maybe one of them nicks his thumb on the edge of an arm guard or wipes his eyes with a hand that got a little too close to a leaking zombie. Live viral particles hit the bloodstream, the cascade kicks off, and amplification begins. In an average-sized human adult, full conversion happens inside of an hour and the whole thing starts again, without warning, without reprieve. The question "Johnny, is that you?" went from horror movie cliché to real-world crisis damn fast when people started facing the infected hand-to-hand.

The closest call I've ever had came when a zombie managed to spit a mouthful of blood in my face. If I hadn't been wearing safety goggles over my sunglasses, I'd be dead. Shaun's come closer than I have; I try not to ask anymore. I don't really want to know.

My armor and pants were clean. I removed them and tossed them onto the plastic sheeting, performing the same check on my sweatshirt and thermal pants before stripping them off and adding them to the pile. A quick examination of my arms and legs revealed no unexpected smears or streaks of blood. I already knew I wasn't wounded; I'd cleared two blood tests since the field. If I'd been so much as scratched, I'd have started amplification before we had hit Watsonville. My socks, bra, and underwear joined the rest. They hadn't been exposed to the outside air. That didn't matter; they went into a hazard zone. They were getting sterilized. There are a lot of folks who advocate for sterilization outside the home. They get shouted down by the people who want to keep it internal, since field sterilization—or even "front-yard chemical shower" sterilization—leaves the risk of recontamination before you reach a secure zone. So far, the groups have been able to keep things deadlocked and we've been able to keep doing our self-examinations in relative peace.

I stepped off the plastic sheet, folded it around my clothes, scooped it up, and carried it to the bedroom door, which I opened long enough to toss the whole bundle into the hamper. It would go through an industrial-grade bleaching guaranteed to neutralize any viral bodies clinging to the fabric, and the clothes would be ready to wear again by morning.

Even that brief blast of white light was enough to make my eyes burn. I scrubbed at them with the back of my hand as I turned toward the bathroom. Shaun's door was still closed. I called, "Showering now!" A thump on the wall answered me.

Shaun and I share a private bathroom with its own fully modernized and airtight shower system. Another little requirement of the household insurance—since we leave safe zones all the time in order to do our jobs, we have to be able to prove we've been properly sterilized, and that means logged computer verification of our sterilizations. The bathroom started life as the closets of our respective bedrooms. Personally, I consider this a much better use of the space.

The bathroom lights switched to UV when my door opened. I walked over and pressed my hand to the shower's keypad, saying, "Georgia Carolyn Mason."

"Accessing travel records," the shower replied. We don't screw with the shower the way we screw with the house system. House security is kept at an absolute minimum, but the shower is governmentally required for journalist use, and we could get in serious trouble if the records don't match up. The fines for posing a contamination risk are more than I could afford in six years of freelancing.

The shower door unsealed. "You have been exposed to a Level 4 hazard zone. Please enter the stall for decontamination and sterilization."

"Don't mind if I do," I said, and stepped in. The door shut behind me, locking with an audible hiss as the air lock seal engaged.

A stinging compound of antiseptic and bleach squirted from the bottommost nozzle on the wall, coating me with icy spray. I held my breath and closed my eyes, counting the seconds before it would stop. They can only legally bathe you in bleach for half a minute unless you've been in a Level 2 zone. At that point, they can keep dunking you until they're sure the viral blocks are clean. Everyone knows it doesn't do any good beyond the first thirty seconds, but that doesn't stop people from being afraid.

Travel in a Level 1 zone means they're not legally obligated to do anything but shoot you.

The bleach stopped. The upper nozzle came on, spraying out water almost hot enough to burn. I cringed but turned my face toward it, reaching for the soap.

"Clean," I said, once the shampoo was out of my hair. I keep it short for a variety of reasons. Most have to do with making myself harder to grab, but showering faster is also a definite motivation. If I wanted it to get any longer, I'd have to start using conditioner and a variety of other hair-care chemicals to make up for the damage the bleach does every day. My one true concession to vanity is dyeing it back to the color nature gave me every few weeks. I look terrible blonde.

"Acknowledged," said the shower, and the water turned off, replaced by jets of air from all four sides. The one good part of our shower system. I was dry in a matter of minutes, leaving only a little residual dampness in my hair. The door unsealed, and I stepped out into the bathroom, grabbing for my bottle of lotion.

Bleach and human skin aren't good buddies. The solution: acid-based lotion, usually formulated around some sort of citrus, to help repair the damage the bleaching does. Professional swimmers did it pre-Rising, and everybody does it now. It also helps to lend a standardized scent tag to people who have scrubbed themselves recently. My lotion was as close to scentless as possible, and it still carried a faint, irritating hint of lemon, like floor cleaner.

I worked the lotion into my skin and retreated to my own room, shouting, "Shaun, it's all yours!" I got the door closed as his was opening, spilling white light into the room. That's not uncommon. We're pretty good about our timing.

I grabbed my robe from the back of the door and shrugged it on as I walked to the main desk. The monitor detected my proximity and switched on, displaying the default menu screen. Our main system never goes off-line. That's where group mail is routed, sorted according to which byline and category it's meant for—news to me, action to Shaun, or fiction, which goes straight to Buffy—and delivered to the appropriate in-boxes. I get the administrative junk that Shaun's too much of a jerk and Buffy's too much of a flake to deal with. Technically, we're a collective, but functionally? It's all me.

Not that I object to the responsibility, except when it fills my in-box to the point of inspiring nightmares. It's nice to know that our licenses are paid up, we're in good with the umbrella network that supports our accreditation, and nobody's suing us for libel. We make pretty consistent ratings, with Shaun and Buffy hitting top ten percent for the Bay Area at least twice a month and me holding steady in the thirteen to seventeen percent bracket, which isn't bad for a strict Newsie. I could increase my numbers if I went multimedia and started giving my reports naked, but unlike some people, I'm still in this for the news.

Shaun, Buffy, and I all publish under our own blogs and bylines, which is why I get so damn much mail, but those blogs are published under the umbrella of Bridge Supporters, the second-largest aggregator site in Northern California. We get readers and click-through traffic by dint of being listed on their front page, and they get a cut of our profits from all secondary-market and merchandise sales. We've been trying to strike out on our own for a while now, to go from being beta bloggers in an alpha world to baby alphas with a domain to defend. It's not easy. You need some story or feature that's big enough and unique enough to guarantee you'll take your readership with you, and our numbers haven't been sustainably high enough to interest any sponsors.

My in-box finished loading. I began picking through the messages, moving with a speed that was half long practice and half the desire to get downstairs to dinner. Spam; misrouted critique of Buffy's latest poem cycle, "Decay of the Human Soul: I through XII"; a threatened lawsuit if we didn't stop uploading a picture of someone's infected and shambling uncle—all the usual crap. I reached for my mouse, intending to minimize the program and get up, when a message toward the bottom of the screen caught my eye.

URGENT—PLEASE REPLY—YOU HAVE BEEN SELECTED.

I would have dismissed that as spam, except for the first word: urgent. People stopped flinging that word around like confetti after the Rising. Somehow, the potential for missing the message that zombies just ate your mom made offering to give people a bigger dick seem less important. Intrigued, I clicked the title.

I was still sitting there staring at the screen five minutes later when Shaun opened the door to my room and casually stepped inside. A flood of white light accompanied him, stinging my eyes. I barely flinched. "George, Mom says if you don't get downstairs, she'll . . . George?" There was a note of real concern in his voice as he took in my posture, my missing sunglasses, and the fact that I wasn't dressed. "Is everything okay? Buffy's okay, isn't she?"

Wordless, I gestured to the screen. He stepped up behind me and fell silent, reading over my shoulder. Another five minutes passed before he said, in a careful, subdued tone, "Georgia, is that what I think it is?"

"Uh-huh."

"They really . . . It's not a joke?"

"That's the federal seal. The registered letter should be here in the morning." I turned to face him, grinning so broadly that it felt like I was going to pull something. "They picked our application. They picked *us*. We're going to do it.

"We're going to cover the presidential campaign."

My profession owes a lot to Dr. Alexander Kellis, inventor of the misnamed "Kellis flu," and Amanda Amberlee, the first individual successfully infected with the modified filovirus that researchers dubbed "Marburg Amberlee." Before them, blogging was something people thought should be done by bored teenagers talking about how depressed they were. Some folks used it to report on politics and the news, but that application was widely viewed as reserved for conspiracy nuts and people whose opinions were too vitriolic for the mainstream. The blogosphere wasn't threatening the traditional news media, not even as it started having a real place on the world stage. They thought of us as "quaint." Then the zombies came, and everything changed.

The "real" media was bound by rules and regulations, while the bloggers were bound by nothing more than the speed of their typing. We were the first to report that people who'd been pronounced dead were getting up and noshing on their relatives. We were the ones who stood up and said "yes, there are zombies, and yes, they're killing people" while the rest of the world was still buzzing about the amazing act of ecoterrorism that released a half-tested "cure for the common cold" into the atmosphere. We were giving tips on self-defense when everybody else was barely beginning to admit that there might be a problem.

The early network reports are preserved online, over the protests of the media conglomerates. They sue from time to time and get the reports taken down, but someone always puts them up again. We're never going to forget how badly we were betrayed. People died in the streets while news anchors made jokes about people taking their zombie movies too seriously and showed footage they claimed depicted teenagers "horsing around" in latex and bad stage makeup. According to the time stamps on those reports, the first one aired the day Dr. Matras from the CDC violated national security to post details on the infection on his eleven-year-old daughter's blog. Twenty-five years after the fact his words— simple, bleak, and unforgiving against their background of happy teddy bears—still send shivers down my spine. There was a war on, and the ones whose responsibility it was to inform us wouldn't even admit that we were fighting it.

But some people knew and screamed everything they understood across the Internet. Yes, the dead were rising, said the bloggers; yes, they were attacking people; yes, it was a virus; and yes, there was a chance we might lose because by the time we understood what was going on, the whole damn world was infected. The moment Dr. Kellis's cure hit the air, we had no choice but to fight.

We fought as hard as we could. That's when the Wall began. Every blogger who died during the summer of '14 is preserved there, from the politicos to the soccer moms. We've taken their last entries and collected them in one place, to honor them, and to remember what they paid for the truth. We still add people to the Wall. Someday, I'll probably post Shaun's name there, along with some lighthearted last entry that ends with "See you later."

Every method of killing a zombie was tested somewhere. A lot of the time, the people who tested it died shortly afterward, but they posted their results first. We learned what worked, what to do, and what to watch for in the people around us. It was a grassroots revolution based on two simple precepts: survive however you could, and report back whatever you learned because it might keep somebody else alive. They say that everything you ever needed to know, you learned in kindergarten. What the world learned that summer was "share."

Things were different when the dust cleared. Some people might find it petty to say "especially where the news was concerned," but if you ask me, that's where the real change happened. People didn't trust regulated news anymore. They were confused and scared, and they turned to the bloggers, who might be unfiltered and full of shit, but were fast, prolific, and allowed you to triangulate on the truth. Get your news from six or nine sources and you can usually tell the bullshit from the reality. If that's too much work, you can find a blogger who does your triangulation for you. You don't have to worry about another zombie invasion going unreported because someone, somewhere, is putting it online.

The blogging community divided into its current branches within a few years of the Rising, reacting to swelling ranks and a changing society. You've got Newsies, who report fact as untainted by opinion as we can manage, and our cousins, the Stewarts, who report opinion informed by fact. The Irwins go out and harass danger to give the relatively housebound general populace a little thrill, while their more sedate counterparts, the Aunties, share stories of their lives, recipes, and other snippets to keep people happy and relaxed. And, of course, the Fictionals, who fill the online world with poetry, stories, and fantasy. They have a thousand branches, all with their own names and customs, none of them meaning a damn thing to anyone who isn't a Fictional. We're the all-purpose opiate of the new millennium: We report the news, we make the news, and we give you a way to escape when the news becomes too much to handle.

—From *Images May Disturb You*,
the blog of Georgia Mason, August 6, 2039

Four

Presidential campaigns have traditionally been attended by "pet journalists" selected to follow the campaign and report on everything from the bright beginning to the sometimes-bitter end. The Rising didn't change that. Candidates announce their runs for the big chair, pick up their little flock of television, radio, and print reporters, and hit the road.

This year's presidential election is different, largely because one of the lead candidates, Senator Peter Ryman—born, raised, and elected in Wisconsin—is the first man to run for office who was under eighteen during the summer of '14. He remembers the feeling of being betrayed by the news, of watching people die because they trusted the media to tell them the truth. So when he announced his candidacy, he made it a point that he wouldn't just be inviting the usual crew to follow his campaign; he'd also invite a group of bloggers to walk the campaign trail with him from before the first primary all the way to the election, assuming he made it that far.

It was a bold move. It was a huge strike for the legitimacy of Internet news. Maybe we're licensed journalists now, with all the insurance costs and restrictions that implies, but we're still sneered at by certain organizations, and we can have trouble getting to information from a lot of the "mainstream" agencies. Having a presidential candidate acknowledge us was an amazing step forward. Of course, he was only going to allow three bloggers to come along. All of them had to have their Class A-15 licenses before they could even apply; if you were in the process of qualifying, your application would be thrown out without any sort of review.

Most of the bloggers we know applied, either singly or in groups, and we wanted that posting so bad that we could taste it. It was our ticket to the big leagues. Buffy had been operating under a Class B-20 license for years; as a Fictional, she didn't need the clearance for field work, political reporting, or biohazard zones, and so she'd never seen the point in paying the license fees or taking the tests. Shaun and I rushed her through her A-level tests and classifications so fast that she just looked sort of stunned when they handed her the upgraded license. We sent in our application the next day.

Shaun was sure we'd get it. I was sure we wouldn't. Now, still staring at my monitor, Shaun said, "George?"

"Yeah?"

"You owe me twenty bucks."

"Yeah," I agreed, before standing and throwing my arms around his neck. Shaun responded by whooping, putting his arms around my waist, and lifting me off the ground in order to whirl me around the room.

"We got the job!" he shouted.

"We got the job!" I shouted back.

After that, we devolved to shouting the words together, Shaun still swinging me in a circle, until the bedroom intercom crackled on and Dad's voice demanded, "Are you two making that racket for a reason?"

"We got the job!" we shouted, in unison.

"Which job?"

"The *big* job!" Shaun said, putting me down and grinning at the intercom like he thought it could see him. "The biggest big job in the history of big jobs!"

"The campaign," I said, aware that the grin on my face was probably just as big and stupid as the grin on Shaun's. "We got the posting for the presidential campaign."

There was a long pause before the intercom crackled again and Dad said, "You kids get dressed. I'll get your mother. We're going out."

"But dinner—"

"Can go into the fridge. If you two are going to go stalk politicians all over the country, we're going out for dinner first. Call Buffy and see if she wants to come. And that's an order."

"Yes, sir," said Shaun, saluting the intercom. It clicked off and he turned on me, holding out his right hand. "Pay up."

I pointed to the door. "Get out. There's about to be nudity, and you'll just complicate things."

"Finally, adult content! Should I turn the

webcams on? We can have a front-page feed in less
than five—" I grabbed my pocket recorder and
flung it at his head. He ducked, grinning again.
"—minutes. I'll go get some nicer clothes on. *You*
can call the Buff one."

"Out," I said again, lips twitching as I fought a
smile.

He walked back to the door between our rooms,
stepping through before he shot back, "Wear a skirt,
and I'll release you from your debts."

He managed to close the door before I found anything else to throw.

Shaking my head, I moved to the dresser, saying,
"Phone, dial Buffy Meissonier, home line. Keep dialing until she picks up." Buffy has a tendency to leave
her phone on vibrate and ignore it while she "follows
her muse," which is basically a fancy way of saying
"screws around online, writes a really depressing
poem or short story, posts it, and makes three times
what I do in click-through revenue and T-shirt sales."
Not that I'm bitter or anything. The truth will make
you free, but it won't make you particularly wealthy.
I knew that when I chose my profession.

Playing with dead things is a little more lucrative,
but Shaun doesn't make enough to support us both—
not yet, anyway—and he isn't willing to move out
without me. A lifetime spent within arm's reach and
counting primarily on each other has left us a little
dependent on one another's company. In an earlier,
zombie-free era, this would have been dubbed "co-
dependence" and resulted in years of therapy, culminat-
ing in us hating each other's guts. Adoptive siblings

aren't supposed to treat each other like they're the center of the world.

Fortunately, or unfortunately, depending on your point of view, that was an attitude for a different world. Here and now, sticking with the people who know you best is the most guaranteed way of staying alive. Shaun won't leave the house until I do, and when we go, we'll be going together.

By the time Buffy picked up her phone, I had actually managed to find a dark gray tweed skirt that not only fit, but that I was willing to wear in a public place. I was digging for a top when the line clicked, and she said, peevishly, "I was writing."

"You're always writing, unless you're reading, screwing with something mechanical, or masturbating," I replied. "Are you wearing clothes?"

"Currently," she said, irritation fading into confusion. "Georgia, is that you?"

"It ain't Shaun." I pulled on a white button-down shirt, jamming the hem under the waistband of my skirt. "We'll be there to pick you up in fifteen. 'We' being me, Shaun, and the 'rents. They're taking the whole crew to dinner. It's just them trying to piggyback on our publicity for some rating points, but right now, failing to care."

Buffy isn't as slow on the uptake as she sometimes seems. Her voice suddenly tight with suppressed excitement, she asked, "Did we get it?"

"We got it," I confirmed. Her ear-splitting shriek of joy was enough to make me wince, even after it had been reduced by the phone's volume filters. Smiling, I pulled a crumpled black blazer out of my drawer and shrugged it on before grabbing a fresh pair of sunglasses from the stack on the dresser. "So we're picking you up in fifteen. Deal?"

"Yes! Yes, yes, deal, hallelujah, yes!" she babbled. "I have to change! And tell my roommates! And change! And see you! Bye!"

There was another click. My phone announced, "The call has been terminated. Would you like to place another call?"

"No, I'm good," I said.

"The call has been terminated," the phone repeated. "Would you like—"

I sighed. "No, thank you. Disconnect." The phone beeped and turned itself off. With the strides they've been making in voice-recognition software, you'd think they could teach the stuff to acknowledge colloquial English. One step at a time, I suppose.

Mom, Dad, and Shaun were in the living room when I came breezing down the stairs, shoving my handheld MP3 recorder into the loop at my belt. The backup recorder in my watch has a recording capacity of only thirty megabytes, and that's barely enough for a good interview. My handheld can hold up to five terabytes. If I need more than that before I can get to a server to dump the contents, I'd better be bucking for a Pulitzer.

Mom was wearing her best green dress, the one that appears in all her publicity shots, and Dad was in his usual professorial ensemble—tweed jacket, white shirt, khaki slacks. Put them next to Shaun, who was wearing a button-down shirt with his customary cargo pants, and they looked just like the last family publicity picture, even down to Mom's overstuffed handbag with all the guns inside it. She takes advantage of her A-5 blogging license in ways that boggle the mind, but it's the government's fault for leaving the loopholes there. If they want to give anybody with a journalist's license ranked Class A-7 or above the right to carry concealed weapons when entering any zone that's had a breakout within the last ten years, that's their problem. At least Mom's responsible about it. She always secures the safety on any gun that she's planning to take into a restaurant.

"Buffy's going to be ready in fifteen," I said, pushing my sunglasses more solidly up the bridge of my nose. Some of the newer models have magnetic clamps instead of earpieces. They won't come off without someone intentionally disengaging them. I would have been tempted to invest in a pair if they weren't expensive enough to require decontamination and reuse.

"The sun's going down; you could wear your contacts," Dad said, sounding amused. He's good at sounding amused. He's been sounding professionally amused since before the Rising, back when he used his campus webcast to keep biology students around the Berkeley area paying attention and doing their homework. Eventually, that same webcast let him coordinate pockets of survivors, moving them from place to place while reporting on the movement of the local zombie mobs. A lot of people owe their lives to that warm, professional-sounding voice. He could've become a news anchor with any network in the world after the dust cleared. He stayed at Berkeley instead, and became one of the pioneers of the evolving blogger society.

"I could also stick a fork in my eye, but where would be the fun in that?" I walked over to Shaun, offering a thin smile. He studied my skirt and then flashed me a thumbs-up sign. I had passed the all-judging court of my brother's fashion sense, which, cargo pants aside, is more advanced than mine will ever be.

"I called Bronson's. They have a table for us on the patio," Mom said, smiling beatifically. "It's a beautiful night. We should be able to see the entire city."

Shaun glanced at me, murmuring, "We let Mom pick the restaurant."

I smirked. "I can see that."

Bronson's is the last open-air restaurant in Berkeley. More, they're the last open-air restaurant in the entire Bay Area to be located on a hillside and surrounded by trees. Eating there is what I imagine it was like to go out to dinner before the constant threat of the infected drove most people away from the wilderness. The entire place is considered a Level 6 hazard zone. You can't even get in without a basic field license, and they require blood tests before they let you leave. Not that there's any real danger: It's surrounded by an electric fence too high for the local deer to jump over, and floodlights click on if anything larger than a rabbit moves in the woods. The only serious threat comes from the chance that an abnormally large raccoon might go into conversion, make it over the fence before it lost the coordination to climb trees, and drop down inside. That's never happened.

Not that this stops Mom from hoping to be there when it near-inevitably does. She was one of the first true Irwins, and old habits die hard, when they die at all. Shouldering her purse, she gave me a disapproving look. "Could you at least pretend to comb your hair?" she asked. "It looks like you have a hedgehog nesting on your head."

"That's the look I was going for," I said. Mom is blessed with sleek, well-behaved ash blonde hair that started silvering gracefully when Shaun and I were ten. Dad has practically no hair left, but when he had it, it was a muted Irish red. I, on the other hand, have thick, dark brown hair that comes in two settings: long enough to tangle, and short enough to look like I haven't brushed it in years. I prefer the short version.

Shaun's hair is a little lighter than mine, but still brown, and when he keeps it short, no one can tell that his is straight and mine wants to curl. It helps us get away with just saying we're twins, rather than going into the whole messy explanation.

Mom sighed. "You two realize the odds are good that someone already knows you got the assignment, and you're going to get swarmed tonight, yes?"

"Mmm-hmmm," I said. "Someone" probably received a quick phone call from one or both of our parents, and "someone" was probably already waiting at the restaurant. We grew up with the ratings game.

"Looking forward to it," said Shaun. He's better at playing nice with our parents than I am. "Every site that runs my picture tonight is five more foxy ladies around the country realizing that they want to hit the road with me."

"Pig," I said, and punched him in the arm.

"Oink," he said. "It's all right, we know the drill.

Smile pretty for the cameras, show off my scars, let George and Dad look wise and trustworthy, pose for anyone who asks, and don't try to answer any questions with actual content."

"Whereas I don't smile unless forced, stay behind my sunglasses, and make a point of how incisive and hard-hitting every report I approve for release is going to be," I said, dryly. "We let Buffy babble to her heart's content about the poetic potential of traveling around the country with a bunch of political yahoos who think we're idiots."

"And we make the front page of every alpha site in the country, and our ratings go up nine points overnight," Shaun said.

"Thus allowing us to announce the formation of our own site early next week, just before heading out on the campaign trail." I slid my sunglasses down my nose, ignoring the way the light stung as I offered a brief smile. "We've thought about this as much as you have."

"Maybe more," Shaun added.

Dad laughed. "Face it, Stacy, they've got it covered. Kids, just in case there isn't another chance for me to tell you this, your mother and I are very proud of you. Very proud of you, indeed."

Liar. "We're pretty proud of us, too," I said.

"Well, then," Shaun said, clapping his hands together. "This is touching and all, but come on—let's go eat."

Getting out of the house is easier with our parents in tow, largely because Mom's minivan is kept ready at all times. Food, water, a CDC-certified bio-hazard containment unit for temperature-sensitive medications, a coffeemaker, steel-reinforced windows . . . We could be trapped inside that thing for a week, and we'd be fine. Except for the part where we'd go crazy from stress and confinement and kill each other before rescue came. When Shaun and I go into the field, we need to check our gear, sometimes twice, to make sure it's not going to let us down. Mom just grabs her keys.

Buffy was waiting at her neighborhood guard station, dressed in an eye-popping combination of tie-dyed leggings and knee-length glitter tunic, with star-and-moon hologram clips in her hair. Anyone who didn't know her would have thought she was completely devoid of sense, fashion *or* common. That's what she was aiming for. Buffy travels with more hidden cameras than Shaun and I combined. As long as people are busy staring at her hair, they don't wonder why she's so careful about pointing the tiny jewels she has pasted to her nails in their direction.

She waved and grabbed her duffel bag when the van pulled up. Then she ran to hop into the back with Shaun and me. The footage of that moment would be on the site within the hour.

"Hey, Georgia. Hey, Shaun—good evening, Mr. and Mrs. Mason," she chirped, buckling herself in while Shaun slammed the door. "I just finished watching your trip to Colma, Mrs. Mason. Really great stuff. I would never have thought to elude a bunch of zombies by climbing a high-dive platform."

"Why, thank you, Georgette," said Mom.

"Thrill as Buffy kisses ass," Shaun said, deadpan. Buffy shot him a poisonous look, and he just laughed.

Content that all was right with the world, I settled back in my seat, folded my arms across my chest, and closed my eyes, letting the chatter in the van wash over me without registering it. It had been a long day, and it was nowhere near over.

When blogging first emerged as a major societal trend, it was news rendered anonymous. Rather than trusting something because Dan Rather looked good on camera, you trusted things because they sounded true. The same went for reports of personal adventures, or people writing poetry, or whatever else folks felt like putting out there for the world to see; you got no context on who created it, and so you judged the work on the basis of what it actually was. That changed when the zombies came, at least for the people who went professional. These days, bloggers don't just report the news; they create it, and sometimes, they *become* it. Landing the position of pet bloggers for Senator Ryman's presidential campaign? That definitely counts as becoming the news.

That's part of why Shaun and Buffy keep me around. My journalistic integrity is unquestioned by our peers, and when we make the jump to alpha— the suddenly feasible jump to alpha—that's going to cement our credibility. Shaun and Buffy will bring in the readers. I'll make it okay for them to trust us. They just have to deal with my depressed personal ratings because part of what makes me so credible is the fact that my news is free from passion, opinion, and spin. I do op-ed, but for the most part, what you'll get from me is the truth, the whole truth, and nothing but the truth.

So help me God.

Shaun elbowed me when we reached Bronson's. I slid my sunglasses back into position and opened my eyes.

"Status?" I asked.

"A least four visible cameras. Probably twelve to fifteen, all told."

"Leaks?"

"That many cameras, at least six sites already know."

"Got it. Buffy?"

"Taking point," she said, and straightened, putting on her best camera-ready smile. My parents exchanged amused looks in the front seat.

"It's all uphill from here," I said.

Shaun leaned over and opened the van door.

Before the Rising, crowds of paparazzi were pretty much confined to the known haunts of celebrities and politicians—the people whose faces could be used to sell a few more magazines. The rise of reality television and the Internet media changed all that. Suddenly, anybody could be a star if they were willing to embarrass themselves in the right ways. People got famous for wanting to get laid, a stunt men have been trying to achieve since the day we discovered puberty. People got famous for having useless talents, memorizing trivia, or just being willing to get filmed twenty-four hours a day while living in a house full of strangers. The world was a weird place before the Rising.

After the Rising, with an estimated eighty-seven percent of the populace living in fear of infection and unwilling to leave their homes, a new breed of reality star was born: the reporter. While you can be an aggregator or a Stewart without risking yourself in the real world, it's hard to be an Irwin, a Newsie, or even a really good Fictional if you cut yourself off that way. So we're the ones who eat in restaurants and go to theme parks, the ones who visit national parks even though we'd really rather not, the ones who take the risks the rest of the country has decided to avoid. And when we're not taking those risks ourselves, we report on the people who are. We're like a snake devouring its own tail, over and over again, forever. Shaun and I have done paparazzi duty when the stories were thin on the ground and we needed to make a few bucks fast. I'd rather go for another filming session in Santa Cruz. Something about playing vulture just makes me feel dirty.

Buffy was the first to flounce into the crowd, looking like a little glittering ball of sunshine and happiness before they closed ranks around her, flashbulbs going off in all directions. Her giggle could cut through steel. I could hear it even after she'd made it halfway to the restaurant doors, distracting the worst of the paparazzi in the process. Buffy's cute, photogenic, a hell of a lot friendlier than I am, and, best of all, she's been known to drop hints about her personal life that can be turned into valuable rating points when the stories go live. Once, she even brought out a boyfriend. He didn't last long, but when she had him, Shaun and I could practically have danced naked on the van without getting harassed. Good times.

Shaun stepped out of the van already smiling. That smile's made him a lot of friends in the female portion of the blogosphere—something about him looking like he'd be just as happy to explore the dangerous wilderness of the bedroom as he is to explore the mysteries of things that want to make him die. They should know by now it's a gimmick, given his continuing lack of a social life that doesn't include the infected, but they keep falling for it. Half the cameras swung around to face him, and several of the chirpy little "anchorwomen"—because every twit who knows how to post an interview on the vid sites is an anchorwoman these days; just ask them— shoved their microphones into his face. Shaun immediately started giving them what they wanted, chattering merrily about our latest reports, offering coy, meaningless come-ons, and basically talking about anything and everything other than our new assignment.

Shaun's smoke screen gave me the opportunity I needed to slip out of the car and start worming my way toward the restaurant doors. Paparazzi gatherings are one of the few times you'll see a crowd in public. I spotted nervous-looking Berkeley Police in riot gear around the edge of the crowd as I made my way toward the thinner concentration of bodies. They were waiting for something to go wrong. They'd just have to keep waiting. There's only been one incident where an outbreak started from a gathering of licensed reporters, and it happened when a nervous celebrity—the real sort, a TV sitcom star, not one of the ones who built themselves celebrity out of boredom—freaked out, pulled a gun out of her purse, and started shooting. The jury found the TV star, not the paparazzi, at fault for the outbreak that followed.

One of the Newsies near the police offered me a

sidelong nod, making no move to draw attention to my position. I nodded back, relieved by his discretion. He was just crowd-surfing, but it was a nice thing to do. I made a note of his face: If his site put in for an interview, I'd grant it.

Irwins get crowd-comfortable the easy way: When you live in the hope that an outbreak will happen where you can observe it, you don't worry about avoiding them the way a sane person might. Fictionals go one of two directions: Some avoid crowds like everybody else. Others refuse to acknowledge that they could possibly get infected when they haven't put it in the script and they go gaily bouncing hither and yon, ignoring the danger. Newsies tend to be more cautious because we know what could happen if we're not. Unfortunately, the demands of our job make it hard for us to be total hermits, and so even those of us who don't need the additional income or exposure from the paparazzi flocks join up with them from time to time, getting accustomed to the feeling of being surrounded by other bodies. The paparazzi flocks are our version of the obstacle course. Stand in them without freaking out and you might be ready for real field work.

My "skirt the crowd and keep your eyes on the door" technique seemed to be working. With Shaun and Buffy providing louder, more visible targets, no one was going for me. Besides, I have a well-established—and well-deserved—reputation for being the sort of interviewee who walks away leaving you with nothing you can use as a front-page quote or saleable sound byte. It's hard to interview someone who refuses to talk to you.

Ten feet to the door. Nine. Eight. Seven . . .

"—and this is my gorgeous daughter, Georgia, who's going to be the head of Senator Ryman's hand-selected blogging team!" Mom's hand caught my elbow just as the gushing, ebullient tone of her voice caught my ears. Trapped. She swung me around to face the crowd of paparazzi, fingers digging into my arm. More quietly, through gritted teeth, she said, "You owe me this."

"Got it," I said, out of the corner of my mouth, and let myself be turned.

Shaun and I figured out early what our purpose was in our parents' lives. When your classmates aren't allowed to go to the movies because they might be exposed to unknown individuals, while your parents are constantly proposing wild adventures in the outside world, you get the idea that maybe something's going on. Shaun was the first to realize how they were using us; it's about the only place where he grew up before I did. I got over Santa. He got over our parents.

Mom kept an iron grip on my arm as she mugged and preened, re-creating her favorite photo opportunity, version five hundred and eleven: the flamboyant Irwin poses with her stoic daughter, polar opposites united by a passion for the news. I once sat down with the news aggregators and compared a public-image search to the collection of private pictures on the house database. Eighty-two percent of the physical affection I've received from my mother has been in public, in careful view of one or more cameras. If that seems cynical, answer this: Why has she reliably, for my entire life, waited to touch me until there was someone with a visible camera in shooting range?

People wonder why I'm not physically affectionate. The number of times I've been a rating-boosting photo opportunity for my parents should be sufficient answer. The only person who's ever hugged me without thinking about the shooting angles and light saturation is my brother, and he's the only one whose hugs I've ever given a damn about.

My glasses filtered camera flashes, although it wasn't long before I had to close my eyes anyway. Some of the newer cameras have lights on them strong enough to take photographs in total darkness that seem to have been taken at noon, and there's not an intelligence check associated with buying that sort of equipment. One of those suckers goes off in your face, you know you've been photographed. I was going to have a migraine for days thanks to Mom's forced photo opportunity. There was no way I could have avoided it; it was give in before dinner or spend the entire meal being harangued about my duties as a good daughter, leading to a much longer photo session afterward. I'd rather kiss a zombie raccoon.

Buffy came to my rescue, slinking through the crowd with the sort of grace that only comes from the kind of practice most of our generation has avoided. Reaching out, she caught hold of my other arm and chirped, all dizzy good cheer, "Ms. Mason, Georgia, Mr. Mason says our table's ready! Only if you don't come now, they may release it, and then we'll have to wait at least a half an hour for another table." She paused before delivering the coup de grace. "An *inside* table."

That was the perfect thing to say. Sitting outside added to the family's mystique, making us look brave and adventurous. Parental opinion, not mine. I think eating outside when you don't have to makes you look like a suicidal idiot dying to get munched by a zombie deer. Shaun sides with everybody on this one—he'd rather eat outside when we have to eat with the parents in public, since that way there's the chance a zombie deer will come along and rescue him. He just agrees that it's a stupid thing to do. Mom doesn't see the stupidity. If it was a choice between an outdoor table where the photographers could get some decent shots and an indoor table where people might gossip about the fearless Stacy Mason losing her nerve, well . . . her answer was obvious.

Flashing her award-winning—literally—smile at the crowd, Mom pulled me into an "impulsive" hug and announced, "Well, folks, our table's ready." Noises of displeasure greeted her statement. Her smile widened. "But we'll be back after food, so if you guys want to grab a burger, we might be able to coax a few wise statements out of my girl." She gave me a squeeze and let go, to the sound of general applause.

I sometimes wonder why none of these news site cluster bombs ever catch the way her smile dies when she's not facing the cameras. They run solemn pictures of her once in a while, but they're as posed as the rest; they show her looking mournfully at abandoned playgrounds or locked cemetery gates, and once—when her ratings dipped to an all-time low during the summer Shaun and I turned thirteen and locked ourselves in our rooms—at the school Phillip had attended. That's our Mom, selling the death of her only biological child for a few points in the ratings game.

Shaun says I shouldn't judge her so harshly, since we make our living doing the same thing. I say it's different when we do it. We don't have kids. The only things we're selling are ourselves, and I guess we have a right to that.

Dad and Shaun were standing outside the restaurant doors, turned just far enough that none of the microphones capable of withstanding the crowd noise without shorting out would be able to make out what they were saying. As I drew closer, I heard Shaun saying, in an entirely pleasant tone, ". . . I really don't care what you consider 'reasonable.' You're not part of our team; you're not getting any exclusives."

"Now, Shaun—"

"Dinnertime," I said, snagging Shaun's arm as I walked past. He came with me as gratefully as I'd gone with Buffy a few moments before. Shaun, Buffy, and I walked into the restaurant practically arm-in-arm, with our parents trailing behind us, both struggling to conceal their irritation. Tough. If they didn't want us embarrassing them in public, they shouldn't have made us go out.

Our table proved to be nice enough to suit Mom's idea of propriety; it was located in the far corner of the yard, close to both the fence keeping out the woods and the fence isolating us from the street. Several enterprising paparazzi had drifted over to that portion of the sidewalk and were snapping candid shots through the bars. Mom flashed them a dimpled grin. Dad looked knowing and wise. I fought the urge to gag.

My handheld vibrated, signaling an incoming text message. I unclipped it from my belt, tilting it to show the screen.

"Think this'll die down when we're on the road? —S"

I smirked, tapping out, *"Once the media machine (aka 'Mom') has been left here? Absolutely. We'll be small potatoes next to the main course."*

He tapped back: *"I love it when you compare people to food."*

"Practicing for the inevitable."

Shaun snorted laughter, nearly dropping his phone into the basket of breadsticks. Dad shot him a sharp look, and he put his phone down next to his silverware, saying angelically, "I was checking my ratings."

Dad's scowl melted instantly. "How's it looking?"

"Not bad. The footage the Buffster managed to clean before we hauled her away from her computer is getting a really good download rate." Shaun flashed a grin at Buffy, who preened. If you want her to like you, compliment her poetry. If you want her to love you, compliment her tech. "I figure once I do the parallel reports and record my commentary, my share's going to jump another eight points. I may break my own top stats this month."

"Show-off," I said, and smacked him on the arm with my fork.

"Slacker," he replied, still grinning.

"Children," said Mom, but there was no heat behind it. She loved it when we goofed around. It made us look more like a real family.

"I'm going to have the teriyaki soy burger," said

Buffy. She leaned forward and said conspiratorially, "I heard from a guy who knows a girl whose boyfriend's best friend is in biotech that he—the best friend, I mean—ate some beef that was cloned in a clean room and didn't have a viral colony, and it tasted *just like* teriyaki soy."

"Would that it were true," said Dad, with the weird sort of mournfulness reserved for people who grew up before the Rising and were now confronted with something that's been lost forever. Like red meat.

That's another nasty side effect of the KA infection that no one thought about until they were forced to deal with it firsthand: Everything mammalian harbors a virus colony, and the death of the organism causes the virus to transmute into its live state. Hot dogs, hamburgers, steaks, and pork chops are things of the past. Eat them, and you're eating live viral particles. Are you sure there aren't any sores in your mouth? In your esophagus? Can you be one hundred percent certain that no part of your digestive tract has been compromised in any way? All it takes is the smallest break in the body's defenses and your slumbering infection wakes up. Cooking the meat enough to kill the infection also kills the flavor, and it's still a form of Russian roulette.

The most well-done steak in the world may have one tiny speck of rare meat somewhere inside it, and that's all that it takes. My brother wrestles with the infected, gives speeches while standing on cars in designated disaster zones, never wears sufficient armor, and generally goes through life giving the impression that he's a suicide waiting to happen. Even he won't eat red meat.

Poultry and fish are safe, but a lot of people avoid them anyway. Something about the act of eating flesh makes them uncomfortable. Maybe it's the fact that suddenly, after centuries of ruling the farmyard, mankind has reason to empathize with the chicken. We always had turkeys at Thanksgiving and geese at Christmas. Just another ratings stunt on the part of our increasingly media-savvy parents, but at least this one had some useful side effects. Shaun and I are some of the only people I know in our generation who don't have any unreasonable dietary hang-ups.

"I'm going to have the chicken salad and a cup of today's soup," I said.

"And a Coke," prompted Shaun.

"And a carafe," I corrected him.

He was still teasing me about my caffeine intake when the waiter appeared, accompanied by the beaming manager. No surprise there. As a family, we've been excellent customers for as long as I can remember. Every time a local outbreak has closed down outside gathering areas, Mom's been at Bronson's, eating in the enclosed dining area and making a point of being the first one outside when they're allowed to reopen it. They'd be stupid not to appreciate what we've done for their business.

The waiter was carrying a tray laden with our usual assortment of drinks: coffee for Mom and Dad, a virgin daiquiri for Buffy, a bottle of sparkling apple cider for Shaun—it looks like beer from any sort of a distance—and a pitcher of Coke for me.

"Compliments of the house," the manager declared, turning his smile on me and Shaun. "We're so proud of you. Going off to be media superstars! It runs in the family."

"It definitely does," simpered Mom, doing her best to look like a giggling schoolgirl. She was only succeeding at looking like an idiot, but I wasn't going to tell her that. We were almost on the campaign trail. It wasn't worth the fight.

"Be sure to sign a menu before you leave?" the manager pressed. "We'll put it on the wall. When you're too big to come to places like this, we'll be able to say, 'They ate here, they ate fries right there, right at that table, while they did their math homework.'"

"It was physics," protested Shaun, laughing.

"Whatever you say," said the manager.

The waiter passed drinks around as we placed our orders. He finished by pouring the first cup of Coke from my pitcher with a flourish of his wrist. I smiled at that, and he winked at me, clearly pleased. I let my smile die, spiking an eyebrow upward. Hours of practice with my mirror have shown me that particular expression's success in conveying disdain. It's one of the few facial expressions that's helped by my sunglasses, rather than being hindered by them. His pleasure faded, and he hustled through the rest of his duties without looking at me.

Shaun caught my eye, mouthing "That wasn't nice" at me.

I shrugged, mouthing "He should have known better" back at him. I don't flirt. Not with waiters, not with other reporters, not with anybody.

Finally, the staff retreated, and Mom raised her glass, clearly signaling for a toast. Choosing the path of least resistance, the rest of us did the same.

"To ratings!" she said.

"To ratings," we agreed and clinked our glasses around the table in doleful adherence to the ritual.

We were on the road to those ratings now. All we had to do was hope that we were good enough to keep them. Whatever it might take.

———

My friend Buffy likes to say love is what keeps us together. The old pop songs had it right, and it's all about love, full stop, no room for arguing. Mahir says loyalty is what matters—doesn't matter what kind of person you were, as long as you were loyal. George, she says it's the truth that matters. We live and die for the chance to maybe tell a little bit of the truth, maybe shame the Devil just a little bit before we go.

Me, I say those are all great things to live for, if they're what happens to float your boat, but at the end of the day, there's got to be somebody you're doing it for. Just one person you're thinking of every time you make a decision, every time you tell the truth, or tell a lie, or anything.

I've got mine. Do you?

—From *Hail to the King*,
the blog of Shaun Mason, September 19, 2039

Five

Ⅰ D?"

"Georgia Carolyn Mason, licensed online news representative, After the End Times." I handed my license and photo identification to the man in black, turning my left wrist over to reveal the blue-and-red ID tattoo I had done when I tested for my first Class B license. Tattooing isn't legally required—yet—but it gives them something to identify your body by. Every little bit helps. "Registered with the North American Association of Internet Journalists; dental records, skin sample, and identifying markings on file."

"Remove the sunglasses."

That was a request I was all too familiar with. "If you'll check my file, you'll see that I have a filed notation of retinal Kellis-Amberlee syndrome. If there's another test we can perform, I'd be happy to—"

"Remove the sunglasses."

"You realize I won't display a normal retinal pattern?"

The man in black offered me the ghost of a smile. "Well, ma'am, if your eyes check normal, we'll know you've been making all this fuss because you weren't who you claimed to be, now, won't we?"

Damn. "Right," I muttered, and removed my glasses. Forcing myself to keep my eyes open despite the pain, I turned to press my face into the retinal scanner being held by the second member of Senator Ryman's private security team. They would compare the scan results to the ocular patterns in my file, checking for signs of degradation or decay that could signify a recent viral flare. Not that they'd get any useful results from me; retinal KA means my eyes *always* register as if I were harboring a live infection.

Buffy and Shaun were going through the standard version of the same process with their own detachments of black-suited security representatives just a few feet away from me. I was willing to bet theirs hurt less.

The light at the top of the retinal scanner went from red to green, and the man pulled it away, nodding to his companion. "Hand," said the first man.

I took a few precious seconds to slide my sunglasses back into place before holding out my right hand, and managed not to grimace as it was grabbed and thrust into a closed-case blood testing unit. Clinical interest took over, wiping away my distaste for the process as I studied the unit's casing.

"Is that an Apple unit?" I asked.

"Apple XH-224," he replied.

"Wow." I'd seen the top-of-the-line units before, but I'd never had the opportunity to use one. They're more sophisticated than our standard field units, capable of detecting a live infection at something like ten times the speed. One of those babies can tell you that you're dead before you even realize that you've been bitten. Which didn't make the process of getting tested any more enjoyable, but it definitely made it more interesting to observe. It was almost worth the pain. Almost.

Five red lights came on along the top of the box, beginning to blink as needles pricked the skin between my thumb and forefinger, at my wrist, and at the tip of my pinkie. Each time, the bite of the needle was followed by a cool blast of antiseptic foam. When all five lights had gone from red to green, the agent pulled the box away and smiled genuinely for the first time.

"Thank you for your cooperation, Miss Mason. You're free to proceed."

"Thanks," I said, and pushed my sunglasses farther up the bridge of my nose. My headache settled back into its previous grumble. "Mind if I wait for the rest of my crew?" Buffy was sticking her hand into the box, and they were waiting for Shaun's retinal check to complete. He has retinal scarring in his left eye from a stupid incident with some crappy Chinatown fireworks when we were fifteen, and that makes his scans take longer than they should. Mine may be weird, but they're a standard weird. His confuse just about every scanner we've ever met.

"Not at all," the agent said. "Just don't cross the quarantine line, or we'll have to start over."

"Got it." I stepped back and studied the area, careful to keep my feet well away from the red line marking the edge of the defined "safe" zone.

We'd been expecting increased security around the campaign, but this was more than I'd been bargaining for. They picked us up from Buffy's house; the senator's security dispatch wasn't even willing to let us near their cars unless they were collecting us from a secured location, which took our place out of the running. Given that they gave us blood tests before they said hello, I don't quite get the reasoning. Maybe they didn't want to deal with a zombie attack before lunch. Or maybe they were avoiding our parents, who were practically panting at the idea of a photo opportunity with the senator's men.

Once in the cars, we were transported to the Oakland Airport, where we had to take another blood test before they loaded us and our portable gear onto a private helicopter. We flew to what was supposedly an undisclosed location but I was pretty sure was the city of Clayton, near the foothills of Mount Diablo. Most of that area was purchased by the government after the original residents evacuated, and it's been rumored for years that they were using some of the old ranches as short-term housing. It's a nice place, assuming you don't mind the occasional threat of zombie coyotes, wild dogs, and bobcats. Rural areas offer a lot where privacy is concerned, but not so much if what you're looking for is safety.

Judging by the stables around the perimeter, our destination started life as a working farm. Now it was clearly a private residence, with electric fences spanning the spaces between buildings and barbed wire strung as far as the eye could see. Factor in the helipad and it didn't take any great leap of logic to conclude that this place confirmed the rumors about the government setting up hidey-holes out in the abandoned boonies. Nice digs, if you can get them. I smiled as I continued looking around. Our first day, and we already had a scoop: Government Use of Abandoned Land in Northern California Confirmed. Read all about it.

Buffy picked up her bags and walked over to me, looking flustered. "I don't think I've ever been poked that many times," she complained.

"At least now you know you're clean," I said. "Cameras rolling?"

"There was a minor EMP band at the entrance that took two and five off-line, but I anticipated for that and built in redundancies. One, three, and four, and six through eight, are all transmitting live and have been since pickup."

I looked at her flatly. "I didn't understand a word of that, so I'm just going to assume you said 'yes' and move on with my life, all right?"

"Works for me," she said, waving at Shaun as he joined us. "You're done?"

"They know Shaun can't be a zombie," I said, adjusting my sunglasses. "You need a brain to reanimate."

He elbowed me amiably and shook his head. "Dude, I'm amazed they didn't strip search us. They should've bought us dinner first, or something."

"Will lunch do?" asked a jocular voice. All three of us turned, finding ourselves facing a tall, generically handsome man whose carefully cropped brown hair was starting to gray but had been left just long enough in the front to fall across his forehead and create the illusion of boyishness. His skin was tan but relatively unlined, and his eyes were very blue. He was casually dressed in tan slacks and a white shirt, with the sleeves rolled up around his elbows.

"Senator Ryman," I said, and offered him my hand. "I'm Georgia Mason. These are my associates, Shaun Mason—"

"Hey," interjected Shaun.

"—and Georgette Meissonier."

"You can call me Buffy," said Buffy.

"Of course," the senator said, taking my hand and shaking it. He had a good grip, solid without being overwhelming, and the teeth he revealed when he smiled were straight and white. "It's a pleasure to meet all three of you. I've been watching your pre-campaign preparations with interest." He released my hand.

"We had a lot to accomplish and not much time to accomplish it in," I said.

"A lot to accomplish" verged on understatement. We had seven baby bloggers contact us before we finished eating dinner, all wanting to know if we were planning to schism. Once people knew the size of the story we'd landed, there was no way striking out on our own would have been a surprise, so we didn't try to make it one. The folks at Bridge Supporters were sorry to see us go and pleased by our severance offer: We took exclusive rights to all campaign-trail stories to our new site, but we allowed them to keep running two of Buffy's ongoing poetry series, gave them first rights on any continuations to Shaun's se-ries on exploring the ruins of Yreka, and guaranteed two op-ed pieces from me per month for the next year. They'd get click-through reads from the folks following us on campaign, and we'd get the same in return as existing Bridge Support readers found their way to our new site through the shared material. My friend Mahir had been looking to move on to new challenges, and he was glad to sign on to help me moderate the Newsies. Shaun and Buffy had their own hiring to do, and I left it to them.

Finding a host for our new site was disturbingly easy. One of Buffy's biggest fans runs a small ISP, and he was willing to put us up and online in exchange for a minimal fee and a lifetime membership to our exclusive features, once we had some to offer. Less than twenty minutes after calling him, we had a URL, a place to put our files, and our very first subscriber. The baby bloggers who contacted us the first night were quickly joined by two dozen others, and that gave us the liberty to pick and choose, looking for people who fit a profile other than "available." We wound up with twelve supporting betas, four in each major category, already producing content for a site that hadn't even officially launched yet. Never in my wildest dreams did I believe it could be that easy to get everything you'd ever wanted . . . but it was.

After the End Times went live six days after we got the notice that we had been chosen to accompany Senator Ryman's campaign, with my name on the masthead as senior editor, Buffy listed as our graphic designer and technical expert, and Shaun responsible for hiring and marketing. Whether we sank or swam, there was no going back; once you make alpha, you can never be a beta again. Blogging is a territorial world, and the other betas would eat you alive if you tried.

I hadn't slept more than four hours a night in two weeks. Sleep was a luxury reserved for people who weren't trying to design their futures around a meal ticket that might still prove to be a rotten apple. I just had to hope the dirt we found on the campaign trail would be enough to support us, or our careers would be short, sour, and too interesting by far.

"Still, you seem to have done all right," Senator Ryman said. His Wisconsin accent was stronger than it sounded on the newscasts; either he didn't realize we were filming, or he figured there was no point in playing fake around the people who were going to be sharing his quarters over the next year. "If you'll come with me, Emily has a nice lunch going, and she's been looking forward to meeting you."

"Is your wife coming with you for the whole campaign?" I asked. He started to walk toward a nearby door, and I followed, gesturing for the others to do the same. We knew the answer already—Emily Ryman was going to be staying on the family ranch in Parrish, Wisconsin, during most of the year, taking care of the kids while her husband did the moving and shaking—but I wanted him to say it for our pickup recordings. The best sound clips are the ones you gather for yourself.

"Em? I couldn't make her come the whole way if I used a tractor pull," the senator said, and opened the door. "Wipe your feet, all three of you. There's no point to making you go through another damned blood test—if you're this far past the gate and you're not clean, we're dead already. May as well be friendly about it." Then he was inside, bellowing, "Emily! The bloggers are here!"

Shaun gave me a look, mouthing "I like him." I nodded. We'd just met the man, and he was probably a master of political bullshit, but I was starting to like him, too. There was something about him that said "I know how pointless all of these political circuses are. Let's see how it long it takes for them to realize that I'm just playing along, shall we?" I had to respect that.

He might be playing us for a bunch of saps, but if he was, he'd slip eventually, and we'd take him apart. That would be almost as much fun as getting along with him, and definitely better for our market share.

The interior of the house was decorated with a distinctly Southwestern flare, all bright, solid colors and geometric patterns. Southwestern art has shifted in the last twenty years; before the Rising, any house with that many potted cacti and Native American–style throw rugs would have boasted a coyote statue or two and possibly a polished steer's skull, complete with horns. I've seen pictures—it was pretty morbid stuff. These days, representations of any animal that weighs more than forty pounds have a tendency to make people uncomfortable, so coyotes and steers are both out of fashion, unless you're dealing with a serious nihilist or some kid playing "creature of the night." Only the painted deserts remain. An enormous picture window took up half of one wall, marking the house as having been put up before the Rising. No one builds windows like that anymore. They're an invitation to attack.

The kitchen was defined by raised counters rather than walls, spilling tile flooring into the hall and attached dining room in an almost organic fashion. Senator Ryman was standing by the big butcher's block at the center when we entered, arms around the waist of a woman in blue jeans and a flannel lumberjack's shirt. Her brown hair was pulled back in a high, girlish ponytail. He was murmuring something in her ear, looking a good ten years younger than he had when we met outside.

Shaun and I exchanged a glance, debating the merits of retreating and allowing them this private time. My journalistic instincts said "stay," and I certainly wasn't turning off the cameras, but my sense of ethics told me that people deserve a chance to unwind before starting on something as huge as a full-on political campaign.

Luckily, Buffy saved us from the conundrum by barreling straight ahead, sniffing the air appreciatively, and asking, "What's for lunch? Wow, I'm starving. That smells like shrimp and mahimahi—am I close? Can I do anything to help?"

Senator Ryman stepped away from his wife, exchanging an amused look with her before turning a grin on Buffy, and said, "I think things are pretty much in hand. Besides which, Emily's too territorial to share her kitchen with another woman. Even if it's a borrowed kitchen."

"Quiet, you," said Emily, jabbing him in the ribs with a wooden spoon. He winced theatrically, and she laughed. The laugh was bright, perfectly in keeping with the practical, elegantly simple kitchen. "Now, let me see if I can guess which of you is which. I know you have two Georges and a Shaun—how is that fair?" She put on an exaggerated pout, not looking a bit like a senator's wife. "Three boys' names for two girls and a boy. It puts me at a disadvantage."

"We didn't get to choose our own names, ma'am," I said, fighting a smile. Shaun and I don't even know what names we were born with. We were orphaned in the Rising, and when the Masons adopted us, we were both listed under "Baby Doe."

"Oh, but one of you did," she said. "One of the Georges is also a Buffy, and if I remember my pop culture right, it should be the blonde one." She turned, extending a hand toward Buffy. "Georgette Meissonier, correct?"

"Absolutely," Buffy said, taking her hand. "You can call me Buffy. Everyone else does."

"It's a pleasure to meet you," Emily replied, and released her hand, turning toward Shaun and me. "That must make you the Masons. Shaun and Georgia. Yes?"

"Got it," Shaun said, saluting her. Somehow, he kept the gesture from looking like he was making fun. I've never understood how he does that.

I stepped forward, offering her a hand. "George is fine by me, or Georgia. Whichever is easier for you, Mrs. Ryman."

"Call me Emily," she said. Her grip was cool, and the glance she cast toward my sunglasses was understanding. "Are the lights too bright for you? They're all soft bulbs, but I can dim the window a bit more if you need me to."

"No, thank you," I said, eyebrows rising as I studied her face more closely. Her eyes weren't dark, as I had first assumed; what I had taken to be deep brown irises were actually her pupils, so dilated that they pushed the natural muddy hazel of her eyes into a thin ring around the edges. "Wouldn't you know if the lights were a problem?"

She smiled, wryly. "My eyes aren't as sensitive as they used to be. I was an early case, and there was some nerve damage by the time they figured out what was going on. You'll tell me if the lights get to be too much?"

I nodded. "Sure will."

"Wonderful. You three make yourselves comfortable. Lunch will be up in a few minutes. We're having fish tacos with mango salsa and virgin mimosas." She raised a finger to the senator, adding playfully, "I don't want to hear a word of complaint from you, Mister. We're not getting these nice reporters drunk before things even get started."

"Don't worry, ma'am," Shaun said. "Some of us can hold our liquor."

"And some of us can't," I said dryly. Buffy weighs ninety-five pounds, soaking wet. The one time we took her out drinking, she wound up climbing onto a table and reciting half of *Night of the Living Dead* before Shaun and I could pull her down. "Thank you, Mrs. . . . Emily."

Her smile was approving. "You can be taught. Now all of you, go sit down while I finish taking care of business. Peter, that means you, too."

"Yes, dear," said the senator, kissing her on the cheek before moving to take a seat at the dining room table. The three of us followed him in an obedient, slightly ragged line. I'll challenge senators and kings for the right to know the truth, but far be it from me to challenge a woman in her own kitchen.

Watching the places everyone took around the table was interesting in a purely sociological sense. Shaun settled with his back to the wall, affording him the best view of the room. He may seem like an idiot, but in some ways, he's the most careful of us all. You can't be an Irwin and not learn some things about keeping your exits open. If the zombies ever mob en masse again, he'll be ready. And filming.

Buffy took the seat nearest the light, where the cameras studded through her jewelry would get the best pickup shots. Her portables work on the principles defined during the big pre-Rising wireless boom; they transmit data to the server on a constant basis, allowing her to come back later and edit it at her leisure. I once tried to figure out how many transmitters she actually had on her, but wound up giving up and wandering off to do something more productive, like answering Shaun's fan mail. He gets more marriage proposals a week than he likes to think about, and he lets me handle them all.

The senator took the seat closest to the kitchen and his wife, thus conveniently leaving me the chair with the highest degree of shadow. So he was a family man *and* someone who understood that consideration was a virtue. Nice. I settled, asking, "You provide home-cooked meals for all your news staff?"

"Just the controversial ones," he replied, his tone easy and assured. "I'm not going to beat around the bush. I read your public reports, your op-ed pieces, everything, before I agreed to your application. I know you're smart and won't forgive bullshit. That doesn't," he held up a finger, "mean I'm going to be one hundred percent straight with you, because there are some things no reporter ever gets to be privy to. Mostly having to do with my home life and my family, but still, there are no-go zones."

"We respect that," I said. Shaun and Buffy were nodding.

Senator Ryman seemed to approve, because he nodded in turn, looking satisfied. "Nobody wanted me to bring blog folks on this campaign," he said, without preamble. I sat up a little straighter. The entire online community knew that the senator's handlers had been recommending against including bloggers in the official campaign press corps, but I'd never expected to hear it put so baldly. "They have this idea that you three will report whatever you damn well want to and not what's good for the campaign."

"So you're saying they're pretty smart, then?" Shaun asked, in a bland surfer-boy drawl that might almost have been believable, if he hadn't been smirking as he said it.

The senator roared with laughter, and Emily looked up from the stove, clearly amused. "That's what I pay them for, so I certainly hope so, Shaun. Yeah, they're pretty smart. They've got you pegged for exactly what you are."

"And what's that, Senator?" I asked.

Sobering, he leaned forward. "The children of the Rising. Biggest revolution that our generations—yours, mine, and at least two more besides—are ever going to see. The world changed overnight, and sometimes I'm sorry I was born too early to be in on the ground level of what it's turned into. You kids, you're the ones who get to shape the real tomorrow, the one that's going to matter. Not me, not my lovely wife, and certainly not a bunch of talking heads who get paid to be smart enough to realize that a bunch of Bay Area blogger kids are going to tell the truth as they see it, and damn the political consequences."

Eyebrows rising again, I said, "That does very little to explain why you felt it was important that we be here."

"You're here because of what you represent: the truth." The senator smiled, boyish once more. "People are going to believe whatever you say. Your careers depend on how many dead folks your brother can prod with a stick, how many poems your friend can write, and how much truth you can tell."

"So what if the things we say don't paint you in a good enough light?" Buffy frowned, tilting her head. It would have looked like a natural gesture if I hadn't known the silver moon-and-star earring dangling from her left ear was a camera that responded to head gestures. She was zooming in on the senator to catch his answer.

"If they don't paint me in a good enough light, I suppose I wasn't meant to be the President of the United States of America," he said. "You want to dig for scandals, I'm sure my opponents have road maps for you to follow. You want to report on this campaign, you report what you see, and don't worry about whether or not I'm going to like it. Because that doesn't matter a bit."

We were still staring at him, trying to frame responses to something that seemed about as realistic coming from a politician's mouth as sonnets coming out of a zombie's, when Emily Ryman walked over and started setting plates onto the table. I was grateful for the interruption. After the way the day had been going, I was running out of "surprised" and moving rapidly into the region of "mild shock," and this was enough to give me a chance to regroup.

Emily sat once she'd finished putting the plates down, reaching for Senator Ryman's hand. "Peter, will you say grace?"

"Of course," he said. Shaun and I exchanged glances before joining hands with each other and the Rymans, closing the circle around the table. Senator Ryman bowed his head, closing his eyes. "Dear Lord, we ask that You bless this table and those who have come to gather around it. Thank You for the good gifts that You have given us. For the health of ourselves and our families, for the company and food we are about to enjoy, and for the future that You have seen fit to set before us. Thank You, oh Lord, for Your generosity, and for the trials by which we may come to know You better."

Shaun and I left our eyes open, watching the senator as he spoke. We're atheists. It's hard to be anything else in a world where zombies can attack your elementary school talent show. Much of the country has turned back toward faith, however, acting under the vague supposition that it can't hurt anything to have God on your side. I glanced at Buffy, who was nodding along with the senator's words, eyes tightly closed. She's a lot more religious than most people would guess. Her family is French Catholic. She's been saying grace at any sort of large gathering since she was born, and she still attends a nonvirtual church on Sundays.

"Amen," said the senator. We all echoed it with varying degrees of certainty.

Emily Ryman smiled. "Everybody, eat up. There's more if you're still hungry, but I want to eat too, so you're going to have to serve yourselves after this round." The senator got a kiss on the cheek to go with his fish tacos; the rest of us just got fed.

Not that Shaun was going to let lunch pass without a little light conversation. Of the two of us, he's the gregarious one. Someone had to be. "Will you be coming along on the whole campaign, ma'am, or just this leg of it?" he asked, with uncharacteristic politeness. Then again, he's always had a healthy respect for women with food.

"You couldn't pay me enough to accompany this dog and pony show," Emily said, dryly. "I think you kids are totally insane. Entertaining as all heck, and I love your site, but insane."

"I'll take that as a 'no,'" I said.

"Uh-uh. For one thing, I am *not* taking the kids out on the road. No way. The tutors they hire for these things are never the sort I approve of." She smiled at the senator, who patted her knee in an unconsciously companionable fashion. "And they wind up seeing way too many reporters and politicians. Not the sort you want keeping company with a bunch of impressionable young kids."

"Look how it's warped us," said Shaun.

"Exactly," she said, unflustered. "Besides which, the ranch doesn't run itself."

I nodded. "Your family still manages an actual horse ranch, don't they?"

"You know the answer to that, Georgia," said the senator. "Been in Emily's family since the late eighteen hundreds."

"If you think the risk of zombie palominos is enough to make me give up my horses, you've never met a real horse nut," she said, grinning. "Now, don't get your back up. I know where you stand on the animal mass restrictions. You're a big supporter of Mason's Law, aren't you?"

"In all recreational and nonessential capacities, yes," I said.

Thanks to the Masons' biological son, Shaun and I have often found ourselves with an element of unasked-for name recognition when dealing with people who work with animals. Before Phillip, no one realized that *all* mammals with a body mass of forty pounds or more could become carriers of the live-state virus, or that Kellis-Amberlee was happy to cross species, going from man to beast and back again. Mom put a bullet through her only son's head, back when that was still something new enough to break you forever—when it felt like murder, not mercy. So yeah, I guess you could say I support Mason's Law.

"I would, too, in your position," Emily said. Her tone carried none of the accusations I'm used to hearing from animal rights activists; she was speaking the truth, and I could deal, or not, as I so chose. "Now, if everyone wants to tuck in, it's the start of a long day—and a longer month."

"Eat up, everybody, before your lunch gets cold," added the senator, and reached for the mimosas. Shaun and I exchanged a look, shrugged in near-unison, and reached for our forks.

One way or another, we were on our way.

———

My sister has retinal KA syndrome. That's where the filovirus does this massive replication thing in the ocular fluid—there's some more advanced technical term for it, but personally, I like to call it "eye goo," because it pisses George off—and the pupils dilate as wide as they can and never close down like they do in a normal person. Mostly only girls get it, which is a relief, since I look stupid in sunglasses. Her eyes are supposed to be brown, but everyone thinks they're black, because of her pupils being broken.

She was diagnosed when we were five, so I don't really remember her without her sunglasses. And when we were nine, we got this really *dumb* babysitter who took George's glasses, said, "You don't need these," and threw them into the backyard, thinking we were spoiled little suburban brats too afraid of the outdoors to go out after them. So it's pretty plain that she was about as bright as a box of zombies.

Next thing you know, there's me and George digging through the high grass looking for her sunglasses, when suddenly she freezes, eyes getting all wide, and says, "Shaun?" And I'm like, "What?" And she's all, "There's somebody else in the yard." And then I turn around, and wham, zombie, *right there*! I hadn't seen it because I don't see as well in low light as she does. So there are some advantages to having your pupils permanently dilated. Besides the part where they can't tell if you're stoned or not without a blood test when you're at school.

But anyway, zombie, in our backyard. So. Fucking. Cool.

You know, it's been more than a decade since that evening, and that is *still* probably the best present that she's ever gotten for me.

**—From *Hail to the King*,
the blog of Shaun Mason, April 7, 2037**

Six

Getting our equipment past the security screening offered by Senator Ryman's staff took six and a half hours. Shaun spent the first two hours getting underfoot as he tried to guard his gear and finally got all of us banished inside. Now he was sulking on the parlor couch, chin almost level with his chest. "What are they doing, taking the van apart to make sure we didn't stuff any zombies inside the paneling?" he grumbled. "Because, gee, *that* would work really well as an assassination tool."

"It's been tried," Buffy said. "Do you remember the guy who tried to kill George Romero with the zombie pit bulls?"

"That's an urban myth, Buffy. It's been disproven about ninety times," I said, continuing to pace. "George Romero died peacefully in his bed."

"And now he's a happy shambler at a government research facility," said Shaun, abandoning his sulk in order to make "zombie" motions with his arms. The ASL for "zombie" has joined the raised middle finger as one of the few truly universal hand gestures. Some points just need to be made quickly.

"It's sort of sad, thinking about him shuffling around out there, all decayed and mindless and not remembering the classics of his heyday," said Buffy.

I eyed her. "He's a government zombie. He eats better than we do."

"It's the principle of the thing," she said.

It took a while for the first Kellis-Amberlee outbreaks to be confirmed as anything but hoaxes, and even after that was accomplished, it took time for the various governmental agencies to finish fighting over whose problem it was. The CDC got sick of the arguing about three days in, jumped into things with both feet, and never looked back. They had squads in the field by the end of week two, capturing zombies for study. It was quickly apparent that there's no curing a zombie; you can't undo the amount of brain damage the virus does with anything gentler than a bullet to the brainpan. But you can work on ways to neutralize Kellis-Amberlee itself, and since all a zombie really does is convert flesh into virus, a few captive shamblers provided the best possible test subjects.

After twenty years of testing and the derailment of almost every technical field that didn't feed directly into the medical profession, we've managed little more than absolutely nothing. At this point, they can completely remove Kellis-Amberlee from a living body, using a combination of chemotherapy, blood replacement, and a nasty strain of Ebola that's been modified to search and destroy its cousin. There are just a few downsides, like the part where it costs upward of ten thousand dollars for a treatment, none of the test subjects has survived, and oh, right, the constant fear the modified virus will mutate like Marburg Amberlee did and leave us with something even worse to deal with. Where the living dead are concerned, we pretty much exist on square one.

It didn't take long for researchers to connect the health of their "pet" zombies to the amount of protein—specifically living or recently killed flesh; soybeans and legumes won't cut it—they consumed. Kellis-Amberlee converts tissue into viral blocks. The more tissue it can find, the less of the original zombie it converts. So if you feed a zombie constantly, it won't wither to the point of becoming useless. Most of the nation's remaining cattle ranches are there to feed the living dead. A beautiful irony, when you consider that cows break the forty-pound threshold, and thus reanimate upon death. Zombies eating zombies. Good work if you can get it.

A lot of folks leave their bodies to science. Your family skips funeral expenses, the government pays a nice settlement so they won't sue if your image winds up on television one of these days, and if you belong to one of those religious sects that believes the body has to remain intact in order to eventually get carried up to Heaven, you don't run the risk of offending God. You just risk eating the research scientists if containment fails, and some people don't see that as being as much of an abomination as cremation.

George Romero didn't mean to save the world any more than Dr. Alexander Kellis meant to almost destroy it, but you can't always choose your lot in life. Most people wouldn't have had the first idea of how to deal with the zombies if it weren't for the lessons they'd learned from Romero's movies. Go for the brain; fire works, but only if you don't let the burning zombie touch you; once you're bitten, you're dead. Fans of Romero's films applied the lessons of a thousand zombie movies to the reality of what had happened. They traded details of the attacks and their results over a thousand blogs from a thousand places, and humanity survived.

In interviews, Mr. Romero always seemed baffled and a little delighted by the power his movies had proven to have. "Always knew there was a reason people didn't like seeing the zombies win," he'd said. If anyone was surprised when he left his body to the government, they didn't say anything. It seemed like a fitting end for a man who went from king of bad horror to national hero practically overnight.

"They better not damage any of my equipment," Shaun said, snapping me back to the present. He was scowling at the window again. "Some of that stuff took serious barter to get."

"They're not going to damage your equipment, dumb ass. They're the government, we're journalists, and they know we'd tell everyone in the whole damn world, starting with our insurance agency." I leaned over to hit him in the back of the head. "They just need to make sure we're not carrying any bombs."

"Or zombies," added Buffy.

"Or drugs," said Shaun.

"Actually," said the senator, stepping into the room, "we're slightly disappointed by the lack of bombs, zombies, or drugs hidden in your gear. I thought you folks were supposed to be reporters, but there wasn't even any illicit booze."

"We're clear?" I asked, ceasing my pacing. Shaun and Buffy were already on their feet, nearly vibrating. I understood their anxiety; the senator's security crew had their hands on all our servers, which had Buffy unhappy, and on Shaun's zombie hunting and handling equipment, which usually makes him so restless that I wind up locking him in the bathroom just to get some peace and quiet. It's times like this that I'm truly glad of my role as the hardnosed reporter in our little crew. Maybe Buffy and Shaun call me a Luddite, but when the government goons take away all our equipment for examination, they lose everything. I, on the other hand, retain my MP3 recorder, cellular phone, notebook computer, and stylus. They're all too basic to require much examination.

Of course, I can't keep my hands on the vehicles, which had me almost as restless as my companions. The van and my bike represent the most expensive articles we travel with, and most of our livelihood depends on their upkeep. At the same time, they're probably the easiest items to repair—a good mechanic can undo almost any damage, and my bike isn't that customized. As long as the feds didn't bust up the van, we'd be fine.

"You're clear," the senator said. He didn't bat an eye as Shaun and Buffy ran out of the room, despite the fact that neither of them said good-bye. I remained where I was, and after a moment, he turned toward me. "I must admit, we *were* impressed by the structural reinforcements on your van. Planning to last out a siege in that thing?"

"We've considered it. The security upgrades were our mother's design. We did the electrical work ourselves."

Senator Ryman nodded as if this explained everything. In a way, it did. Stacy Mason has been the first name in zombie-proof structural engineering for a long time. "I have to admit, I don't really understand most of your professional equipment, but the security systems . . . Your mother did a truly lovely job."

"I'll give her your compliments." I gestured toward the door. "I should join the feeding frenzy. Buffy's going to want to start assembling today's footage, and she always goes overboard without me standing over her."

"I see." The senator paused for a moment. His voice was uncharacteristically stiff as he continued, "I wondered if I might ask you a small favor, Miss Mason."

Ah, the first demand for censorship. I was going to owe Shaun ten bucks; I'd been betting that Senator Ryman could make it at least until we hit the actual campaign trail before he started trying to control the media. Keeping my voice level, I said, "And that would be, Senator?"

"Emily." He shook his head, a smile tugging at his lips. "I know you'll release whatever you want to, and I look forward to having the chance to read and watch it all. I don't figure we caught half the cameras and recorders you three had on you—some of the ones Miss Meissonier was carrying were barely in the range of our sensors, which leads me to believe that she had others we couldn't see at all, and if she ever wishes to pursue a career in espionage, I only pray she offers her services to us first—so you've doubtless got some great footage. And that's fabulous. But Emily, you see, well . . . she's not so comfortable with a lot of media attention."

I looked at him, thoughtfully. "So you want me to minimize the use of your wife?" That was odd. Emily Ryman was friendly, photogenic, and, except for the horses, just about the sanest politician's wife I'd ever met. I expected him to milk her as the asset she was. "She's going to have to feature in this campaign. And if you win—"

"She understands her role in things, and she doesn't mind being written about, but she'd rather her picture wasn't used excessively," he said. He was clearly uncomfortable with the request. That made me a lot more likely to grant it. "Please. If it's at all possible, I would see it as a great personal favor."

Lowering my sunglasses enough to let him see my eyes, I asked, "Why?"

"Because she raises horses. I know you don't approve of keeping mammals that meet the size for Kellis-Amberlee amplification, but you're polite about it. You write articles and you lobby for stricter controls, and that's fine, that's your right as an American citizen. Given your family connections, it's even unavoidable. Some people, however, get a little more . . . aggressive."

"You're talking about the bombing in San Diego, aren't you?" It was the darling of the news feeds for a while, because it was such a huge event: the world's largest remaining zoo and wild animal conservatory, bombed by activists who believed Mason's Law should be used to shut down every facility in the world that kept animals capable of undergoing viral amplification. The same fringe group, in other words, that supports lifting the bans on big-game hunting across the world, and wiping out North America's large indigenous mammals. They call themselves "pro-life," but what they really are is pro-genocide. Their proverbial panties get wet just thinking about the opportunity to go out and slaughter something under the illusion of following the law. Hundreds died in San Diego because of what they did, and I'm not just talking about the animals. We got a lot of firsts out of that stunt. "First confirmed Kellis-Amberlee transmission through giraffe bite" wasn't the weirdest.

Senator Ryman nodded, lips pressed into a thin line. "I have three daughters. All of them are at the ranch with their grandparents, waiting for their mother to rejoin them."

"Trying to avoid making them a target?"

"That's unavoidable, unfortunately. It's the nature of modern politics. But I can keep them out of the spotlight for as long as I can."

I kept my sunglasses pulled down, studying him. Unlike most people, he met my eyes without flinching. Having a wife with retinal KA probably helped with that. Finally, I slid my glasses back into place and nodded. "I'll see what I can do."

He offered a quick, boyish smile, his relief showing clearly. "Thank you, Miss Mason. Don't let me keep you any longer. I'm sure you're anxious to check the state of your vehicles."

"If your goons scratched my bike, I'll have to get bitchy," I cautioned, and left the room, following the path Shaun and Buffy had taken to the yard. Leaving Emily out of things would be relatively easy. The way the kitchen was lit meant we could limit footage of her without changing the overall tone of the afternoon, and without being too blatant—looking like you're hiding something is the fastest way to bring the vultures down. I'd have to leave it up to Buffy, of course. She's our graphics wiz.

The interesting part was that he was willing to ask for it at all. Senator Ryman knew he'd only get to ask us to leave things out so many times before we started resisting, and once that happened, he wasn't going to be a happy man. So why introduce us to Emily at all, if the introduction meant he'd have to use one of his limited "get out of jail free" cards to keep her out of a puff piece about meeting the candidate over some good old-fashioned fish tacos? It was possible he was just trying to play on our sympathies—"Golly, my wife doesn't like to be seen on camera, and it could endanger the kids, so you'll be good to us, right?"—but that didn't seem likely. It seemed a lot more realistic to me that she'd wanted the chance to meet us, and he was willing to go along with it, as long as it kept her happy with him. I've learned to trust my hunches, and they were telling me now that the senator and his wife were generally good folks, with the bad taste to choose politics and horse breeding as their respective careers.

Our vehicles were parked out front. The van had been scrubbed until it gleamed, and even the relay towers were clean. All the chrome on my bike had been buffed until it was almost too bright to contemplate, even through my sunglasses. "I don't think that thing's been this clean since before I bought it," I said, shoving my glasses back up my nose. The sunset was on the way, and as far as I was concerned, it was taking a little too much of its own sweet time about things.

Shaun stuck his head out of the van's rear door and waved, calling, "Hey, George! They got the fruit punch stain out of the upholstery!"

"Really?" I couldn't help being impressed. That stain had been in the van since three days after the parents gave it to us, and that was on our eighteenth adoption day. "Class A license means Class A equipment," Dad said, and that—well, that, and roughly three hundred hours of back-breaking work—was that.

"And they moved *all* Buffy's wires around," he said, with a certain degree of sadistic glee, before retreating back into the van.

I smothered a smile as I started toward the van, pausing to run one hand down the sleekly polished side of my bike. If the security crew had scratched the paint, they'd also buffed the scratch clean without leaving a trace. It was impressive work.

Things were less peaceful inside the van. Shaun was sprawled in a chair, cleaning his crossbow, while Buffy was flat on her back under one of the desks, heels drumming against the floor as she yanked wires out of their current, incorrect locations and jammed them into new holes. Every time she yanked a wire, one or more of the van's monitors would start to roll or be consumed by static, turning the scene into something abstract and surrealistic, like a bad B-grade horror movie. She was also swearing like a merchant marine, displaying a grasp of profanity that was more than a little bit impressive.

"Do you kiss your mother with that mouth?" I asked, stepping over the spools of discarded cabling and taking a seat on the counter.

"Look at this!" She shoved herself out from under the desk and into a kneeling position, brandishing a fistful of cables in my direction. I raised my eyebrows, waiting. "*All* of these were connected wrong! All of them!"

"Are they labeled?"

Buffy hesitated before admitting, "No."

"Do they follow any sort of normal, sane, or predictable system?" I knew the answer to that one. Shaun and I did most of the electrical work, but the actual wiring is all Buffy's, and she thought most people were too conservative with the way they managed their inputs. I've tried to understand her system a few times. I've always come away with a migraine and the firm conviction that, sometimes, ignorance really *is* bliss.

"They didn't have to unplug *everything*," Buffy muttered, and crawled back under the desk.

Shaun pulled back the string on his crossbow with one finger, checking the tension, and said, "You can't win. Logic has no power over her when her territory has been invaded by the heathens."

"Got it," I said. The monitor next to me rolled to static before it began displaying a video feed of the yard outside. "Buffy, how long before we're fully operational again?"

"Fifteen minutes. Maybe twenty. I haven't checked the wires on the backup consoles yet, so I don't know how big of a mess they made *there*." The irritation in her voice was unmasked. "No data loss so far, but none of the van's exterior cameras got anything but static for over an hour, thanks to their stupid monkeying."

"I'm sure we can live without an hour's recordings of the security team," I said. "Shaun, get the lights?"

"On it." He put his crossbow aside and rose, moving to drop the shade over the van's window and pull the rear door closed. Buffy made a small grunt of protest, and he flicked the switch to turn on the interior lights. The area was promptly bathed in a soft, specially formulated light designed to be gentle on sensitive eyes. The bulbs cost fifty bucks each, and they're worth it. They're even better than the black lights I use in my room at home. They don't just prevent headaches; sometimes, they *cure* them.

I removed my glasses with a sigh, massaging my right temple with my fingertips. "All right, folks, we have our first official, on-the-record encounter. Impressions?"

"Like the wife," said Shaun. "She's photogenic, and a definite asset. I still need a handle on the senator. He's either the biggest Boy Scout ever to make it past the local level, or he's playing us."

"The fish tacos were good," said Buffy. "I like Senator Ryman, actually. He's nice even when he doesn't have to be. This could be a pretty fun gig."

"Who cares about fun as long as it brings in the green?" asked Shaun, with a philosophical shrug. "We're made when this is over. Everything else is gravy."

"I agree with both of you, to a degree," I said, still massaging my temple. I could already tell I was going to need painkillers before we wrapped for the night. "Senator Ryman can't be as nice as he wants us to think he is, but he's also nicer than he has to be; it's not entirely a put-on. There's a degree of sincerity there that you can't fake. I'll do a pull-and-drop profile on him tonight, something like 'First Impressions of the Man Who Would Be President.' Puff piece, but still. Buff, how long is it going to take you to splice our footage?"

"Once everything is ready to run again, I'll need an hour—two, tops."

"Try for an hour. We want to hit the East Coast while they're still awake. Shaun, care to do a review of the security precautions? Hit up a few of the guards, find out what sort of ordnance they're carrying with them?"

His face split in a wide grin. "Already on it. You know the big blond guy? Built like a linebacker?"

"I did notice the presence of a giant on the security team, yes."

"His name's Steve. He carries a baseball bat." Shaun made an exaggerated swinging motion. "Can you imagine him hitting one out of the park?"

"Ah," I said, dryly. "The classics. Grab a few cameras, harass the locals until you get what you want. Which brings us to my last order of business—we have a request from the senator."

Buffy slid out from under the desk again, another bundle of wires in her hands, and gave me a curious look. Shaun scowled.

"Don't tell me we're being censored *already*."

"Yes and no," I said. "He wants us to keep Emily out of things as much as we can for right now. Minimize her inclusion in the lunch footage, that sort of thing."

"Why?" asked Buffy.

"San Diego," I said, and waited.

I didn't have to wait long. Shaun doesn't feel as strongly as I do about the universal application of Mason's Law, but he still follows the debate. Expression changing from one of incomprehension to complete understanding, he said, "He's afraid somebody's going to target her at the ranch if we make too big a deal of things."

"Exactly." I switched my massaging to my other temple. "Their kids are out there with their grandparents, and he sort of wants the family alive. A little risk is unavoidable, but he'd like to keep them low-profile as long as he can."

"I can manage the footage edits," said Buffy.

"She wouldn't feature in my piece at all," said Shaun.

"And I'll sidebar her. So we're in agreement?"

"Guess so," said Shaun.

"Great. Buffy, let me know when we're back to live-feed capacity on all bands. I'm going to step outside for a few minutes." I slid my sunglasses back on and stood. "Just getting a little air."

"I'll get to work," said Shaun, and stood as I did, exiting the van a few steps ahead of me. He didn't stop or look back as I came out; he just kept going. Shaun knows me better than anyone else in the world. Sometimes I think he knows me better than I do. He knows I need a few minutes by myself before I can start working. Location doesn't matter. Just solitude.

The afternoon light had dimmed without dying, and my bike wasn't quite as painful to look at. I walked over and leaned against it, resting my heels on the driveway as I closed my eyes and tilted my face up into the dying light. Welcome to the world, kids. Things were moving now, and all we could do was make sure that the truth kept getting out, and getting where it needed to be.

When I was sixteen and told my father that I wanted to be a Newsie—it wasn't a surprise by that point, but it was the first time I had said it to his face—he pulled some strings and got me enrolled in a history of journalism course at the university. Edward R. Murrow, Walter Cronkite, Hunter S. Thompson, Cameron Crowe . . . I met the greats the way you should meet them, through their words and the things they did, when I was still young enough to fall in love without reservations or conditions. I never wanted to be Lois Lane, girl reporter, even though I dressed like her for Halloween one year. I wanted to be Edward R. Murrow, facing down corruption in the government. I wanted to be Hunter S. Thompson, ripping the skin off the world. I wanted the truth, and I wanted the news, and I'd be damned before I settled for anything less.

Shaun's the same, even if his priorities are different. He's willing to let a good story come before the facts, as long as the essential morals stay true. That's why he's so good at what he does, and why I double-check every report he writes before I release it.

One thing I did learn from those classes is that the world is not, in any way, what people expected thirty years ago. The zombies are here, and they're not going away, but they're not the *story*. They were, for one hot, horrible summer at the beginning of the century, but now they're just another piece of the way things work. They did their part: They changed everything. Absolutely everything.

The world cheered when Dr. Alexander Kellis announced his cure for the common cold. I've never had a cold, thanks to Dr. Kellis, but I understand they were pretty annoying; people didn't enjoy spending half their time sniffling, sneezing, and getting coughed on by total strangers. Dr. Kellis and his team rushed through testing at a pace that seems criminal in retrospect, but who am I to judge? I wasn't there.

What's really funny is that you can blame this whole thing on the news. One reporter heard a rumor that Dr. Kellis was intending to sell his cure to the highest bidder and would never allow it to be released to the man on the street. This was ridiculous if you understood that the cure was a modified rhino-virus, based on the exact virulence that enabled the common cold to spread so far and so fast. Once it got outside the lab, it was going to "infect" the world, and no amount of money would prevent that.

Those are the facts, but this guy didn't care about the facts. He cared about the scoop and being the first to report a great and imaginary injustice being perpetrated by the heartless medical community. If you ask me, the real injustice is that Dr. Alexander Kellis is viewed as responsible for the near-destruction of mankind and not Robert Stalnaker, investigative reporter for the *New York Times*. If you're going to lay blame for what happened, that's where it belongs. I've read his articles. They were pretty stirring stuff, condemning Dr. Kellis and the medical community for allowing this to happen. Mankind, he said, had a right to the cure.

Some people believed him a bit too much. They broke into the lab, stole the cure, and released it from a crop duster, if you can believe that. They flew that bastard as high as it would go, loaded balloons with samples of Dr. Kellis's work, and fired them into the atmosphere. It was a beautiful act of bioterrorism, conducted with all the best ideals at heart. They acted on a flawed assumption taken from an incomplete truth, and they screwed us all.

To be fair, they might not have screwed things up as badly as they did if it hadn't been for a team working out of Denver, Colorado, where they were running trials on a genetically engineered filovirus called "Marburg EX19," or, more commonly, "Marburg Amberlee." It was named for their first successful infection, Amanda Amberlee, age twelve and a half. She'd been dying of leukemia and considered unlikely to see her thirteenth birthday. The year Dr. Kellis discovered his cure, Amanda was eighteen, finishing her senior year of high school, and perfectly healthy. The folks in Denver took a killer, made a few changes to its instructions, and cured cancer.

Marburg Amberlee was a miracle, just like the

Kellis cure, and together they were primed to change the course of the human race. Together, that's what they did. No one gets cancer or colds anymore. The only issue is the walking dead.

There were ninety-seven people in the world infected with Marburg Amberlee when the Kellis cure was released. The virus never left the system once it had been introduced; it would kill off cancerous cells and go dormant, waiting. All those people were quiet, noninfectious hot zones, living their lives without a clue of what was about to happen. Amanda Amberlee wasn't among them. She died two months earlier, in a car crash following her senior prom. She was the only one of the Marburg Amberlee test cases not to reanimate; she provided the first clue that it was the interaction of the viruses and not Marburg Amberlee itself that caused the apparently dead to rise.

The Kellis cure swept the globe in days. Those responsible for the release were hailed, if not as heroes, then at least as responsible citizens, cutting through red tape to better the lives of their fellow men. No one knows when the first Marburg Amberlee test subjects came into contact with the cure or how long it took from exposure to mutation. How long for the formerly peaceful filovirus to seize on the newly introduced rhinovirus and begin to change? Best estimates say that within a week of the introduction of the Kellis cure to Marburg Amberlee, the two had combined, creating the airborne filovirus we know as Kellis-Amberlee. It went on to infect the world, hopping from person to person on the back of the virulence coded into the original Kellis cure.

There is no index case for viral amplification. It happened in too many places at the same time. We can only pinpoint things to this degree because of what the movies got wrong: Infection wasn't initially universal. People who died before getting dosed with Kellis-Amberlee stayed dead. Those who died after infection didn't. Why it brings its hosts back to literal, biological life is anyone's guess. The best theories hold that it's an enhanced version of normal filovirus behavior, the urge to replicate taken to a new and unnatural level, one that taps into the nervous system of the host and keeps it moving until it falls apart. Zombies are just sacks of virus looking for something to infect, being "driven" by Kellis-Amberlee. Maybe it's true. Who knows? Whether it is or not, the zombies are here, and everything has changed.

That includes the shape of the political world, because a lot of the old issues shifted once the living dead were among us. The death penalty, animal cruelty, abortion—the list goes on. It's hard to be a politician in this world, especially given the xenophobia and paranoia running rampant through most of our more well-off communities. Senator Ryman was going to have a long, hard fight to the White House, assuming he could get there at all. And we'd be with him every step of the way.

I sat with my face toward the sun, ignoring the way my head was throbbing, and waited for Buffy to tell me that the time had come to begin.

BOOK II

Dancing with
the Dead

You tell the truth as you see it, and you let the people decide whether to believe you. That's responsible reporting. That's playing fair. Didn't your parents teach you anything?

—GEORGIA MASON

Darwin was right. Death doesn't play fair.

—STACY MASON

To explain my feelings for Senator Peter Ryman, I must first note that I am a naturally suspicious soul: that which seems too good to be true, in my experience, generally is. It is thus with the natural cynicism that is my hallmark that I make the following statement:

Peter Ryman, Wisconsin's political golden boy, is too good to be true.

As a lifelong member of the Republican party in an era when half the party has embraced the idea that the living dead are a punishment from God and we poor sinners must do "penance" before we can enter the Kingdom of Heaven, it would be easy for him to be a bitter man, and yet he shows no signs of it. He is friendly, cordial, intelligent, and sincere enough to convince this reporter, even at three in the morning when the convoy has broken down in the middle of Kentucky for the third time and the language has turned saltier than the Pacific tide. Rather than preaching damnation, he counsels tolerance. Rather than calling for a "war on the undead," he recommends improving our defenses and the quality of life in the still-inhabited zones.

He is, in short, a politician who understands that the dead are the dead, the living are the living, and we need to treat both with equal care.

Ladies and gentlemen, unless this man has some truly awe-inspiring skeletons in his closet, it is my present and considered belief that he would make an excellent President of the United States of America, and might actually begin to repair the social, economic, and political damage that has been done by the events of these past thirty years. Of course, that can only mean that he won't win.

But a girl can dream.

—From *Images May Disturb You*,
the blog of Georgia Mason, February 5, 2040

Seven

The civic center had been prepared for Senator Ryman's visit with row upon row of folding chairs and video screens angled to broadcast his image all the way to the rear of the cavernous room. Speakers were mounted every fifth row to make sure his words remained crystal clear as they fell upon the ears of the twenty or so brave souls who had actually dared to come hear him speak. The attendees were clustered in the front four rows, leaving the back of the room for the senator's entourage, security folks, and, of course, the three of us. Put together, we outnumbered the voting public almost two to one.

Not that this was a unique occurrence. We'd seen this scene play out in nearly two dozen states and more than three times as many locations in the six weeks since we had left California. People don't come out to "press the flesh" the way they used to, not even for the primaries that determine which candidates will be making it all the way to the presidential elections. They're too worried about contagion and too afraid that the weird guy who keeps muttering to himself isn't actually insane—there's always a chance that he's going through massive viral amplification and will take a chunk out of someone at any moment. The only safe people are the ones you know so well that they can't surprise you with the personality changes the virus causes during replication. Since few people have enough close personal friends to fill an auditorium, most folks don't come out.

That doesn't mean that things have been going unobserved. Judging by the ratings, page hits, and downloads, the campaign has been maintaining some of the highest viewer numbers since Cruise versus Gore in 2018. People want to know how it's going to turn out. There's a lot riding on this election. Including, incidentally, our careers.

Shaun's always said that I take things too seriously; since the start of the campaign, he'd started saying my sense of humor had been surgically removed to make room for more anal-retentiveness. Anyone else who said that would probably have gotten slapped, but from Shaun, I had to admit to an element of truth. Still, if I left things up to him, we'd be living with our parents and pretending we didn't mind the lack of privacy until we died. Someone has to watch the bottom line, and someone has pretty much always been me.

Glancing to Buffy, I stage-whispered, "How do our numbers look?"

She didn't look up from the text scrolling rapidly across her phone. The data feed was moving so fast I didn't have a prayer of following it, but it obviously meant something to Buffy because she nodded, with a small smile on her lips as she said, "We're looking at a sixty percent local audience on the video feed, and we just hit top six percent on the Web. The only candidate getting a higher feed ratio is Congresswoman Wagman, and she's lagging in the actual polls."

"And we know why *she's* getting the feeds, now, don't we children?" drawled Shaun, continuing to test the links in his favorite chain-mail shirt with a pair of lightweight pliers.

I snorted. Word on the blog circuit is that Kirsten "Knockers" Wagman had serious breast augmentation surgery before she went into politics, acting under the assumption that in today's largely Internet-based demographic, looking good is more important than sounding like you have two brain cells to knock together. That worked for a while—it got her a seat in Congress, partially because people enjoy looking at her—but it isn't going to get her very far in a presidential race. Especially not now that she's up against folks who understand the issues.

Senator Ryman didn't appear to have noticed the emptiness of the hall or the nervous expressions on his few actual, physical attendees. Most were probably local politicians coming out to show that they believed in the safety of their community, since several of them looked like they'd explode if you snuck up behind them and said "boo" in a commanding tone of voice. Most, not all. There was one little old lady, at least seventy years old, sitting dead center in the front row. She held her purse primly in her lap, lips set into a thin, hard line as she watched Senator Ryman go through his paces. She didn't look nervous at all. If any zombies tried to invade *this* political event, she'd probably wind up giving them what-for and driving them back outside to wait their turn.

The senator was winding down. You can only give your political platform in so many ways, no matter how much practice you have at saying the same thing from sixteen different angles. I adjusted my sunglasses, settling in my chair as I waited for the real fun to begin: the question-and-answer period. Most of the questions people come up with have something to do with the infected, as in, "What are you going to do about the zombies that the other guys haven't tried already?" The answers can get seriously entertaining, and honestly, so can the questions.

Most questions are e-mailed in by the home audiences and asked by the polite, slightly bland voice of the senator's digital personal assistant, which has been programmed to sound like a well-educated female of indeterminate age and race. Senator Ryman calls it "Beth" for no reason anyone has been able to get him to explain. I intend to keep trying. The *best* questions are the ones that come from the live audiences. Most of them are scared out of their minds after being out of the house for more than half an hour, and nothing loosens the tongue like fear. If I had my way, all questions would be asked by people who had just taken a trip through a really well-designed haunted house.

"—and now I'd like to take a few questions from our audience—both those watching this event through the electronic methods provided by my clever technicians," Senator Ryman chuckled, managing to telegraph his utter lack of understanding of such petty details as "how the video feeds work," "and the good people of Eakly, Oklahoma, who have been good enough to host us this evening."

"Come on, lady, don't let me down," I murmured. Sure enough, the lady in the front row had her hand in the air almost before the senator finished speaking, arm jutting upward at a fierce, near-military angle. I settled back in my chair, grinning. "Jackpot."

"Huh?" Buffy looked up from her watch.

"Live one," I said, indicating the lady.

"Oh." Suddenly interested in something other than the data feed, Buffy sat forward. She knows potential ratings when she sees them.

"Yes—the lady in the front row." Senator Ryman indicated the woman, whose tight-lipped face promptly filled half the monitors in the room. Buffy tapped two buttons on her phone, directing her cameras to zoom in. The senator's tech team is good, and even Buffy admits it; they understand camera angles, splicing footage, and when to go for a tight shot. Thanks to Chuck Wong, who does all their planning and design, they're probably near the top of their field. But Buffy is better.

The lady in question lowered her hand, fixing the senator with a stern gaze. "What is your stance on the Rapture?" Her voice was as clipped and thin as I'd expected. The sound system picked it up clear as a bell, reproducing every harsh edge and disapproving inflection flawlessly.

Senator Ryman blinked, looking nonplussed. It was the first time I'd seen a question take him completely by surprise. He recovered with admirable speed, though, saying, "I beg your pardon?"

"The Rapture. The event in which the faithful will be elevated to the Heavens, while the unfaithful, sinners, and infidels will be left to suffer Hell on Earth." Her eyes narrowed. "What is your stance on this holy, foreordained event?"

"Ah." Senator Ryman continued to look at her, thoughtfulness clearing away his confusion. I heard a faint clink and glanced to my left; Shaun had put down his chain mail and was watching the stage with open interest. Buffy was staring at her phone, furiously tapping buttons as she angled her cameras. You can't edit or pause a live feed, but you can set up the data to give you the best material to work from later. And this was the sort of material you just can't stage. Would he bow to the religious nuts who have been taking over more and more of the party in recent years? Or would he risk alienating the entire religious sector of the voting public? Only the senator knew. And in a moment, so would we.

Senator Ryman didn't break eye contact with the woman as he stepped out from behind his podium, walked to the edge of the stage, and sat, resting his elbows on his knees. He looked like a schoolboy approaching confession, not a man jockeying for the leadership of the most powerful country on the planet. It was a well-considered position, and I applauded it inwardly, even as I began to consider an article on the showmanship of modern politics. "What's your name, ma'am?"

"Suzanne Greeley," she said, pursing her lips. "You haven't answered my question, young man."

"Well, Ms. Greeley, that would be because I was thinking," he said, and looked out at the small gathering, a smile spreading across his face. "I was taught that it's rude to answer a lady's question without giving it proper thought. Sort of like putting your elbows on the table during dinner." A ripple of laughter passed through the crowd. Ms. Greeley didn't join in.

Turning back toward her, the senator continued: "You've asked me about my position on the Rapture, Ms. Greeley. Well, first, I think I should say that I don't really have 'positions' on religious events: God will do as He wills, and it isn't my place or my position to judge Him. If He chooses to lift the faithful into Heaven, He will, and I doubt all the politicians in the world saying, 'I don't believe you can do that' would stop him.

"At the same time, I doubt He's going to do anything like that, Ms. Greeley, because God—the God I believe in, anyway, and as a lifelong Methodist, I feel I know Him about as well as a man who doesn't devote his life to the Church can—doesn't throw good things away. God is the ultimate recycler. We have a good planet here. It has its troubles, yes. We have overpopulation, we have pollution, we have global warming, we have the Thursday night television lineup," more laughter, "and, of course, we have the infected. We have a lot of problems on Earth, and it might seem like a great idea to hold the Rapture now—why wait? Let's move on to Heaven, and leave the trials and tribulations of our earthly existence behind us. Let's get while the getting's good, and beat the rush.

"It might seem like a great idea, but I don't think it is, for the same reason I don't think it's a great idea for a first grader to stand up and say that he's learned enough, he's done with school, thanks a lot but he's got it from here. Compared to God, we're barely out of kindergarten, and like any good teacher, I don't believe He intends to let us out of class just because we're finding the lessons a little difficult. I don't know whether I believe in the Rapture or not. I believe that if God wants to do it, He will . . . but I don't believe that it's coming in our lifetime. We have too much work left to do right here."

Ms. Greeley looked at him for a long moment, lips still pressed into a thin line. Then, so slow that it was almost glacial, she nodded. "Thank you, young man," she said.

Those four words couldn't have been sweeter if they'd been backed by the hallelujah choir.

"Internet share just jumped to top three percent," Buffy reported, raising her head. Her eyes were very wide. "Georgia, we're getting a *top-three feed.*"

"Ladies and gentlemen," I murmured, leaning back in my chair, "I do believe we've got ourselves a presidential candidate."

Top-three feed. The words were, if you'll pardon the cliché, music to my ears. The world of Internet percentages and readership shares is complicated. It all comes down to server traffic. There are thousands of machines dedicated to calculating the flow of data, then reporting back which sites are getting the most access requests from outside sources, and which subsidiaries are attracting the biggest number of hits. Those turn into our ratings, and those are what the advertisers and financial backers base their investments on. Top three was the top of the heap. Anything more would require adding click-through porn.

The rest of the question-and-answer period was pretty standard stuff, with a few hardballs thrown in just to keep things interesting. Where did the senator stand on the death penalty? Given that most corpses tended to get up and try to eat folks, he didn't see it as a productive pursuit. What was his opinion on public health care? Failure to keep people healthy enough to stay alive bordered on criminal negligence. Was he prepared to face the ongoing challenges of disaster preparedness? After the mass reanimations following the explosions in San Diego, he couldn't imagine any presidency surviving without improved disaster planning. Where did he stand on gay marriage, religious freedom, free speech? Well, folks, given that it was no longer possible to pretend that any part of the human race was going to politely lie down and disappear just because the majority happened to disagree with them, and given further the proof that life is a short and fragile thing, he didn't see the point of rendering anyone less free and equal than anybody else. When we got to the afterlife, God could sort us out into the sinner and the saved. Until we got there, it seemed to him that we were better off just being good neighbors and reserving our moral judgments for ourselves.

After an hour and a half of questions, more than half of which originated in the auditorium—a campaign first—the senator stood, wiping his forehead with the handkerchief he'd produced from a back pocket. "Well, folks, much as I'd like to stay and chat a while longer, it's getting on late, and my secretary has informed me that if I don't start cutting off these evening discussions, I'm going to seem a little dull to the folks I'm visiting in the morning." Laughter greeted this comment. Relaxed laughter; sometime in the previous hour, he'd managed to ease the audience out of their fear and into the sort of calm most people don't experience outside of their homes. "I want to thank you for having me, and for all your questions and viewpoints. I sincerely hope I'll have your vote when the time comes, but even if I don't, I have faith that it will be because you managed to find someone who was better for this great land."

"We're following *you*, Peter!" shouted someone from the back of the room. I twisted around in my seat and blinked, realizing that the shouter wasn't someone from the campaign; it was a woman I'd never seen before, holding up a hand-painted Senator Ryman for President sign.

"The campaign has groupies," observed Shaun.

"Always a good sign," said Buffy.

The senator laughed. "I certainly hope that you are," he said. "You'll have the chance to make me put my money where my mouth is soon enough. In the meantime, good night, and God bless you all." Waving to the audience, he turned and walked off the stage as "The Star-Spangled Banner" began to play from speakers around the room. The applause wasn't exactly thunderous—there wasn't enough audience for that—but it was enthusiastic. More so than it had been at the last engagement, and that one had been more enthusiastic than the one before it, and so on, and so on. Maybe you couldn't tell by looking at it, but the campaign was gathering steam.

I stayed where I was, observing the audience as they rose, and, surprisingly, began to talk among themselves rather than fleeing the hall for the safety of their cars. That was a new development, just like the applause. People were *talking*. Face-to-face, real-time *talking*, inspired by the senator and the things he had said.

More and more, I was beginning to feel like we were following a president.

"Georgia?" said Buffy.

"Go ahead and check the backstage feeds," I said, and nodded toward the knot of chattering attendees. "I'm going to go see what the buzz is."

"Make sure you're recording," she said, and started for the stage, gesturing for Shaun to follow. Grumbling good-naturedly, he snagged his chain mail and went.

I walked toward the group of attendees. A few of them glanced over at my approach, took note of my press pass, and went back to talking. The news is either invisible or something to be avoided, depending on what's going on and how many cameras the people around you can see. Since I didn't have any visible recording equipment, I was just part of the scenery.

The first cluster was discussing Senator Ryman's stance on the death penalty. That's one that's been going around since the dead first started getting up and walking. If you're killing someone for the crime of killing people, doesn't it sort of contradict the spirit of the thing if their corpse is going to get up and immediately start killing *more* people? Most death-row inmates stay there until they die of natural causes, at which point the government seizes their shambling corpses and adds them to the ongoing research on the cure. Everybody wins, except for the unlucky prisoners who get eaten by the newly deceased before they can be recovered.

The next group was talking about the potential candidates. Senator Ryman was definitely getting a favorable reception, since they were calling his closest competition respectively "a cheap show-biz whore"—that would be Congresswoman Wagman—and "an arrogant tool of the religious right"—that would be Governor Tate, originally of Texas, and currently the single loudest voice claiming the zombies would only stop eating good American men and women when the country got back to its moral and ethical roots. Whether this would stop the zombies from eating people of different national backgrounds never seemed to come up, which was a pity, since I liked the idea of zombies checking your passport before they decided whether or not they were allowed to bite down.

Satisfied that I wasn't likely to hear anything new in this crowd, I started casting around for a conversation worth joining. The one nearest the doors looked promising; there was a lot of scowling going on, and that's usually a sign that interest is warranted. I turned, walking close enough to hear what was going on.

"The real question is whether he can keep his promises," one man was saying. He looked to be in his late fifties, old enough to have been an adult during the Rising and part of the generation that embraced quarantine as the only true route to safety. "Can we trust *another* president who won't commit to an all-out purge of the zombie population of the national parks?"

"Be reasonable," said one of the women. "We can't simply wipe out endangered species because they might undergo amplification. That kind of rash action isn't going to do anything to make the average man safer."

"No, but it might keep another mother from burying her children after they get attacked by a zombie deer," countered the man.

"Actually, it was a moose, and the 'children' were a group of college students who crossed a proscribed stretch of the Canadian border looking for cheap weed," I interjected. All heads turned my way. I shrugged. "That's a Level 1 hazard zone. It's forbidden to almost everyone outside the armed forces and certain branches of the scientific community. Assuming you're talking about the incident last August and I didn't somehow miss an ungulate attack?" I knew I hadn't. I religiously follow animal attacks on humans, filing them under one of two categories: "We need stricter laws" and "Darwin was right." I don't think people should be allowed to keep animals large enough to undergo amplification, but I also don't believe wiping out the rest of the large mammals in the world is the answer. If you want to go foraging into the wilds of Canada without proper gear, you deserve what you get, even if that happens to include being attacked by an undead moose.

The man reddened. "I don't think I was talking to you, miss."

"Fair enough," I said. "Still, the facts of the event are pretty well documented. Again, assuming I didn't miss something."

Looking mildly amused, one of the other men said, "Well, come on, Carl, did the young lady miss an attack, or are you referring to the incident with the moose?"

He didn't need to answer; his glare was answer enough. Turning his back pointedly on the three of us, he moved to join a vigorous condemnation of the senator's stance on the death penalty that was going on just a few feet away.

"I don't think I've ever seen him deflated with facts before," said the woman, and offered her hand. "I'll have to remember that. Rachel Green. I'm with the local SPCA."

"Dennis Stahl, *Eakly Times*," said the remaining man, flashing his press pass in a brief show of solidarity.

Relieved that my sunglasses would cover the more subtle points of my expression, I took Ms. Green's hand, shook once, and said, "Georgia Mason. I'm one of the bloggers covering Senator Ryman's campaign."

"Mason," said Ms. Green. "As in . . . ?"

I nodded.

She winced. "Oh, dear. Is this going to be unpleasant?"

"Not unless you're in the mood for a debate. I'm here to record reactions to the senator's agenda, not forward my own. Besides," I nodded to Carl's back, "I'm not as hard-line as some. I just have strong opinions about large animals being kept in urban areas, and I think we can agree to disagree on that point, don't you?"

"Fair enough," she said, looking relieved.

Mr. Stahl laughed. "Rachel gets a lot of flack from the local media for what she does," he said. "How's the campaign trail treating you?"

"Are you saying you haven't been reading our reports?" I asked the question lightly, but I wanted to hear the answer. Journalistic acceptance is one of the last things any blog gets. We may be accepted inside the community, but it's not until the traditional news media starts to take our reports seriously that a new feed can honestly be said to have established itself.

"I have," he said. "They're good. A little rough, but good. You care about what you're reporting, and it shows."

"Thanks," I replied, and glanced to Ms. Green. "Did you enjoy the presentation?"

"Is he as sincere as he seems?"

"I haven't seen any signs that he's not," I said, and shrugged. "Illusions of journalistic objectivity aside? He's a nice guy. He has good ideas, and he presents them well. Either he's the best liar I've ever met, or he's going to be our next President. Not that the two are mutually exclusive, but still."

"Mind if I quote you on that?" asked Mr. Stahl, with a sudden predatory intensity that I recognized quite well from my peers.

I smiled. "Go right ahead. Just make sure to give your readers a link to our site, if you would be so kind?"

"Of course."

The three of us chatted for a bit longer, eventually exchanging pleasantries and going our separate ways. I resumed moving from group to group, now mostly listening, and was amused to see that Carl—no last name given or requested—continually moved away from me, as if afraid that I'd taint his ranting with more of my unfortunate facts. I've encountered his type before, usually at political protests. They're the sort who would rather we paved the world and shot the sick, instead of risking life being unpredictable and potentially risky. In another time, they were anti-Semitic, antiblack, antiwomen's liberation, antigay, or all of the above. Now, they're antizombie in the most extreme ways possible, and they use their extremity to claim that the rest of us are somehow supporting the "undead agenda." I've met a lot of zombies. Not as many as Shaun and Mom have, but I'm not as suicidal as they are. In my experience, the only "undead agenda" involves eating you, not worming their way into public acceptance and support. There will always be people for whom hate is easier when it's not backed up by anything but fear. And I will always do my best to hoist them by their own petards.

The hallway lights dimmed once before returning to their original brightness, a sign that moving along was requested by the management. I glanced at my watch. It was a quarter to ten. Most zombie attacks occur between the hours of ten and two. Allowing people to gather during the "high risk" period can triple your insurance rate, especially if you live in an area with recently documented outbreaks. That includes much of the Midwest, where coyotes, feral dogs, and farm animals create a constant low-grade threat.

It doesn't take much to get most people moving after they realize they've managed to stay out past the unspoken world curfew. The conversational groups broke up as people grabbed their coats, bags, and traveling companions and turned to head for the doors. All of them had someone to walk with, even Carl. We are a nation equally afraid of gathering together and being alone. Is it any wonder that the average American is in therapy by the age of sixteen?

My ear cuff beeped, signaling a call. I reached up and tapped it on. "Georgia."

"You coming to join the party soon, or should I drink this beer by myself?" I could hear laughter in the background. The senator's entourage was celebrating another series of political minefields navigated with grace and charm. They were right to celebrate. If the numbers we'd been getting were anything to go by, Senator Ryman was a shoo-in for the Republican Party nomination once the convention rolled around.

"Just finishing out here, Shaun," I said. The hall lights began coming up from their ambient "event" setting, heading for the blazing fluorescents that would keep things lit for the cleaning crew. I squinted my eyes closed, turning to walk toward the stage exit. "Let folks know I'm coming through?"

"On it," he said. My ear cuff beeped again, signaling disconnection. I'm not much for jewelry, but disguised cellular phones are another matter. They're more convenient than walkie-talkies and have a longer battery life, with an average talk time of fifty hours before the battery gives out. Once the batteries go, it's cheaper to buy a new phone than it is to pay to have the case cracked and a new battery installed, but we all have to pay the price of progress. I have at least three phones on me at any given time, and only Shaun has all the numbers.

Two of the senator's security guards were waiting by the door, dressed in identical black suits, with sunglasses covering their eyes and blotting out most of their expressions. I nodded to them. They nodded back.

"Steve, Tyrone," I said.

"Georgia," said Tyrone. He produced a portable blood testing unit from his pocket. "If you would?"

I sighed. "You know they're just going to test me again before they let me into the convoy."

"Yes."

"And you know that a clean result now would be a clean result after the five-minute walk to the buses."

"Yes."

"But you're still going to make me prick my damn finger, aren't you?"

"Yes."

"I hate protocol." My ritual grumbling finished, I extended my hand, pressing my index finger against the contact pad. The lights on the top of the box flashed in the familiar red-green pattern, settling on a steady, uninfected green. "Happy?"

"Overjoyed," Tyrone replied, a faint smile on his lips as he withdrew a biohazard bag from his other pocket and dropped the test kit into it. "Right this way."

"How gracious," I said. Steve smothered a wider

smile, and I smiled back, starting across the parking lot toward the distant lights of the convoy. The bodyguards fell into step beside me, flanking me as we walked. Being escorted through every open area we encountered had been a little annoying at first, but I was getting used to it.

The senator's crew—Shaun, Buffy, and I included—had been traveling in a convoy consisting of five luxury RVs, two buses, our van, and three converted military transport Jeeps, which were ostensibly for scouting runs before entering open territory but were mostly used for off-road rallies in whatever fields presented themselves. There were several smaller vehicles, ranging from my bike to the more substantially armored motorcycles favored by the bodyguards. With as much equipment as we need to carry to meet legal safety standards, it wouldn't make sense to break camp and check into hotels for anything less than a four-day stay, and so we often found ourselves spending a lot of nights "roughing it" in mobile homes that were better outfitted than my room back home.

Shaun, Buffy, and I had been assigned to share one of the RVs, although Buffy usually slept in the van with her equipment, claiming that the perpetual gloom of my special lights gave her, quote, "the heebie-jeebies." The senator's crew had been taking it as another sign that our resident techie is a little bit unhinged, and Shaun and I hadn't been making any efforts to discourage them, even though we knew that it was less of an obsessive-compulsive desire to protect the cameras and more of an ongoing quest for something resembling privacy. Unlike most of our generation, Buffy is an only child, and life in the convoy had been getting on nerves she may not have known she had.

Life in the convoy was also creating a new issue: her religion, and our lack thereof. Buffy prayed before she went to sleep. Buffy said grace before she ate. And Shaun and I . . . didn't. It was better to avoid the conflict by letting her have a little space. Besides, that gave Shaun and me the sort of privacy *we* were accustomed to—the kind that never actually leaves you alone, but doesn't put people in your personal space when you don't want them there, either.

Two more guards waited at the perimeter gates. Unlike Steve and Tyrone, who kept their pistols concealed beneath their jackets, these two openly held autofeed rifles I vaguely recognized from Mom's magazines. They could probably hold off the average zombie mob without outside assistance.

"Tracy, Carlos," I said, and extended my hand, palm down. "I'm tired, I'm filthy, and I'm ready to get drunk with the rest of the good boys and girls. Please confirm my uninfected status so that I can get on with it."

"Bring me a beer later, and it's a deal," Carlos replied, and shoved one of the tester units over my hand, while Tracy did the same for Steve. Tyrone stepped back, waiting his turn. These were midrange units, performing a more sensitive scan and taking a correspondingly longer time to return results. It would be possible for the finger-prick test to declare someone clean and for the full-hand unit to revoke that status less than five minutes later.

My results came back clean, as did Steve's. Tyrone

stepped up to start his own tests and waved us off, toward the third RV in the chain. I could claim that my finely honed journalistic instincts told me which way to go, but they didn't have nearly as much to do with my choice of destinations as with the fact that it was the only RV with an open door, and was definitely the source of the pounding rock music that was assaulting our ears. The Dandy Warhols. The senator is a man who loves his classics.

Senator Ryman was standing on a coffee table inside the RV with his shirt half-unbuttoned and his tie draped over his left shoulder, saluting the room with a bottle of Pabst Blue Ribbon beer. People were cheering too loudly for me to tell what he was saying, but from the look of things, I'd just walked into the middle of a toast. I stopped by the door, stepping out of the way to let Steve get inside behind me, and took a wine cooler offered by one of the interns. I've given up trying to keep them straight; this was one of the brunette ones, which made her a Jenny, a Jamie, or a Jill. I swear, they should come with name tags.

Shaun pushed through the crowd, nodding to Steve before settling next to me. "Word?"

"Generally positive. People like our boy." I nodded to the senator, who had pulled a Jenny up onto the table with him. The audience cheered louder. "I think we might be able to ride this one all the way."

"Buffy said the same thing," Shaun agreed, taking a swig from his beer. "Ready to review tonight's footage?"

"What, and miss the bacchanal? Let me think . . . *yes*." I shook my head. "Get me out of here."

The first postappearance party was fun. So was the third. And the fifteenth. By the twenty-third, I had come to recognize them as a clever method of controlling the locals: let the peons blow off some steam, reinforce the idea that you're just "one of the gang," and get down to the real business after most of the campaign had gone to bed. It was cunning, it was productive, and I salute Senator Ryman for thinking of it. All that being what it is, I saw no reason to spend any more time in an overly bright, overly crowded RV drinking crappy wine coolers than I absolutely had to.

Steve smiled wryly as we turned to push past him. "Leaving so soon?"

"I'll be back for the midnight football game," Shaun promised, and propelled me out the door with a solid push to the middle of my back. The dimness outside was like a benediction.

"Midnight football?" I asked, giving him a sidelong look as we moved away from the raucous RV, heading for our much quieter van. "Do you *sleep*?"

"Do you?" he countered.

"Touché."

Shaun spends his time moving, planning to move, and coming up with new ways to move, many of them involving heavy explosives or the undead. I spend my time writing, thinking about writing, and trying to come up with new things I can write about. Sleep has never been high on the priority list for either of us, which is probably a blessing in disguise. We kept each other amused as kids. If one of us had actually wanted to get some rest, we would have made each other crazy.

The van lights were on and the back door was un-locked. Buffy looked up as we entered, her expression remaining distracted even as she made note of our ar-rival. Once she was sure that we weren't being pur-sued by a rampaging horde of zombies, she turned back to her keyboard.

"Working on?" I asked, putting the wine cooler down next to my station.

"Splicing the footage from tonight and synchro-nizing the sound feeds. I'm thinking of doing a music video remix once it's all finished. Pick some-thing retro and rock the house. Also, I'm chatting with Chuck. He's going to let me access his cam-paign footage to date and see if I can't put together a sort of retrospective."

I raised an eyebrow as I grabbed a Coke from the fridge. "Because you couldn't get at that footage without help?"

Buffy's cheeks reddened. "He's being helpful."

"Buffy has a crush," Shaun sing-songed.

"Play nice," I said, and sat, cracking my knuckles. "I need to hit the op-ed sites, see who's saying what, and start prepping the morning headlines. It's going to be a fun night, and I don't need you starting a fight and spoiling it."

Shaun rolled his eyes. "Riiiiight. You girls feel free to stay cooped up in here screwing around all night—"

"It's called 'making a living', dumb-ass," I said, flicking the screen on and entering my password.

"Like I said, screwing around all night. I'm going out with the boys. We're going to find some action, and I'm going to fuck with it, and tomorrow, we'll have a ratings bonanza like you've never seen." Shaun spread his hands, framing his illusionary triumph. "I can see it now: 'Flagging News Site Saved by Intrepid Irwin.'"

"Get glasses," said Buffy.

I snickered.

Shaun gave Buffy his best wounded look, opening his mouth to rebut.

Whatever he was going to say was drowned out by the gunshots from outside.

You want to talk hypocrisy? Here's hypocrisy: the people who claim Kellis-Amberlee is God's punishment on humanity for daring to dabble where He never intended us to go. I might buy it if zombies had some sort of supernatural scientist-detecting powers and only went for the heretics, but when I look at the yearly lists of KA-related casualties—you can see the raw lists at the official CDC Web site, and a more detailed list is posted on the Wall every Rising Day—I don't see many scientists. What do I see?

I see children. I see Julie Wade, age seven, of Discovery Bay, California; I see Leroy Russell, age eleven, of Bar Harbor, Maine; I see a lot more than just them. Of the two thousand six hundred and fifty-three deaths directly attributed to Kellis-Amberlee within the United States over the past year, *sixty-three percent* were persons under the age of sixteen. Doesn't sound like a merciful God to me.

I see the elderly. I see Nicholas and Tina Postoloff, late of the Pleasant Valley Nursing Home in Warsaw, Indiana. Reports say Nicholas would have survived if he hadn't gone back for Tina, his wife of forty-seven years. They died and were reanimated by the virus before help could arrive. They were put down in the street like wild animals. Doesn't sound like divine judgment. Doesn't sound like divine *anything*.

I see men and women like you and me, people trying to live their lives without making any mistakes that will come back to haunt them later. I don't see sinners or people who have called down some sort of righteous plague. So stop. Stop trying to make people even more afraid than they already are by implying that, somehow, this is just a taste of the torments to come. I'm tired of it, and if there's a God, I bet He's tired of it, too.

—From *Images May Disturb You*,
the blog of Georgia Mason, January 12, 2040

Eight

Shaun didn't hesitate. Putting his beer on the nearest counter, he grabbed a crossbow off the wall and ran for the door. I was only a few feet behind him, Coke in one hand. Unlike my idiot brother, I have no intention of becoming a footnote on the Wall, but that doesn't mean I can't watch from a safe remove.

"Georgia!" There was enough anxiety in Buffy's voice to make me turn. She lobbed a handheld camera in my direction. I caught it, raising my eyebrows in question. "Better picture quality and sixty hours of battery life."

And audiences love a little hand-shot footage, as long as you cut to the smoother computer-operated stuff before they get motion sickness. "Got it," I said, and followed Shaun, opening my soda as I went.

The encampment was ablaze with activity. Guards swarmed everywhere I turned, weapons out and ready. I couldn't blame them for their excitement. Anyone who goes into private security in this day and age is likely to be a lot like Shaun, and he'd slowly been going nuts from the lack of dangerous things to pester.

More gunshots sounded from the south. I turned in that direction, flipping on the camera, and tapped my soda twice against the pressure pad on my belt. My ear cuff beeped. A moment later, Shaun's slightly breathless voice was in my ear: "Kinda busy, George. What gives?"

"Need a position if you want this on film." Distant moaning was audible as a whisper on the wind. Buffy's microphones are pretty sensitive. If she could get any sort of audio track, she'd be able to intensify it and play it back with the report, twice as loud and ten times as chilling.

"Location?"

"Just outside the van."

"Northwest. I'm at the fence."

That was directly away from the loudest signs of combat. "You sure about that?"

"Hurry and get over here!" he snapped, and clicked off. Shrugging, I turned toward the northern fence, breaking into a trot. I've learned not to argue with Shaun where zombies are concerned; he knows more about their behavior than I can imagine wanting to, and if he says "north," he's probably right. Gunshots continued to sound as the moaning, faint as it was, began getting louder.

The glare from the perimeter lights confused my night vision; I heard Shaun before I saw him. He was swearing merrily, using language that would make a longshoreman blush, as he taunted the infected closer to the fence. There were five of them, all fresh enough to look almost human, assuming you discounted the extreme dilation of their pupils and the slack, hungry way they stared at my brother as their fingers clawed against the fence. They'd died within the past few hours. I raised the camera, zooming in on their faces.

Shaun didn't even realize I was there until my soda hit the pavement. He stopped taunting the infected, stepping clear of the fence as he turned to stare at me. "George? What's wrong? You look like you've seen a ghost."

"I have." I indicated one of the zombies. Before amplification, she'd been a slender young woman, no heavier than Buffy. The wound that killed her the first time stood out livid and red against the still-pink flesh of her throat, and the fabric of her pale gray University of Oklahoma sweatshirt was stained bloody. "Recognize her?"

"Should I?" Shaun leaned closer to the fence. The zombie bared her teeth and hissed, increasing her attempts to break through. "She's definitely not one of my exes, George. I mean, she's cute, but way too dead for my tastes."

"Like you *have* any exes?" Shaun has dated as much as I have, which is to say "not at all." Buffy usually has five or six paramours at any given time, but Shaun and I haven't ever bothered. Other things keep getting in the way.

"Well, if I *did* have exes, they wouldn't look like her. Fill me in?"

"She was the cheering section at the senator's presentation." She'd looked a hell of a lot better when she was alive. I didn't remember seeing her after the

Q&A broke up. If she left promptly and got caught on the street . . . given her body mass, she'd have had plenty of time to reach full amplification and rise again. It wasn't a difficult scenario to imagine. A young college student comes alone to a risky meeting in a public place and leaves the same way. No one would have been there to help her. A single bite is a death sentence, and not everyone has the guts to call the police and request a bullet to the brain before it gets too late to avoid rising.

Whoever she was, she died alone, and she died stupid. I couldn't help feeling bad for her.

"Oh, jeez, you're right." Shaun leaned closer still, moving well out of what most people would call the safe zone. All five zombies were clustering around the same stretch of fence now, hissing and snarling at him. "That was *fast*."

"This isn't the primary pack. They're too fresh." The most decayed of the zombies would still have been able to pass for human in a dark alley, assuming he could keep himself from trying to eat anyone in range. "Something had to bite them."

"Or one of 'em dropped dead of a heart attack," Shaun said. "You're right. The rest are south, harassing the guards." He gave the fence an assessing look. "I'd put this at what, twelve feet?"

"Shaun Phillip Mason, you are *not* thinking what I think you're thinking."

"Sure as hell am. Keep 'em distracted, okay?" He didn't wait for a reply before backing up, getting a running start, and launching himself at the fence. His fingers caught well above the reach of the tallest of the zombies. His toes didn't fare quite as well, but that didn't matter much—steel-toed combat boots are too tough for even the infected to gnaw their way through. Laughing at their moans, Shaun began pulling himself up toward the top of the fence.

"Next up, we have my brother, committing suicide," I muttered and focused the camera on him, tapping the pad at my belt again to dial Buffy. "Don't fall, asshole, or I'm telling Mom you did it for love of the dead girl."

"Bite me," Shaun called back. He swung his leading leg over the top of the fence and stood astride it, with one foot hooked into the chain on either side. Unhooking the crossbow from his belt, he loaded the first quarrel.

"Not while I'm breathing, oh brother mine."

"Buffy here," said Buffy's voice in my ear.

"Buffy, you getting the feeds on this? I want any positive IDs you can pull on our friends. You can cross-reference the one in the sweatshirt with footage from the—"

"I'm on it. Her name was Dayna Baldwin, age twenty-three, political science major at the University of Oklahoma. I'm running lookups on the other four. I have a few possible matches, but there's nothing confirmed."

Shaun pulled back the catch, taking careful, almost affectionate aim on the nearest of his admirers. I directed the handheld camera toward the mob as a crossbow bolt appeared in the center of their leader's forehead. He fell and two of the remaining four were suddenly distracted with cannibalizing his remains, leaving two to menace Shaun. The virus that drives the infected is only in it for the meat. Zombies generally choose the living over the dead, but something that won't put up a fight is always better than nothing at all.

"Keep looking," I said. Shaun reloaded his crossbow, moving with calm, unhurried precision. I have to give my brother this: He's damn good at what he does.

"Of course," said Buffy, sounding affronted. She hung up, presumably to focus on her cameras. We'd get a clearer picture of everything that had happened once Shaun finished having his fun and we could get back to the van. If there's a square inch of convoy that Buffy can't get on film, I'll eat my sunglasses.

Shaun was taking aim on the third zombie when I realized there was something wrong with the quality of the moans. They were getting louder and moving against the prevailing wind. I dropped the camera, hearing its case crack as it hit the ground, and turned to look behind me.

The leader of the zombies—another familiar face, opinionated Carl from the after-meeting—was ten feet away and closing fast, moving at that horrible, disconnected half-run that only the freshest zombies can sustain for long. He must have died even more recently than Dayna, because he'd been up and moving around less than an hour before. That implied multiple bites and a group attack, possibly by the pack that Shaun was in the process of dispatching.

Six more zombies followed the ill-fated Carl, moving at speeds ranging from a half-run to a shamble. Pulling the pistol from my belt, I shot Carl twice in the head, turning to aim at the zombie behind him. I didn't have enough bullets. Even if I were as good of a shot as Shaun, which I'm not, eight bullets and seven zombies didn't leave me in a position with much of a margin for error. I was already down below the one-for-one divide, and that made survival a lot less likely. I pulled the trigger and the second zombie fell.

The sound of gunshots attracted Shaun's attention. I heard his sharp intake of breath as he turned, surveying my attackers. "Holy—"

"We're past saying it and all the way to doing it," I snarled, and fired again. The shot went wild. Four bullets and only two zombies down; the odds were not in my favor. *"Buffy!"*

Buffy never sends out a camera without a two-way sound pickup. She says she doesn't trust us to manage our own levels, but really, I think she just likes being able to eavesdrop without leaving the van. Her voice emerged from the speaker a moment after I called her name, coming through crackly and distorted. "Sorry for the delay—distracted. We've had a perimeter breech on the south fence. One of the gates went down and they're reporting casualties. How're you two faring?"

"Let's just say that if you have a broadcast point near some unoccupied men with heavy weaponry, now would be a swell time to use it." I fired twice more. The second bullet hit its target. Six bullets and three zombies down, while the remaining four continued to approach. I fired at the new leader of the pack and missed. A crossbow bolt whizzed by my shoulder and the zombie toppled, the end of the bolt protruding from its forehead. Three zombies. "I didn't come out here expecting to actually *fight* anything—I'm only carrying a pistol, and I'm about to be out of bullets. Shaun?"

"Three bolts left," he called. "Think you can make it up this fence?"

"No." I'm a decent sprinter and I can gun a motorcycle from zero to suicidal in less than ten seconds, but I'm not a climber. I nearly washed out of the physical section of my licensing exams, twice, thanks to my lack of upper-body strength. If I was lucky, I'd be able to cling to the fence until the zombies grabbing my ankles hauled me down and ate me. If I wasn't, I'd just fall.

The speaker crackled. "There's a group of guards on the way," Buffy said. "They're having some problems, but they said they'd be there as fast as they could."

"Hope it's fast enough," I said. I started backing up toward Shaun and the fence. My father has always had just one piece of advice about zombies and ammunition, one he's drilled into my head enough times that it's managed to stick: When you have one bullet left and there's no visible way out of the shit you're standing in, save it for yourself. It's better than the alternative.

Two more crossbow bolts whizzed by, and two more zombies fell, leaving just one to shamble toward us, still moaning. There were no answering moans, either from the sides or from behind. Shaun's pack was down, and there didn't seem to be any further reinforcements coming.

"Fire any time now, Shaun," I said tightly.

"Not until I know that there aren't more coming," he said.

I kept backing up until I hit the fence and stopped, keeping my gun in front of me, muzzle aimed toward the shambler. Between the two of us, we had the ammo to take it down . . . as long as that was all there was. "It figures," I said.

"What figures?"

"We finally crack the global top five, so of course we're going to get eaten by zombies that same night."

Shaun's laughter managed to be bitter and amused at the same time. "Are you ever *not* a pessimist?"

"Sometimes. But then I wake up." The zombie was continuing to advance, moaning as it came. There were no answering moans. "I think it's alone."

"So shoot, genius, and we'll see."

"I may as well." I steadied my hands, lining up on the zombie's forehead. "If it eats me, I hope you're next."

"Always gotta go first, don't you?"

"You know it." I fired.

My shot whizzed past the zombie, punching a barely visible hole in the nearest RV. Still moaning, the zombie raised its arms in the classic "embracing" gesture of the undead, moving slightly faster now. No one's ever figured out how the zombies can tell when their victims are unarmed, but they manage somehow.

"Shaun . . ."

"We have time."

"Yeah, sure," I said. The zombie was still twelve feet away, well out of attack range, but it was closing on us. "I hate you."

"It's mutual," Shaun said. I risked a glance up at him, and saw that he was aiming for the zombie's forehead, waiting for the perfect shot. One bolt, one chance. Maybe that sounds like the odds he'd been playing before, but it wasn't. It's easier to get a bull's-eye when there's nothing actually at risk.

"Just so we're clear," I said, and closed my eyes.

The gunfire came from two directions at the same time. I opened my eyes to see the last zombie mowed down by a hail of chain-fed bullets being fired by no fewer than four of the guards, two closing on either side. Above me, Shaun gave a loud war whoop.

"The cavalry has *arrived*!"

"God bless the cavalry," I muttered.

Our tense stand-off was over in a matter of seconds. I ignored the fallen camera as I pushed away from the fence and strode toward the nearest pair of guards. The camera was a write-off. Buffy had the footage downloaded by now, and they were going to insist on destroying the damn thing anyway, since it had almost certainly been spattered with blood when the guards started firing. The electronics were too delicate to survive a full decontamination. That sort of thing is why we keep our insurance paid up.

Steve was there, scowling at the fallen infected like he was challenging them to get up and let him kill them again. Sorry, Steve, the virus only reanimates a host once. His partner was a few feet away, scanning the fence. It wasn't Tyrone. I paused, starting to get the vaguest idea of how the zombies had broken through the fence.

Ideas never drew ratings without confirmation. "What happened?"

"Not now, Georgia," said Steve, with a tight shake of his head. "Just . . . not now."

I considered pressing the matter. If this were a normal zombie attack, one of the hit-and-run outbreaks that can happen anywhere, I probably would have. It's always best to question the survivors before they can start deluding themselves about the reality of what they just went through. After the adrenaline fades, half the people who survive a zombie attack turn into heroes, having gunned down a thousand zombies with nothing but a .22 and a bucket of guts, while the other half deny that they were ever close enough to the undead to be in any actual danger. If you want the real story, you have to get it fast.

But Steve was a professional bodyguard, and that made him less likely than most men to lie to himself. Factor in the fact that unless he left the convoy after the paperwork was completed, I'd have to continue interacting with him on a regular basis, and getting the scoop wasn't worth alienating the large, potentially violent man who managed a lot of my blood tests. Shaking my head, I took a step back.

"Sure, Steve," I said. "Just let us know if there's anything we can do."

There was a clatter as Shaun jumped down from the fence. I didn't turn, and he trotted to a stop beside me, eyes narrowing as he took note of the attending guards. "Christ, Steve, where's Tyrone?" he said.

Shaun has done more to get close to the guards than I have. A little friendliness is unavoidable, but he'd actually gotten out there and made *friends*. Maybe that's why Steve answered his question with a quiet, "Conversion was confirmed at twenty-two hundred hours, twenty-seven minutes. Tracy put him down, but not before he was able to pass on the infection."

Shaun whistled, long and low. "How many down?"

"Four casualties from the convoy and an as-yet-undetermined number of locals. The senator and his aides are being moved to a secure location. If you'll gather your things and collect Miss Meissonier, we'll take the three of you to decontamination before relocating you as well."

"Are all the zombies down?" I asked.

Steve frowned at me. "Miss Mason?"

"The zombies. Shaun and I just eliminated the better part of two packs," ignoring the part where one of us nearly got eaten in the process, "and you seem to have handled the mess at the gates. Are all the zombies down?"

"Channels are showing a negative on infected activity within the area."

"Channels are not a one hundred percent guarantee," I said, keeping my tone reasonable. "You're down hands, and we've already been in primary contact, which means we'll need the same decon you will. Why not let Shaun and me stay and help? We're licensed, and if you have ammo, we're armed. Remove Buffy, but let us stay."

The guards exchanged uneasy glances before looking to Steve. Whatever he said would go. Steve frowned down at the bodies littering the tarmac, and finally said, "I hope you both understand that I won't hesitate to shoot either one of you."

"We wouldn't go out with you if we thought

you'd hesitate," said Shaun. He held up his crossbow. "Anybody got bolts for this thing?"

———

Cleanup is the worst thing about a small-scale outbreak. For many people, this part of a rising is pretty much invisible. Anyone without a hazard license is confined outside the contaminated zones until the burials, burnings, and sterilizations are done. When the cordons come up, life goes back to normal, and this sort of thing is routine enough that, unless you know the signs, you could even fail to realize that there was an incident. We've had a lot of practice at cover-ups.

That changes if you have to be involved. Part of getting your hazard license is going along on a cleanup run, just to make sure you understand what you're getting into. George and I both threw up when we made our first cleanup run, and I almost passed out twice. It's horrible, messy work. Once a zombie's been shot through the head, it doesn't look like a zombie anymore. It just looks like somebody who was in the wrong place at the wrong time, and I hate the whole process.

Sterilization is horrific. You burn any vegetation the zombies came into contact with, and if they walked on any open ground, you drench it with a solution of chlorinated saline. If it's a rural or suburban area, you kill any animals you find. Squirrels, cats, whatever; if it's mammalian and can carry the virus in its live state, it dies, even if it's too small to undergo amplification. And when you're done, you shuffle back to the hazmat center that's been established for agent decon, and you go inside, and you spend two hours having your skin steamed off, which is a nice way to prepare for the two weeks of nightmares that you're going to have to live through.

If you ever start to feel like I have a glamorous job, that maybe it would be fun to go out and poke a zombie with a stick while one of your friends makes a home movie for your buddies, please do me a favor: Go out for your hazard license first. If you still want to do this crap after the first time you've burned the body of a six-year-old with blood on her lips and a Barbie in her hands, I'll welcome you with open arms.

But not before.

—From *Hail to the King*,
the blog of Shaun Mason, February 11, 2040

Nine

I collapsed onto our bed at the local four-star hotel a little after dawn, my aching eyes already squeezed shut. Shaun was a bit steadier on his feet and he stayed upright long enough to make sure the room's blackout curtains were drawn. I made a small noise of approval and felt him pulling my sunglasses off my face a moment later. I swatted ineffectually at the air.

"Stop that. Give those back."

"They're on the bedside table," he said. The bedsprings creaked as he sat down, taking the side of the bed that was closer to the window. Rustling followed as he removed his shoes and slumped sideways. I didn't have to open my eyes to know what he was doing. We shared the same room until puberty hit, and since then we've never been more than a closed door away from one another. "Christ, George. That was a clusterfuck."

"Mmm," I replied, and pulled the covers over my head. I was still wearing my shoes. The staff was paid to wash the sheets after every visit, and by the point we left the field, I'd dressed and undressed so many times in the course of decontamination that I never wanted to remove my clothes again. I'd just wear them until they dissolved, and then spend the rest of my life naked.

"How the hell did we get an outbreak that close to the convention hall? Primaries are coming up. We didn't need this, even if it's going to be great for ratings. Think Buffy has the initial edits up? I know you hate it when she releases footage without your say-so, but cleanup ran long. She probably won't wait. Waiting could mean we get scooped."

"Mmm."

"Bet this spikes us another half-point. More when I can get my POV stuff edited together. Think there were faults in the fencing? Maybe they broke through. Steve wasn't clear on where the attack started, and we lost both guards stationed on the gate."

"Mmm."

"Poor Tyrone. Jesus. Did you know he was putting his teenage son through college with this gig? Kid wants to be a molecular virologist—"

Somewhere in the middle of explaining the hopes, dreams, and character failings of the fallen guards, Shaun's voice trailed off, replaced by the soft, rhythmic sound of his breathing. I sighed, rolling over, and followed him into sleep.

The curtains were pulled away from the window some unknown length of time later, allowing sunlight to stream into the room and jerk me unceremoniously back into awareness. I swore, fumbling for the nightstand I vaguely remembered Shaun mentioning in conjunction with my sunglasses. My hand hit the side of the bed, and I squinted my eyes more tightly closed, trying to ward off the light.

Shaun was less restrained in his profanity. "Fuck a duck, Buffy, what are you trying to do, blind her?" My sunglasses were thrust into my hand. I unfolded them and slid them into place, opening my eyes to see Shaun, clad only in his boxer shorts, glaring at an unrepentant Buffy. "Knock next time!"

"I did knock, three times," she said. "And I tried the room phone, twice. See?" Both Shaun and I glanced toward the phone. The red message light was blinking. "When you kept not answering, I re-routed the locks to make them think your room was my room and let myself in."

"You didn't just shake us because?" I mumbled. A splitting headache was rushing in to fill the void left by my disrupted REM cycle.

"Are you kidding? You two sleep armed. I like having four limbs and a head." Seeming oblivious to the hostility in the room, Buffy activated the terminal on the wall, pulling down the foldable keyboard. "I'm guessing you guys haven't seen the daily returns, huh?"

"We haven't seen anything but the insides of our eyelids," Shaun said. He wasn't making any effort to hide his irritation, which was only increasing as Buffy ignored it. "What time is it?"

"Almost noon," Buffy said. The hotel start-up screen came up and she began typing, shunting the connection to one of our own server relays. The logo of After the End Times filled the screen, replaced a moment later by the black-and-white grid of our secure staff pages. "I let you guys sleep for, like, six hours."

I groaned and reached for the phone. "I am so calling room service for a gallon of Coke before she can do any more talking."

"Get some coffee, too," said Shaun. "A whole pot of coffee."

"Tea for me," said Buffy. The screen shifted again as she pulled up the numerical display that represents our feed from the Internet Ratings Board. It measures server traffic, unique hits, number of connected users, and a whole bunch of other numbers and factors, all of them combining to make one final, holy figure: our market share. It's color-coded, appearing in green if it's more than fifty, white for forty-nine to ten, yellow for nine to five, and red for four and above.

The number at the top of screen, gleaming a bright, triumphant red, was 2.3.

I dropped the phone.

Shaun recovered his composure first, maybe because he was more awake than I was. "Have we been hacked?"

"Nope." Buffy shook her head, grinning so broadly that it seemed like the top of her head might fall off. "What you're seeing is the honest to God, unaltered, uncensored Ratings Board designation for our site traffic over the past twelve hours. We're running top two, as long as you discount porn, music download, and movie tie-in sites."

Those three site types make up the majority of the traffic on the Internet—the rest of us are just sort of skimming off the top. Rising unsteadily, I crossed the room and touched the screen. The number didn't change.

"Shaun . . ."

"Yeah?"

"You owe me twenty bucks."

"Yeah."

Turning to Buffy, I asked, "How?"

"If I attribute it to the graphic design, do I get a raise?"

"No," said Shaun and I, in unison.

"Didn't think so, but a girl has to try." Buffy sat down on the edge of my bed, still beaming. "I got clean footage from half a dozen cameras all the way through both attacks. No voice reports, since someone went and volunteered to help with cleanup—"

"Not that going through decon without helping would have left me able to record," I said dryly, retreating back toward the phone. Incredible ratings or not, I needed to kill this headache before it got fully established, and that meant I needed something caffeinated to wash down the painkillers. "You know that wipes me out."

"Details," said Buffy. "I spliced together three basic narrative tracks—one following the outbreak at the gate as closely as possible, one following the perimeter, and one that followed the two of you."

I glanced in her direction as I waited for room service to pick up. "How much of our dialogue did you get?"

Buffy beamed. "All of it."

"That explains some of the jump," Shaun said dryly. "We always get a point spike when you say you hate me in a published report."

"Only because it's true," I said, quashing the urge to groan. It was my own fault for leaving Buffy alone with the unedited footage. She had to put *something* up. A news blackout doesn't heighten suspense; it just loses readers.

Shaun snorted. "Right. So you had three tracks, and . . . ?"

"I tossed them up in their raw form, tapped some beta Newsies to throw down narrative tracks, got straight bio files on the confirmed casualties, and wrote a new poem about how fast everything can fall apart." Buffy cast an anxious glance my way, smile slipping. "Did I do it right?"

Room service confirmed that the assorted drinks were en route, along with an order of dry wheat toast. I hung up the phone. "Which betas?"

"Um, Mahir for the gate, Alaric for the perimeter, and Becks for the attack on the two of you."

"Ah." I adjusted my sunglasses. "I'm going to want to review their reports." It was a formality, and from the look on her face, Buffy knew it; she'd selected the same betas I would have chosen. Mahir is located in London, England, and he's great for dry, factual reporting that neither pretties things up nor dumbs them down. If I have a second in command, it's Mahir. Alaric can build suspense almost as well as an Irwin, fitting his narration and description into the natural blank spots in a recording. And Becks would have been a horror movie director if we weren't all practically living in a horror movie these days. Her sense of timing is impeccable, and her cut shots are even better. Of the betas we've acquired, I count my Newsies as the best of the bunch. They're good. They're hoping to ride our success to alpha positions of their own, and that makes them ambitious. Ambition is worth more than practically anything else in this business, even talent.

"Of course you will," Buffy said, clearly waiting for me to break down and say the words.

I smiled, faintly, and said them: "You did good."

Buffy punched the air. "She shoots, she scores!"

"Just don't get cocky," I said. There was a knock at the door. This hotel must have the fastest room service in the Midwest. "Remember, one successful set of executive decisions does *not* prepare you to take my—"

I opened the door to reveal Steve and Carlos. They were impeccably dressed, matching black suits so crisply pressed that you'd never have guessed they'd been in the field incinerating the bodies of their fallen comrades less than eight hours previous. I stood there in my slept-in clothes, with my uncombed hair sticking up in all directions, and stared at them.

"Miss Mason," said Steve. His tone was flat, even more formal than it was on our first encounter. Dipping a hand into his pocket, he produced the familiar shape of a handheld blood testing unit. "If you and your associates would care to come with us, a debriefing has been scheduled in the boardroom."

"Couldn't you have called first?" I asked.

He raised his eyebrows. "We did."

Shaun and I really had been sleeping like the unrisen dead. I pressed my lips into a thin line, and said, "My brother and I have only been awake for a few minutes. Can we have time to make ourselves presentable?"

Steve looked past me into the room, where Shaun—still clad only in his boxers—offered a sardonic wave. Steve looked back to me. I smiled. "Unless you'd prefer we came as we are?"

"You have ten minutes," Steve said, and shut the door.

"Good morning, Georgia," I muttered. "Right. Buffy, get out. We'll see you in the boardroom. Shaun, put clothes on." I raked a hand through my hair. "I'm going to wash up." One good thing about going to bed straight from a cleanup operation: Even after six hours of sleeping and sweating into my clothes, they were still cleaner than they'd been when I bought them. After you've been sterilized seven times for live virus particles, dirt doesn't stand much of a chance.

"Georgia—" Buffy began.

I pointed to the door. "Out." Not waiting to see whether she obeyed me—largely because I was pretty certain she wasn't going to—I grabbed my overnight bag off the floor by the foot of the bed and went into the bathroom, closing the door behind me.

There's only one way to prevent a migraine from the combination of too little sleep and too much light from fully establishing itself, and that's to wear my contacts. They come with their own little complications, like making my eyeballs itch all damn day, but they block a lot more light than my sunglasses. I pulled the case out of my bag, popped off the top, and withdrew the first of the lenses from the saline solution where they customarily floated.

Normal contact lenses are designed to correct problems with the wearer's eyesight. My eyesight is fine, except for my light issues, which the lenses can compensate for. Unfortunately, while normal contacts enhance peripheral vision, these ones kill the greater part of mine by covering the iris and most of the pupil with solid color films that essentially create artificial surfaces for my eyes. I'm not legally allowed to go into field situations while wearing contacts.

Tilting my head back, I slipped the first lens into place, blinking to settle it against my eye. I repeated the process with the other eye before lowering my head and looking at myself in the mirror. My reflection gazed impassively back at me, eyes perfectly normal and cornflower blue.

The blue was my choice. When I was a kid they got me brown lenses that matched the natural color of my eyes. I switched to blue as soon as I was old enough to have a say. They don't look as natural, but they also don't make me feel like I'm trying to lie about my medical condition. My eyes aren't normal. They never will be. If that makes some people uncomfortable, well, I've learned to use that to my own advantage.

I straightened my clothes, tucked my sunglasses into the breast pocket of my shirt, and ran a brush through my hair. There, that was as presentable as I was going to get. If the senator didn't like it, he could damn well refrain from allowing any more late-night attacks on the convoy.

Buffy was gone when I emerged from the bathroom. Shaun handed me a can of Coke and my MP3 recorder, wrinkling his nose. "You know your contacts creep me out, right?"

"That's the goal." The soda was cold enough to

make my back teeth ache. I didn't stop gulping until the can was empty. Tossing it in the bathroom trash, I asked, "Ready?"

"For hours. You girls always take *forever* in the bathroom."

"Bite me."

"Not without a blood test."

I kicked his ankle, grabbed three more Cokes from the room service tray, and left the room. Steve was waiting in the hall, blood test unit still in his hand. I eyed it.

"Isn't this going a bit far? We went from cleanup to bed. I doubt there was a viral reservoir in the closet."

"Hand," Steve replied.

I sighed and switched my pilfered sodas to my left hand, allowing me to offer him the right. The process of testing me, and then Shaun, took less than a minute. Both of us came up unsurprisingly clean.

Steve dropped the used units into a plastic bag, sealed it, and turned to walk down the hall, obviously expecting us to follow. Shaun and I exchanged a glance, shrugged, and did exactly that.

The boardroom was three floors up, on a level you needed an executive keycard to access. The carpet was so thick that our feet made no sound as we followed Steve down the hall to the open boardroom door. Buffy was seated on a countertop inside, keying information into her handheld and trying to stay out of the way of the senator's advisors. They were moving back and forth, grabbing papers from one another, making notes on whiteboards, and generally creating the sort of hurricane of productive activity that signals absolutely nothing happening.

The senator was at the head of the table with his head in his hands, creating an island of stillness in the heart of the chaos. Carlos flanked him to the left, and as we crossed the threshold, Steve abandoned us to cut across the room and flank Senator Ryman to the right. Something must have alerted the senator to Steve's presence because he raised his head, looking first toward the bodyguard and then toward us. One by one, the bustling aides stopped what they were doing and followed the direction of the senator's gaze.

I raised a can of soda and popped the tab.

The sound seemed to snap the senator out of his fugue. He sat up, clearing his throat. "Shaun. Georgia. If the two of you wouldn't mind taking your seats, we can get things started."

"Thanks for holding the briefing until we got here," I said, moving toward one of the open chairs and setting my MP3 recorder on the table. "Sorry we took so long."

"Don't worry," he said, waving a hand. "I know how late you were out with the cleanup crews. A little sleep is hardly repayment for going above and beyond the call of duty like that."

"In that case, I'd like some groupies," said Shaun, settling in the chair next to mine. I kicked him in the shin. He yelped but grinned, unrepentant.

"I'll see what we can do." The senator rose, rapping his knuckles against the table. The last small eddies of conversation in the room died, all attention sliding back to him. Even Buffy stopped typing as the senator leaned forward, hands on the table, and said, "Now that we're all here . . . how the *hell* did that happen?" His voice never rose above a conversational level. "We lost four guards last night, three of them at our own front gate. What happened to the concept of security? Did I miss the meeting where we decided that zombies weren't something we needed to be concerned about anymore?"

One of the aides cleared his throat and said, "Well, sir, it looks like there was a power short on the anterior detection unit, which resulted in the doors failing to shut fast enough to prevent the incursion from—"

"Speak English at this table or I will fire you so fast you'll wind up standing at the airport wondering how the hell you got from here to there without any goddamn pants on," the senator snapped. The aide responded by paling and dropping the papers he'd been holding. "Can *anyone* here tell me what happened and how, in simple English words of two syllables or less?"

"Your screamer wasn't working," said Buffy. Every head in the room turned to her. She shrugged. "Every perimeter rig has a screamer built in. Yours didn't switch on."

"A screamer being . . . ?" asked one of the aides.

"A heat-sensitive motion sensor," said Chuck Wong. He looked anxious—and with good reason. Most of his job involves the design and maintenance of the convoy's automated perimeter defenses. If there'd been a mechanical failure, it was technically his fault. "They scan moving objects for heat as well as motion. Anything below a certain range sets off an alert of possible zombies in the area."

"A really fresh one can fool a screamer, but the

packs we saw last night were too mixed for that. They should have set off the alerts, and they didn't." Buffy shrugged again. "That means we had a screamer failure."

"Chuck? Care to tell us why that happened?"

"I can't. Not until we can arrange for a physical inspection of the equipment."

"It's arranged. Carlos, get three of your men and take Chuck for an inspection run. Report back as soon as you have anything." Carlos nodded, heading for the door. Three of the other bodyguards moved away from the walls and followed, not waiting to be asked.

"I'll need my equipment—" Chuck protested.

"Your equipment should be with the convoy, and since that's where you're going, I'm sure you'll have everything you need," the senator said. There was no arguing with his tone. Chuck obviously saw that. He stood, thin-boned hands twitching by his sides as he turned toward the door.

"Mind if I go along?" asked Buffy. The room looked at her again. She flashed her most winning smile. "I'm pretty good at seeing why field equipment decided to fry. Maybe I could be a second opinion."

And maybe she could get us some footage for a follow-up report. I nodded, and caught the senator watching the gesture before he, in turn, began to nod. "Thank you for volunteering, Miss Meissonier. I'm sure the group will be glad to have you along."

"I'll ring back," Buffy said, and hopped off the counter, trotting out the door after Chuck and the bodyguards.

"There she goes," Shaun muttered.

"Jealous?" I asked.

"Tech geeks trying to figure out why a screamer broke? Please. I'll be jealous if she comes back saying there were actual dead guys to play with."

"Right." He was jealous. I folded my arms, returning my attention to the senator.

He wasn't looking his best. He was leaning forward with his hands braced against the table, but it was clear even in that well-supported position that he hadn't had nearly as much sleep as Shaun and I. His hair was uncombed, his shirt was wrinkled, and his collar was open. He looked like a man who'd been faced with the unexpected, and now, after a little time to consider the situation, was getting ready to ride out and kick its ass.

"Folks, whatever the cause of last night's catastrophe, the facts are this: We lost four good men and three potential supporters right before the first round of primaries. This does *not* send a good message to the people. This sort of thing doesn't say 'Vote Ryman, he'll protect you.' If anything, it says 'Vote Ryman if you want to get eaten.' This isn't our message, and I refuse to let it become our message, even though that's the way my opponents are going to try to spin it. What's our game plan?" He glared around the room. "Well?"

"Sir, the bloggers—"

"Will be staying for this little chat. We try covering it up, they'll report it a lot less kindly when they manage to root it out. Now please, can we get down to business?"

That seemed to be the cue the room had been

waiting for. The next forty minutes passed in a blaze of points and counterpoints, with the senator's advisors arguing the finer aspects of spin while his security heads protested any attempts to categorize their handling of the campaign to date as "lax" or "insufficient." Shaun and I sat and listened. We were there as observers, not participants, and after the argument had a little time to develop, it seemed as if most of the room forgot we were there at all. One camp held that they needed to minimize media coverage of the attack, make the requisite statements of increased vigilance, and move on. The other camp held that full openness was the only way to get through an incident of this magnitude without taking damage from other political quarters. Both camps had to admit that the reports released on our site the night before were impacting their opinions, although neither seemed aware of exactly how much traffic those reports had drawn. I opted not to inform them. Observing the political process without interfering with it is sometimes more entertaining than it sounds.

One of the senator's advisors was beginning a rant on the evils of the modern media when my ear cuff beeped. I rose, moving to the back of the room before I answered. "Georgia here."

"Georgia, it's Buffy. Can you patch me to the speakerphone?"

I paused. She sounded harried. More than that, she sounded openly nervous. Not frightened, which meant she probably wasn't being harassed by zombies or rival bloggers, but nervous. "Sure, Buff. Give me a second." I strode back to the table and leaned across two of the arguing aides to grab the speaker phone. They squawked protests, but I ignored them, yanking off my ear cuff and snapping it into the transmission jack at the base of the phone.

"Miss Mason?" inquired the senator, eyebrows rising.

"Sorry, this is important." I hit the Receive button.

". . . testing, testing," said Buffy's voice, crackling slightly through the speaker. "Am I live?"

"We can hear you, Miss Meissonier," said the senator. "May I ask what was so important that it required breaking in on our conference?"

Chuck Wong spoke next; apparently, ours wasn't the only end on speakerphone. "We're at the perimeter fence, sir, and it seemed important that we call you as quickly as possible."

"What's going on out there, Chuck? No more zombies, I hope?"

"No, sir—not so far. It's the screamer."

"The one that failed?"

"Yes, sir. It didn't fail because of anything my team did." Chuck didn't keep the relief out of his tone, and I couldn't blame him. Carelessness can be a federal offense when it applies to antizombie devices. No one has managed to successfully charge a security technician with manslaughter—yet—but the cases come up almost every year. "The wires were cut."

The senator froze. "Cut?"

"The screamer shows detection of the zombies we saw last night, sir. The connection that should have set off the perimeter alarms wasn't made because those wires had been cut before the alarm was sounded."

"Whoever did it did a pretty good job," Buffy

said. "All the damage is inside the boxes. Nothing visible until you crack the case, and even then you have to dig around before you find the breaks."

The senator sagged backward, paling. "Are you telling me this was sabotage?"

"Well, sir," said Chuck, "none of my men would have cut the wires on a screamer protecting the convoy that they were inside. There's just no reason for it."

"I see. Finish your sweep and report back, Chuck. Miss Meissonier, thank you for calling. Please, call again if you need anything further."

"Roger. Georgia, we're on server four."

"Noted. Signing off now." I leaned over and cut the connection before pulling my ear cuff out of the jack and sliding it back onto my ear. Only when this was done did I glance back up at Senator Ryman.

The senator looked like a man who'd been hit, hard and unexpectedly, from behind. He met my gaze, despite the alien appearance of my contacts, and gave a small, tightly controlled shake of his head. Please, that gesture said, not right now.

I nodded, taking Shaun's arm. "Senator, if you don't mind, my brother and I should be getting to work. We're a bit behind after last night."

Shaun blinked at me. "What?"

"Of course." The senator smiled, not bothering to conceal his relief. "Miss Mason, Mr. Mason, thank you for your time. I'll have someone notify you before we're ready to check out and move on."

"Thank you," I said, and left the room, hauling the still-bewildered Shaun along in my wake. The boardroom door swung closed behind us.

Shaun yanked his arm out of my hand, subjecting me to a sharp sidelong gaze. "Want to tell me what that was all about?"

"The man just found out his camp was sabotaged," I said. "They're not going to come up with anything useful until they finish panicking. That's going to take days. Meanwhile, we have reports to splice together and update, and Buffy's dumping her footage to server four. We should take a look."

Shaun nodded. "Got it."

"Come on."

Back in our hotel room, I turned the main terminal over to Shaun while I plugged my handheld into the wall jack and settled down to work. We couldn't both record voice feeds at the same time, but we could edit film clips for our individual sections of the site and we could write as much text as we needed. I skimmed the reports Buffy authorized while Shaun and I were on cleanup. All three of the betas had done excellent jobs. Mahir, especially, had done an amazing amount with his relatively straightforward video feed, and I saw from the server flags that both the footage and his voice tracking had already been optioned by three of the larger news sites. I tapped in a release, authorizing use of the footage under a standard payment contract that would give Mahir forty percent of the profits, with clear credit for the narrative. His first breakout report. He'd be so proud. After a pause, I added a note of congratulations, directed to his private mailbox. He and I have been friends outside of work for years, and it never hurts to encourage your friends to succeed.

"How're things in your department?" I asked,

pulling up the raw footage of the attacks and setting it to run sequentially on my screen. I wasn't sure what I was looking for, but I had a hunch, and I've learned to follow my hunches. Buffy knows visual presentation, and Shaun knows shock value, but me? I know where to find the news. There had been sabotage. Why? When? And how had our saboteur been able to cut those wires without coming into the range of Buffy's cameras?

"I'm taking Becks away from you," he said. I glanced over. Shaun's screen was dominated by the footage of the two of us against the fence, holding off the last of the zombies. The audio was being fed directly to him via the earpiece plugged into his left ear. His expression was serious. "She wants to go Irwin. She's been begging for weeks. And this report—this isn't a Newsie report, George. You know that."

I scowled, but it wasn't like the request was a surprise. Good Irwins are hard to come by because the death rates during training are so damn high. You don't have time for a learning curve when you're playing with the infected. "What are her credentials?"

"You're stalling."

"Humor me." The footage on my screen was set to play in real-time, which meant some of the feeds would pause to let the others catch up again. The gate cameras had chunks missing from their narrative, while the attack at the fence was almost complete. I couldn't help wincing when I saw one of the women from the political rally come staggering up, clearly among the infected. I didn't need the dialogue tracks to tell me what Tyrone was saying: He was telling her to halt in her approach, back off, and present her credentials. But she just kept coming.

"Rebecca Atherton, age twenty-two, BA in film from New York University, Class A-20 blogging license, upgraded from a B-20 six months ago, when she passed her final marksmanship tests. She's testing for an A-18 next month."

An A-18 license would mean she was cleared to enter Level 4 hazard zones unaccompanied. "If you take her, my side of the site retains a six percent interest in her reports for the next year." The infected girl was sinking her teeth into Tyrone's left forearm. He screamed soundlessly and fired into the side of the zombie's head. Too late. The damage was done.

"Three percent," Shaun countered.

"Done," I said, not taking my eyes off the screen. "Draft an offer letter. If she agrees, she's yours." Tyrone was staggering in circles, clutching his arm against his body. I could see Tracy barking orders; Carlos turned and ran for the convoy, presumably to get reinforcements. That's why he survived—because he ran away. How must that kind of thing sit with a man like him? I can't imagine that it sits very well.

"George? What's up? I expected you to fight me more than that."

Instead of answering, I pulled the headphone jack out of my machine and let the sound start broadcasting to the room.

"Oh God Tracy oh God oh God," Tyrone was babbling. The moaning in the background was low and constant; the infected were coming, and the gate in the convoy fence was standing open.

"Shut up and help me close this thing," Tracy

snarled, grabbing the gate with both hands. After a moment's hesitation, Tyrone ran over and joined her, placing his hands well away from hers. It was a good way of dealing with things. As long as she didn't encounter any of the live virus, she wouldn't begin amplification, and in someone Tyrone's size, full conversion would take longer than was needed to close a simple gate, even one that heavy. Once it was shut, she could wave him off to a safe distance and put a bullet through his brain. It wouldn't be pretty, but elimination of contagion rarely is.

The tape jumped. Tyrone was on the ground in a spreading pool of his own blood while Tracy screamed and struggled against the zombie gnawing at the side of her neck. The gate was closed, and yet there were six zombies on the screen, one chewing on Tracy, three closing, and the other two lurching onward, toward the convoy.

Shaun frowned. "Pause the feed."

I tapped my keyboard. The image froze.

"Rewind to the jump."

I tapped my keyboard again and the image ran backward to the blank spot. I left it there, frozen, and looked to Shaun for further instructions.

He wasn't looking at me at all. "Start it up again, half-speed."

"What are you—"

"Just start the feed, George."

I tapped my keyboard. The image began to move again, much more slowly now. Shaun scowled, and snapped, "Freeze!"

The frozen image showed Tracy screaming, the zombies shambling, and Tyrone dead on the ground.

Shaun's finger stabbed out like an accusation, indicating the leg of Tracy's suit. "She didn't run because she *couldn't*," he said. "Someone shot out her kneecap."

"What?" I squinted at the screen. "I don't see it."

"Take out your damn contacts and try again."

I leaned back, blinking my right contact free and removing it with the tip of my index finger. After a moment to let my eye adjust, I closed my left eye and considered the screen again. With my low-light vision restored, it was much harder to miss the wetness of Tracy's leg, or the way the blood on the snow around her fanned out from her body, rather than falling straight down as I would have expected.

I sat up straight. "Someone shot her."

"During the missing footage," Shaun agreed, voice tight. I glanced to him, and he turned his face away, rubbing a hand across his eyes. "Christ, George. She was just doing this because it looked good on her résumé."

"I know, Shaun. I know." I put a hand on his shoulder, staring at my frozen video display, where Tracy battled for a life that was already lost. "We'll find out what's going on here.

"I promise."

*   *   *

——————

. . . they come to us, these restless dead,
Shrouds woven from the words of men,
With trumpets sounding overhead
(The walls of hope have grown so thin
And all our vaunted innocence
Has withered in this endless frost)
That promise little recompense
For all we risk, for all we've lost . . .

**—From *Eakly, Oklahoma,*
originally published in *By the Sounding Sea*, the blog
of Buffy Meissonier, February 11, 2040**

Ten

We were approaching the polls on Super Tuesday, and the mood in the senator's camp was grim. People should have been nervous, elated, and on edge; we were hours away from finding out whether the gravy train was about to take off like a rocket or come grinding to a halt. Instead, a funereal atmosphere ruled the camp. The guards continued to triple-check every protocol and step, and no one was willing to go out without an assigned partner. Even the interchangeable interns were beginning to get antsy, and they didn't notice much beyond their duties. It was bad.

The convoy was holding a position three blocks from the convention center, parked in what used to be a high school football field before the Rising rendered outdoor sports too dangerous. It was a good location for our purposes, providing power, running water, and sufficient clear ground for the perimeter fence to be established without anything—either physical or visual—obstructing the cameras. The number of people packed into Oklahoma City for the festivities necessitated running secure buses to the convention center every thirty minutes. Each of them was equipped with state-of-the-art testing units and armed guards.

We had received the final confirmation that Tracy McNally was shot through the right kneecap during the attack two days after Shaun and I first reviewed the tape and brought it to the attention of the senator's security team. This, on top of the cut wires in the perimeter screamers, had provided absolute confirmation that the attack had been a poorly managed assassination attempt. The convoy had been preparing to leave Eakly at the time, and it felt like we'd left the last of our high spirits behind.

It was Shaun who first identified the assassination attempt as poorly-managed. When the senator asked him to defend his position, he shrugged and said, "You're alive, aren't you?" It wasn't a comforting point, but it was a good one. A few more zombies in the original wave or a few more guards taken out like Tracy and the convoy could have been overrun rather than suffering a few casualties. Either it hadn't been a full-fledged assassination attempt, or it was an incredibly badly planned one. The former seemed unlikely. They used infected humans.

The attraction of attempting to weaponize the infected has decreased exponentially since the Raskin-Watts trail of 2026, when it was officially declared that any individual who used live-state Kellis-Amberlee as a weapon would be tried as a terrorist. What's the point of using a sloppy, difficult-to-manage weapon if even failure means you're likely to be one of the few lucky souls to still qualify for the death penalty?

The screamers were the only piece of the convoy's equipment that seemed to have been sabotaged. Reviewing the cameras at the gate confirmed that the blank spots were caused by a localized EMP burst— something focused enough that it took out only the cameras within a certain range and didn't attract the attention of most of Buffy's sensors. You can get that sort of tech at RadioShack. It's portable, disposable, and entirely untraceable, unless you happen to have the make and model of the unit, which we don't. The senator's men had been going over every scrap of available evidence since the incident, and they were still no closer to finding answers. If anything, they were further away, because the trail had time to get cold.

Who would want to kill Senator Ryman? Try "practically everyone," and you'd be off to a good start. Senator Peter Ryman started out as a long shot, and somehow became a front-runner in the presidential race. Everything could change before the official party conventions, but there was no denying that he'd been doing well in the polls, that he'd been performing solidly across a wide spectrum of potential voters, and that his views on the issues tended to appeal to the majority. Being the first candidate to open his campaign to the blogging world certainly didn't hurt—he'd enjoyed a substantial boost in awareness among voters aged thirty-five and below. The other candidates took too long to realize that they might have missed a trick, and they'd all been scrambling to catch up. Two of our betas received invitations to follow competing politicians in the week immediately after Eakly. Both refused the offers, citing conflict of interest. When you've got a good thing going, you don't shoot it before you have to.

Beyond Senator Ryman's standing lead, he was photogenic, well-liked, and well-placed in the Republican Party, with no major scandals in his background. No one makes it that far in politics and stays completely clean, but he's about as close as they come. Literally, the biggest scandal I've been able to find on the man is that his oldest daughter, Rebecca, was either three months premature or was conceived out of wedlock. That's it. He's like a big, friendly Boy Scout who just woke up one day and decided to become the President of the United States of America.

He doesn't even seem to belong to any of the major special-interest groups. Despite his wife's horse ranch, he supports the enforcement of Mason's Law, which means he's not in the pocket of the animal rights organizations, but he also opposes wide-scale hunting and deforestation, which means he doesn't belong to the militant antinature groups. He neither preaches damnation nor asserts that secular humanism was the only answer for a post-Rising world. I haven't even been able to find proof that his campaign received funding from the tobacco companies, and *everyone's* campaign receives funding from the tobacco companies. Once lung cancer stopped killing their customers, they rapidly became the number one contributors to most political campaigns. There's big money to be had in cigarettes that don't give anybody cancer.

A lot of people would benefit if Peter Ryman

turned up dead. So maybe it's no surprise that things were fairly bleak around the convoy as the primaries approached. The playful atmosphere that had dominated the campaign for the first six weeks was gone, replaced by blank-faced, by-the-book bodyguards who sometimes seemed to think they should demand blood tests after you used a public toilet. Buffy was handling things pretty well, largely by spending her time either inside the van or with Chuck and his team over in the senator's equipment rig, but it was driving Shaun and me out of our minds.

We both have our own ways of dealing with crazy. That's why Super Tuesday found Shaun off with every other Irwin who'd shown up to cover the convention, looking for dead things to irritate, while I was packed onto a bus with six dozen other deeply uncomfortable-looking reporters, heading for the convention center. I didn't know why they looked so uneasy; I had to get my press pass scanned three times and my blood tested twice before they'd even let me board. The only way anyone was going into conversion before we hit the convention center was if they suffered from cardiac arrest from the strain of being surrounded by other human beings.

A tense-looking man whose shirt was deformed in a way that telegraphed "I am wearing poorly fitted Kevlar" got onto the bus, and the driver announced, "We are at capacity. This bus is now departing for the convention center." This garnered a smattering of applause from the riders, most of whom looked like they were rethinking their choice of careers. No one ever told them that being a reporter would mean *talking* to people!

If it seems as if I have little respect for the other members of my profession, that's because it's true: I frequently don't. For every Dennis Stahl who's willing to go out and chase down the story, you have three or four "reporters" who'd rather edit together remotely taped feeds, interview their subjects by phone, and never leave their homes. There's a fairly popular news site, Under the Lens, that makes that one of their selling points: They claim they must be truly objective, because none of their Newsies ever go into the field. None of them have Class A licenses, and they act like this is something to brag about, like being distanced from the news is a good thing. If the paparazzi clouds serve one purpose, it's keeping that attitude from spreading.

Fear makes people stupid, and Kellis-Amberlee has had people scared for the last twenty years. There comes a point when you need to get over the fear and get on with your life, and a lot of people don't seem to be capable of that anymore. From blood tests to gated communities, we have embraced the cult of fear, and now we don't seem to know how to put it back where it belongs.

The ride to the convention center was almost silent, punctuated only by the various beeps and whirrs of people's equipment recalibrating as we passed in and out of the various service zones and secure bands. Wireless tech has reached the point where you'd practically have to be in the middle of the rain forest or standing on an iceberg in uncharted waters to be truly "out of service," but privacy fields and encryption have progressed at roughly the same rate, which frequently results in service being present but unavailable unless you have the security keys.

No one's supposed to interfere with the standard phone service channels. This doesn't stop overenthusiastic security crews from occasionally blanking everything but the emergency bands. It was amusingly easy to spot the freelance journalists in the crowd: They were the ones hitting their PDAs against their palms, like this would somehow make the proper security keys for the convention center access points appear. Fortunately for the security techs of the world, this approach has yet to work for anyone, and the freelancers were still quietly abusing their equipment when we reached the convention center.

The bus stop was located in the underground parking garage, in a clear, well-lighted area equidistant from both the entrance and exit. The bus approached, the entry gate rose; the bus entered the garage, the gate descended. Assuming it was a standard security setup, there were circuit breakers in place to prevent the entry and exit gates from opening at the same time, and sounding the internal alarm would cause them both to descend and lock. In modern security design, "death trap" isn't always a bad phrase. The idea is minimizing casualties, not preventing them entirely.

Blank-faced security men approached the bus as the doors opened, each holding a blood testing kit. I bit back a groan as I exited and approached the first free guard, adjusting the strap of my shoulder bag before extending my hand toward him. He slipped the unit over my hand and clamped it down.

"Press pass," he said.

"Georgia Mason, After the End Times." I unclipped the pass from my shirt and offered it to him. "I'm with Senator Ryman's group."

He fed the pass into the scanner at his waist. It beeped and popped the pass out again. He handed it back and glanced at the testing unit, which was showing a flashing green light. He frowned. "Please remove the glasses, Ms. Mason."

Lovely. Some of the extremely sensitive units can get confused by the elevated levels of inactive virus particles caused by retinal KA. I didn't exactly want to expose my eyes to the harsh lights of the parking garage, but I didn't feel like getting shot as a security precaution either. I removed by sunglasses, fighting the urge to squint.

The guard leaned forward, studying my eyes. "Retinal Kellis-Amberlee," he said. "Do you carry a med card?"

"Yes." No one with naturally elevated virus levels goes out without a med card if they enjoy breathing. I withdrew my wallet and produced the card, handing it over. He slotted it into the back of the testing unit. The green light stopped flashing, turned yellow, and finally turned a solid green, apparently having satisfied itself that my virus levels were within normal parameters and nothing to be concerned with.

"Thank you for your cooperation." He returned my card. I replaced it in my wallet before sliding my glasses back on. "Will your associates be joining us?"

"Not today." The scan of my press pass would have told him everything there was to know about our organization: Our work history, what our ratings share was like, any citations we'd received for sloppy reporting or libel, and, of course, how many of us were traveling with the senator and his group. "Where can I find—"

"Information kiosks are inside, up the stairs, and to your left," he said, already turning toward the next of the waiting journalists.

Assembly-line hospitality. Maybe it's not that welcoming, but it gets the job done. I turned to head through the glass doors into the convention center proper, where I could hopefully locate a bathroom in short order. The light had left dazzling spots dancing in front of my eyes, and the only way I was going to make them go away was by swallowing some painkillers before the migraine had time to finish developing. It was a small hope, but as I didn't exactly relish the idea of spending the day mingling with politicians and reporters while suffering from a headache, it was the best one I had.

The air conditioning inside was pumping full volume, ignoring the fact that it was February in Oklahoma. The reason for the arctic chill was evident: The place was packed. Despite the xenophobia that's gripped the world since the Rising, some things still have to happen face-to-face, and that includes political rallies. If anything, the rallies have gotten larger, growing as the smaller events dwindled. There's always the chance of an outbreak when you gather more than ten or twenty people in one place, but man is by his very nature a social animal, and once in a while, you just need an excuse.

Before the Rising, Super Tuesday was a big deal. These days, it's a three-ring circus. Beyond the expected political factions and special-interest groups, the convention center has exhibit halls and even a temporary mini-mall of service and sales kiosks. Place your vote for the next presidential candidate and buy a new pair of running shoes! You know everyone in here has been screened for signs of viral amplification, so have a ball!

The combination of sudden cold and the press of that many bodies was enough to make my impending headache throb. Hunching my shoulders, I began cutting my way diagonally across the crowd, aiming for the escalators. Presumably, the information kiosk would identify the locations of both the bathrooms and whatever was serving as a press staging area in this zoo.

Getting there was easier said than done, but after swimming my way upstream against the delegates, merchants, voters, and tourists who felt that the inconvenience of going through security was worth the chance to have a little fun, I managed to reach the escalator and stepped on, clinging to the rail for all that I was worth. I think the average American's tendency to hide inside while life goes whizzing by is an overreaction to a currently unavoidable situation, but I'm still a child of my generation; for me, a large crowd is fifteen people. The wistful looks older people sometimes get when they talk about gatherings of six and seven hundred are completely alien to me. That's not the way I grew up, and shoving this many bodies into one space, even a space as large as the Oklahoma City Convention Center, just feels *wrong*.

Judging from the makeup of the crowd, I wasn't alone in that attitude. Except for the people dressed in the corporate colors of one exhibitor or another, I was the youngest person in sight. I'm better crowd-socialized than most people born after the Rising because I've forced myself to be; in addition to the paparazzi swarms, I've attended technology conventions and academic conferences, getting myself used to the idea that people gather in groups. If I hadn't spent the past several years working up to this, just stepping into the hall would have made me run screaming, probably causing security to decide there was an outbreak in progress and lock us all inside.

That's me. The eternal optimist.

I saw the information kiosk as soon as I stepped off the escalator: a brightly colored octagon surrounded by scantily clad young women handing out packs of cigarettes. I pushed past them, refusing three packs on the way, and squinted at the posted map of the convention center. "You are here," I muttered. "That's great. I already found me. The drinking fountain, on the other hand, would be exactly where?"

"Nonsmoker?" inquired a voice at my elbow. I turned to find myself facing Dennis Stahl of the *Eakly Times*. He was smiling and had a press pass clipped to the lapel of his slightly wrinkled jacket. "I thought you looked familiar."

"Mr. Stahl," I said, eyebrows rising. "I didn't expect to see you here."

"Because I'm a newspaperman?"

"No. Because this hall holds roughly the population of North America, and I wouldn't expect to see my brother without a tracking device."

Mr. Stahl laughed. "Fair enough." One of the scantily clad young women took advantage of his distraction and pushed a pack of cigarettes into his hand. He eyed it dubiously before holding it toward me. "Cigarette?"

"Sorry. Don't smoke."

He tilted his head to the side. "Why not? I'd expect a cigarette to be the perfect capper on your 'look at me, I'm hard as nails' air of journalistic integrity." I raised my eyebrows farther. He laughed. "Come on, Ms. Mason. You wear all black, carry an actual hand-held MP3 recorder—I haven't seen anyone use one of those in years—and you never remove your sunglasses. You really think I don't know how to spot an image when I see one?"

"First off, I have retinal KA. The sunglasses are a medical necessity. Second . . ." I paused, smiling. "You got me. It's an image. But I still don't smoke. Do you know where the bathrooms are in this place? I need some water."

"I've been here three hours, and I haven't seen a bathroom yet," he said. "But there *is* a cunningly concealed Starbucks at the end of one of the exhibitors' rows, if you wouldn't mind my walking you?"

"If it gets me water, I'm all for it," I said, waving off another pack of cigarettes.

Mr. Stahl nodded, opening a path through the crowd with a sweep of his arm as he led me through. "Water, or a suitable substitute thereof," he agreed. "In exchange, I have a question for you . . . Why don't you smoke? Again, it seems like the perfect capper to your image. Personal reasons?"

"I like having sufficient lung capacity to run away from the living dead," I replied, deadpan. Mr. Stahl raised an eyebrow, and I shrugged. "I'm serious.

Cigarettes won't give you cancer, but they still cause emphysema, and I have no desire to get eaten by a zombie just because I was trying to look cool. Besides, the smoke can interfere with some delicate electronics, and it's hard enough to keep most kits working in the field. I don't need to add a second level of pollution to the crap they're already trying to function through."

"Huh. And here I thought that once you took cancer out of the equation, we'd be back to a world where every hard-hitting journalist was up to eight packs a day."

The exhibitors' row was packed with people selling things of every shape and size, from freeze-dried food guaranteed to stay good for the duration of a siege to medieval weaponry with built-in splatter guards. If you were looking for fluffier entertainments, there were the usual assortment of new cars, hair-care accessories, and toys for the kids, although I had to admit a certain affection for the Mattel booth advertising Urban Survival Barbie, now with her own machete and blood testing unit.

"That assumes every 'hard-hitting journalist' comes equipped with parents who don't mind them living at home and stinking up the curtains," I said. "What about you? I don't see you lighting up."

"Asthma. I could smoke if I wanted to. I could also collapse in the middle of the sidewalk clutching my chest, and somehow, that makes it substantially less fun." He pointed to the end of the row. "There's the Starbucks. What brings you out this way?"

"The usual: following the Senator around like a kitten on a string. Yourself?"

"A little bit of the same, on a somewhat more general scale." There was no line at the Starbucks, just three bored-looking baristas leaning on the counter and trying to seem busy. Mr. Stahl stepped up to them and said, "Large black coffee, please, to go."

The baristas exchanged a glance, but they'd clearly had their fill of arguing with men wearing press passes. One of them moved to start filling his order.

Glancing to me, Dennis asked, "Want anything?"

"Just a bottled water, thanks."

"Got it." He collected his coffee and handed me my water, passing a debit card to the barista at the register.

I dug a hand into my pocket. "What do I owe you?"

"Forget it." He reclaimed his card and turned to head for an open table near the edge of the exhibit line. I followed, sitting down across from him. He smiled. "Consider it payback for the circulation figures I got off that little incident out at your encampment after the rally the other week. Remember?"

"How could I forget?" I pulled a bottle of prescription-strength painkillers out of my shoulder bag, uncapping them with my thumb. "That 'little incident' has been defining my life for weeks."

"Got any juicy details for an old friend?"

It had been impossible to keep from releasing the fact that the screamers had been sabotaged. Even if we'd wanted to damage our ratings that way, the families of the victims could have sued us for interfering with a federal case if we'd attempted to suppress details. I shook my head. "Not that the press hasn't already released."

"The dangers of pumping industry sources," Mr.

Stahl said, and sipped his coffee. "Seriously, though, how have things been around the camp? Everything going smoothly?"

"Relatively so," I said, shaking four pills into my palm and slamming them down with a long gulp of icy water. Once I finished swallowing, I added, "Tense, but smooth. There haven't been any real leads on who sabotaged our perimeter. Causes a bit of internal strife, if you understand what I'm saying."

"Unfortunately, I do." Mr. Stahl shook his head. "Whoever it was must have been careful to cover their tracks."

"With good reason. People died in that attack. That makes it murder and that means they could be tried under Raskin-Watts. Most folks don't commit acts of terrorism expecting to get caught." I took another slower sip of water, waiting for the painkillers to kick in.

Mr. Stahl nodded, lips pressed into a thin line. "I know. Carl Boucher was a blowhard and an opinionated bastard, but he didn't deserve to die like that. None of those folks did. Good or bad, people deserve better deaths than that." He pushed away from the table, taking his coffee with him. "Well, I need to go meet up with my camera crew. We're interviewing Wagman in half an hour, and she likes it when her news crews are prompt. You take care of yourself, Miss Mason, all right?"

"Do my best," I replied, with a nod. "You've got my e-mail address."

"I'll keep in touch," he assured me, and turned, striding off into the crowd. It swallowed him up, and he was gone.

I stayed where I was, sipping my water and considering the atmosphere of the room. In some ways, it was like a cross between a carnival and a frat party, with people of all ages, stripes, and creeds bent on having as much fun as they could before it was time to leave for less well-secured climes. Signs hanging from the ceiling directed voters of the various districts where they should go if they wanted to place their votes in the old, physical way, rather than doing them from home via real-time electronic ballot. From the way most folks were ignoring the signs, I guessed the majority had placed their votes online before hitting the convention center. The paper-voting booths are more of a curiosity than anything else, maintained because the law insists that anyone who wishes to do so be able to place their ballot via physical, nonelectronic means. What this really means is that we can't get exact results on any election until the paper ballots have been tabulated, even when ninety-five percent of the votes have been already placed electronically.

The tobacco companies weren't the only ones working the time-honored selling power of half-clothed female flesh to push their wares. Girls wearing little more than a bikini and a smile were weaving their way in and out of the crowd, offering buttons and banners with political slogans to the passersby. More than half the swag was finding its way into nearby trash cans or onto the floor. Most of the buttons that stayed on, I noted, were either promoting Senator Ryman or Governor Tate, who was definitely shaping up to be Ryman's closest in-party competitor. Congresswoman Wagman had been able to ride her one-trick pony pretty far, but the buzz was pretty uniform in agreeing that it wouldn't get her much further. You can take the "porn star" platform a long way, but it's never going to get you to the White House. Signs indicated it would either be Ryman or Tate for the Republican nomination.

The results of the day would probably solidify one of them in the lead and make the upcoming convention nothing but a formality. I'd been hoping for a third candidate to mix things up at least a little, but there hadn't been any real breakouts on the campaign trail. Among the Republican voters—and even some of the Democrats and Independents—it was either Ryman's brand of laid-back "we should all get along while we're here," or Tate's hellfire and damnation that was attracting the attention, and hence the potential support, of just about everyone.

Tapping my watch to activate the memo function, I raised my wrist and murmured, "Note to self: See what you can do about getting an interview out of Tate's camp sometime after the primary closes, whatever the results." Technically, Shaun, Buffy, and I count as "rival journalists," given that we're mostly devoted to following Ryman's campaign. At the same time, we've all taken public oaths of journalistic integrity, and that means we can—at least supposedly—be trusted to provide a fair and unbiased report on any subject we address, unless it's in a clearly flagged editorial. Getting close enough to Tate to see how the man ticks might help with my growing objections to his political standpoints. Or it might not, and that could give me a renewed reason to rally for Ryman. Either way, it would make for good news.

My water was nearly gone, and I hadn't come to the convention center to people watch and cadge free beverages from the local newspapermen, no matter how much of an improvement that was over life at the convoy. I tapped my ear cuff. "Call Buffy."

There was a pause as the connection was made, and then Buffy's voice was in my ear, asking, "What glorious service may this unworthy one perform for her majesty on this hallowed afternoon?"

I smirked. "Interrupt your poker game?"

"Actually, we were watching a movie."

"You and Chuckles are getting a little cozy there, don't you think?"

Buffy's reply was a prim, "You don't ask about my business, and I won't ask about yours. Besides, I'm off-duty. There's nothing to edit, and all my material for the week has already been uploaded to the time-release server."

"Fine with me," I said. Contrary to my earlier fears, the painkillers were preventing the headache from becoming more than an annoying throb at the back of my temples. "Can you get me a current location on the senator? I'm over at the convention center, and the place is a madhouse. If I try to find him on my own, I may never be heard from again."

"I'd be able to track a government official because . . . ?"

"I know you have at least one transmitter planted on the man, and you never let a piece of equipment out of your sight without a tracking device."

Buffy paused. Then she asked, "Are you near a data port?"

I looked around. "There's a public jack about ten yards from me."

"Great. They don't have wireless maps of the convention center up for public access—something about 'preserving the security of the hall' or whatever. Go over and plug yourself in, and I can give you Senator Ryman's current location, assuming he's not standing within ten yards of a scrambler."

"Have I mentioned recently that I adore you?" I rose, chucked my bottle into a recycler, and walked toward the jack-in point. "So, Chuck, huh? I guess he's cute, if you like the weedy techie type. Personally, I'd go for something a little taller, but whatever floats your boat. Just make sure you know where he's been."

"Yes, mother," Buffy replied. "Are you there yet?"

"Plugging in now." Hooking my handheld to the wall unit was a matter of seconds. The standardization of data ports has been a true blessing to the technically inept computer users of the world. My system took a few seconds to negotiate a connection with the convention center servers, and most of that was verifying compatibility of antiviral and anti-spam software. It beeped, signaling its readiness to proceed. "I'm in."

"Great." Buffy quieted. I could hear typing in the background. "Got it. You're in the exhibition zone on the second level, right?"

"Right. Near the Starbucks."

"Drop the singular; there are eight Starbucks

kiosks on that level alone. Bring me a sugar-free vanilla raspberry mocha when you come back. The senator is on the conference floor three levels down. I'm dropping you a map." My handheld beeped, acknowledging receipt. "That should have everything you need, assuming he doesn't move."

"Thanks, Buffy." I unplugged myself from the wall. "Have fun."

"Don't call back for at least an hour." The connection cut itself off.

Shaking my head, I focused on the map dominating my screen. It was fairly simplistic, representing the convention center in clear enough lines that my route was difficult to misinterpret. The senator's last known location was marked in red, and a thin yellow line connected him to the blinking white dot representing the data port where I'd downloaded the information. Nicely done. Pushing my sunglasses back up, I began making my way down the exhibition hall.

The crowd had grown thicker during my water break. That wasn't a problem: Buffy's mapping software was equipped with a full overview of the pedestrian routes through the convention center and had been programmed to come up with the fastest route between points, rather than the shortest. After estimating congestion levels, it displayed a route that made use of little-used hallways, half-hidden shortcuts, and a lot of stairwells. Since most people will use escalators whenever possible, taking the stairs is often the best way to avoid getting yourself lost in a crowd.

The human tropism toward illusionary time-saving devices has been the topic of a lot of studies since the Rising. There were an estimated six hundred casualties in one large Midwestern mall due entirely to people's unwillingness to take the stairs during a crisis. Escalators jam if you overload them. People got stuck on elevators or ambushed by zombies that had been able to worm their way into the crush of people trying to force their way up the frozen escalators, and that was all she wrote. You'd think that after something like that, folks would start getting better about expending a little extra effort, but you'd be wrong. Sometimes, the hardest habit to break is the habit of doing nothing beyond the necessary.

It took about fifteen minutes to descend three levels and make it past the cursory security checkpoint between the exhibition levels and the conference floor, which was closed to everyone save the candidates, members of their immediate family, official staff, and the press. The security check consisted of scanning my press pass to confirm that it wasn't a fake, patting me down for unlicensed weapons, and performing a basic blood check with a cheap handheld unit from a brand that I know for a fact returns false negatives three times out of ten. I guess once you're past the door in these places, they don't worry as much about your health.

The quiet of the conference floor was a welcome change from the hustle and bustle of the levels above. Down here, the business of waiting for results was exactly that: business. There are always a few hopefuls who stick it out even after the numbers indicate they don't have much of a shot at the big seat, but the fact of the matter is that the party nominations almost always go to the folks who take Super Tuesday, and without party backing, your odds of taking the presidency are slim to none. You're welcome to try, but you're probably not going to win. Nine out of ten of the folks who've been out pounding the pavement for the last few months will be heading home after the polls close. It'll be four more years before they have another shot at the big time, and for some of them, that's too long to wait; a lot of this year's candidates will never try for it again. Dreams are made and broken on days like this.

The senator and his team were in a plushly appointed boardroom about halfway down the hall. A placard on the wall identified the room's inhabitants as "Senator Ryman, Rep., WI," but I still knocked before trying the door, just in case something was going on that I wasn't meant to interfere with.

"Come in," called a brisk, irritated voice. I nodded, satisfied that I wasn't interrupting, and stepped inside.

When I first met Robert Channing, the senator's chief aide, my initial impression was of a fussy, egotistical man who resented anything that might get in his way. After a few months of acquaintanceship, I haven't been forced to revise that impression, although I've come to understand that he's very good at what he does. He doesn't travel with the convoy. He's usually at the senator's office in Wisconsin, arranging bookings, setting up the halls where Senator Ryman speaks, and coordinating outside news coverage, since "three amateur journalists with a vanity site doesn't exactly constitute wide-scale exposure." Oddly, much of my respect for him comes from the fact that he's willing to say things like that to my face. He's been very upfront about everything that affects the senator's chances at the White House from day one, and if that means stepping on a few toes, he's okay with that. Not a nice guy, but a good one to have on your side.

At the moment, he was looking at me with narrowed eyes, and it was clear that whoever's side he was currently on, it wasn't mine. His tie was askew, and his jacket had been tossed over a nearby chair. That, more than the senator's unbuttoned jacket and missing tie, told me they'd been having a rough day. Senator Ryman is quick to shed the trappings of propriety, but Channing only takes his jacket off when the stress is too much to tolerate in tweed.

"Thought I'd come see how things were going at the fort," I said, closing the door behind myself. "Maybe get some decent reaction quotes as the numbers come down."

"Miss Mason," acknowledged Channing stiffly. Several of the interchangeable interns were occupied at the back of the room, taking notation from the various monitors into their handhelds and PDAs. "Please try not to get underfoot."

"I'll do my best." I sat in the first unoccupied chair, folding my hands behind my head as I stared in his direction. Channing is one of those people who can't stand the fact that my sunglasses make it hard for him to tell whether I'm actually looking at him.

He met my stare with a disgruntled glower before grabbing his jacket and striding for the door. "I'm getting coffee," he said, and stepped out into the hallway, slamming the door as he went.

Senator Ryman didn't bother to conceal his amusement. Instead, he roared with it, as though my driving his chief aide out of the room was the funniest thing he'd seen in years. "Georgia, that wasn't nice," he said, finally, between gusts of laughter.

I shrugged. "All I did was sit down," I said.

"Wicked, wicked woman. I assume you're here to find out whether you still have a job?"

"I have a job whether you have a campaign or not, Senator, and I can monitor the public polls from the convoy just as well as I can monitor them from here. I wanted to get an idea of the mood around the camp." I looked around the room. Most of the people present had shed their jackets, and in some cases their shoes. Empty coffee cups and half-eaten sandwiches littered random surfaces, and the whiteboard was largely dedicated to a series of tic-tac-toe grids. "I'm going with 'guardedly optimistic.'"

"We're ahead by twenty-three percent of the vote," the senator said, with a short nod. "'Guardedly optimistic' is an accurate assessment."

"How are you feeling?"

He frowned at me. "How do you mean?"

"Well, sir, at some point in the next," I made a show of checking my watch, "six hours, you find out whether you have a shot at the party nomination, and hence the presidency, or whether you're looking at the second-banana consolation prize, or worse, nothing at all. Today begins the process of winning or losing the election. So, bearing all of that in mind, how are you feeling?"

"Terrified," the senator said. "This is a long way from turning to my wife and saying, 'Well, honey, I think this is the term when I make a run for the office.' This is the real deal. I'm a bit anticipatory, but not that much. Whatever the polls say, the people will have spoken, and I'll just have to abide with what they have to say."

"But you're expecting them to speak in your favor."

He fixed me with a stern eye. "Georgia, has this just turned into an interview?"

"Maybe."

"Thanks for the warning."

"Warnings aren't in my job description. Did you need me to repeat the question?"

"I hadn't realized it was a question," he said, tone suddenly wry. "Yes, I'm expecting them to speak in my favor, because you don't make it as far as I have without developing an ego, and I'm of the opinion that the average American is an intelligent person who knows what's best for this country. I wouldn't be running for office if I didn't think I was the best man for the job. Will I be disappointed if they don't pick me? A bit. It's natural to be disappointed when you don't get chosen for this sort of thing. But I'm willing to believe that if the American public is smart enough to choose their own president, then the American public is smart enough to know what they want, and if they don't choose me, I need to do some serious self-examination to see where I got it all wrong."

"Have you given any thought to your next steps, assuming you show strongly enough in today's polls to continue with the campaign?"

"We'll keep taking the message to the people. Keep getting out there and meeting people, letting them know that I won't be the sort of president who sits in a hermetically sealed room and ignores the problems plaguing this country." His dig at President Wertz was subtle but well-deserved. No one's seen our current president set foot outside a well-secured urban area since before he was elected, and most critiques of his administration have centered around the fact that he doesn't seem to realize not everyone can afford to have their air filtered before it gets to them. To listen to him talk, you'd think zombie attacks only happened to the careless and the stupid, rather than being something ninety percent of the people on the planet have to worry about on a daily basis.

"How does Mrs. Ryman feel about this?"

Senator Ryman's expression softened. "Emily is as pleased as can be that things are going so well. I'm on this campaign with the full support and understanding of my family, and without them, I'd never have been able to make it half as far as I have."

"Senator, in recent weeks, Governor Tate—who many view as your primary in-party opponent—has been speaking out for stricter screening protocols among children and the elderly, and increased funding for the private school system, on the basis that overcrowding in the public schools only increases the risk of wide-scale viral incubation and outbreak. How do you stand on this issue?"

"Well, Miss Mason, as you know, all three of my daughters have attended the excellent public schools in our home town. My eldest—"

"That would be Rebecca Ryman, age eighteen?"

"That's correct. My eldest will be graduating high

school this June and expects to start at Brown University in the fall, where she'll be studying political science, like her old man. Supporting a free and equal public school system is one of the duties of the government. Which does mean increased blood screening for children under the age of fourteen, and additional funding for school security, but it seems to me that taking money from our public schools because they might be threatened at some point in the future is a bit of burning down the barn to keep the hay from going bad."

"How do you speak to the criticisms that your campaign depends too heavily on the secular issues facing our nation, while ignoring the spiritual?"

Senator Ryman's lips quirked in a smile. "I say when God comes down here and helps me clean my house, I'll be more than happy to help Him with cleaning His. Until then, I'll trouble myself with keeping people fed and breathing, and let Him tend the parts I can't do anything to help."

The door opened as Channing returned, balancing a tray of Starbucks cups on his outstretched arms. The interchangeable interns promptly mugged him. An open can of Coke was somehow deposited in front of me in the chaos that followed. I acknowledged it with a grateful nod, picked it up, and sipped before saying, "If the campaign ends today, Senator, if this is the culmination of your work to date . . . was it worth it?"

"No," he said. The room went quiet. I could almost hear heads turning toward him. "As your readers are no doubt aware, an act of sabotage committed at my headquarters earlier this month led to the deaths of four good men and women who were dedicated to supporting this campaign. They signed on to draw a paycheck and maybe, along the way, help an ideal find a place in this modern world. Instead, they passed on to whatever reward may be waiting for us—for heroes—in the *next* world. If those men and women had lived, then yes, I could have walked away from this a little sadder, a little wiser, but convinced that I'd done the right thing, I'd done my best, and next time, I'd be able to make that run all the way to the end of the road. At this point?

"Nothing I do is bringing them back, and if there *were* something I could do to change what happened in Eakly, I would have done it ten times over. From where I sit, there's only one thing left that I *can* do, and that's win. For the ideal they died supporting, and for the sake of their memories. So if I lose, if I have to go home empty-handed, if the next time I contact their families it's to say, 'Sorry, but I couldn't make it after all' . . . then no, it wasn't worth it. But it was the only thing I knew to do."

There was a long, stunned pause before the room erupted in applause. Most of it came from the interchangeable interns, but the technicians were applauding as well—and so, his hands devoid of coffee cups, was Channing. I noted this with thoughtful interest before turning back to the senator and nodding.

"Thank you for your time," I said, "and best of luck in today's primaries."

Senator Ryman flashed a practiced grin. "I don't need luck. I just need the waiting to be over."

"And I just need the use of one of your data ports,

so that I can clean this up and transmit it over for upload," I said, pulling out my MP3 recorder and holding it up to the room. "It'll take me about fifteen minutes to do the surface edits."

"Will we be permitted to review your report before release?" asked Channing.

"Down, boy," said the senator. "I don't see where we need to. Georgia's been square with us so far, and I don't see where that's going to change. Georgia?"

"You can review it if you'd like, but all that's going to do is delay release," I said. "Leave me to work, and this hits my front page before the polls have closed."

"Go to it," said the senator, and indicated a free space on the wall. "You have all the data ports you need."

"Thanks," I said, and took my Coke, moving over to the wall to settle down and set to work.

Editing a report is both easier and harder for me than it is for Shaun or Buffy. My material rarely depends on graphics. I don't need to concern myself with camera angles, lighting, or whether the footage I use gets my point across. At the same time, they say a picture is worth a thousand words, and in today's era of instant gratification and high-speed answers, sometimes people aren't willing to deal with all those hard words when a few pictures supposedly do the job just as well. It's harder to sell people on a report that's just news without pictures or movies to soften the blow. I have to find the heart of every subject as fast as I can, pin it down on the page, and then cut it wide open for the audience to see.

"Super Tuesday: Index Case for a Presidency"

wouldn't win me any awards, but once I cleaned up my impromptu interview with Senator Ryman and intercut the text with a few still shots of the man, I was reasonably sure that it *was* going to catch and hold an audience, and tell the truth as I understood it. Anything beyond that was more than I had a right to ask.

With my report uploaded and turned in, I settled to do what a lifetime of reporting the truth has equipped me for best of all: I settled to wait. I watched the interchangeable interns come and go, watched Channing pace, and watched the senator, aware that his fate was already determined, holding calm and implacable sway over them all. He just didn't know what that determination was.

The polls closed at midnight. Every screen in the room was turned to the major media outlets, a dozen talking heads conflicting with one another's words as they tried to string the suspense out and drive their ratings just a few degrees higher. I couldn't blame them for it, but that didn't mean that I had to be impressed with it.

My ear cuff beeped. I tapped it.

"Go."

"Georgia, it's Buffy."

"Results?"

"Senator Ryman took the primary with a seventy percent clean majority. His position jumped eleven points as soon as your report went live."

I closed my eyes and smiled. One of the talking heads had just revealed the same information, or something similar; whoops and cheers were filling the room. "Say the words, Buffy."

"We're going to the Republican National Convention."

Sometimes, the truth *can* set you free.

The importance of the Raskin-Watts trial and the failure of all subsequent attempts to overturn the ruling have been often overlooked in the wake of more recent, more sensational incidents. After all, what bearing can two long-dead religious nutcases from upstate Indiana have on the state of modern politics?

Quite a lot. For one thing, the current tendency to dismiss Geoff Raskin and Reed Watts as "religious nut-cases" is an oversimplification so extreme as to border on the criminal. Geoff Raskin held a degree in psychology from UC Santa Cruz, with a specialization in crowd control. Reed Watts was an ordained priest who worked with troubled youth and was instrumental in bringing several communities "back to God." They were, in short, intelligent men who recognized the potential for turning the waves of social change engendered by the side effects of Kellis-Amberlee to their own benefit, and to the benefit of their faith.

Did Geoff Raskin and Reed Watts work for the common good? Read the reports on what they did to Warsaw, Indiana, and see if you think so. Seven hundred and ninety-three people died in the primary infection wave alone, and the cleanup from the secondary infections took six years to complete, during which time Raskin and Watts were held in maximum security, awaiting trial. According to their own testimony, they were intending to use the living dead as a threat to bring the people of Warsaw, and eventually of the United States, around to their point of view: that Kellis-Amberlee was the judgment of the Lord, and that all ungodly ways would soon be wiped from the Earth.

It was the finding of the courts that the use of weaponized live-state Kellis-Amberlee, as represented by the captive zombies, was considered an act of terrorism, and that all individuals responsible for such acts would be tried under the International Terrorism Acts of 2012. Geoff Raskin and Reed Watts were killed by lethal injection, and their bodies were remanded to the government to assist in the study of the virus they had helped to spread.

The moral of our story, beyond the obvious "don't play with dead things": Some lines were never meant to be crossed, however good your cause may seem.

—From *Images May Disturb You*,
the blog of Georgia Mason, March 11, 2040

Eleven

Georgia! Shaun! It's so lovely to see you!" Emily Ryman was all smiles as she approached, arms spread wide in an invitation to an embrace. I glanced at Shaun and he stepped forward, letting her hug him while he blocked her from reaching me. I don't like physical contact from semistrangers, and Shaun knows it.

If Emily noticed the deliberate way we positioned ourselves, she didn't comment. "I never quite believe you're alive after those reports you do, you foolish, foolish boy."

"It's good to see you, too, Emily," Shaun said, and hugged her back. He's much easier with that sort of thing than I am. I blame this on the fact that he's the kind of person who believes in shoving his hand into the dark, creepy hole, rather than sensibly avoiding it. "How have you been?"

"Busy, as usual. Foaling season kept us hopping, but that's mostly over, thank God. I lost two good mares this year, and neither managed to reanimate on

the grounds, thanks to the help being on the ball."
Emily detangled herself from Shaun, still smiling,
and turned to offer her hand. Not a hug, just her
hand. I gave her a nod of approval as I took it. Her
smile widened. "Georgia. I can't thank you enough
for your coverage of my husband's campaign."

"It hasn't just been me." I reclaimed my hand.
"There are a lot of reporters keeping a close eye on the
senator. Word on the street is he's receiving the party
nomination tonight." The other political journalists
were starting to smell "White House" in the water
and were gathering like sharks, hoping for something
worth seizing on. Buffy spent half her time disabling
cameras and microphones set up by rival blog sites.
She spent the other half writing steamy porn about the
senator's aides and hanging out with Chuck Wong,
who'd been spending a disconcerting amount of time
in our van recently, but that was her business.

"Yes, but you're the only one I've met who's reporting on *him*, rather than the interesting things his
campaign drives out from beneath the rocks, or the
fictional affairs of his office aides," Emily said, wryly.
"I know I can trust what you say. That's meant a lot
to me and the girls while Peter was on the road, and
it's going to mean a lot more from here on out."

"It's been an honor."

"What do you mean, 'it's going to mean a lot
more'?" asked Shaun. "Hey, George, are you finally
going to learn to write? Because that would be awesome. I can't carry you forever, you know."

"Sadly, Shaun, this doesn't have anything to do
with how well your sister can write." Emily shook
her head. "It's all about the campaign."

"I understand," I said. Glancing to Shaun, I continued, "Once he accepts the nomination—assuming he gets nominated—this gets real. Up until now, it's been a weird sort of summer vacation." After the nominations, it would be campaigning in earnest. It would be debates and deals and long nights, and she'd be lucky to see him before the inauguration. Assuming all that work didn't turn out to be for nothing; assuming he could win.

"Exactly," said Emily, expression going weary. "That man is lucky I love him."

"Statements like that make me wish that I didn't have quite so much journalistic integrity, Emily," I said. The statement was mild, but the warning wasn't. "You, expressing unhappiness with your husband? That's about to become sound-bite gold for both sides of the political fence."

She paused. "You're telling me to be careful."

"I'm telling you something you already know." I smiled, changing the subject to one that would hopefully make her look less uncomfortable. "Will the girls be joining you? I still need to meet them."

"Not for this silly convention," she said. "Rebecca is getting ready for college, and I didn't have the heart to drag Jeanne and Amber away from the foals to get their pictures taken by a thousand strangers. *I* wouldn't be here if it wasn't absolutely necessary."

"Understandable," I said. The job of a candidate's spouse at the party convention is simple: stand around looking elegant and attractive, and say something witty if you get a microphone shoved in your face. That doesn't leave much time for family togetherness, or for protecting kids from reporters itching to find something scandalous to start chewing on. Everything that happens at a party convention is on the record if the press finds out about it. Emily was doing the right thing. "Mind if I drop by later for an interview? I promise not to bring up the horses if you promise not to throw heavy objects at my head."

Emily's lips quirked up in a smile. "My. Peter wasn't kidding when he said that the convention had you feeling charitable."

"She's saving up her catty for her interview with Governor Tate," Shaun said.

"He's agreed to an interview?" asked Emily. "Peter said he'd been putting you off since the primaries."

"That would be why he's finally agreed to an interview," I replied, not bothering to keep the irritation from my voice. "Doing it before now was dismissible. I mean, what was I going to say about the man? 'Governor Tate is so busy trying to get elected that he doesn't have time to sit down with a woman who speaks publicly in support of his in-party opposition'? Not exactly a scathing indictment. Now we're at the convention and if he doesn't talk to me when he's talking to everyone else, it looks like censorship."

Emily considered me for a moment. Then, slowly, she smiled. "Why, Georgia Mason, I do believe you've entrapped this poor man."

"No, ma'am, I've merely engaged in standard journalistic practice," I said. "He entrapped himself."

An exclusive six weeks before the convention would have been something he could bury or buy off: No matter how good it was, unless I somehow got him to confess to a sex scandal or drug abuse, it wasn't going to be enough to taint the shining purity of his "champion of the religious and conservative right" reputation. Senator Ryman is moderate leaning toward liberal, despite his strong affiliation to and affection for the Republican Party. Governor Tate, on the other hand, is so far to the right that he's in danger of falling off the edge of the world. Few people are willing to stand for both the death penalty and an overturning of *Roe v. Wade* these days, but he does it, all while encouraging loosening the Mason's Law restrictions preventing family farms from operating within a hundred miles of major metro areas and encouraging tighter interpretation of Raskin-Watts. Under his proposed legislation, it wouldn't be a crime to own a cow in Albany, but it would be considered an act of terrorism to attempt to save the life of a heart attack victim before performing extensive blood tests. Did I want a little time alone with him, on the record, to see how much of a hole he could dig for himself when faced with the right questions?

Did I ever.

"When's your interview?"

"Three." I glanced at my watch. "Actually, if you don't mind Shaun escorting you from here, that would be a big help. I need to get moving if I don't want to make the governor wait."

"I thought you *did* want to make the governor wait," said Shaun.

"Yes, but it has to be on purpose." Making him wait intentionally was showing strategy. Making him wait because I didn't allow enough time to get to his office was sloppy. I have a reputation for being a lot of things—after the article where I called Wagman a "publicity-seeking prostitute who decided to pole-dance on the Constitution for spare change," "bitch" has been at the top of the list—but "sloppy" isn't among them.

"Of course," said Emily. "Thank you for coming out to meet me."

"It was my pleasure, Mrs. Ryman. Shaun, don't make the nice potential First Lady poke any dead things before you deliver her to security."

"You never let me have any fun," Shaun mock-grumbled, offering Emily his arm. "If you'd like to come with me, I believe I can promise an utterly dull, boring, and uneventful trip between points A and B."

"That sounds lovely, Shaun," said Emily. Her security detail—three large gentlemen who looked just like every other private security guard at the convention—fell in behind her as Shaun led her away down the hall.

When she'd e-mailed asking us to meet her, she said she'd be arriving at one of the delivery doors, rather than the VIP entrance. "I want to avoid the press" was her quixotic, but sadly understandable, justification. Despite the snide implications that have been made by some of my colleagues, my team and I aren't the lapdogs of what will hopefully become the Ryman administration. We're twice as critical as anyone else when the candidate screws up because, quite frankly, we expect better of him. He's *ours*. Win or lose, he belongs to *us*. And just like any proud parent or greedy shareholder, we want to see our investment make it to the finish line. If Peter screws the pooch, Shaun, Buffy, and I are right there in the thick of things, pointing to the wet spot and shouting for people to come quick and bring the cameras . . . but we're also the ones who won. We have no interest in embarrassing the senator by harassing his family or dragging them inappropriately into the spotlight.

An example: Rebecca Ryman fell off her horse during a show-jumping event at the Wisconsin State Fair three years ago. She was fifteen. I don't understand the appeal of show-jumping—I don't care for large mammals under any circumstances, and I like them even less when you're stacking adolescents on their backs and teaching them to clear obstacles—so I can't say what happened, just that the horse stepped wrong somehow, and Rebecca fell. She was fine. The horse broke a leg and had to be put down.

The euthanasia was performed without a hitch; as is standard with large mammals, they used a captive bolt gun to the forehead, followed by a stiletto to the spinal column. Nothing was hurt except the horse, Rebecca's pride, and the reputation of the Wisconsin State Fair. The horse never had a prayer of reanimating. That hasn't prevented six of our rivals from airing the footage from that fair for weeks on end, as if the embarrassment of a teenage girl somehow cancels out the fact that they didn't make the cut. "Ha-ha, you got the candidate, but we can mock his teenage daughter for an honest mistake."

Sometimes I wonder if my crew is the only group of professional journalists who managed to avoid the asshole pills during training. Then I look at some of my editorials, especially the ones involving Wagman and her slow political suicide, and I realize that we took the pills. We just got a small portion of journalistic ethics to make them go down more easily. Emily knew she was safe with us because, unlike our peers, Shaun and I don't abuse innocent people for the sake of a few marketable quotes. We have politicians to abuse when we need that sort of thing.

I checked my watch as I strode down the hall toward the main entrance. A shortcut through the press pen would take me to the governor's offices, where his chief of staff would be happy to stall me for as long as possible. My interview wasn't for a guaranteed sixty minutes; I'd need a lot more pull if I wanted to achieve something like that. No, I just got whatever questions I could ask and have answered in the span of an hour, no matter what else came up during that time. I wanted to make him wait no more than ten minutes. That would make a point but still leave me the time to get the answers I both wanted and needed to have. His chief of staff would not only want to make *me* wait, he'd want to make me wait for at least half an hour, thus gutting the interview and proving once more exactly who was in control of the situation.

There are moments when I look at the world I'm living in, all the cutthroat politics and the incredibly petty, partisan deal mongering, and I wonder how anyone could be happy doing anything else. After this, local politics would seem like a bake sale. Which means I need to stay exactly where I am, and *that* means making sure everyone sees how good I am at my job.

People called greetings my way as I cut through the press pen. I waved distractedly, attention focused on the route ahead. I have a reputation for aloofness in certain parts of the press corps. I guess I deserve it.

"Georgia!" called a man I vaguely recognized from Wagman's press pool. He shouldered his way through the crowd, drawing up alongside me as I continued toward the door to Governor Tate's offices. "Got a second?"

"Not so much," I said, reaching for the doorknob.

He put a hand on my shoulder, ignoring the way I tensed, and said, "The congresswoman just dropped out of the race."

I froze, swinging my head around to face him before tugging my sunglasses down enough to allow me an unobstructed view of his face. The overhead lights burned my eyes. That didn't matter; I could see his expression well enough to know that he wasn't lying. "What do you want?" I asked, pushing my glasses back up.

He looked over his shoulder toward the rest of the gathered journalists. None of them seemed to have realized that there was blood in the water. Not yet, anyway. They'd catch on fast, and once they did, we were cornered.

"I bring you what I have—and there's footage, too, lots of stuff, all the votes, details on where she's throwing what's left of her weight—and you let me on the team."

"You want to follow Ryman?"

"I do."

I considered this, keeping my face impassive. Finally, incrementally, I nodded. "Be at our rooms in an hour, with copies of all your recent publications, and everything you've got on Wagman. We'll talk there."

"Great," he said, and stepped back, letting me continue on my way.

Governor Tate's security agents nodded as I stepped through the doorway into the governor's offices, holding up my press pass for their review. It passed muster; they didn't stop me.

Governor Tate's quarters looked just like Senator Ryman's, and were, I'm sure, close to identical to Wagman's. Since presidential hopefuls are packed into contiguous convention centers these days, the folks organizing the conventions go out of their way to prevent the appearance that they're "showing favor" to any particular candidate. One of our guys was going to come away the Crown prince of the party while the other went begging for scraps, but until the votes were counted, they'd be standing on equal footing.

The office was full of volunteers and staffers, and the walls were plastered with the requisite "Tate for President" posters, but the atmosphere still managed to be quiet and almost funereal. People didn't look frightened, just focused on what they were doing. I tapped the button on my lapel, triggering its internal camera to start taking still shots every fifteen seconds. There was enough memory to keep it doing that for two hours before I needed to dump the pictures to disk. Most of the shots would be crap, but there would probably be one or two that I could use.

I killed a few minutes pouring myself an unwanted cup of coffee and doctoring it to my supposed satisfaction before walking over to show my press pass to the guards waiting at the governor's office door.

"Georgia Mason, After the End Times, here to see Governor Tate."

One of them looked over his sunglasses at me. "You're late."

"Got held up," I replied, smiling. My own sunglasses were firmly in place, making it difficult, if not impossible, to tell whether the smile was reaching my eyes.

The guards exchanged a look. I've found that men in sunglasses really hate it when they can't see your eyes—it's like the air of mystique they're trying to create isn't meant to be shared with anyone else, especially not a silly little journalist who happens to suffer from an ocular medical condition. I held my ground and my smile.

Late or not, they didn't have a valid reason to keep me out. "Don't do it again," said the taller of the two, and opened the door to the governor's private office.

"Right," I said, and let my smile drop as I walked past them. They closed the door behind me with a sharp click. I didn't bother to turn. I'd only get one first look at the private office of the man who stood the best shot at putting me out of a job. I wanted to savor it.

Governor Tate's office was decorated austerely. He'd chosen to cover the room's two windows; shelves blocked them almost completely, and the ambient light was provided by soft overhead fluorescents. Two massive flags covered most of the rear wall, representing, respectively, the United States and Texas. There were no other personal touches in evidence. This office was a stopping place, not a destination.

The governor himself was behind his desk,

carefully placed so he was framed by the flags. I could imagine his handlers spending hours arguing about how best to create the image that he was a man who would be strong, both for his country and for the world. They'd done it; he looked perfectly presidential. If Peter Ryman was all boyish good looks and all-American charm, Governor David Tate was the embodiment of the American military man, from his solemn demeanor down to his respectable gray crew cut. I didn't need to call up his service record; the fact that he had one while Senator Ryman didn't has been the source of a lot of ads paid for by "concerned citizens" since the campaign cycle began. Three-star general, saw combat in the Canadian Border Cleansing of '17, when we took back Niagara Falls from the infected, and then again in New Guinea in '19, when a terrorist action involving aerosolized live-state Kellis-Amberlee nearly cost us the country. He'd been wounded in battle, he'd fought for his nation and for the rights of the uninfected, and he understood the war we fight every day against the creatures that used to be our loved ones.

There are a lot of good reasons the man scares the crap out of me. Those are just the beginning.

"Miss Mason," he said, indicating the chair on the far side of his desk with a sweep of one hand as he rose. "I trust you didn't get lost? I was beginning to think you weren't intending to come."

"Governor," I replied. I walked over and sat down, pulling my MP3 recorder from my pocket and placing it on the table. The action triggered at least two video cameras concealed in my clothing. Those were the ones I knew about; I was sure Buffy had hidden half a dozen more in case someone got cute with an EMP pulse. "I was unavoidably detained."

"Ah, yes," he said, sitting back down. "Those security checks can be murder, can't they?"

"They certainly can." I leaned over to turn on the MP3 recorder with a theatrical flick of my index finger. Smoke and mirrors: If he thought that was my only recording device, he'd worry less about what was really going on the record. "I wanted to thank you for taking the time to sit down with me today and, of course, with our audience at After the End Times. Our readers have been following this campaign with a great deal of interest, and your platform is something that they're eager to understand in more depth."

"Clever folks, your readers," the governor drawled, settling back in his seat. I glanced up without moving my head; the ability to see your interviewees when they don't know you're looking is one of the great advantages to living your life behind tinted glass.

It was easier to look than it was to avoid flinching at what I saw. The governor was watching me with undisguised blankness, like a little boy watching a bug he intended to smash. I'm used to people disliking reporters, but that was a bit much. Sitting up again, I straightened my glasses and said, "They are among the most discriminating in the blogging community."

"Is that so? Well, I suppose that explains their unflagging interest in this year's race. Been glorious for your ratings, hasn't it?"

"Yes, Governor, it has. Now, your run for president was a bit of a surprise—political circles held that you wouldn't be reaching for the office for another cycle. What prompted this early entrance into the race?"

The governor smiled, erasing the blankness from his eyes. Too late; I'd already seen it. In a way, the sudden life in his expression was even more frightening. He was on script now. He thought he knew how to handle me.

"Well, Miss Mason, the long and the short of it is that I've been getting a mite worried watching the way things have been going around here. I looked out at the field and realized that, unless I was on it, there just wasn't anyone out there that I'd trust to watch after my wife and two boys when the dead decided it was time for another mass uprising. America needs a strong leader in this time of turmoil. Someone who knows what it means for a man to fight to hold what's his. No offense against my esteemed opponent, but the good senator hasn't ever fought for what he loves. He doesn't understand it the way he would if he'd ever bled to keep it." His tone was jovial and almost jocular, a father figure imparting wisdom on a privileged student.

I wasn't buying it. Keeping my expression professional, I said, "So you see this as a two-man race—between yourself and Senator Ryman."

"Let's be honest here: It *is* a two-man race. Kirsten Wagman is a good woman with strong Republican values and a firm grasp of the morals of this nation, but she's not going to be our next president. She isn't prepared to do what's needed for the people and the economy of this great land."

Resisting the urge to point out that Kirsten

Wagman believed in using her breasts in place of an informed debate, I asked, "Governor, what do you feel is needed for the people of America?"

"This country was based on the three Fs, Miss Mason: Freedom, Faith, and Family." I could hear the capital letters in his voice; he said the words with that much force. "We've gone to great lengths to preserve the first of those things, but we've allowed the other two to slip by the wayside as we focused on the here and now. We're drifting away from God." The blankness was back in his eyes. "We're being judged; we're being tested. I'm afraid we're coming direly close to failing, and this isn't a test you get to take more than once."

"Can you give me an example of this 'failure'?"

"Why, the loss of Alaska, Miss Mason; a great American territory ceded to the dead because we didn't have the guts to stand up for what was rightly ours. Our boys weren't willing to put their faith in God and stand that line, and now a treasured part of our nation is lost, maybe forever. How long before that happens again, in Hawaii or Puerto Rico or, God forbid, even the American Heartland? We've gotten soft behind our walls. It's time to put our trust in God."

"Governor, you saw action in the Canadian Border Cleansing. I'd expect you to understand why Alaska had to be abandoned."

"And I'd expect you to understand why a true American never lets go of what's his. We should have fought. Under my leadership, we *will* fight, and we will by God win."

I suppressed the unprofessional urge to shudder. His voice held all the hallmarks of a fanatic. "You're requesting relaxation of Mason's Law, Governor. Is there a particular reason for that?"

"There's nothing in the Constitution that says a man can't feed his family however he sees fit, even if that way isn't exactly popular. Laws that limit our freedoms are needless as often as not. Why, look what happened when the Democrats stopped fighting for their unconstitutional gun control laws. Did gunshot deaths climb? No. They declined by forty percent the first year, and they've been dropping steadily ever since. It stands to reason that relaxation of other antifreedom legislation would—"

"How many of the infected are killed with guns every year?"

He paused, eyes narrowing. "I don't see what bearing that has on our discussion."

"According to the most recent CDC figures, ninety percent of the Kellis-Amberlee victims that are killed in clashes with the uninfected are killed by gunshot."

"Guns fired by licensed, law-abiding citizens."

"Yes, Governor. The CDC has *also* said that it's virtually impossible to tell a murder victim killed by a shot to the head or spinal column from an infected individual put down legally in the same fashion. What is your answer to critics of the relaxed gun control laws who hold that gun-related violence has actually *increased*, but has been masked by the postmortem amplification of the Kellis-Amberlee virus?"

"Well, Miss Mason, I suppose I'd have to ask them for proof." He leaned forward. "You carry a gun?"

"I'm a licensed journalist."

"Does that mean yes?"

"It means I'm required to by law."

"Would you feel safe entering a hazard zone without it? Letting your kids enter a hazard zone? This isn't the civilized world anymore, Miss Mason. The natives are always restless now. Soon as you get sick, you start to hate the folks who aren't. America needs a man who isn't afraid to say that your rights end where the grave begins. No mercy, no clemency, and no limits on what a man can do to protect what's his."

"Governor, there have been no indications that infected individuals are capable of emotions as complex as hate. Further, they're not dead. If rights end where the grave begins, shouldn't they be protected by law like any other citizen?"

"Miss, that's the sort of thinking you can afford when you're safe, protected by men who understand what it means to stand strong. When the dead—sorry, the 'infected'—are at your door, well, you'll be wishing for a man who speaks like me."

"Do you feel that Senator Ryman is soft on the infected?"

"I don't think he's ever been put into a position to find out."

Nicely said. Cast doubt on Senator Ryman's ability to fight the zombies *and* imply that he might be overly sympathetic to the idea of "live and let live"—a concept that gets floated now and then by the members of the far left wing. Usually for about fifteen minutes, until another lobbyist gets eaten. "Governor, you've spoken on wanting to do away with the so-called Good Samaritan laws that currently make it legal to extend assistance to citizens in trouble or distress. Can you explain your reasoning?"

"Simple as pie. Someone in distress likely got that way for a reason. Now, I'm not saying that I don't feel terrible for anyone who winds up in that sort of a position, but if you rush to my aid when I've been bit, and you violate a quarantine line to do it, well, odds are good that you're not saving me anyway, but you've also just thrown your own life aside." The governor smiled. It might have seemed warm if it had come close to reaching his eyes. "It's always the young and the idealistic who die that way. The ones America needs most of all. We have to protect our future."

"By sacrificing our present?"

"If that's what it takes, Miss Mason," he said, smile widening and turning beatific. "If that's what America requires."

———

Now that I've had my long-delayed meeting with the man, there's one question on everybody's mind: What did I think of Governor David "Dave" Tate of Texas, elected three times in a landslide of votes, each time from voters from both sides of the partisan fence, possessed of an incredible record for dispensing justice and settling disputes in a state famed for its belligerence, hostility, and political instability?

I think he's the scariest of the many frightening things I've encountered since this campaign began. And that includes the zombies.

Governor Tate is a man who cares so much about freedom that he's willing to give it to you at gunpoint.

He's a man who cares so deeply about our schools that he supports shutting down public education in favor of vouchers distributed only to schools with government safety certifications. A man who cares so deeply about our farmers that he would reduce the scope of Mason's Law to allow not only large herding dogs but livestock up to a hundred and thirty pounds back into residential neighborhoods. Governor Tate wants us all to experience the glories of his carefree youth, including, it would seem, pursuit by infected collies and zombie goats.

To make matters worse, he has a good speaking manner, a parochial appearance that polls well in a large percentage of the country, and a decorated history of military service. In short, ladies and gentlemen, he is a legitimate contender to hold the highest office in our nation, as well as being the man who seems most likely to escalate the unending conflict between us and the infected into a state of all-out war.

I can't tell you to choose Senator Ryman as the Republican Party candidate just because I don't like Governor Tate. But I can tell you this: The governor's biases, like mine, are a matter of public record. Do your research. Do your homework. Learn what this man would do to our country in the name of preserving a brand of freedom that is as destructive as it is impossible to secure. Know your enemy.

That's what freedom really means.

—From *Images May Disturb You*,
the blog of Georgia Mason, March 14, 2040

Twelve

George?"

"Yeah?" I didn't look up. Editing Governor Tate's remarks into a coherent interview was easy, especially since I wasn't forcing myself to be evenhanded. The man didn't like me; there was no reason to pretend it wasn't mutual. Compiling everything into a readable format took less than fifteen minutes, and we were already getting a satisfactory number of hits. It was the follow-ups that were taking time. Not only did I have a lot of photographs and video footage to wade through, but the phenomenal amount of gossip and hearsay posted about the man bordered on appalling. The folks running the convention were about to start calling the votes—we'd have a formal party nominee inside the hour—and I wasn't anywhere near prepared to leave my computer.

"No, seriously, George?"

"*What?*"

"There's a man."

Now I did look up, squinting in the glare from the

open office door before I reached for my sunglasses. The room faded into a comforting monochrome. Anyone who values colors has never had to deal with a KA-induced migraine. "You want to try that again? Because you almost told me something, and I'm thinking you might want to obfuscate your verbiage just a little more. Just for, y'know, giggles."

"He says you invited him here." Shaun leaned forward and smirked, his tone dripping with affected smarm. "Got a little election night itch you want scratched? I mean, he's not completely hideous, although I didn't think the corn-fed farm boys were your type—"

"Wait. Sandy brown hair, about your height, blue eyes, older than us, looks like butter wouldn't melt in his mouth?"

"Or anywhere else you wanted to shove it," Shaun confirmed, eyes narrowing. "You mean you really *did* tell him to come here?"

"He's a defector from Wagman's press corp. She's pulling out, and he's bringing everything he's got, providing it nets him a spot with us for the duration of Ryman's campaign."

Shaun's eyebrows rose. "Public domain materials?"

"Or he wouldn't be trying to bribe us with them. Buffy!" I hit Save and stood, looking toward the closet our resident Fictional had drafted as her private office. The door cracked open, and her head poked out. "Drop me all the personnel files you can pull on Wagman's press corps and get out here. We have an interview to conduct."

"Okay," she said, and withdrew back into the closet. My terminal beeped a moment later, signaling receipt of the files I'd requested. We're nothing if not efficient.

"Good." I looked to Shaun. "Let's find out whether the man's wasting our time. Go get him."

"Your wish, my command," Shaun said, and turned, closing the door behind him.

Buffy emerged from her closet, moving to take the seat next to me. She had her hair skimmed back in a loose ponytail and was wearing a blue button-up shirt I was reasonably sure belonged to Chuck. She looked about as professional as your average fifteen-year-old, which was close to perfect: If this guy couldn't handle us in our natural working environment, he didn't really want to work with us.

"You really thinking of hiring this guy?" she asked.

"Depends on what he's got and what his credentials say," I said.

She nodded. "Fair enough."

Further conversation was forestalled as the door swung open. Shaun stepped into the room, followed by the man from the press room. He was carrying a sealed folder under one arm, which he tossed to me as soon as he was clear of the door. I caught it and raised one eyebrow, waiting. Buffy sat up a little straighter, attention fixed on the newcomer.

"That's everything," he said. "Video, hardcopy, data files. Six months of following Wagman, plus the details on the deals she cut as she made for the door. Your boy's getting confirmed tonight, and it's going to be partially because of the amount of pull she tossed his way."

"I doubt she shifted the balance," I said. Handing

the folder to Buffy, I said, "Run this. See if there's anything we can use."

"Got it." She stood and paused, tossing a studied, impish grin toward the newcomer. "Hey, Rick. You're looking all downtrodden and desperate."

The newcomer—Rick—returned the smile with one that looked substantially more sincere, and even, I thought, slightly relieved. "Ah, Buffy," he said. "You, meanwhile, look like you're wearing your boyfriend's clothes again. I hope this one is at least a Catholic?"

"That's between me and my prayers," she said, blowing him a kiss.

I turned to eye him, pulling my sunglasses far enough down my nose to make my expression plain. "I take it you two know each other?"

"No, I just call every strange blonde I see 'Buffy.' You'd be amazed how often I'm right." He offered his hand. Buffy snorted, amusement evident, and retreated to her closet.

I could pursue that line of questioning later. "Well, you've tagged our Fictional, and I know you know who I am. Care to even the odds?" I took his hand and shook it.

His grip was firm, but not overly so. "Richard Cousins—Rick to my friends. Newsie, currently unaffiliated, although I'm hoping we're about to change that; my biases are registered with Talking Points and Unvarnished Truth."

"Huh," I said, releasing his hand. Talking Points and Unvarnished Truth are two of the larger blogger databases; anyone can register a bias page with them and get it certified. Still, their signal-to-noise ratio is surprisingly good, largely because they self-police on a constant basis, looking for people who claim one set of biases while espousing another. "License level?"

"A-15. Wagman required it when she started aping your boy." He produced a data pad from inside his coat. "My credentials are there and ready for link, along with my most recent medical records and blood test results."

"Fabulous." I slid the data pad into the docking slot on my terminal. Files promptly filled my screen. I skimmed them as I unhooked the pad and passed it back to him. "No publications before two years ago, but you're already reporting at an A-15 level? I don't know whether that's impressive or suicidal."

"I vote 'blackmailed the license committee,'" contributed Shaun.

"Actually—" said Rick.

"Open the file on his print media pubs," said Buffy, emerging from the closet. "That'll explain everything. Won't it, Ricky?"

"Print media?" Shaun's eyebrows shot upward. "Like magazines?"

"Try newspapers," said Buffy, eyes on Rick. I had to give him this much: He was taking her poking with good grace, and he wasn't squirming. Yet. "That's why he's such a golden oldie."

"Newspapers," I repeated, disbelieving, and pulled up the next page in his file. The rest of his credentials filled the screen. I slid my glasses back up to cover my surprise. "Here we go—Buffy's right. Staff writer, *St. Paul Herald*, five years. Field reporter, the *Minnesota News*, three years. How old *are* you?"

"My recertification to virtual media was fully processed eighteen months ago. I got on Wagman's team fair and square," said Rick, before adding, "And I'm thirty-four."

"Fair and square means, what, you got on by waiting for her to realize Ryman had the right idea and then chasing her ambulance?" asked Buffy sweetly.

"All right, that's enough." Removing my glasses, I looked from Rick to Buffy and back. "What's the story, you two?"

"Richard 'Rick' Cousins, Newsie, stated biases are left-wing Dem without crossing any lines into actual psychosis, solid writer, good with deadlines, not too adept at use of imagery, and the bastard beat me in an essay contest six years ago," Buffy said.

"You can't hold that against me," Rick protested. "It wasn't a teen competition. You were sixteen."

"I can hold anything I *want* against you," said Buffy, glowering at him before her face split in a wide grin. "You didn't say you wanted the files on *Rick*, Georgia. Finally looking for a real story, you perverted ambulance chaser?"

"Don't flatter yourself, Buffy. Any story you've had your hands on can't possibly be real," Rick countered.

Shaun and I exchanged a look. "Think they know each other?" he asked.

"Getting the feeling. Buffy?"

She looked, briefly, like she didn't want to explain. Then she shrugged and said, "After Rick beat me, we started writing. He's a pretty cool guy, once you get past the part that he's older than the dawn of time."

"I choose to take that in the spirit in which it was offered," said Rick. "Especially since it comes from someone who thinks Edgar Allen Poe is socially relevant."

Buffy sniffed.

"Right, you know each other," I said. "How's his bribe? Do we hire him?"

"He's got good footage of Wagman from the last six months, a couple exclusive interviews, and a full recording of her chief of staff making the resignation calls," Buffy said.

I shot Rick a startled look.

He grinned. "He didn't say I had to stop taping."

"If I was interested in boys, I'd kiss you right now," said Shaun, deadpan. "George, in Newsie-speak, what does that mean for ratings?"

"Three percent increase for starters, more if he can write well enough to sustain an audience. Rick, we can take you as a beta, you get your own byline but you run everything through me or my second, Mahir Gowda, no direct access to the candidate; if Ryman doesn't get the nomination, you're on a six-month base contract. I can e-mail you the legalese."

"And if he does get the nomination?"

"What?"

"If he gets the nomination—which he will—what do I get?"

I smiled. "You get to stay with us until the bitter end, or until I fire your ass, whichever comes first."

"Acceptable." He held out his hand.

I shook it. "Welcome to After the End Times."

Shaun clapped him on the back before he had a chance to let go. "More testosterone on the field team! My man! What do you think about poking dead things with sticks?"

"It's a good way to get ratings and commit suicide at the same time," Rick said.

I snorted. "All right. You can stay."

There was a knock at the door. It opened before any of us had a chance to react, and Steve entered, sunglasses obscuring the majority of his expression. I stood.

"Is it time?" I asked.

Steve nodded. "Senator asked me to make sure you were ready."

"Right. Thanks, Steve." Grabbing my bag, I hooked a thumb toward our newest addition. "Rick, you're with me; we're on the floor. Buffy, I need you here, working the terminals. Hit my remotes and tell them we're streaming raw footage starting in ten minutes, and they should be ready to start doing the forum-facing clean and jerk."

"Editorial power?"

"Fact only, no opinions until I log on and start setting the baselines." I was checking equipment as I spoke, hands moving on autopilot. My recorder was charged, and the readout on my watch indicated that all cameras were operating at seventy percent or above. "See if you can rouse Mahir, and yes, I know what time it is in London, but I need *someone* sane stomping on the trolls. Shaun—"

"Outside the convention hall with my skateboard and my stick, watching to see if the protestors and picketers do anything worth reporting on," Shaun said, snapping an amiable salute. "I know my strengths."

"Play to them, and don't get dead," I said, turning to head for the door. Steve stepped out of the way, giving me a sidelong look as Rick followed in my wake. "It's okay, Steve. He's on the squad."

"They liked my backflip," Rick said, looking up at Steve. There was a lot of "up" to look at. "You're very tall."

"You *must* be a reporter," Steve said. He closed the door behind us, leaving Shaun and Buffy inside.

The convention center had seemed busy before. Compared to the madhouse that greeted us as we proceeded toward the main meeting hall, it was a mausoleum. People were everywhere. They ranged from staffers I recognized from the various campaigns to private security, members of politicians' families, and reporters who'd somehow managed to get out of the press pit and into the wild. Soon, they'd go feral and start inventing scandals for the sake of their ratings.

Rick greeted the scene with calm professionalism, sticking close as I followed in Steve's massive, crowd-clearing wake. Rick didn't seem to have any problems taking orders from a woman ten years his junior, either, which can be an issue with guys trying to jump from the traditional news media to the blogging world. They don't mean to bring their prejudices with them when they make the transition, but some things are harder to get rid of than an addiction to seeing your stories physically printed. If Rick continued to listen as well as he had been, things were going to be fine.

Steve steered a course through the back halls and into the screaming furor of the auditorium, where politicos and onlookers of every age, race, and creed were gathered for the solemn practice of screaming at the top of their lungs whenever they thought they caught a glimpse of one of the prospective candidates. A satisfying percentage of the crowd was sporting "Ryman for President" buttons. A group of clean-cut sorority girls in tight white T-shirts hung over one of the rails, shrieking with delight over the entire political process.

I elbowed Rick, indicating the girls. "See their shirts?"

He squinted. "'Ryman's My Man'? Who comes up with this stuff?"

"Shaun, actually. He's got an amazing ear for doggerel." I tapped my ear cuff. "Buffy, we're in. How's my signal?"

"Loud and clear, O glorious recorder of really jumbled footage. Try to get yourself to a clean shot, I'm only getting fifty percent signal off the stationary cameras."

"You mean the stationary cameras that belong to the convention center and were installed for security purposes? The ones with the supposedly unbreakable signal feeds?"

"Those would be the ones. I won't be able to use them for anything but pan shots, and the networks have the wall-mount cameras under exclusive coding that I *can't* break through, so get something good!"

"Yes, ma'am," I said.

"Buffy out."

The connection clicked off, and I turned to Steve. "Where are we?"

"Mrs. Ryman has said you can sit backstage with

her if you'd like, or you can stay out here and film the crowd," Steve said. "Either way, I need to head back there. We're hitting the wire."

"Got it." I looked to Rick, unclasping the recording array from my left wrist. "Take this. Three cameras, direct feed back to Buffy in the closet—just lift it up, the lenses are set to autofocus."

He took the wristband and snapped the Velcro around his own wrist. "You'll be backstage?"

"Got it. Meet back in the office when the crowd disperses, and we'll see where we're going from there." The footage I got backstage wouldn't be as sensational, but it would be more intimate, and that sort of thing has a staying power that crowd shots lack. We'd hook readers with the screaming and keep them with the silence. Plus, this was a good opportunity to test Rick's reactions in a field situation. The term "probationary period" doesn't mean much in the news. He'd work out or he wouldn't, starting tonight.

"Right." He turned toward the stage, raising his arm to give the cameras the best view. Satisfied that he wasn't going to screw around, I followed Steve along the edge of the hall toward the curtained-off area behind the stage.

You wouldn't think one little canvas curtain could make that much of a difference. Most little canvas curtains aren't equipped with enough private security to stop a full-scale invasion. The men at the entrance eyeballed our credentials but didn't bother to stop us or ask for blood tests—once we were this deep into the convention center, either we were clean or we were all dead already. So we just sailed on through, out of the chaos and into the calm harbor on the other side.

Once upon a time, in a political process far, far away, the candidate selection results were known before they were announced to the general public. With necessary enhancements in security and increases in the number of delegates who chose to vote remotely, this has changed over the last twenty years. These days, no one knows who's taking the nomination until the announcement is made. Call it part of a misguided effort to reinsert drama into a process that has become substantially more cut-and-dried as the years went by. Reality television on the grandest of scales.

Emily and Peter Ryman were sitting in a pair of folding chairs near the stage, his left hand clasped in both of hers as they watched the monitor that was scrolling current results. David Tate was pacing not far away; he shot me a poisonous look as I entered.

"Miss Mason," he said. "Looking for more muck to rake?"

"Actually, Governor, I was looking for more facts to pass along," I said, and continued for the Rymans. "Senator. Mrs. Ryman. I hope you're ready for the results?"

"Ask not for whom the bell tolls, Georgia," said the senator gravely. Then he laughed, releasing his wife's hand and standing to grasp and shake mine. "Whatever the numbers say, I want to thank you and your crew. You may not have changed the race, but you made it a hell of a lot more fun for everyone involved."

"Thank you, Senator," I said. "That's good to hear."

"After Peter's had a few weeks to rest, all three

of you *must* come and visit the farm," Emily said. "I know the girls would love to meet you. Rebecca's very fond of your reports, especially. It would be a real treat for them."

I smiled. "We'd be honored. But let's not assume a break just yet."

"Far from it," said the senator, with a glance at Governor Tate. Governor Tate's return look wasn't a friendly one. "I think we're going to go all the way."

A bell rang as if to punctuate his words, and a hush fell over the convention. I stepped back, lifting my chin to bring the camera on my collar to a better angle.

"Let's see if you mean that," I said.

Over the loudspeaker, the voice of a third-rate celebrity who'd gone from bad sitcoms to convention announcements blared: "And now, the Republican Party's man of the hour, and the next President of these fabulous United States of America—Senator Peter Ryman of Wisconsin! Senator Ryman, come on out here and greet the people!"

The cheers were almost deafening. Emily gave a little squeal that was only half-surprise, and wrapped her arms around the senator's shoulders, kissing him on both cheeks as he lifted her off the ground in a hug. "Well, Em?" he said. "Let's go make the people happy." Beaming, she nodded her agreement, and he led her onto the stage. The cheers doubled in volume. Some of those people wouldn't be able to talk at all the next day. Right then, I doubted any of them particularly cared.

Tate stayed where he was, expression blank. Before I moved toward the stage exit, still filming, I paused long enough to get a reaction shot of a man whose dreams had just been dashed. "Go, Pete, go," I murmured, unable to keep from smiling. He had the nomination. That was our man out there on that stage, accepting the nomination.

We were going on the road.

My ear cuff beeped three times, signaling an emergency transmission. I tapped it, stepping away from the opening. "Shaun, what did you—"

Buffy's voice cut me off. It was all business, and so cold I almost didn't recognize it at first. "Georgia, there's an outbreak at the farm."

I froze. "What farm?"

"The Ryman farm. It's on all the feeds, it's *everywhere*. They think one of the horses went into spontaneous conversion. No one knows why, and they're still digging in the ashes and setting the perimeter. No one knows where the . . . where the—oh, God, Georgia, the girls were in there when the alarms went off, and no one knows—"

Slowly, as if in a dream, I turned back toward the opening. Buffy was talking, but her words didn't matter anymore. Senator Ryman had formally accepted the nomination and was standing there grinning, his beautiful wife holding his arm, waving to the crowd that chose him to bear their banner toward the highest office in the country. They looked like the happiest people in the world. People who had never known what a real tragedy was. God help them, they were about to learn.

"—you there? Mahir's trying to control the forums, but he needs help, and we need you to find the valid news feed into all this, we—"

"Tell Mahir to contact Casey at Media Breakdown and arrange a fact-only feed-through of the situation at the farm; tell him we'll trade an early release on my next candidate interview," I said, tonelessly. "Wake Alaric, get him backing Mahir until Rick finishes on the floor, then throw him in there, too. He wanted to join the party? Well, here's his invitation."

"What are you going to do?"

Emily Ryman was laughing, hands clasped together. She had no idea.

Grimly, I said, "I'm going to stay here and report the news."

BOOK III

Index
Case Studies

The difference between the truth and a lie is that both of them can hurt, but only one will take the time to heal you afterward.

—GEORGIA MASON

We live in a world of our own creation. We've made our bed, ladies and gentlemen, whether we intended to or not. Now, we get the honor of lying down in it.

—MICHAEL MASON

I've done a lot of difficult things over the course of my journalistic career. Few, in the end, were pretty; most of the supposed "glamour" of reporting the news is reserved for the people who sit behind desks and look good while they tell you about the latest tragedy to rock the world. It's different in the field, and even after doing this for years, I don't think I grasped how different it was. Not until I looked into the faces of presidential candidate Peter Ryman and his wife and informed them that the body of their eldest daughter had just been cremated by federal troops outside their family ranch in Parrish, Wisconsin.

You've heard about Rebecca Ryman by now. Eighteen years old, scheduled to graduate high school in less than three months, ranked fifth in her class, and already accepted at Brown University, where she was planning to study law and follow in her father's footsteps. She'd been riding since she was old enough to walk; that's how she was able to bridle that postamplification horse and get her baby sisters off the grounds. She was a real American hero—at least, that's what all the papers and news sites say. Even mine.

If you'll allow a reporter her brief moment of sentiment, I'd like to tell you about the Rebecca that I met, if only for a moment, in the words and the faces of her parents.

Rebecca Ryman was a teenage girl. She was petu-
lant. She was sulky. She hated being asked to sit for
her sisters on a Friday night, especially when there was
a new Byron Bloom movie opening. She liked to read
trashy romances and eat ice cream straight from the
container, and nothing made her happier than working
with the horses. She stayed home from the Republican
National Convention partially to get ready for college
and partially to be with the horses. Because of that decision, she died, and her sisters lived. She couldn't save
her grandparents or the men who worked the ranch, but
she saved her sisters, and in the end, what more could
anyone have asked of her?

I told her parents she was dead. That, if nothing
else, qualifies me to say this:

Rebecca, you will be deeply missed.

—From *Images May Disturb You*,
the blog of Georgia Mason, March 17, 2040

Thirteen

The funeral services for Rebecca Ryman and her grandparents were held a week after the convention at the family ranch. The delay wasn't for mourning or to allow family members time to travel; that's how long it took for regional authorities to downgrade the ranch from a Level 2 hazard zone to a Level 5. It was still illegal to enter unarmed, but now at least nonmilitary personnel could enter unescorted. The area would return to its original Level 7 designation if it could go three years without signs of further contamination. Until then, even the kids would need to carry weapons at all times.

Most public opinion held that it wouldn't matter how long it took for the hazard rating to drop; no family would choose to stay in a home and a profession—viewed by many as a dangerous, glorified hobby—that claimed the life of one of their children. They said the ranch would be long deserted by the time that happened.

I wish I could say that attitude was confined to the

conservative fringe, but it wasn't. Within six hours of Rebecca's death, half the children's safety advocacy groups were clamoring for tighter guidelines and attempting to organize legislation that would make the life led by the Rymans illegal. No more early riding classes or family farms; they wanted it shut down, shut down now, and shut down hard. It wasn't a surprise to anyone but the Rymans, I think: Peter and Emily never attempted to map out the scenarios leading to the martyrdom of their eldest daughter, and so they'd never considered what a boon her death would be to certain organizations. Americans for the Children was the worst. Its "Remember Rebecca" campaign was entirely legal and entirely sleazy, although its attempts to use pictures of Jeanne and Amber had been quashed by the Rymans' legal team. It didn't matter. The images of Rebecca with her horses—and of postamplification horses attempting to disembowel the federal authorities putting them down—had already done their damage.

In the chaos and noise surrounding the outbreak at the ranch, it wasn't really a surprise that Senator Ryman's selection of a running mate barely made anyone's radar, save for the hardcore politicos who couldn't care less that people were dead . . . and me. I wasn't surprised, although I must admit that I was more than slightly disappointed when it was announced that Governor Tate would accompany Senator Ryman on the ballot. It was a good, balanced ticket; it would carry most of the country, and it stood a good chance of putting Senator Ryman in the White House. The tragedy at the ranch had already put him twenty points up on his opponent in the early polls. The Democratic candidate, Governor Frances Blackburn, was a solid politician with an excellent record of service, but she couldn't compete with a teenage heroine who sacrificed herself to save her sisters. This early in the race, people weren't voting for the candidate. They were voting for his daughter. And she was winning.

My team and I offered to head back to California until after the services. While our contract with the senator said "constant access," there's a difference between honest reporting and playing the ghoul. Let the local news film the funeral. We'd do our laundry, give Buffy a chance to upgrade the equipment, and introduce Rick to the parents. Nothing says "crash course in working as a team" like starting with a major political convention, then moving on to meeting my mother on her home turf. Shaun can seem like a minor natural disaster sometimes, but Mom's *always* a seven point five on the Richter scale.

That plan was scotched on the drawing board by Senator Ryman, who took me aside the day after the convention and informed me that it would mean a great deal to everyone if we would attend—and cover—the funeral. Rebecca loved our coverage of the elections, and given his position as the Republican Party candidate, he knew there would be reporters trying to get in to report on the funeral. This way, he'd know the press was reputable.

What was I supposed to say? Buffy can order most of what she needs online, and they have Laundromats everywhere. The only thing that might have been a sticking point was Rick, since he was still moving his personal belongings out of the hotel that had been the base camp for the Wagman campaign, but I didn't anticipate it being much of a problem. He'd been forced to hit the ground running, and he'd done it without a murmur of complaint. His footage of Senator Ryman's acceptance speech was top-notch, especially after we had cut it with the video feed of the assault on the ranch. Our viewer numbers have jumped more than eighteen percent since the convention, and they're still climbing; I attribute it partially to adding Rick to the team. No one else got an exclusive on the Wagman pullout. Add that to the acceptance and the tragedy, and well . . .

Sometimes in the news, "luck" is just a matter of "capitalizing on someone else's pain."

March in Wisconsin is very different from March in California. The day of the funeral was gray and cold, with patches of snow dotting the struggling lawn of the O'Neil family cemetery. Emily's family had been in the area long enough to have their own graveyard. If the old zombie flicks had been right about the dead clawing their way out of the ground, the funeral would have been a blood bath.

Fortunately, that's one detail the movies got wrong. The earth was smooth beneath its uneven blanket of snow, save for the darker, recently dug patches in front of three headstones near the west wall. Folding chairs were set up on the central green and people sat close together, steadfastly not looking toward the displaced ground. A woman who bore a vague resemblance to Peter—enough that I was willing to tentatively place her as a cousin, if not a sister—murmured to her companion, "They're so *small*."

Of course. Cemeteries are an oddity in this modern

world; since most bodies are cremated, there's no need for them unless you're fabulously wealthy, strongly religious, or clinging to tradition with both hands. When you do have an actual burial, you're not looking at the iconic rectangles of disturbed earth that you find in pre-Rising movies. Modern graves are little circles in the grass, big enough to hold a handful of ash.

The mingled Ryman and O'Neil clans were dressed in the mourning editions of their Sunday best: all blacks and charcoal grays, with the occasional hint of off-white or cream in someone's shirtfront or blouse. Even the little girls, Jeanne and Amber, were wearing black velvet. Shaun, Buffy, and I were the only attendees who weren't related to the family; the senator's security detail—a combination of the campaign agents and the new guys from the Secret Service—had stopped at the cemetery gates, guarding the perimeter without disturbing the ceremony. We were the privileged few, and everyone knew it. More than a few unpleasant looks had been tossed our way by the relatives as we moved into position.

Not that I cared. We were there for Peter, for Emily, and for the news. What the rest of the family thought didn't matter.

". . . and so we have come together, in the sight of God, to commend the mortal remains of His beloved children into His keeping, to be held in trust, no longer subject to the dangers of the world, until the day we may be reunited in the Kingdom of Heaven," said the priest. "For His is the Kingdom, the life and the glory, and through His grace may we be granted everlasting life. Let us pray." The family bowed their heads. So did Buffy, who was raised to a faith beyond "tell the truth, know the escape routes, and always carry extra ammunition."

Shaun and I didn't bow. Someone has to keep the lookout. After checking to make sure my shoulder cameras were still recording on an even keel, I turned my head, surveying the cemetery. It was completely indefensible; the low stone walls were more for delineation of boundaries than anything else and wouldn't have kept a determined horde of zombies out for more than a few minutes. The gates were spaced widely enough to make the whole place little more than a big corral for humans. I shuddered.

Shaun caught the gesture and put a hand at the small of my back, steadying me. I flashed him a smile. He knows I don't like being outside in poorly defended areas. He doesn't feel the same way; open spaces just make him think something worth poking is bound to come along sooner than later.

The service was winding down. I schooled my expression back to grim serenity and turned to face forward as the priest closed his Bible. The family rose, many of them in tears. Most turned to head for the gates, where cars were waiting to take them to the reception at the funeral home. Nothing says "deeply in mourning" like canapés and free beer. A few remained, still looking toward the graves as if shell-shocked.

"I just feel so bad," murmured Buffy. "How can things like this happen?"

"Luck of the draw?" Shaun shrugged. "Play with big animals, a little amplification is almost guaranteed. They're lucky it waited this long."

"Yeah," I said, frowning. "Lucky." Something wasn't right about this whole setup. The timing, the scope—you need safety precautions on a scale most millionaires wouldn't bother with to operate a horse ranch, even several miles from the nearest town, and you need to have them upgraded on a regular basis. If something went wrong, it would be contained in a matter of minutes. They might have to torch a barn, but they shouldn't have lost *anyone*. Certainly not three family members and half the working staff. "Shaun, get Buffy back to the van, okay? I'm going to give my regrets to the family."

"Shouldn't we come, too?" asked Buffy.

"No, you go back to the van. Call Rick, make sure nothing's caught fire while we were away from our screens."

"But—"

Shaun reached around me to take Buffy's arm. "C'mon, Buff. If she's sending us away, it's because she wants to poke something with a stick and see what happens."

"Something like that," I said. "I'll be there in a few minutes."

"Okay," said Buffy, letting Shaun guide her toward the cemetery gates. I turned to study the remaining members of the family. Peter and Emily were there, along with several other adults who looked enough like one another to be close relations. Emily had one arm around each of her two remaining daughters. She didn't look like she'd slept for a week, and both Jeanne and Amber looked like they were finding their mother's embrace more than a little smothering. Peter seemed older, somehow, his farm boy good looks strained by the speed and severity with which everything had gone wrong.

He caught the motion of my head as I looked toward them. He nodded slightly, indicating that it was safe for me to approach. I answered with a thin smile, beginning to pick my way across the slushy ground.

"Georgia," said Emily, as I reached them. Letting go of Jeanne and Amber, she put her arms around me in a too-tight hug. The girls moved to stand behind an elderly woman who looked like she might be their paternal grandmother, blocking their mother from grabbing them again once she was done with me. I couldn't blame them; Emily's grief had given her a measure of hysterical strength that seemed likely to crack one of my ribs. "We're so glad you came."

"I'm sorry for your loss," I said, patting her awkwardly on the back. "Buffy and Shaun send their regrets."

"Emily, let the nice girl go," said Peter, tugging his wife's arm until she released me. I stepped quickly backward, and both Jeanne and Amber cast understanding glances my way. They'd been their mother's targets since she ran out of the convention to get to them. "Georgia."

"Senator Ryman." He didn't try to hug me. I appreciated that. "It was a beautiful ceremony."

"It was, wasn't it?" He glanced toward the churned-up earth. "Becky hated these things. Said they were morbid and silly. She would've stayed home, if she weren't a required attendee." He laughed, bitterly. "She really wanted to meet you."

"I'm sorry she never got the chance," I said, pushing

my sunglasses up to shield my eyes from the light glinting off the patchy snow. "Would you mind if I took you aside for a moment? It won't take long."

"No, of course not." He kissed Emily on the forehead, and said, "You just get back to the girls, all right, sweetheart? I'll only be a moment."

"All right," said Emily. She managed to force a wavering smile, and said, "We'll see you at the reception, won't we, Georgia?"

"Of course, Mrs. Ryman," I replied.

The senator and I walked until we were about eight feet from the group, far enough that they couldn't hear us, but close enough to maintain visual contact. "Now, Georgia," he said, without preamble. "What's this all about?"

I tilted my chin up until I was looking directly at him, and said, "Senator, if you don't mind, my team and I would like permission to go up to the ranch and take a look around." He was silent. I continued: "If we walk the grounds and post our footage . . ."

"You think it'll reduce trespassers looking for a little excitement?"

I nodded.

Senator Ryman looked at me for a long moment. Then, shoulders sagging, he nodded his acquiescence. "I hate this, Georgia," he said, in a voice that was a million miles away from the proud, self-confident man I'd followed most of the way across the country. "This is supposed to be the start of the most exciting fight in my career, and instead I'm standing here consigning my eldest unto God when I just want to shake the bastard until he gives her back to me. It's not fair."

"I know, Senator," I said. Glancing back to where Emily had managed to recapture her surviving children, I added, "But you're not the only one it isn't fair to."

"Are you telling me to mind my family, young lady?" he asked, with a mirthless chuckle.

"Sometimes family is all we have, sir."

"Very true, Georgia. Very true." He followed my gaze back to Emily and the girls. "I'll tell Em I've given you folks permission to go to the ranch. She'll understand. The guards, now . . ."

"We have the proper licenses."

"Good." Raking his hair back from his forehead with one hand, he sighed. "Ain't this just one hell of a mess?"

"Very much so," I agreed.

We made our good-byes without much conviction; he needed to get back to the business of mourning, and I needed to get back to my team before Shaun decided to go hiking or Buffy took the wireless network off-line for upgrading. Rick hadn't been with us long enough for me to know what I didn't want him doing, but I was sure he'd come up with something. He was a journalist, after all, and we're all incurably insane.

I walked toward the cemetery gates, tapping my ear cuff. "Shaun, what's your twenty?"

"We're parked behind the security vans," Shaun said. Someone asked a question in the background, and he added, "Buffy wants to know if we need her or if she can go with Chuck. He's pretty torn up, and she wants to get in some 'couple time.'"

"Shaun Mason, you may be the only boy above

the age of nine who still says 'couple time' like it was a dead rat." I nodded to the guards as I passed through the gates and scanned the parking lot for the security vans.

"I do not," said Shaun, sounding affronted. "I *like* dead rats."

"Sorry. My bad. Tell Buffy she's free to go, but I want her to have the field equipment ready, and she needs to be back for editing by nine."

"The field equipment . . . ?"

"I have Senator Ryman's clearance. We're heading for the ranch." I grimaced at Shaun's whooping and tapped my ear cuff again, cutting off the connection. The van was in sight; I could let him yell in my ear once I was inside, rather than putting up with it remotely.

Buffy was seated on a counter doing something arcane to a shoulder-mount camera when I stepped through the rear door. She'd changed out of her funeral clothes into something more comfortable, if still subdued, and when she looked up, it was obvious that she'd redone her makeup to match. "Hey."

"Hey." I looked around, starting to unbutton my jacket. "Where's Shaun?"

"Up front checking his armor for holes." She peered into the camera, blew lightly on the exposed circuitry, and snapped the cover back into place. "Chuck's going to come pick me up, so you can leave me here when you head out. It'll only take a few more minutes to review the field equipment."

"Anybody call Rick?" I tossed my jacket onto a chair and started unbuttoning my dress shirt. I had a tank top under that; swap my skirt for jeans, add a

Kevlar vest, my motorcycle jacket, and combat boots, and I'd be ready for a low-hazard field op. Most girls learn how to accessorize for dinner parties and dates. I learned to do it for hazard zones.

"He said he'd meet you at the ranch." Buffy offered me the camera. "Here. This whole generation is on its last legs. We're gonna need new ones sooner than later."

"I'll get it into the budget," I said. Peeling off my shirt, I dropped it to the floor and took the camera, eyeing Buffy over my glasses. "Something on your mind, Buff?"

"No. Yes. Maybe." She sat back on the counter, her gaze dropping to her hands. "You're going to the ranch."

"Yes."

"It's . . ."

"The area's been downgraded. We have the licenses to enter, as long as we're armed."

Buffy's head snapped up. "It's *disrespectful*."

Ah. The crux of the problem. "Disrespectful to whom, Buffy? To the dead?" She gave a small, almost imperceptible nod. "Buffy, the dead aren't there. They've been buried." After they were cremated to prevent their corpses from coming back to life and doing disrespectful things to the living.

"They *died* there," she said, fiercely. "They died there, and now you're going to turn it into more *news*."

"We aired the attack."

"That was different. That was something dangerous. This is just ghosts. Souls trying to sleep."

Her expression turned pleading. "Can't we let them sleep? Please?"

"We're not going to disturb them. If anything, we're going so that they *can* sleep. The Rymans trust us to be respectful, and we will be, and by showing that there's nothing of any interest in those buildings, we'll keep *less* respectful journalists from breaking in looking for an 'exposé.'" I might be wrong—journalists seeking a scoop will break into almost anything—but I needed to get in there, and I needed Buffy to stay calm. Without her to enhance any footage we got, we might well come up with less than nothing.

She sniffled. "You swear you're not intending to upset their ghosts?"

"I'm not sure I believe in ghosts, but I swear we won't do anything to disturb any spirits that might be resting there." I put down the camera she'd handed me and shook my head as I opened the van closet and pulled out the rest of my field gear. I always keep a few pairs of thick denim jeans on hand, the kind with steel fibers woven into the fabric. "Be prepared" isn't just the Boy Scouts' marching song anymore. "Zombies are enough. I don't need to add poltergeists to the ranks of 'things that want to kill me.'"

She studied me for a moment before she nodded, offering a small smile. "All right. It just seems ghoulish to go there on the day of the funeral."

"I know, but time is sort of important right now," I said. A horn honked outside. I glanced over my shoulder toward the door. "Sounds like your ride's here."

"That didn't take long." Buffy slid off the counter.

"Your kits are packed. I didn't review the auxiliary batteries, but you'd only need those if everything else failed. Technically, they're not even required."

"I know," I said. "Get out of here. Have a nice evening with Chuck, and I'll see you at the hotel at nine for editing and data consolidation."

"Work, work, work," she complained, but she was almost laughing as she stepped outside. I caught a glimpse of Chuck waving from his rental car before the van door banged shut, blocking them from view.

"Have a nice date, Buffy," I said to the closed door and pulled on my jacket before moving to assess the field kits.

Normally, Buffy would have done all the checks before she went anywhere. Normally, where she was going was "back to the van" or "home to her room," not out with her boyfriend. It's not like she's never dated; she's had at least six boyfriends since we met, and unlike a large percentage of our generation, they've all been face-to-facers, not virtuals. She doesn't date people she meets online unless they live locally and are willing to meet in the flesh, with all the security checks and blood tests that entails, and even then, she likes to keep her romantic relationships as off-line as possible. Partly because she likes the interaction—it's a change from the amount of time she spends online—but I think it's partly been to keep them untraceable. She's never been comfortable with the fact that Shaun and I won't talk about why we don't date. She eventually gave up trying to hook us up with people she knew, but Chuck is still the first of her boyfriends who we've been allowed to spend any real time around, and I suspect it's only because they met on the campaign trail.

Everyone has their own little quirks. My brother and I avoid romantic entanglements, and Buffy runs hers like acts of international espionage.

Checking the field kits took about five minutes. Shaun emerged from the front of the van carrying a crossbow and moving with a slight stiffness that signaled how much body armor he was wearing. Straightening, I tossed him his pack.

"Light," he said, hefting it. "Did we decide to skip the cameras this time?"

"Actually, I decided to skip the weapons." Picking up the other two kits, I brushed past him on my way up front. "If we meet any zombies, we'll pacify them with Hostess snack cakes."

"Even the living dead love Hostess snack cakes."

"Precisely." I hooked open the door between the sections of the van with my foot and tossed Rick's field kit back to Shaun. "I'm driving."

"I'm not surprised," he said, with a mock annoyed look. Following me, he settled in the passenger seat and asked, "So what are we *really* doing?"

"Really doing? We're really visiting the scene of a tragic accident to determine whether it was caused by gross human negligence or a simple series of unavoidable events." I sat and pulled my seat belt across my lap. "Buckle up."

He did. "You aren't implying what I think you're implying."

"What am I not implying, Shaun?"

"They had to torch and burn the infection. Don't

you think someone would have noticed if things weren't right?"

"Repeat the first part of your statement again."

"They had to torch and . . ." He stopped. "You're not serious."

"Shaun, the O'Neils have been raising horses for generations. They didn't even take a break after the Rising." I pulled out of the lot and started down the road. The countryside around us was wide, flat, and relatively unbroken by anything as plebian as signs of human habitation. Not the best hunting territory for the living dead. "They don't make mistakes on the level of allowing a massive outbreak that kills nearly half the hired help. It just doesn't happen. So either somebody screwed up big time—"

"—or someone cut the screamers," Shaun finished, hushed. "Why wouldn't anyone have found anything?"

"Was anyone going to *look*? Shaun, if I say, 'A big animal amplified and killed its owners,' do you think, 'Something is rotten in the state of Denmark,' or do you think, 'It was bound to happen sometime'?"

Shaun was quiet for several minutes as we drove toward the ranch. Finally, in a pensive tone, he said, "How big is this, George?"

I tightened my hands on the wheel. "Ask Rebecca Ryman."

"What are we going to do about it?"

"We're going to tell the truth." I glanced toward him. "Hopefully, that's going to be enough."

He nodded, and we drove on in silence.

—————————

A lot of time was spent looking into the science and application of forensics before the Rising. How did this man die? What did he die for? Could he have been saved? It's been different since the Rising, as the possibility of infection makes it too dangerous for investigators to pry into any crime scene that hasn't been disinfected, while the strength of modern disinfectants means that once they've been used, there's nothing to find. DNA testing and miraculous deductions brought about by a few clinging fibers are things of the past. As soon as the dead started walking, they stopped sharing their secrets with the living.

For modern investigators, whether with the police or the media, this has meant a lot of "going back to our roots." An active mind is worth a thousand tests you can't run, and knowing where to look is worth even more. It's all a matter of learning how to think, learning how to eliminate the impossible, and admitting that sometimes what's left, however improbable, is going to be the truth.

The world is strange that way.

—From *Images May Disturb You*,
the blog of Georgia Mason, March 24, 2040

Fourteen

Rick was a good match for our team in more ways than one: He had his own transport, and he didn't leave home without it. I'd heard about the armor-plated VW Beetles—they're in a lot of Mom's antizombie ordnance reports, which she tends to leave lying all over the house—but I'd never actually seen one before Rick's. It looked like a weird cross between an armadillo and a pill bug.

An electric blue armadillo.

With headlights.

He was parked outside the ranch gates, leaning against the side of his car and typing something into his PDA's collapsible keyboard. He lifted his head as we drove up, folding the keyboard and stowing the entire unit in his pocket.

Shaun was out of the van before we'd stopped moving, pointing to Rick. "You do not lower your eyes in the field!" he snapped. "You do not split your attention, you do not focus on your equipment, and you *especially* do not do these things when you're alone at an off-grid rendezvous point!" Rick blinked, looking more confused than anything else.

I stopped the van, leaning over to close Shaun's door before opening my own. A lot of people don't think my brother has a temper. It's like they assume I somehow sucked up the entire quota of "cranky," and now Shaun's perpetually cheery and ready for a challenge while I glower at people from behind my sunglasses and plot the downfall of the Western world. They're wrong. Shaun has a bigger temper than I do. He just saves his fits of fury for the important things, like finding one of our team members acting like an idiot in the vicinity of a recent outbreak.

Rick was realizing he had a problem. Putting up his hands in a placating gesture, he said, "The area was cleared, and they did a full disinfect. I looked it all up before I came out here."

"Did they get a one hundred percent scratch-and-match between mammals meeting the KA amplification barrier, known victims, registered survivors, and potential vector points?" Shaun demanded. He knew they hadn't, because there's *never* been a one hundred percent return on the Nguyen-Morrison test array, not even under strict laboratory conditions. There's always the chance something capable of carrying the virus, either in its own bloodstream or by carrying tainted blood or tissue on its person, got away.

"No," Rick admitted.

"No, because it doesn't happen. Which means you? Have basically been standing naked in the middle of the road, waving your arms and shouting, 'Come get it, dead guys, I wanna be your next snack.'" He flung Rick's field kit at his chest. Rick caught it and stood there, blinking as Shaun spun on his heel and stalked off toward the gates. I let him go. Someone needed to start the process of presenting our credentials to the guards on duty, and it would calm him down. Bureaucracy generally did.

Rick stared after Shaun, still looking shell-shocked.

"He's right, you know," I said, squinting at him through my sunglasses. The glare outside the van was bad enough to make me wish it were safe to take painkillers in the field. It's not; nothing that dulls your awareness of your body and what it's doing is a good idea. "What made you get out of your car?"

"I thought it was safe," Rick stammered.

I shook my head. "It's never safe. Get your pack on, activate your cameras, and let's go." I started along Shaun's path to the ranch gates. Getting out of the car alone was a rookie mistake, but Rick's record wasn't heavy on field work. His reporting was good, and he knew enough to stick with the senior reporters in an area. He'd learn the rest if he lived long enough to get the chance.

If getting out of the car was a rookie mistake, going into the ranch on foot was blatant stupidity, but we didn't have any real choice. Not only would our vehicles have been impossible to fit into any of the standing structures, we wouldn't have been able to avoid getting hung up in potholes or in the ruts opened by the government cleaning equipment. Better on foot and paying attention than sucked into a false sense of security and taken out by hostile road conditions.

Shaun was outside the guard station, where two

wary, clean-shaven men watched from behind thick sheets of safety glass. Both were wearing plain army jumpsuits. From the looks on their faces, this was their first outbreak, and we didn't fit their expectations of the sort of folks who would walk into a sealed-off hazard zone, even one that was due to be unsealed within the next seventy-two hours and had been the scene of a complete Nguyen-Morrison testing, including bleach bombs and aerosol decontamination. If it'd been the sort of ranch that grew crops instead of livestock, they'd have been forced to shut it down for at least five years while the chemicals worked their way out of the soil. As it was, they'd be importing feed and water for eighteen months, until the groundwater tested clear again.

The things we're willing to do to avoid the possibility of exposure to the live virus are sometimes awe inspiring. "Any trouble?" I asked, stopping next to Shaun and casting a tight-lipped smile toward the army boys. "My, don't they look happy to see us?"

"They were happier before I showed them we had Senator Ryman's permission to be here and the proper clearances to enter the property. Although I think they were kind of relieved when they realized our clearance levels mean they don't have to come in with us." Shaun grinned almost maliciously as he handed me and Rick the metal chits that served as our passes into the zone. Any hazard seals would react to the ID tags on the chits, opening to let us pass. "Somehow, I don't think the boys want to meet a real live infected person of their very own. It's amazing that they passed basic training."

"Don't tease the straights," I said, pressing the

chit against the strap of my shoulder bag. It adhered to the fabric with a nearly unbreakable seal, turning on and beginning to flash a reassuring green. "How long's our clearance?"

"Standard twelve-hour passage. If we're inside the zone when the chits run out, we'll have to call for help and hope help answers." Shaun pressed his own chit to the collar of his chain-mail shirt. It flashed before dimming to standard metallic gray.

"Any recent signs of movement in or around the zone?" Rick asked. His chit was clinging to the earpiece of his wireless phone, where its green flashes contrasted with the blinking yellow LED.

"Not a one." Shaun jerked his up, indicating the guards. "Shall we move on before they book us for loitering outside a hazard zone?"

"Can they do that?" asked Rick.

"We're within a hundred yards of a recent outbreak," I said. "They can do just about whatever they want." I walked toward the gates. The chit on my bag flashed and they swung open, letting me enter the ranch grounds. There were no blood tests on this side of the hazard zone. If I wanted to enter a known infection site when I was already infected, I'd just finish my transition behind a pre-established barrier. Not exactly what most people would consider a loss.

The gates shut behind me, only to open again as Shaun approached, and a third time for Rick. Only one person was allowed to pass at a time. If they'd followed standard procedure, the gates would also be electrified, with a current set to increase exponentially if anything grabbed hold. It wouldn't do much to stop a horde of zombies that really wanted to get through, but it was better than nothing.

"Dropping the first fixed-point camera, setting the feed to channel eight, and activating screamers," Shaun said, planting a small tripod. It extended an antenna, flashing yellow as it caught the local wireless. It would record everything it saw and feed it to the databases in the van. We wouldn't get anything useful unless there was an outbreak while we were on the grounds, but it never hurts to cover your bases. More important, it would sound the alarm if it detected any motion not connected to one of the team's identifying beacons. "George, we have a map?"

"We have a map," I confirmed, pulling out my PDA and unfolding the screen to its full extension. "Buffy pulled it down before she left." God bless Buffy. No team is complete without a good technician, and the word for an incomplete team is usually "fatality." "Cluster round, guys." They did.

The Ryman family ranch was laid out in the pre-Rising style, with a few adjustments to account for the increased security required by the senator's political career and the possibility of invasion by the rampaging undead. Most of the buildings were unconnected, with four separate horse barns—one for foaling, one for yearlings, one for older horses, and the last, constructed in isolation and using modern quarantine procedures, for the sick. The main house had more windows than any sane person would be comfortable with, but that had apparently suited the Rymans just fine.

Shaun studied the map before asking, "Do we have the outbreak grid?"

"We do." I started tapping. "Either of you boys care to place a bet as to where the outbreak started?"

"Isolation ward," Rick said.

"Foaling," said Shaun.

"Wrong." I hit enter. A grid appeared, crisscrossing the map with streaks of red. The largest red zone surrounded the yearling barn, covering the entire building and extending out in all directions. "The first outbreak was in the yearling barn. Where the strongest, healthiest, most resistant horses were housed."

Shaun frowned. "I don't know much about horses, but that seems a little funny to me. We have a full match-up on the index case?"

"Ninety-seven percent certainty on the Nguyen-Morrison," I said, pulling up a picture of a pale gold horse with a white streak down its nose. "Ryman's Gold Rush Weather. Yearling male, not gelded, clean vet reports every three months since birth, and a clean blood test registered every week for the same time period. No history of elevated virus levels. If you were looking for the cleanest horse on the planet, epidemiologically speaking, you'd have trouble going wrong with this one."

"And he's our index?" said Rick. "That's bizarre. Maybe something bit him?"

"They logged every movement these horses made, all day, every day." I closed the files, snapping the screen of my PDA into its collapsed formation before slipping it into my shoulder bag. "Goldie went out for a run the night before the outbreak, was rubbed down, and checked out clean, with no wounds or scratches. He didn't leave the barn again before things went south."

"None of the other horses top out in the Nguyen-Morrison?" Shaun reached into his own bag, pulling out a collapsible metal rod that he began uncollapsing as the three of us moved, by unspoken accord, toward the side of the ranch where the barns were clustered. If there was evidence to be found, it would be in the barns.

"The closest is the horse in the stall next to his, Ryman's Red Sky at Morning, which tested out at a ninety-one *and* had visible bite marks. Six percent pretty much says Goldie's our index."

"The only way that could happen is spontaneous amplification," Shaun said, with a deep frown. He snapped the last segment of the rod into place and hit a button on the handle, electrifying the metal. "No chance of heart attack or other natural death?"

"Not in a place like this," Rick said. We both looked toward him. Shaking his head, he said, "I did a piece on modern ranching a few years back. They have those animals so monitored that if they just up and die—a heart stops, or they suffocate on a piece of feed, or whatever—someone will know immediately."

"So you're saying the people on duty would have received some sort of notification that the horse had died, and they'd have been able to get there before he got up and started biting the other horses," I said, slowly. "Why didn't they?"

"Because when you convert instead of reanimating, there's no interruption in your vital signs," said

Shaun. He was starting to sound almost excited. "One minute you're fine, the next minute, bang, you're a shambling mass of virus-spreading flesh. The monitors wouldn't catch a spontaneous conversion because a machine wouldn't be able to tell that anything was *wrong*."

"And people say modern technology doesn't do enough to protect us," I deadpanned. "All right, so if the horse checked out clean at a seven o'clock rubdown and went into spontaneous amplification in the night, the monitors wouldn't have caught it. That still doesn't tell us why it happened."

Spontaneous amplification is a reality. Sometimes, the virus sleeping inside a person decides it's time to wake up, and there's nothing anyone can do to stop it. Roughly two percent of the recorded outbreaks during the Rising were traced back to spontaneous amplifications. It usually hits only the very young or the very old, as the virus reacts to their rapidly changing body weight by making some rapid changes of its own. I'd never heard of spontaneous amplification occurring in livestock, but it's never been proven that it *couldn't* happen . . . and it seemed way too pat. The index case for equine spontaneous amplification happened to be in Senator Ryman's barn, on the day he was confirmed as the next Republican candidate for president? Coincidences like that don't exist outside of a Dickensian tragedy. They certainly don't wander around happening in the real world.

"I don't buy it," said Rick, voicing my thoughts. "It's too cut-and-dried. Here's a horse, the horse is healthy, now the horse is a zombie, lots of people die, isn't that tragic? It's what I would write if you asked me to pen a front-page human interest story that would never happen."

"So why isn't anyone digging deeper?" Shaun stopped in the courtyard between the four barns, looking first at Rick, then at me. "Not to be rude or anything, but Rick, you're new on this beat, and George, you're sort of professionally paranoid. Why isn't anyone else punching holes in this crap?"

"Because no one looks twice at an outbreak," I said. "Remember how pissed you got when we had to do all that reading about the Rising back in sixth grade? I thought you were going to get us both expelled. You said the only way things could've gotten as bad as they did was if people were willing to take the first easy answer they could find and cling to it, rather than doing anything as complicated as actually *thinking*."

"And you said that was human nature and I should be thankful we're smarter than they are," Shaun said. "And then you hit me."

"That's still your answer: human nature."

"Give people something they can believe, especially something like a personal tragedy and a teenage girl being heroic to save her family, and not only will everyone believe it, everyone will *want* to believe it." Rick shook his head. "It's good news. People like to believe good news."

"Sometimes it's great living in a world where 'good' and 'news' don't always combine to mean 'positive information.'" I looked to Shaun. "Where do we start?"

I'm in charge in the editing studio and the office. It's different in the field. Shaun calls the shots unless

I'm demanding an immediate evac. Both of us are smart enough to know where our strengths lie. His involve poking dead things with sticks and living to blog about it.

"Everyone armed?" he asked—more for Rick's benefit than mine. He knows I'd stick my hand in a zombie's mouth for fun before I'd enter a field situation unarmed.

"Clear," I said, pulling out my .40.

"Yes," said Rick. His own gun was larger than mine, but he handled it easily enough for me to think it was a matter of preference, not machismo. He slid it back into the holster in his vest, adding, "I'd offer to take some marksmanship tests, but this doesn't seem like the place."

"Later," said Shaun. Rick looked amused. I smothered a snort of laughter. Poor guy probably thought my brother was kidding. "Right now, we're splitting up. George, you take the foaling barn. Rick, you hit the adult quarters. I'll take the hospital barn, and we'll meet up back here to go through the yearling barn together. Radio contact at all times. If you see anything, scream as loudly as you can."

"So we can all come together to help?" asked Rick.

"So the rest of us have time to get away," I said. "Cameras on, people, and look alive; this is not a drill. This is the *news*."

Splitting up made the most sense: All four barns were involved in the outbreak, but it started in a single place. We'd search the other areas individually, get some good atmospheric shots for background, and then get back together where we might actually find something. That didn't stop my heart from racing as I opened the door to the foaling barn feed room and stepped inside. The barn was dark. I removed my glasses and the burning in my eyes stopped almost immediately, pupils abandoning their futile efforts to contract and relaxing into full expansion as I walked into the main barn. This unvaried twilight was the sort of light they're best suited to. I saw in it the way the infected did, and like the infected, I saw everything.

The ranch was clearly a state-of-the-art establishment, on top of all the latest developments in animal husbandry. The stalls were spacious, designed to maximize the comfort of all parties involved. It was actually possible to ignore the federally mandated hazmat suits hanging from one wall and the yellow-and-red biohazard bins that marked the barn's four corners.

The smell of bleach was harder to ignore, and once I admitted it was there, the rest came clear. The stains on the walls that weren't paint or spilled feed. The way the straw in the stalls was matted down with the remains of some thick, tacky liquid. They hadn't finished the biohazard cleanup in here yet. That's standard operating procedure. First you remove all infected bodies and any . . . chunks . . . that were left behind. Then you seal the building as well as you can and fill the air with bleach. Finally, you set off the aerosol disinfectants and formalin bombs. Formalin is a formaldehyde-based compound that can kill almost anything, including the mobile infected, and standard decontamination procedures call for five waves of the stuff, releasing a new batch as the previous one is depleted by the organic materials around you. It's only after the area has been bleached so thoroughly that anything living is pretty much toast and has been allowed to sit long enough for all fluids to dry to a splatter-free state that it's considered safe to start removing and incinerating potentially infected materials, like the straw in the stalls.

My shoulder cam was already recording. I activated three more cameras, one attached to my bag, one at my hip, and one concealed in my barrette, and began to make my first slow turn, looking around the barn.

A pile of dead cats was under the hayloft, their multicolored bodies twisted from the brutal abdominal hemorrhaging that killed them. They'd survived the outbreak and the chaos that followed, but they couldn't outrun the formalin. I spent several seconds standing there, looking at them. They looked so small and harmless . . . and they were. Cats don't reach the Mason barrier. They weigh less than forty pounds. Kellis-Amberlee isn't interested in them, and they don't reanimate. For cats, dead is still dead.

I made it almost to the wall before I threw up.

It was easier once the initial wash of disgust was out of my system. My first pass brought up nothing. There were no signs that anything unusual had happened; it was just the site of an outbreak, tragic and horrible, but not *special*. Here was the place where one of the infected horses kicked its way inside, knocking the barn's sliding door off its rails. It would have hit the nursing mares in the first three stalls without slowing down, and the humans on duty were probably totally undefended. They had no idea anything was wrong until it was too late. If they were lucky, they died fast, either bleeding out or ripped to pieces before the virus had a chance to take hold and start rewriting them into another iteration of it. That was sadly unlikely. A fresh mob wants to infect, not devour.

It was easy to picture infected horses rampaging through the place, biting everything in sight and rushing on to bite still more. It was a nightmare image; it's how we almost lost the world at the beginning of the century, and it was probably accurate. We know how this sort of outbreak goes, even though we wish we didn't. The virus is dependable, not creative.

It took me twenty minutes to sweep the barn. By the time I was done, I was in such a hurry to get out of there that I forgot to put my sunglasses on before rushing out into the sunlight. The sudden glare was more than I could take. I staggered and caught myself against the barn door, eyes squinting shut.

"This is how we can tell she hasn't converted," Shaun commented to my left. "Real zombies don't get flash-blinded by sunlight when they forget their sunglasses."

"Fuck you, too," I muttered, as Shaun got his arm around me and hoisted me away from the barn.

"You kiss our mother with that mouth?"

"Our mother and you both, dickhead. Give me my sunglasses."

"Which are where?"

"Left-hand vest pocket."

"I've got it." That was Rick's voice, and it was Rick who pressed my glasses into my hand.

"Thanks." I snapped the glasses open, continuing

to lean against Shaun as I pushed them on. Both their cameras were catching this. I really didn't care. "Either of you find anything?"

"Not me," said Shaun. For some reason, he sounded like he was . . . laughing? His barn couldn't have been any better than mine; if anything, it should have been worse, since more of the medical staff would have been on duty overnight. "Looks like Rick's the only one who got lucky."

"I've always had a way with the ladies," said Rick. Unlike Shaun and his evident amusement, Rick sounded almost embarrassed.

I clearly needed to see whatever was going on to understand it. Wary of the light, I opened first one eye, and then the other. There was Shaun, his arm still around me, holding me upright as best he could; my eyes are a lot of why I'm so leery to go into live field situations, and no one understands that better than him. And there was Rick, standing just a few feet away, his expression a mixture of anxiety and confusion.

Rick's shoulder bag was moving.

I jerked upright, demanding, "What is *that*?"

" 'That' would be Rick's new lady friend," Shaun said, snickering. "He's irresistible, George. You should've seen it. He came out of that barn and she was all *over* him. I've seen clingy girlfriends before, but this one doesn't just take the cake, she takes the entire *bakery*."

I eyed the junior member of my reporting staff warily. "Rick?"

"He's right. She latched on once she realized I was in the barn, not aiming a bleach gun at her face, and not planning to hurt her." Rick opened the flap of his shoulder bag. A narrow orange-and-white head poked out, yellow eyes regarding me warily. I blinked. The head withdrew.

"It's a cat."

"All the others were dead," Rick said, closing his bag. "She must have managed to burrow farther under the hay than they did. Or maybe she was outside when the cleaners came through and somehow got trapped inside when they left."

"A *cat*."

"She tests clean, George," Shaun said.

Mammals under forty pounds can't convert—they lack some crucial balance between body and brain mass—but they can sometimes carry the live virus, at least until it kills them. It's rare. Most of the time, they just shrug it off and carry on, uninfected. In the field, "rare" isn't something you can gamble on.

"How many blood tests?" I asked, looking toward Shaun.

"Four. One for each paw." He held up his arms, anticipating my next question. "No, I didn't get scratched, and yes, I'm sure the kitty's clean."

"And he already yelled at me for picking her up before I was certain," Rick said.

"Don't think that means I'm not planning to yell at you, too." I pushed away from Shaun. "I'll just do it when we're back inside. We have three clean barns and one live cat, gentlemen. Are we ready to proceed?"

"I've got nothing better planned for the afternoon," Shaun said, his tone still cheerful. This was Irwin territory. Very little makes him happier. "Cameras on?"

"Rolling." I glanced at my watch. "We have clean feeds and more than enough memory. You going to grandstand?"

"Do I ever not?" Shaun backed away until he was standing at the proper angle in front of the remaining barn, backlit by the afternoon sun. I had to admire his flare for the theatrics. We'd do two reports on the day's events—one for his side of the site, playing up the dangers of entering an area that had suffered such a recent outbreak, and one for my side, talking about the human aspects of the tragedy. My opening spiel could be recorded later, when I had a better idea of what happened. Irwins sell suspense. Newsies sell the news.

"What's he doing?" Rick asked, raising his eyebrows.

"You've seen those video clips of Irwins talking about fabulous dangers and horrible lurking monsters?"

"Yeah."

"That. On your count, Shaun!"

That was his cue. Suddenly grinning, suddenly relaxed, Shaun directed the smile that sold a thousand T-shirts toward the camera, flicked sweat-soaked hair out of his eyes with one gloved hand, and said, "Hey, audience. It's been pretty boring around here lately, what with all the politics and the sealed-room stuff that only the heavy-duty news geeks care about. But today? Today, we get a treat. Because today, we're the *only* news team being allowed into the Ryman ranch before decon is finished. You're gonna see blood, guys. You're gonna see stains. You're gonna

do everything but taste the formalin in the air—"
He was off and running.

I admit it: I tuned him out as he started getting
into his spiel, preferring to watch rather than ac-
tively listening. Shaun has working his audience into
a frenzy down to a science; by the time he's done with
them, they get excited by the mysterious discovery
of pocket lint. It's impressive, but I'd rather watch
him move. There's something wonderful about the
way he lets go, becoming all energy and excitement
as he outlines what's coming next. Maybe it's geeky
for a girl my age to admit she still loves her brother. I
don't care. I love him, and one day I'll bury him, and
until then, I'm going to be grateful that I'm allowed
to watch him talk.

"—so come with me, and let's see what *really* happened here on that cold March afternoon." Shaun
grinned again, winking at the camera, and turned
to head for the barn doors. As he reached them, he
called, "Cut segment!" and turned back, joviality
gone. "We ready?"

"Ready," I said.

With all chances to gracefully decide, "You know
what? This is a job for the authorities—the people
we *pay* to risk their lives for information" behind us,
Rick and I followed Shaun through the feed room
and into the last of the Ryman's four barns.

The smell hit first. There's a stench to an outbreak
site that you never find anywhere else. Scientists have
been trying for years to determine why it is that we
can smell the infection even when it's been declared
safely dead, and they've been forced to conclude that

it's the same viral sense that lets zombies recognize each other, just acting on a somewhat smaller scale. Zombies don't try to kill other zombies on sight unless they haven't had anything to eat in weeks; the living can tell where an outbreak started. It's probably another handy function of the virus slumbering in our own bodies—not that anyone can say for sure. No one has ever been able to put the smell into words. Not really. It smells like death. Everything in your body says "run." And, like idiots, we didn't.

Once the feed room door was shut, the barn was washed with the same dimness I experienced before. "George, Rick, lights," Shaun called. I had time to raise my arm to shield my eyes before the overhead lights clicked on. Rick made a faint gagging noise, and I heard him throwing up somewhere behind me. Not a real surprise. Everyone tosses their cookies at least once on this sort of trip—I had, after all.

When enough time had passed to let my eyes adjust to the limits of their capacity, I lowered my arm. What I saw was sheer chaos. The foaling barn seemed bad at first, but it was really nothing, just a few odd stains and some dead cats. The dead cats were here, too, strewn around the floor like discarded rags. As for the rest . . .

My first thought was that the entire barn had been drenched with blood. Not just sprayed; literally drenched, like someone took a bucket and started painting the walls. That impression passed as it became clear that the majority of the blood was in one of two locations—either smeared along the walls in a band roughly three feet off the floor, or soaking the floor itself, which had turned a dozen different shades of brown and black as the mixture of bleach, blood, and fecal matter dried into an uneven crust. I stared at it, unblinking, until I was over the urge to vomit. Once was fine. Twice was not, especially when round two happened in front of the others.

"These are labeled with the names of the horses," Shaun called. He was on the far side of the barn, studying one of the stalls. "This one was called 'Tuesday Blues.' What kind of name is that for a horse?"

"They liked weather names. Look for Gold Rush Weather and Red Sky at Morning. If anything odd happened here, we might find signs of it around their stalls."

"Under the six hundred gallons of gore," Rick muttered.

"Hope you brought a shovel!" Shaun called, sounding ungodly cheerful.

Rick stared at him. "Your brother is an alien."

"Yeah, but he's a cute one," I said. "Start checking stalls."

I was halfway down my own row of stalls—between "Dorothy's Gale" and "Hurricane Warning" —when Rick called, "Over here." Shaun and I looked toward him. He was indicating a corner stall. "I found Goldie."

"Great," Shaun said, and we started toward him. "Did you touch anything?"

"No," Rick replied. "I was waiting for you."

"Good."

The stall door hung askew. The hinges had been broken from the inside, and the wood was half-splintered in places, dented with the crescent shapes of a horse's hooves. Shaun whistled low. "Goldie wanted out pretty darn bad."

"Can't say that I blame him," I said, leaning forward to study the broken wood. "Shaun, you've got gloves on. Can you open that?"

"For you, the world. Or at least an open door on a really disgusting horse stall." Shaun swung the door open, latching it with a small hook to keep it that way. I bent forward, letting my camera record every inch, as Shaun stepped past us into the stall itself.

Something crunched under his feet.

Rick and I whipped around to face him. My shoulders were suddenly tight with tension. Crunching noises in the field are almost never good. At best, they mean a close call. At worst . . .

"Shaun? Report."

Face pale, Shaun lifted first one foot, and then the other. A piece of sharp-edged plastic was wedged in the sole of his left boot. "Just some junk," he said, expression broadcasting his relief. "No big deal." He reached down to pull it loose.

"Wait!"

Shaun froze. I turned to stare at Rick. "Explain."

"It's sharp." Rick looked between us, eyes wide. "It's sharp-edged, in a *horse stall*, on a breeding ranch. Do you see any broken windows around here? Any broken equipment? Neither do I. What is something *sharp* doing in the stall? Horses have hard hooves, but they're soft on the inside, and they get cut up really easily. Competent handlers don't allow anything with a sharp edge loose near the stalls."

Shaun lowered his foot, careful to keep his weight

balanced on his toe, not pressing on the plastic. "Son of a—"

"Shaun, get out of there. Rick, find me a rake or something. We need to turn that straw."

"Got it." Rick turned and headed for the rear corner of the barn where, I supposed, he'd seen some cleaning equipment. Shaun was limping out of the stall, still pale-faced.

I hit him on the shoulder with the heel of my right hand as soon as he came into range. "Asshole," I accused.

"Probably," he agreed, calming. If I was calling him names, it couldn't be too bad. "You think we found something?"

"It seems likely, but it's not your concern right now. Get the pliers, get that goddamn thing out of your shoe, and get it bagged. If you touch it, I'll kill you."

"Gotcha."

Rick came trotting back, rake in hand. I took it from him and leaned over, starting to poke through the straw. "Rick, keep an eye on my stupid brother."

"Yes, ma'am."

Using the rake to turn over the straw where Shaun had stepped uncovered several more chunks of plastic, and a long, bent piece of snapped-off plastic in a familiar shape. Behind me, Shaun breathed in sharply. "George . . ."

"I see it." I continued stirring the straw.

"That's a needle."

"I know."

"If there's no reason for the plastic to be in there, why is there a *needle* in there?"

"For no good reason," said Rick. "Georgia, try a little bit to the right."

I glanced toward him. "Why?"

"Because that's where the hay is less crushed. If there's anything else to find, it's more likely to be intact if it's off to the right."

"Good call." I turned my attention to the right-hand side of the stall. The first three passes found nothing. I had already decided the fourth pass would be the last in that area when the tines pulled an intact syringe into view. Not just intact: loaded. The plunger hadn't been pushed all the way home, and a small amount of milky liquid was visible through the mud-smeared glass. The three of us stared at it.

Finally, Shaun spoke. "George?"

"Yeah?"

"I don't think you're a paranoid freak anymore."

"Good." I gingerly used the rake to pull the syringe closer. "Check the sharps bin and see if there are any isolation bags left. We need to vacuum seal this before we take it out of here, and I don't trust our biohazard baggies."

"Why?" Rick asked. "They did the Nguyen-Morrison."

"Because there's only one thing I can think of that someone would inject into a perfectly healthy animal that then turns around and becomes the index case for an outbreak," I said. Just looking at the syringe was making me feel nauseous. Shaun could have stepped on that. He could have put his foot down wrong and . . .

New thought, Georgia. New thought.

"Syringes are watertight," Shaun said, as he turned

to head for the sharps bin. "Bleach wouldn't have been able to get inside."

"You mean—"

"Unless I'm wrong, we're looking at enough Kellis-Amberlee to convert the entire population of Wisconsin." I smiled without a trace of humor. "How's that for a front-page headline?

"Rebecca Ryman was murdered."

———

The Kellis-Amberlee virus can survive indefinitely inside a suitable host, which is to say "inside a warm-blooded, mammalian creature." No cure has been found, and while small units of blood can be purged of viral bodies, the virus cannot be removed from the body's soft tissues, bone marrow, spinal fluid, or brain. Thanks to the human ingenuity that created it, it is with us every day, from the moment of our conception until the day that we die.

We'll have multiple "infections" of the original Kellis strain during our lifetimes. It manifests to fight invading rhinoviruses seeking to attack the body and it acts to support the immune system. Some will also have minor flares of Marburg Amberlee, which wakes when there are cancerous growths to be destroyed. The synthesis of these wildly different viruses has not changed their original purposes, which is a good thing for us. If we're going to have to live with the fact that formerly dead people now rise up and attempt to devour the living, we may as well get a few perks out of the deal.

We only have problems when the conjoined form of these viruses enters its active state. Ten microns of live Kellis-Amberlee are enough to begin an unstoppable viral cascade that inevitably results in the effective death of the original host. Once the virus is awake, you cease to be "you" in any meaningful sense. Instead, you're a living viral reservoir, a means of spreading the virus, which is always hungry and always waiting. The zombie is a creature with two goals: to feed the virus in itself, and to spread that virus to others.

An elephant can be infected with the same amount of Kellis-Amberlee as a human. Ten microns. Speaking literally, you could pack more viral microns than that onto the period of this sentence. The horse that started the infection that killed Rebecca Ryman was injected with an estimated 900 *million* microns of live Kellis-Amberlee.

Now look me in the eye and tell me that wasn't terrorism.

—From *Images May Disturb You*,
the blog of Georgia Mason, March 25, 2040

Fifteen

It turns out that calling a United States senator from inside a quarantined biohazard zone to report that you've found a live cat and a syringe containing what you suspect to be a small but terrifying amount of live Kellis-Amberlee is a *great* way to get the full and immediate attention of both the army and the Secret Service. I've always known radio and cellular transmissions out of quarantine zones were monitored, but I'd never seen the fact so clearly illustrated. The words "intact syringe" were barely out of my mouth before we were surrounded by grim-faced men carrying large guns.

"Keep filming," I hissed to Rick and Shaun. They answered with small nods but were otherwise as frozen as I was, staring at the many, many guns around us.

"Put the syringe and any weapons you may be carrying on the ground and raise your hands above your heads," boomed a dispassionate voice, distorted by the crackle of a loudspeaker.

Shaun and I exchanged a look.

"Uh, we're journalists?" called Shaun. "On Class A-15 licenses with the concealed carry allowance? We've been following Senator Ryman's campaign? So we're carrying a lot of weapons, and we're sort of uncomfortable with this whole 'syringe' thing. Do you really want to wait while we take off *everything*?"

"God, I hope not," I muttered. "We'll be here all day."

The nearest of the armed men—one of the ones in army green rather than Secret Service black—tapped his right ear and said something under his breath. After a long pause, he nodded and called, in a much less intimidating voice than the one from the loudspeaker, "Just put down the syringe and any visible weapons, raise your hands, and don't make any threatening moves."

"Much easier, thanks," said Shaun, flashing a grin. At first, I couldn't figure out why he was wasting the energy to show off for the crowd, which was probably pretty high-strung and might be trigger-happy. Then I followed his line of sight and had to swallow a smile. Hello, fixed-point camera number four. Hello, ratings like you wouldn't believe, especially with Shaun doing his best to keep it interesting.

I stepped forward and placed the syringe on the ground. It was safe inside its reinforced plastic bubble, which was safe inside a second plastic bubble. A thin layer of bleach separated them. Anything that leaked out of that syringe would die before it hit the open air. Still moving with extreme care, I put my gun a few feet away, followed by my Taser, the pepper spray I keep clipped to my shoulder bag—there are dangerous things out there other than the infected, and most of them hate getting stinging mist in their eyes—and the collapsible baton Shaun gave me for my last birthday. Holding up my hands to show that I didn't have anything else, I began to step back into the line.

"The sunglasses too, ma'am," said the soldier.

"Oh, for crying—she's got retinal KA! You have our files from when we came in here, you should know that!" Shaun's earlier grandstanding was gone, replaced by genuine irritation.

"The sunglasses," repeated the soldier.

"It's all right, Shaun; he's just doing his job," I said, gritting my teeth and squeezing my eyes closed before tugging off my sunglasses and dropping them. Again, I moved to step back into the line.

"Please open your eyes, ma'am," said the soldier.

"Are you prepared to provide me with immediate medical attention?" I asked, not bothering to conceal my own anger. "My name is Georgia Carolyn Mason, license number alpha-foxtrot-bravo-one-seven-five-eight-nine-three, and like my brother said, you *have* my file. I have advanced retinal Kellis-Amberlee. If I open my eyes without protection, I risk permanent damage. Again, we're journalists, and I *will* sue."

There was another pause as the soldier conferred with whoever was giving him his orders. This one took longer; they were presumably calling up my file and confirming that no one was attempting to use a pair of sunglasses and some big words to conceal my impending conversion. "Return to your group," he said, finally. I stepped backward, letting Shaun's hand on my elbow guide me to a stop.

It took nearly ten minutes for Shaun and Rick to finish putting their weapons down and move back into place beside me, Shaun's hand going to my elbow in case we needed to move. I'm basically blind in daylight without my glasses. Maybe worse, since a real blind person doesn't have to worry about migraines or damaging their retinas just because there's no cloud cover.

"Under whose authority have you entered these premises?" asked the soldier.

"Senator Peter Ryman," said Rick, speaking with a calm that clearly said that he'd done more than his share of dealing with the authorities. "I believe it was Miss Mason's call to the senator that you intercepted?"

The soldier ignored his barb. "Senator Ryman is aware of your current location?"

"Senator Ryman gave full consent for this investigation," said Rick, stressing the word 'senator.' "I'm sure he'll be very interested in our findings."

There was another pause as the soldier conferred. This one was interrupted by a crackle of static, and Senator Ryman's voice came over the loudspeaker, saying, "Give me that thing. What are your people doing? That's my press corps, and you're acting like they're trespassers on *my* land—you don't see something wrong with that?" Another voice mumbled contrition outside the range of the speaker's microphone, and Senator Ryman boomed, "Damn right, you didn't think. You folks all right? Georgia, have you gone mental, girl? Get your glasses back on. You think a blind reporter's going to be much good at uncovering all my dirty little secrets?"

"These nice men told me to take them off, sir!" I called.

"These nice men with all the guns," Shaun added.

"Well, that was very neighborly of them, but now I'm asking you to put them back on. Georgia, you got a spare set?"

"I do, but they're in my back pocket—I'm afraid I'll drop them." Never go out without a spare pair of sunglasses. Preferably three. Of course, that anticipates contamination, not army-induced flash-blinding.

"Shaun, get your sister her glasses. She looks naked without them. It's creeping me out."

"Yes, sir!" Shaun let go of my elbow and reached into my pocket. A moment later, I felt him pressing a fresh pair of glasses into my palm. I let out a relieved sigh, snapped them open, and slid them on. The glare receded. I opened my eyes.

The scene hadn't changed much. Shaun and Rick were still flanking me, the armed men were still surrounding us, and fixed-point camera number four was still transmitting the whole thing back to the van on a band so low that it would look like white noise to most receivers. Buffy stays on top of what's happening in the field of wireless technology for just that reason; the more she knows, the harder it is to jam our signals. I didn't know whether our higher-band cameras were being blocked—probably, considering the army—but our low-band was going to be fine.

"Are your eyes all right, Georgia?" asked the senator. Shaun was giving me a look that asked the same question, in fewer words.

"Absolutely, sir," I called. That wasn't entirely true. My migraine was reaching epic proportions and would probably be with me for days. Still, it was close enough for government work. "We need to talk when these nice men are done, if you have time."

"Of course." There was a tension in the senator's voice that belied his earlier friendliness. "I want to know everything."

"So do we, sir," said Rick. "For one thing, we'd very much like to know what's in this syringe. Unfortunately, we lack the facilities to test its contents."

"The item in question is now in the custody of the United States Army," said the first voice, reclaiming the loudspeaker from Senator Ryman. "What it does or does not contain is no longer your concern."

I straightened. Shaun and Rick did the same.

"Excuse me," Rick said, "but are you saying that potential proof that live Kellis-Amberlee was used to cause an outbreak on American soil, on the property of a candidate for President of the United States of America, is *not* the concern of the people? Of, to be specific, three fully licensed and accredited representatives of the American media, who located that proof after being invited to perform an investigation that the armed forces had neglected to carry out?"

The soldiers surrounding us stiffened, and their guns were suddenly at angles that implied that accidents can happen, even on friendly soil. The Secret Service men frowned but remained more relaxed; after all, the original investigation hadn't been under their control.

"Son," said the original voice, "I don't believe you want to imply what you're implying."

"What, that you're saying we don't get to know what we found, even when we have a worldwide audience that really, *really* wants to know?" Shaun asked, folding his arms and sliding into a hip-shot pose that seemed casual, if you didn't know him well enough to see how pissed off he was. "That doesn't scream 'freedom of the press' to me."

"It won't say 'freedom of the press' to our readers, either," I said.

"Miss, there are things called 'nondisclosure forms,' and you'll find that I can have all three of you signing them before you take step one outside of this property."

"Well, *sir*, that might work if we hadn't been streaming our report live all along," I replied. "If you don't believe me, hit our Web site and see for yourself. We have a live feed, a transcript, the works." There was a pause before the sound of muffled swearing drifted through the loudspeaker. Somebody looked online. I allowed myself to smile. "If you wanted this kept secret, you shouldn't have left it for the journalists to find."

"And what I'd like to know," said Senator Ryman, in a voice that was suddenly colder than it had been before, "is what gives you the authority to seize materials found on my property without giving full disclosure to me, as the owner. *Especially* if said materials may have been involved in the death of my daughter and her grandparents."

"All sealed hazard zones—"

"Remain the property of the original owners, who must continue to pay taxes but will not benefit from any natural resources or profitable development of the land," said Rick. I gave him a sidelong look. Smiling serenely, he said, "*Secor v. the State of Massachusetts*, 2024."

"That aside, covering up evidence is rarely smiled upon in this country," Senator Ryman said. "Now, I believe what you intended to tell these nice folks was that they were free to leave the zone as soon as they've passed their mandatory blood tests, and that you'll be contacting me *and* them with an analysis of the contents of that syringe, given as how they found it and it was found on my property."

"Well—"

Senator Ryman cut him off. "I hope you understand that arguing with a senator—especially one who intends to be president, if only so he can make you realize what an imbecilic move this was—is not the best way to further your career."

There was a longer pause before the first voice spoke again, saying carefully, "Well, sir, I think perhaps you've gotten the wrong idea about this situation . . ."

"I hoped that was the case. I assume my people are free to go?"

Now falsely jovial, the first voice said, "Of course! My men are just there to escort them to their blood tests. Men? Get those citizens out of the field!"

"Sir, yes sir!" barked the soldiers. The Secret Service just looked faintly disgusted with the entire situation.

The soldier who asked me to remove my sunglasses consulted with the speaker on his shoulder before saying, reluctantly, "If the three of you would retrieve your weapons and follow me, I'll take you to the gate for testing and release. Please don't attempt to touch the article you removed from the outbreak site."

Rick looked like he was going to contest the phrase "the article" by bringing up the fact that we'd removed more than one thing from the outbreak site. Since I didn't think the cat would be happy to be dissected by army scientists, I kicked Rick in the ankle.

He glared at me. I ignored him. He'd thank me later. Or the cat would.

Picking our weapons back up took longer than putting them down, since all the safeties had to be checked. The area was certified as clean as was reasonable under the Nguyen-Morrison—as clean as any area where you found a syringe full of potential live-state Kellis-Amberlee could be—but shooting yourself in the foot in the vicinity of a recent outbreak still strikes me as an all-around rotten plan. Our escort waited as we armed ourselves and then walked with us in lockstep to the gates, where, I was pleased to see, Steve and two other men from Senator Ryman's security detail were waiting with the blood test units.

I caught my breath as I saw the boxes. Leaning over slightly, I nudged Shaun with my elbow. He followed my gaze and whistled. "Pulling out the big guns, there, Steve-o?"

Steve cracked a thin smile. "The senator wants to be certain you're all right."

"My brother's never been all right, but Rick and I are clean," I said, holding out my right hand. "Rock me."

"My pleasure," he said, and slid the box over my hand.

Blood testing kits range from your basic field units, which can be wrong as often as thirty percent of the time, to the ultra-advanced models, which are so sensitive that they've been known to trigger false positives as they pick up the live Kellis infection harbored by nearly every human on Earth. The most advanced handheld kits are the Apple XH-237s. They cost more than I care to think about, and since they're field kits, they can only be used once without replacing the needle array, a process that costs more than most independent journalists make in a year. Once is more than enough. Needles so thin they can barely be felt, hitting at sites on all five fingers, the palm, and the wrist. Viral detection and comparison mechanisms so advanced that the Army supposedly bought the right to use several of Apple's patents after the XH-237 came out.

Shaun and I carry one—only one—in the van. We've had it for five years. We've never felt rich or desperate enough to use it. You only use the XH-237 when you need to be sure, right here and now, with no margin for error. It's a kit for use after actual exposure. The army didn't wonder what was in that syringe. Somehow, they *knew*. The implications of that were more than a little disturbing.

Steve activated the kit. The lid locked down, flattening my palm until I felt the tendons stretch. There was a moment of pain. I tensed, but even waiting for it, I couldn't feel the needles as they began darting in and out of my hand and wrist. The lights atop the unit began to cycle, flashing red, then yellow, and finally settling, one by one, into a steady, unblinking green. The entire process took a matter of seconds.

Steve smiled as he dropped the unit into a biohazard bag. "Despite all natural justice, you're still clean."

"That's one more I owe to my guardian angel," I said. A glance to the side showed me that Shaun's unit was still cycling, while Rick's test was just getting started.

"Yeah, well, stop making that angel work so hard," said Steve, more quietly. I looked back to him, surprised. His expression was grave. "You can leave the zone now."

"Right," I said. I walked to the gate, where two blank-faced men in army green watched me press my forefinger against the much simpler testing pad. Another needle bit deeply, and the light switched from green to red to green again before the gate clicked open. Shaking my stinging hand, I stepped out.

Our van and Rick's car had been joined by a third vehicle: a large black van with mirrored windows that gleamed with the characteristic patina of armor plating. The top bristled with enough antennae and satellite dishes to make our own relatively modest assortment of transmitters look positively sparse. I stood, considering it, as Shaun and Rick made their own exits from the ranch and moved to stand beside me.

"That look like our friendly order-giver to you?" Shaun asked.

"Can't imagine who else it would be," I said.

"Well, then, let's go up, say hello, and thank them for the welcome. I mean, *I* was touched. A fruit basket might have been more fitting, but an armed ambush? Definitely a unique way to show that you care." Shaun went bounding for the van. Rick and I followed at a more sedate pace.

Shaun banged on the van door with the heel of his hand. When there was no reply, he balled his hand into a fist and resumed banging, louder. He was just starting to get a good rhythm going when the door was wrenched open by a red-faced general who glared at us with open malice.

"I don't think he's a music lover," I commented to Rick. He snorted.

"I don't know what you kids think you're doing—" began the general.

"Pretty sure they were looking for me," said Senator Ryman, stepping up behind him. The general cut off, shifting the force of his glare to the senator. Ignoring him, Senator Ryman moved around him and out of the van and clasped Shaun's hand. "Shaun, good to see you're all right. I was a bit concerned when I heard that transmission had been intercepted."

"We got lucky," Shaun said, with a grin. "Thanks for getting us through the red tape."

"My pleasure." Senator Ryman looked back at the glowering general. "General Bridges, thank you for your concern for the well-being of my press pool. I'll be speaking to your superiors about this operation, and I'll make sure they know your part in it."

The general paled. Still grinning, Shaun waggled his fingers at him.

"Nice to meet you, sir. Have a nice day." Turning back to Rick and me, he slung his arms around our shoulders. "So, my beloved partners in doing really stupid shit for the edification of the masses, would you say I bought us another three percent today? No, that's too conservative, for I am a God among men and a poker into unpokeable places. Make that five percent. Truly, you should all worship me in the brightness of my glory."

I turned my head enough to glance at the Senator. He was still forcing himself to smile, but the expression wasn't reflected in his eyes. That was the face of a man under considerable strain.

"Maybe later," I said. "Senator Ryman? Did you drive out here?"

"Steve was listening to your report," the senator said. "When he heard you'd found something, he called me, and we came out here immediately."

"Thank you for that, sir," said Rick. "If you hadn't, we might have had a few issues to contend with."

"Permanent blindness," said Shaun, looking at me.

"An all-expenses paid stay at a government bio-hazard holding facility," I countered. "Sir, did you want us to follow you back to the house and give you the details on what we found?"

"Actually, Georgia, thank you, but no. Right now, I'd like the three of you to return to your hotel and do whatever it is you need to do. Go do your jobs." There was something broken in his expression. I'd thought he looked old at the funeral, but I was wrong; he looked old *now*. "I'll call you in the morning, after I've had time to explain to my wife that our daughter's death wasn't an accident, and to get very, very drunk."

"I understand," I said. Looking to Rick, I said, "Meet us at the hotel." He nodded and turned to head for his car. I didn't want him to ride with us and leave it here. We'd just annoyed the army. A little accidental "vandalism" wasn't outside the realm of possibility. "You'll call if you need anything, sir?"

"You can count on it." The senator's voice was mirthless. So was his expression as he walked over to his government-issue SUV. Steve was already standing next to the passenger-side door, holding it open. I couldn't see any other security guards, but I knew they were there. They wouldn't be taking any chances with a presidential candidate this close to a recent hazard zone. Especially not after the things we'd just learned.

I watched the senator climb into the car. Steve shut the door behind him, nodded toward us, and got into the driver's side, pulling out. Rick's little armored VW followed a few minutes later, rumbling down the road toward civilization.

Shaun put his hand on my shoulder. "George? We okay to get going before the jerks in power come up with a reason to detain us? Other than the cat. Rick took the cat with him, so if there's going to be detention, it'll just be him. Beating erasers, getting electrodes strapped to sensitive parts of his body . . ."

"Huh?" I twisted around to look at him. "Right, leaving. Yeah, I'm ready to go."

"You feeling okay?" He peered at me. "You're pale."

"I was thinking about Rebecca. You drive? My head hurts too much for it to be safe."

Now Shaun was really starting to look concerned. I don't like to let him drive when I'm a passenger. His idea of traffic safety is going too fast for the cops to catch up. "You sure?"

I tossed him the keys. Usually, I don't like to be in the car when he's behind the wheel, but usually, I don't have a bunch of dead people, a distraught presidential candidate, and a splitting headache to contend with. "Drive."

Shaun gave me one last worried look and turned to head for the van. I followed and climbed into the passenger seat, closing my eyes. Showing rather uncharacteristic concern for my well-being, Shaun opted to drive like a sane human being, pulling out at a reasonably sedate fifty or so miles per hour, and actually acknowledging that the brakes could be used in situations other than "band of zombies blocking the road ahead." I settled deeper into my seat, keeping my eyes closed, and started to review.

When I said that the facts on the outbreak at the ranch didn't add up, I'd been half-expecting to find some sign of human neglect or possibly of an intruder who kicked off the whole mess and managed to get overlooked in the carnage, leaving it to be blamed on the horses. Some small thing that was nonetheless enough to trigger my sense of "something isn't right here." In short, a blip, a little bit of nothing that didn't change anything.

Rebecca Ryman was murdered.

This changed *everything*.

We'd known for weeks that Tracy's death—and thus probably the entire Eakly outbreak, although there wasn't anything conclusive that could be used to prove it—wasn't an accident, but we'd had no real proof that it was anything more than some lunatic taking advantage of an opportunity to cause a little chaos. Now . . . the chances of two random acts of malicious sabotage happening to the same group of people were small to nil. They just got smaller when you stopped to consider that the man who connected both incidents was one of the current front-runners for the office of President of the United States of America. This was big. This was very, very big.

And it was also very, very bad, because whoever was behind it thought nothing of violating Raskin-Watts, and that meant they'd already crossed a line most people don't even realize is there. Murder is one thing. This was terrorism.

"George? Georgia?" Shaun was shaking my shoulder. I opened my eyes, squinting automatically before

I realized that I was facing blessed dimness. Cocking an eyebrow, I turned toward him. He smiled, looking relieved. "Hey. You fell asleep. We're here."

"I was thinking," I said primly, unbuckling my belt before admitting, "and maybe also dozing a little bit."

"It's no big. How's the head?"

"Better."

"Good. Rick's already here, and your crew is driving him up a wall—he's called three times to find out when we'd be on site."

"Any word from Buffy?" I grabbed my bag and opened the door, sliding out of the car. The parking garage was cool and fairly full. Not surprising; when the senator booked our rooms, he put us in the best hotel in town. Five-star security doesn't come cheap, but it comes with perks, like underground parking with motion sensors that keep constant track not only of who's where, but how long they've been there and what they're doing. Stay down here walking in circles for a while, and Shaun and I could get a whole new view of hotel security. That might have been appealing if we hadn't already been working a story that was almost too hot to handle. I was starting to miss the days when toying with rich people's security systems was enough to make our front page.

"She's still at Chuck's, but she says the servers are prepped to handle whatever load we ask them to and that the Fiction section won't have a response for a day or two anyway; we should go ahead and run without her." Shaun slammed his door, starting toward the elevators that would let us into the main hotel. "She seemed pretty shaken up. Said she'd probably sleep over there tonight."

"Right."

Like most of the senator's men, Chuck was staying at the Embassy Suites Business Resort, a fancy name for a series of pseudo-condos that offered less transitory lodgings than our own high-scale but strictly temporary accommodations. His place came with a kitchen, living room, and a bathtub a normal human being could actually take a bath in. Ours came with a substantial array of cable channels, two queen-sized beds that we'd shoved together on the far side of the room in order to make space for the computers, and a surprisingly robust electrical system. We'd only managed to trip the circuit breakers twice, and for us, that's practically a record.

The elevators were protected by a poor-man's air lock. The sliding glass doors opened at our approach, then slid closed, sealing us into a small antechamber. A second set of glass doors barred us from the elevator. Being a high-end hotel, they were configured to handle up to four entrances at a time, although most people wouldn't be foolish enough to take advantage of that illusionary convenience. If anyone failed to check out as clean, the doors would lock and security would be called. Going into an air lock with someone you weren't certain was uninfected was a form of Russian roulette that few cared to indulge in.

Shaun took my hand, squeezing before we split up. He took the leftmost station while I took the one on the right.

"Hello, honored guests," said the warm, mock-maternal voice of the hotel. It was clearly designed to conjure up reassuring thoughts of soft beds, chocolates on your pillow every morning, and no infections ever getting past the sealed glass doors. "May I have your room numbers and personal identifications?"

"Shaun Phillip Mason," said Shaun, grimacing. Our usual games worked on the security system at home, but with a setup this advanced, there was too much potential that the computer would mistake "messing around" for "confused about your own identity" and call security. "Room four-nineteen."

"Georgia Carolyn Mason," I said. "Room four-nineteen."

"Welcome, Mr. and Ms. Mason," said the hotel, after a fifteen-second pause to compare our voice prints to the ones on file. "Could I trouble you for a retinal scan?"

"Medical dispensation, federal guideline seven-fifteen-A," I said. "I have a registered case of non-active retinal Kellis-Amberlee and would like to request a pattern recognition test, in accordance with the Americans with Disabilities Act."

"Hang on while I check your records," said the hotel. It fell silent. I rolled my eyes.

"Every time," I muttered.

"It's just trying to be thorough."

"*Every* time."

"It only takes the system a few seconds to find your file."

"How many times have we gone through this garage now?"

"Maybe they figure that if you were infected, you'd forget that stupid federal guideline."

"I'd like to forget your stupid—"

The speaker clicked back on. "Ms. Mason, thank you for alerting us to your medical condition. Please look at the screen in front of you. Mr. Mason, please proceed to the line marked on the floor, and look at the screen in front of you. Tests will commence simultaneously."

"Lucky disabled bitch," muttered Shaun, placing his toes on the indicated line and opening his eyes wide.

My screen flickered, resetting from scanning to text mode, and displayed a block of text. I cleared my throat and read, "Ah, distinctly I remember, it was in the bleak December, and each separate dying ember wrought its ghost upon the floor. Eagerly I wished the morrow, vainly I had sought to borrow from my books surcease of sorrow."

"Please hold," said the hotel. The black plastic doors on two of the test panels slid upward, revealing the metal testing panels. "Mr. and Ms. Mason, please place your hands on the diagnostic panels."

"Don't you love how it doesn't tell us whether we've passed or not?" said Shaun, putting his hand flat on the first panel. "They could be calling security right now and just stalling us until they get here."

"Gee, thanks, Mr. Optimism," I said. I pressed my hand to the second panel, feeling the brief sting of a needle against the base of my palm. "Got any other cheery thoughts?"

"Well, if Rick's frantic, Mahir may have experienced spontaneous human combustion by now."

"I hope somebody got it on film."

"Mr. and Ms. Mason, welcome to the Parrish Weston Suites. We hope you enjoy your stay; please let us know if there's anything we can do to make you more comfortable." The hotel finished delivering its sugar-soaked greeting as the doors between us and the elevator slid open, allowing us to proceed. They closed as soon as we were through, locking us out of the air lock. "Thank you for choosing the Weston family of hotels."

"Same to you," I said, and hit the Call button.

The science of moving people from point to point has improved over the past twenty years, since the infected have done a lot to discourage the once-natural human desire to linger alone in dark, poorly defended places. The Weston had nine elevators sharing a series of corridors and conduits. They were controlled by a central computer that spent the day dispatching them along the most efficient, collision-free routes. It took less than five seconds for the elevator doors to open. It promptly skidded sideways twenty yards once we were inside, beginning the rapid ascent to the elevator access closest to our hotel rooms.

"Priorities?" asked Shaun, as the elevator shot upward.

"Clear the message boards, perform a general status check-in, and debrief," I said. "I'll get my crew online if I have to haul them out of their beds. You get yours."

"What about the Fictionals?"

"Rick can handle them." If Buffy wanted to skip out on what might be the most important scoop the two more realistic sections of the site ever had, that was her prerogative, but she'd have to cope with us rousing her junior bloggers. Her department didn't get to hang up the blackout curtains just because she wanted to get laid.

Shaun grinned. "Can I tell him?"

The elevator slowed as it approached our floor, dumping inertia at such a rate that you'd never guess it had just been traveling in excess of twenty miles per hour. The doors slid open with a ding. "If it'll make you happy, by all means, tell him. Make sure he knows Magdalene is his to abuse. That should help things a bit." I approached our room, pressing my thumb against the access panel. It flashed green, acknowledging my right to enter. Shaun opened the door and shoved past me, leaving me standing in the hall. I sighed. "After you."

"Don't mind if I do!" he called back.

Rolling my eyes, I followed him.

When the senator booked our rooms, he gave us a pair of adjoining suites, assuming Buffy and I would take one room while Shaun and Rick took the other. It didn't work out that way. Buffy refuses to sleep without a nightlight, which I can't tolerate for obvious reasons; Shaun tends to respond violently to unexpected noises in the night. So Rick and Buffy wound up in one room, while Shaun and I were in the other with all the computers, turning it into our temporary headquarters.

Rick was at a terminal when we came in. The cat he'd saved was curled up in his lap, purring. I'd be purring, too, if I'd just eaten the better part of a tuna fish sandwich from room service.

"Lucky cat," I commented.

"Oh, thank God," said Rick, looking up. "Everyone wants to know what we're doing next. The raw footage has been downloaded so many times I thought we were going to blow up one of the servers, Mahir won't stop pinging me, and the message boards are—"

I interrupted him with a wave of my hand. "What are the numbers like, Rick?"

"Ah . . ." He recovered quickly, glancing to the top of his screen. "Up seven percent in all markets."

Shaun whistled. "Wow. We should uncover terrorist conspiracies more often."

"We haven't uncovered it yet; we've just found out that it existed," I said, and sat down at my own terminal. "Hit your boards and start pinging your people. We're doing the debrief in thirty, and then we start to edit and recap for the evening reports."

"On it." Shaun grabbed a chair and looked to Rick, adding carelessly, "You get to ping the Fictionals. Buffy isn't coming."

"Oh, great," said Rick, wrinkling his nose. He was already pulling up his IM lists as he asked, "Why do I get the honor?"

"Because you kept the cat," I said. "Kick Magdalene. She'll help you. Hush now. Mommy's working." He snorted but turned back to his computer. Shaun and I did the same.

It took thirty minutes to beat the message boards into something that looked less like a combination of a forest fire and a conspiracy theorist convention. No one had quite reached the point of linking the outbreak at the Ryman family ranch with the initial release of the Kellis cure and the death of JFK, but they'd have gotten there before much longer. As I'd expected, everyone in my department was already up, online, and doing their best to moderate the mess, and from the crossover threads, it looked like the same was mostly true for the Irwins and the Fictionals. Behold the power of the truth. When people see its shadow on the wall, they don't want to take the time to look away.

"My boards are clear," Shaun called. "Ready when you are."

"Same," Rick said. "The chat relay is humming nicely, and the volunteer mods have things under control."

"Excellent." Since the volunteers weren't technically employees of After the End Times, they didn't need to be included in the debriefing. I pulled up the employee chat and typed, *Log on now.* "Turn on your conference functions, boys. We're about to see the swarm."

"Logged on."

"Logged on."

"Logging on now. Room eleven, maximum security." Our conferencing system is half the standard Microsoft Windows VirtuParty setup—allowing people to share real-time socialization through webcams and a common server—and half Buffy's own homebrew. All eleven of our channels have varying degrees of security, from the base three, which clever readers can break into with relative ease, to eleven, which has never been successfully violated. Not even by the people we've paid to try.

Windows began spawning on my screen, each containing the small, pixelated face of one of our bloggers. Shaun, Rick, and I appeared first, followed almost immediately by Mahir, who looked like he hadn't slept in several days, Alaric, and Suzy, the girl I'd hired to replace Becks after she jumped ship to the Irwins. Becks herself appeared a moment later, along with a trio of Irwins I only vaguely recognized. Five more faces followed them as the Fictionals logged in; three of them were sharing one screen, proving that Magdalene was hosting another of her infamous grindhouse parties.

When all was said and done, we were only missing Dave—one of Shaun's Irwins, who was on a field trip in the wilds of Alaska and probably couldn't get to a conferencing setup—and Buffy. I looked from face to face, studying their expressions while the initial quiet still held. They looked worried, confused, curious, even excited, but none of them looked like they had anything to hide. This was our team. This was what we had to work with. And we had a conspiracy to break.

"All right, everyone," I said. "This afternoon, we led an expedition onto the Ryman family ranch. You've seen the footage by now. If you haven't, please log out, watch it, and come back. Here's the topic at hand: 'What happens next?'"

Following the campaign of Congresswoman Kirsten Wagman taught me one important fact about politics: Sometimes, style *can* matter more than substance. Let's face it: We're not talking about one of the great political minds of our age. We're talking about a former stripper who got her seat in Congress by promising her constituency that for every thousand votes she got, she'd wear something else inappropriate to the floor. Judging by the landslide of that first win, we'll be seeing congressional hearings graced by a lady in lingerie long after the end of her term in office.

But she didn't win. Despite the general malaise of the voting public and their willingness to put "interesting" above "good for them" in nine out of ten cases, Wagman's run for the presidential seat proved to be the tenth event. Why was this? I place the blame partially on Senator Peter Ryman, a man who proved that style and substance can be combined to the benefit of both, and, more important, that integrity is not actually dead.

I also blame After the End Times and Georgia Mason, for their willingness to get into the campaign in a way that has seldom been seen in this century. Their reporting hasn't been impartial or perfect, but it has something we see even more rarely than integrity.

It has heart.

It is with great joy that I report that the youth of America aren't actually riddled with ennui and apathy; that the truth hasn't been fully forsaken for the merely entertaining; that there's a place in this world for reporting the facts as accurately and concisely as possible and allowing people to draw their own conclusions.

I've never been more proud of finding a place where I can belong.

—From *Another Point of True*,
the blog of Richard Cousins, March 18, 2040

Sixteen

The discussion lasted late into the morning. People dropped off the conference one by one, until it was just Rick, Mahir, and me. Shaun had long since passed out at his terminal, leaning back in his chair and snoring. Rick's newly acquired cat was curled up on his chest with its tail tucked over its nose, occasionally opening an eye to glare at the room.

"I don't like this, Georgia," said Mahir, worry and exhaustion blurring his normally crisp English accent into something much softer. He ran his hand through his hair. He'd been doing that for hours, and it was sticking up in all directions. "The situation is starting to sound like it isn't exactly safe."

"You're on the other side of the planet, Mahir. I don't think you're going to get hurt."

"It's not my safety I'm concerned with here. Are you sure we want to continue to pursue the situation? I'd rather not be reporting your obituary." He sounded so anxious that I couldn't be angry with him. Mahir's a good guy. A little conservative, and generally inclined to avoid taking risks, but a good guy and a fabulous Newsie. If he couldn't understand why we were pursuing things, I just needed to make them clearer.

"Everyone who died at the ranch was murdered," I said. His image winced. "The people who died in Eakly were murdered, too, and that set of casualties nearly included me and Shaun. There's something connected to this candidate and this campaign that someone wants to see destroyed, and they're not above causing a little collateral damage. You want to know if we want to continue pursuing the situation. I want to know what makes you think we can afford not to."

Mahir smiled, reaching up to adjust his glasses. "I was assuming you'd say something along those lines, but I wanted to be certain of it. Rest assured that you have the full support of everyone here. If there's anything I can do, all you have to do is say so."

"You know, Mahir, your support is something I never worry about. I may have something for you very soon," I said. "Although if you play 'test the boss' again, I may kill you. For now, it's almost four in the morning, and the senator's going to want to talk before much longer. I hereby declare this discussion over. Rick, Mahir, thanks for sticking it out."

"Any time," said Rick, voice echoing as the relay raced to keep up with him. His window blinked out.

"Cheers," said Mahir, and logged off. I closed the conference, standing. I was so stiff that it felt like my spine had been replaced with carved teak, and my eyes were burning. I removed my sunglasses and rubbed my face, trying to relieve some of the tension. It wasn't working.

"Bed?" asked Rick.

I nodded. "Don't take this the wrong way, but—"

"Get out. I know. Wake me when it's time to go?"

"I will."

"Good night, Georgia. Sleep well." Rick opened the adjoining door with a faint creak. I opened my eyes, turning to wave as he slipped out.

"You too, Rick," I said. Then the door was closed, and I staggered to the bed, shedding clothes as I went. When I was down to T-shirt and panties, I abandoned the notion of looking for nightclothes and crawled under the covers, closing my eyes again as I sank into blessed darkness.

"Georgia."

The voice was vaguely familiar. I pondered its familiarity for a moment, and then rolled over, deciding I didn't need to give a damn.

"Georgia."

There was more anxiousness to the voice this time. Maybe I needed to pay attention to it. It wasn't the sort of anxiousness that said "Pay attention or something is going to eat your face." I made a faint grumbling noise and didn't open my eyes.

"George, if you don't wake up *right now*, I'm going to pour ice water over your head." The statement was made in an entirely matter-of-fact manner. It wasn't a threat, merely a comment. "You won't like that. I won't care."

I licked my lips to moisten them and croaked, "I hate you."

"Where's the love? *There's* the love. Now get out of bed. Senator Ryman called. You slept through me talking to him for, like, the whole time I was getting dressed. How late were you up last night?"

I opened my eyes and squinted at Shaun. He was wearing one of his bulkier shirts, the ones he puts on only when he needs to cover body armor. I pushed myself unsteadily into a sitting position, holding out my left hand. He dropped my sunglasses into it. "Sometime around four. What time is it?"

"Almost nine."

"Oh, my God, kill me now," I moaned, and rose, shuffling toward the bathroom. The hotel had been happy to switch our standard light bulbs for lower-wattage soft lights that wouldn't hurt my eyes, but management didn't have a way to swap out the built-in bathroom fluorescents. "What time will he be here? Or are we going to him?"

"You've got fifteen minutes. Steve's picking us up." There was a distinctly amused note in Shaun's voice as he relayed this piece of information. "Buffy's *pissed*. She and Chuck are already with the Rymans, and she didn't have spare clothes with her. I got the world's angriest text message while I was on the phone."

"She wants to have her night on the town, she can take the walk of shame the day after." The bathroom lights were searingly bright, even through my sunglasses. I looked in the mirror and groaned. "I look like death."

"Cute journalistic death?"

"Just plain death." I was washed-out and sallow, and it had been too long since I had my hair trimmed; it was getting long enough to tangle. My head wasn't throbbing, but it would be soon. The light seeping in around the edges of my glasses was telling me that. There was a way I could avoid that, if I was willing to deal with the inconvenience. Muttering under my breath, I grabbed my contact case off the sink and clicked the bathroom lights off. Even with as little as I voluntarily wear my contacts, the nature of my medical condition means I need to be able to put them in despite near or total darkness. Doing otherwise means risking retinal scarring, and I have things to do that require having eyes.

Shaun's feet shuffled on the carpet as he crossed to the bathroom door. "George? What are you doing in there in the dark?"

"Putting in my contacts." I blinked, and felt the first slide into place. "Find me clean clothes."

"What do I look like, your maid?"

"Nah, she's *way* better looking." I blinked my second lens into place before clicking the bathroom lights back on. Harsh white light flooded the room. I squinted slightly, studying my blue-eyed reflection before I turned to the important matter of brushing my hair and teeth. "Any time now, Shaun. I can't go see the senator in my undies."

"Hunter S. Thompson would go see a senator in his undies. Or your undies, for that matter."

"Hunter S. Thompson was too stoned to know what undies were." The bathroom door opened. I turned, catching the clothes Shaun pitched in my direction. "There, now, was that so hard? Go grab our gear. I'll be there in a second."

"Next time, I'll let you sleep in," he grumbled,

backing up. "And those contacts make you look like an alien!"

"I know," I said, and shut the bathroom door.

Ten minutes later, Shaun and I were back in the elevator. I was running the final diagnostic checks on my equipment, and Shaun was doing the same, fingers tapping over the screen of his PDA in a series of increasingly complex patterns. This wasn't a field op, and odds were that Senator Ryman would request a privacy screen on anything we recorded, but that didn't matter. Leaving the hotel without our cameras and recorders set and primed to go would have been like leaving naked, and neither of us was up for that.

Some of my cameras were starting to show signs of misalignment, and the memory in my watch was almost full. Making a note to have Buffy take a look at things, I stepped out into the lobby with Shaun half a beat behind.

"Thank you for choosing the Parrish Weston Suites as your home away from home," the hotel chirped as we approached the air lock. "We know you have many choices, and we are grateful for your business. Please place your right hand—"

"That's enough," I said, slamming my palm down on the test panel as soon as it finished opening. Getting *out* of the hotel requires nothing but a clean blood test. They don't care if you want to go into massive viral amplification as long as you have the common courtesy to do it outside, preferably after you've paid your bills.

Shaun and I checked clean and the outer doors slid open, allowing us to exit while the automated voice of the hotel chirped pleasantries to an empty ante-chamber. It was cold and bright outside; a perfect Wisconsin day. There was only one car idling in the passenger pickup lane.

"Think that's us?" asked Shaun.

"That, or there's a pro-wrestling convention in town," I said. We started toward it.

When the senator sends a car, he doesn't screw around. Our intended transport was a solid-looking black SUV. The windows were tinted, and I would have placed bets on their being bulletproof. Possessing a personal fortune has its perks. Shaun nudged me and whistled, pointing to the inset gunner's windows on the back windshield.

"Even *Mom* doesn't have those," he murmured.

"I'm sure she'll be jealous," I said.

Steve was standing by the rear passenger door, holding it open for us—as much, I'm sure, as a reminder that we weren't allowed to ride up front as a gesture of civility. His eyebrows rose when he saw my contacts. To his credit, he didn't comment on them; he just held the door open a little wider. "Shaun. Georgia."

"I see you drew the short straw this morning," I said, hoisting myself into the SUV and scooting over to make room for Shaun. Rick was already inside. I offered him a small wave, which he dolefully returned.

"The senator prefers this meeting be conducted in a more secure location and thought you might appreciate the chance to take a break from driving." Steve glanced toward the parking garage and tapped his earpiece. I frowned. They thought our van had been bugged? It was possible—without Buffy running a full diagnostic on our systems, there was no way to tell—but it seemed a little paranoid.

I stopped that line of thought. Rebecca Ryman was murdered by someone who was willing to use live-state Kellis-Amberlee in an uncontrolled situation to achieve their goals, whatever they happened to be. There was no such thing as paranoia anymore.

"Looking good, Steve-o," said Shaun, slapping the security agent a high five as he slid into the car.

"One day you're going to call me that, and I'm going to punch your head clean off," said Steve, and slammed the door. Shaun laughed. The sound of Steve's footsteps moved around the car, where the driver's-side door opened and closed again. A sheet of one-way glass separated the front seat from the passenger compartment. He could see us, but we couldn't see him. How encouraging.

"He probably means that, you know," said Rick.

"As long as I get it on film, I'll be happy," said Shaun. Folding his hands behind his head, he stretched out on the seat and propped his feet in my lap. "This is awesome. We're being driven to a clandestine meeting with a man who wants to be president. Anybody else feel like James Bond right now?"

"Too female," I said.

"Too aware of the fact that I'm not immortal," said Rick.

"You realize you're both wimps, right?" scolded Shaun.

"Yes, but we're wimps with a life expectancy, and I have to respect that," I replied.

"I'll trade my life expectancy for a cup of coffee and a nice dark room," said Rick.

I craned my head to look at him. He was rubbing his eyes. He looked groggy, and I wasn't entirely sure he'd changed his shirt. "Didn't sleep well?"

"Cat kept me up all night," he said. Dropping his hands from his face, he did a classic double-take, eyes going wide. "Georgia? What's wrong with your eyes?"

"Contacts," I said. "They irritate the shit out of my eyes, but at least this way, I can't have some hopped-up asshole with a megaphone take my sunglasses away."

He tilted his head, studying me. "That really upset you, didn't it?"

"What, you mean the part where the nice guys with the big guns demonstrated over a live feed that I can be incapacitated by taking my glasses away? That didn't bother me a bit." I shoved Shaun's feet off my lap. "Sit up. This isn't a cruise."

"Behold the bitchiness of George when she hasn't had her beauty sleep," said Shaun, pushing himself upright. Twisting around to face Rick, he said, "So, Ricky-boy, you seen your ratings? Because I have some ideas to spice things up. Let's start with nudity—" And he was off and running, offering a plethora of insane suggestions as my overwhelmed fellow Newsie looked on in dismay.

Grateful for the save, I pulled out my PDA and started scrolling through the headlines. There'd been another outbreak in San Diego; that city hasn't had a break since the Rising, when bad timing and worse luck caused amplification to occur during the annual International Comic Convention, an event that drew over a hundred and twenty thousand attendees. The results were less than pleasant. In other news, Congresswoman Wagman had been asked to leave the floor for showing up in an outfit more suitable for a Vegas showgirl. Another nutcase in Hong Kong was claiming that Kellis-Amberlee had been engineered specifically to undermine those religions that depended on ancestor worship. In other words, a pretty quiet day . . . if you cut out the headlines that directly referenced or connected back to our expedition to the Ryman family ranch. At a rough glance, I estimated that sixty to seventy percent of the news sites were carrying us as their top story. *Us*.

I tapped my ear cuff. There was a pause as the connection was made; then Buffy was on the line, sounding irritated from her first curt "Go."

"Buffy, I need numbers. We're everywhere, and I have to know whether I'm hauling Mahir's ass out of bed to start manning the walls."

"Sec." We all have live feeds, but Buffy's are the most up-to-date. I need special equipment to get the data she pulls as a matter of course. That's why she's the techie, while I'm just in charge.

There was a long pause. Longer than I'm used to; Buffy can normally give me numbers in a matter of seconds. "Buffy?" Shaun stopped talking as both he and Rick turned toward me. I held up my hand, signaling for quiet. "Are you still there?"

"I'm here. I, uh . . . I think I'm here, anyway." She sounded a little bit scared. "Georgia? We're number *one*, Georgia. We have more current hits, references, link-backs, and quotations than any other news site on the planet."

My entire body seemed to go numb. I licked my lips. "Say that again."

"Number one, Georgia."

"You're sure?"

"I'm positive." There was a pause before she said, plaintively, "What do we do now?"

"What do we do now? What do we do *now*? Wake them up, Buffy! Call your people and wake them up!"

"Senator Ryman—"

"We're on our way! Ignore him! Get your people on the phone, and get them on the damn site!" I hit my ear cuff to kill the connection and twisted to face the others. "Shaun, start dialing. I want your entire team updating, ten minutes ago, and that means Dave, too. They have phones in Alaska. Rick, check your in-box, start clearing out any merchandise queries that got routed to you by mistake."

"George, what—"

"We have the ratings, Shaun. *We have the top slot.*" I nodded at his stunned expression. "Yeah. Now get them on the phone."

The rest of the ride was a blur of telephone calls, text messages, e-mails, and rousing person after person out of their well-earned rest in order to throw them back into the fray. Most of my crew was too disoriented by lack of sleep to argue when I ordered them out of bed and to their terminals, where the freshly updated site message that appeared as each of them logged in read "Number One News Site IN THE WORLD" in flashing red letters. If that wasn't enough to jolt them into consciousness, they were probably already dead.

Mahir put it best: When I called him, he responded first with stunned silence, then by swearing a blue streak and hanging up on me so he could get to his computer. I love a man who keeps his priorities straight.

All three of us were so engrossed in work that we missed the rest of the drive to the senator's "secure location." I was in the process of giving Alaric and Suzy their marching orders when the car doors opened, filling the back seat with light and nearly spilling Shaun—whose feet were braced against the left-hand passenger window—into the parking lot.

"We're here," said Steve. The three of us continued frantically typing on our various handheld PDAs and output screens. Rick was managing to type on his Palm and his phone at the same time, using his thumbs for data entry. Steve frowned. "Uh, guys? We're here. The senator is waiting."

"Sec," I said, freeing one hand long enough to hold it up to him in the universal "stop" gesture. While he gaped at me, I finished tapping out the instructions Alaric and Suzy would need to keep their portions of the site functional until I could get back online. I wasn't confident they'd survive the day, but Mahir would back them up as much as he could, and he had most of the same administrative permissions as Shaun and I; it would have to do. I lowered my PDA. "All right. Where do we go?"

"You sure you don't need a few more minutes to check your e-mail or anything?"

I glanced to Shaun. "I think he's making fun of us."

"I think you're right," Shaun said, and slid out of

the car, offering me his hands. "Ignore the philistine and get out here. We have government officials to annoy."

We were parked in a covered garage less than a quarter the size of the one at the hotel. The lights were bright enough that I hadn't even noticed the transition from real to artificial illumination. I used Shaun's hands for balance as I stepped out of the car, sliding my PDA into the carrier on my belt before turning to help Rick down. He glanced to me, and I nodded.

That was his cue. Rick goggled, sparing Shaun and me the trouble of playing hick, before asking, "Where *are* we?"

"The senator considers it wise to keep a second local residence for meetings of a sensitive nature," said Steve.

I gave him a sharp look. "Or meetings with people who didn't feel comfortable being around the horses?"

"I'm sure I wouldn't be qualified to speak to that, Miss Mason."

That meant yes. "Fine. Where do we go?"

"This way, please." He led us to a steel-reinforced door, where I was surprised to see a lack of the customary blood testing units. There also wasn't a doorknob. Shaun and I exchanged a glance as Steve tapped his earpiece, saying, "Base, we're at the west door. Release."

Something clicked, and a light above the door frame flashed green. The door slid open. There was a soft outrush of air as the hall on the other side was revealed; it was a positive-pressure zone, designed to force air out rather than allowing it to flow in and cause a contamination risk.

"No wonder they don't need blood tests." I followed Steve into the hall with Shaun and Rick close behind me. The hallway door slid shut behind us.

The lights in the hall were bright enough to hurt my eyes even through my contacts. I squinted, stepping closer to Shaun and letting the blurry motion of his silhouette guide me toward the door at the far end, where two more guards waited, each holding a large plastic tray.

"The senator would prefer this meeting not be broadcast or recorded," Steve said. "If you would please place all nonessential equipment here, it will be returned to you at the end of the meeting."

"You have *got* to be kidding," said Shaun.

"I don't think he is," I said, turning toward Steve. "You want us to walk in there naked?"

"We can put up an EMP privacy screen if you don't think we can trust you to leave your toys behind," said Steve. His tone was mild, but the tightness around his eyes said he knew exactly how much he was asking and he wasn't happy about it. "The choice is yours."

An EMP privacy screen sufficient to secure an area would fry half of our more sensitive recording devices and could do serious damage to the rest. Replacing that much gear would kill our operating budget for months, if not the rest of the year. Grumbling, all three of us began stripping off our equipment—and in my case, jewelry—and dumping it into the trays. The guards stood there impassively, waiting for us to finish.

Dropping my ear cuff into my hand, I looked to Steve. "So do we have to be totally radio silent, or are we allowed to keep our phones?"

"You can keep any private data recorders that will be used solely for the purposes of taking personal notes, and any telecommunications devices that can be deactivated for the duration of the meeting."

"Swell." I dropped my ear cuff into the tray and slipped my PDA back onto my belt. I felt strangely exposed without my small army of microphones, cameras, and data storage devices, as if the world held a lot more dangers than it had a few minutes before. "How's Buffy taking this?"

Steve smirked. "They said they wouldn't cut her off until we got here."

"So you're telling me your men are in there, right now, trying to take Buffy's equipment away?" Shaun said, and looked toward the closed door with a sort of wary fascination. "Maybe we should stay out here. It's a *lot* safer."

"Unfortunately, Senator Ryman and Governor Tate are waiting for you." Steve nodded to the guards. The one on the left leaned over and took the tray from the one on the right, who opened the door. There was another inrush of air as the hallway's positive-pressure zone met the house beyond. "If you don't mind?"

"Tate's here?" My eyes narrowed. "What do you mean, Tate's here?"

Steve walked through the open door without answering me. Eyes still narrowed, I shook my head and followed, with Rick and Shaun close behind me. Once the last of us was through the door, the guards closed it, remaining outside in the garage.

"What," muttered Shaun, "no blood test?"

"Guess they figure there's no point," said Rick.

I kept my mouth shut, busying myself with studying the house. The décor was simple but refined, all clean, sleek lines and well-lit corners. Overhead lighting provided a steady level of illumination, with no visible dimmer switches or controls; it was either light or darkness, with nothing in between. It was less glaring than the hallway lights, but I still grimaced. The lights answered one question—this was nothing but a show home, intended for meetings and parties, but never for living in. Emily, with her retinal KA, couldn't possibly have lived here.

There were no windows.

We walked through the house to the dining room, where a brisk-looking security guard in a black suit was finishing the process of taking Buffy's equipment away. If looks could kill, the way she was glaring would have left us with an outbreak on our hands.

"We about done here, Paul?" asked Steve.

The guard—Paul—shot him a harried look and nodded. "Miss Meissonier has been quite cooperative."

"Liar," said Shaun, so close to my ear that I don't think anyone else heard him.

"Buffy," I said, swallowing my smile. "What's the sitrep?"

"Chuck's in there with the senator and Mrs. Ryman," Buffy said, as she continued glaring at Paul. "Governor Tate just got here. They didn't tell me he was coming, or I would've warned you."

"It's all right." I shook my head. "He's a part of this campaign now, like it or not." I looked to Steve. "We're ready when you are."

"This way, please." He opened a door on the far side of the room, holding it as the four of us filed through. When Rick stepped through the doorway, Steve closed the door behind him. The lock slid home with a final-sounding "click."

We were standing in a sitting room decorated in stark blacks and whites, with stylized white art deco couches flanked by glossy black end tables and carefully arranged spotlight lamps illuminating tiny pieces of art that probably cost more individually than our operating budget for the year. The only spots of color came from the faces of the senator and his wife, both red-cheeked from crying, and from Governor Tate, who was wearing a tailored dark blue suit that screamed "money" in a politely subdued way. All three turned toward us, and the senator rose, tugging his suit jacket down before offering his hand to Shaun. Shaun shook it. I looked past them to where Governor Tate was endeavoring to cover his own expression of disgust.

"Thank you for coming," said Senator Ryman, releasing Shaun's hand and reclaiming his seat. Emily's eyes were hidden behind mirrored sunglasses. She mustered a tiny smile as she folded her hands around her husband's. He tugged her closer, seemingly unaware of the gesture. He didn't have much strength to offer, but what he did have was hers without question. That's the kind of guy we need running this country.

"We had a choice?" asked Shaun, dropping onto one of the couches and sprawling with intentional untidiness. He'd clearly caught Tate's look, too; that, combined with the confiscation of our equipment, had him primed and ready to offend. Good. It's always easier to seem reasonable when my brother is providing a handy contrast.

"We were glad to come, Senator, but I'm afraid I don't understand why our equipment had to be confiscated. Some of those cameras are delicate, and I'm not comfortable leaving them with anyone who's not a member of our staff. If we'd been informed of the need for privacy before we left the hotel, we could have left them behind."

Tate snorted. "You mean you could have brought cameras that were easier to hide."

"Actually, Governor, I meant what I said." I turned to look him in the eyes, unblinking. One of the few handy side effects of retinal KA is the lack of a need for repeated ocular lubrication—or, in layman's terms, I don't blink much. Being stared at by someone with retinal KA can be very unnerving, at least according to Shaun. "I'm aware that you're a recent addition to this campaign, and may not be used to working with members of the reputable news media. We can make allowances for that. I would, however, appreciate it if you could also keep in mind that we've been working with Senator Ryman and his staff for some time now, and not once have we broadcast or distributed material we were asked to withhold. Now, I'll admit that part of that can be attributed to the fact that we've never been asked to withhold information without good reason. I still believe it establishes that we're capable of behaving ourselves with tact, propriety, and, above all, the patriotism inherent in the duty of serving as media corps of a major political campaign."

"Well, missy," said Tate, meeting my eyes without a flinch, "those are a lot of pretty words, but I hope you'll forgive me if I've been burned a few times by the media before landing here, and I prefer to proceed with caution."

"Well, *sir*," I replied, "you'll forgive *me* if I believe that our track record should count for something, given that we've never been anything other than appropriate in our dealings with sensitive information; further, if I might be so bold, there's a chance that the media has 'burned' you so many times because you persist in treating honest people like they're waiting for the opportunity to be criminals. For a man who says he's standing for American values, you're sure devoted to the suppression of media freedom."

The governor's eyes narrowed. "Now see here, young lady—"

"My name is neither 'young lady' nor 'missy,' and I think I see all too well." I turned to the others. "Shaun, get up. Rick, Buffy, come on."

"Where do you think you're going?" demanded Tate.

"Back to our hotel, where we'll cheerfully explain to our many readers that we have no news for them today because—after uncovering an act of criminal bioterrorism on United States soil—we were unable to attend a conference with our candidate since, oopsie, the new man on the ticket thinks the media can't be trusted." I smiled. "Won't that be fun?"

"Georgia, sit down," said Senator Ryman. He sounded exhausted. That was no surprise. "You, too, Shaun. Buffy, Rick, you can sit or not, as you prefer. And you, David, will please try to remember that these folks are the only ones who cared enough to really *look* at the ranch rather than writing it off as a simple outbreak. You'll be courteous, and we'll trust them to keep on being as they have been: perfectly reasonable and willing to work with us."

"There's still the matter of our recording devices, Senator," I said, staying still.

"That was a bad decision, and I'm sorry. That being said, I'm going to stand by it for now, and ask that you allow me to conduct this meeting."

I raised an eyebrow. "And what do we get?"

Governor Tate sputtered, growing red in the face. Senator Ryman waved him down, looking at me squarely, and said, "An exclusive interview with me, no editing, regarding what you found yesterday."

"No deal," said Shaun. The senator and I looked toward him, surprised. My brother was sitting up, suddenly alert. "No offense, sir, but you're not that impressive anymore. Our readers know you. They respect you, and if you keep on the way you have been, they'll elect you, but they won't be razzled and dazzled by the fact that we managed to *get* you."

The senator ran a hand through his hair, looking pained. "What do you want, Shaun?"

"Her." He nodded to Emily. "We want an interview with her."

"Absolutely n—"

"Yes," said Emily. Her voice was weary but clear. "I'm happy to. I only wanted to be left out of things for the sake of . . . for the sake of my family." Her voice broke. "That's not a concern anymore."

"You aren't worried about the safety of your younger daughters?" I asked.

"They aren't at the ranch. They have the best security in the world. They're safe. If I can prevent people from going out and killing other people's pets because of what happened to Rebecca and my parents, well." She managed to muster a smile. "It'll be worth the strain."

Senator Ryman reached for her arm. "Emily . . ."

"Accepted." I sat next to Shaun, ignoring the senator's stricken look. "We'll be setting up interview times with both of you later this afternoon. Now, I assume there's a reason we're all here?"

"The senator would like to discuss the tragic evidence of tampering that your crew discovered at his family ranch, Miss Mason," said Governor Tate smoothly, all traces of his earlier aggravation gone. The man was a natural politician; I had to give him that, even if I wasn't willing to let him have anything else if I could help it. "Now, I realize this may seem as if I'm questioning your journalistic integrity—"

"Hey, Rick, ever notice how dickheads only say that when they're about to question your journalistic integrity?" asked Shaun.

"Oddly, yes," Rick said. "It's like a nervous twitch."

The governor shot them a glare and continued. "Please understand that I don't ask this for personal reasons, but simply because we need to determine the truth of the situation."

I looked at him. "You're wondering if somehow, to drive up our ratings, we smuggled evidence of terrorist activity through the checkpoints and managed to plant it while our own cameras were broadcasting over a live feed to an audience that can be conservatively estimated, judging by yesterday's ratings, as being somewhere in the millions."

"I wasn't intending to put it in quite those—"

I held up my hand to cut him off, turning to face Senator Ryman. "Senator, you know I'll ask this again when I'm permitted to film the exchange, but in the interests of killing this line of questioning here and now, I'm going to sacrifice spontaneity in favor of clarity. Have the lab results come back on the syringe?"

"Yes, Georgia, they have," said the senator, jaw set in a hard line.

"Can you tell us what those results were?"

"I don't see how that's relevant to the original question," said Tate.

"Senator?" I said.

"The contents of the syringe were determined to be a suspension of ninety-five percent live-state virus, common designation 'Kellis-Amberlee' or 'KA', isolated in iodized saline solution," the senator said. "We're waiting on additional information."

"Like the viral substrain?" I asked. "Right. Governor Tate, my crew and I were several hundred miles from the ranch at the time of the outbreak at the Ryman family home, and security records will support this. Further, with the exception of Mr. Cousins, we were all traveling with the campaign for months prior to the outbreak. Mr. Cousins was traveling with the convoy of Congresswoman Wagman, who should be able to vouch for his whereabouts. I'm not a virologist, but I'm fairly sure it takes special equipment to isolate the live virus without risking infection, and that said special equipment would not only be delicate, but would require special training to operate and maintain. Do you see where I'm going with this, Governor Tate, or should we draw you a diagram?"

"She's right," said Emily. Governor Tate looked toward her, eyes narrowing. She met his gaze and said, "I took virology courses at college; they're required for an animal husbandry degree. What Peter is describing is lab quality. You'd need a clean room and excellent biohazard protections just to isolate it, much less load it into any sort of a . . . a weapon. They just didn't have the resources. You'd need something a lot more secure than a pressure cooker in a hotel room to do something like this."

"Furthermore," I said, cutting Tate off before he could speak again, "even assuming we could somehow come up with the resources to do something like this, *and* had some sort of 'silent partner' we could get out to the ranch while we were occupied at the convention, we'd have to be *idiots* to turn around and be the ones who found the proof that the outbreak was man-made. So now that you've insulted our patriotism, our sanity, and our intelligence, how about we move on?"

Governor Tate leaned back in his seat, eyes narrowed. I kept my own eyes wide, playing off just how disturbing the unbroken, too-too-blue of my contacts is to most humans. He looked away first.

Satisfied, I turned toward Senator Ryman. "So now that we've had that little throwdown, what else did you feel needed to be handled behind a firewall?"

To his credit, he looked embarrassed as he said, "We were wondering, given the circumstances, if, well . . . if it might not be the best idea for the four of you to go home."

I gaped at him. Rick did the same. Buffy, who had been uncharacteristically silent through the entire exchange with Tate, continued staring at her hands.

In the end, it was Shaun who spoke, slamming his feet flat against the floor as he stood up and demanded, "Are you people *fucking insane*?!"

"Shaun—" said Senator Ryman, raising both hands in a placating gesture. "If you'd just be reasonable here—"

"Pardon me, *sir*, but you gave up your right to ask me to do that when you suggested we run out on the story," Shaun snapped, voice tight. Out of everyone in the room, I was the only one who understood how much that degree of self-control was costing him. Shaun's temper doesn't show itself often, but when it does, "duck and cover" is the best approach. "Don't you think we owe it to our viewers to finish what we started? We signed up for the long haul! We don't get to cut our losses and run as soon as things start getting a little bit uncomfortable!"

"My daughter *died*, Shaun!" said the senator. He was suddenly on his feet, leaving Emily abandoned and looking lost on the couch. "Do you understand that this is more than a story to us? Rebecca is *dead*! Telling the truth isn't going to bring her back to life!"

"Neither is telling a lie," said Rick, his tone so calm that it seemed almost out of place among the heated exchanges. We all turned to look at him. His head was up, his expression clear as he looked from Senator Ryman to Governor Tate. "Senator, believe me when I say I understand your pain more than you can know. And I understand that concern is making you listen to bad advice," he glanced toward the governor, who had the grace to redden and scowl, "that says we're civilians, and you should get us out of harm's way. But, sir, it's too late for that. This is news. If you send us away, you're just going to get other reporters sniffing around, looking for a story. Reporters who, if you'll allow me to beg your pardon, you can't control. Now, we have a working relationship, and you know we'll listen to you. Can you honestly expect that from anyone else who might be attracted to this scoop?"

"I think we should go," said Buffy. I turned to her, eyes going wide. Still looking at her hands, she continued. "We didn't sign up for this. Maybe Rick's right, and maybe other people will come, but who cares?" She glanced up through the fringe of her hair and licked her lips. "If they want to come and die, that's their problem. But I'm scared, and he's right. We shouldn't be here anymore. If we were ever supposed to be here at all."

"Buffy," said Shaun, sounding stung. "What are you talking about?"

"This is just a *story*, Shaun, and everywhere we've gone, horrible things have happened." She raised her head, expression miserable. "Those poor people in Eakly. The thing at the ranch. Senator Ryman, I think you're a wonderful man, but this is just a story, and we shouldn't be in it. We're going to get hurt."

"That's exactly why we have to stay," I said. My disappointment didn't show in my voice; I found that astonishing. I wanted to slap Buffy. I wanted to shake her and demand to know how she could be so blind to the importance of telling the truth after everything we'd been through together. Instead, I faced the room, and my voice stayed calm as I said, "Everything is 'just a story.' Tragedy, comedy, end of the world, whatever, it's just a story. What matters is making sure it's *heard*."

"That attitude, young lady, is why it's time for you to go," said Governor Tate. "We can't trust you to keep your mouth shut when *you* decide it's time for the story to be told. Your judgment isn't the yardstick here. National security is. And I don't think you fully understand the dangers you could place us in."

"Now, David——" said the senator.

"Nice stand for freedom there, Governor," I snapped.

"Can you *believe* this bullshit?" demanded Shaun.

"On the plus side, 'Faithful Reporters Fired from Campaign as Veil of Censorship Descends' has a nice ring to it," said Rick. "I figure that's a rating spike, right there."

"Ratings! All you concern yourself with——"

"Be quiet," said Emily.

"——is your precious by God ratings!" Governor Tate was getting into it now, his face flushing with religious fire. He'd found his latest opponents, now that Senator Ryman was off the menu. Us. "A little girl dies, a family is shattered, a man's run to the presidency may not recover, and what do you care about? Your damn *ratings*! Well, you can take those ratings, and——"

We never found out what we could do with our

ratings. The sound of Emily's palm striking Governor Tate's cheek rang through the room like a branch breaking; the only thing that could have been louder was the silence that came after it. Governor Tate raised his hand to his cheek, staring at her like he couldn't believe what he was seeing. I couldn't blame him. I couldn't believe what I was seeing either, and I wasn't the one who'd been slapped.

"Emily, what—" began Senator Ryman. She raised her hand for silence, and then slowly, deliberately, removed her sunglasses, eyes on Governor Tate the whole time. The unforgiving light flooding the room had caused her pupils to expand until her irises were entirely gone, drowning in blackness. I winced. I knew how much that had to be hurting her, but she didn't flinch. She kept staring at Tate.

"For the sake of my husband's political career, I will be pleasant to you; I will smile at you at public functions, and I will, whenever a camera or member of the undiscriminating press is present, endeavor to treat you as if you were a human being," she said, in a calm, almost reasonable tone. "But understand this: If you *ever* speak to these people in that sort of manner in my presence again? If you *ever* behave as if they have no judgment, no compassion, and no common sense? I'll make you wish you'd never joined this ticket. And if I come to believe that your attitude is in any way changing my husband—not damaging his oh-so-precious career, but changing who he is *as a man*—I will repudiate you, and I will *end* you. Do we have an understanding, Governor?"

"Yes, ma'am," said Governor Tate, sounding about as stunned as I felt. A glance to Shaun showed that he was probably feeling much the same. "I think you've made yourself clear."

"Good." Emily turned toward us. "Shaun, Georgia, Buffy, Rick, I hope you won't let this unpleasant little scene sour you against my husband's campaign. I speak for both of us when I say that I very much hope you'll continue doing exactly what you've been doing for us."

"We signed on for the good and the bad alike, Mrs. Ryman," said Rick. "I don't believe any of us are planning on going anywhere."

Looking at Buffy, I wasn't sure. "He's right, Emily," I said. "We're staying. Assuming, of course, the senator wants us to . . . ?" I looked his way, and waited.

Senator Ryman looked uncertain. Then, slowly, he nodded and rose, moving to put his arm around his wife's shoulders. "David, I'm afraid I'm going to have to vote with Emily on this one. I very much want them all to stay."

"Well, Senator," I said, "I think our partnership is still good."

"Good," he replied. Reaching out, he took my hand and shook it.

* * *

The trouble with the news is simple: People, especially ones on the ends of the power spectrum, like it when you're afraid. The people who have the power want you scared. They want you walking around paralyzed by the notion that you could die at any moment. There's always something to be afraid of. It used to be terrorists. Now it's zombies.

What does this have to do with the news? This: The truth isn't scary. Not when you understand it, not when you understand the repercussions of it, and not when you aren't worried that something's being kept from you. The truth is only scary when you think part of it might be missing. And those people? They like it when you're scared. So they do their best to sit on the truth, to sensationalize the truth, to filter the truth in ways that make it something you can be afraid of.

If we didn't have to fear the truths we didn't hear, we'd lose the need to fear the ones we did. People should consider that.

—From *Images May Disturb You*,
the blog of Georgia Mason, April 2, 2040

Seventeen

We spent three weeks in Parrish before it was time for the campaign to get back on the road. The voters would forgive the senator taking time to mourn for his daughter, but unless he got out there and made sure people remembered him as more than the victim of a senseless tragedy, he'd never make up the ground he was already losing. Voters are a fickle bunch, and Rebecca Ryman's heroic death was already yesterday's news. Instead, the news was buzzing with Governor Blackburn's exciting plans for heath-care reform, her suggestions for increasing school security, and her proposed alterations to the animal husbandry and care laws. In some ways, her campaign was using Rebecca as much as the senator's was, because when she said "tougher restrictions on keeping large animals," it was Rebecca's face people saw. The senator needed to get rolling or there wouldn't be anywhere for him to roll to.

Unfortunately, our swift departure from Oklahoma City left the convoy of RVs and equipment trucks we'd been depending on to get us across the country several states behind us. This became an issue as we were preparing to set out from Wisconsin, especially since our newly tightened schedule didn't leave time to go back and get them. How were we supposed to get ourselves, the senator, his staff, the security detail, and the equipment—some of which was new to the campaign, having joined us with Governor Tate—to our destination when we didn't have a means of protected travel?

The answer was simple: We weren't. Instead, the senator, his wife, the governor, their respective campaign managers, and the bulk of the staff flew ahead to our next stop in Houston, Texas, where they could meet up with the convoy and really get things started. The rest of us were left with the exciting task of getting ourselves and the equipment that *hadn't* been abandoned in Oklahoma to Texas via the overland express. There was no train from Parrish to Houston large enough to haul the additional equipment, but that worked out since Shaun and I were unwilling to abandon our vehicles. One way or another, we were driving it.

We initially planned to make the drive alone: just the After the End Times crew, reconnecting with one another through the time-honored ritual of the road trip. This plan got shouted down on all fronts, starting with Senator Ryman and moving down the chain to Steve. The argument that we'd travel faster without a bunch of extra bodies didn't hold water where they were concerned, but we managed to find a compromise after three days of shouting. We'd take a security team. We were exhausted enough after that fight to give in on the matter of Chuck, who needed to monitor the transportation of some of the more sensitive equipment. Besides, his presence might keep Buffy a little calmer, and we needed all the help we could get in that regard.

The tension between Buffy and the rest of us had been getting worse since our meeting with the Rymans and Governor Tate. None of us had expected her to endorse the idea that we should walk away. It was a betrayal of everything we worked for, and it came out of nowhere. Rick took it hardest. As far as I knew, he hadn't spoken to Buffy since we got back to the hotel. Buffy looked at him sorrowfully, like a dog that knew it had done something wrong, and went back to the task of getting our equipment ready for the road. By the time we were ready to roll, I think she'd rebuilt every piece of camera equipment we owned at least twice, in addition to upgrading our computers and replacing the memory chips in my PDA.

Shaun and I didn't have anything that practical to concern ourselves with. I managed to stay distracted by conducting remote interviews with every politician I could get my hands on, working with Mahir to update our merchandising, and cleaning up the message boards. Shaun lacked those outlets. The government had banned him from going back to the ranch during the investigation, and Parrish was otherwise short of things for him to poke at. He was restless, unhappy, and making me insane. Shaun doesn't handle idleness well. Make him sit still too long, and he winds up silent, sullen, and, above all, touchy as hell.

Shaun's crankiness, combined with everything else, was the reason for our caravan traveling arrangements. Rick was in his little blue armadillo with the barn cat, which he'd named "Lois" after it received a clean bill of health from the Ryman family veterinarian. Shaun was in our van, blasting heavy metal and brooding, while Buffy was riding with Chuck in the equipment truck at the rear of the convoy.

My own place in the driving order was a little less predictable since I was on my bike and unconstrained by the shape of the road. I kept my cameras running the whole time, privately hoping I'd find a shambler for Shaun to amuse himself with. That was all he'd need to bring his spirits up. We'd been driving for two days, with another two still ahead of us, and the silence was starting to wear on me.

My helmet speaker crackled. "On," I said to activate the connection, following it with, "Georgia here."

"It's Rick. What do you think about dinner?"

"The sun went down an hour ago, and dinner is traditionally the evening meal, so I think dinner is logically our next stop. What are we looking at?"

"GPS says there's a truck stop about two hours up the road that has a pretty decent diner."

"Any record on their screening protocols?" We'd run into multiple truck stops where the security agents wouldn't let us eat because their blood tests weren't good enough to guarantee we wouldn't have to worry about an outbreak between the coffee and the pie. I'd been driving all day. If we stopped, I wanted it to be for more than fifteen minutes and an argument.

"They're government certified. All their licenses up to date, all their inspection scores posted."

"Sounds good to me. I'll see if I can rouse Shaun and let him know what the plan is. You call Steve and the guys, give them the address, and tell them we'll meet there."

"Deal."

"Coffee's on me. Georgia out."

"Rick out."

"Great." I followed it with, "Disconnect and re-dial Shaun Mason." The speaker beeped acknowledgment, and began to ring as it signaled my brother.

He never picked up the call. He didn't have the time.

I didn't hear the gunshots until I went back to review the tapes and turned the low-level frequencies up enough to undo the work of the silencers. Eight shots were fired. The first two trucks, the ones containing the campaign guards and lower-level personnel, passed by unmolested. They were rolling ahead of the rest of the crew and passed out of the shallow valley without incident. The gun didn't start going off until Rick's car pulled into the ideal position, halfway between the valley's entrance and its exit.

Two shots were fired at Rick's little blue armadillo, two more were fired at the van, and the two after that were fired at my bike. The last two shots were fired at the equipment truck at the back of the caravan, the one Chuck was driving, with Buffy riding shotgun. The shots were very methodical, one following the other as fast as the skill of the shooter would allow. I'd have been impressed if they hadn't been aimed so effectively at me and mine.

The first shot fired at my bike punched a hole in my front tire, sending me weaving out of control. I screamed and swore, fighting with the handlebars as I tried to steady my trajectory enough to keep me from becoming a stain on the side of the road. Even with my body armor, falling wrong would kill me. I was focusing so hard on not toppling over that my driving became impossible to predict, and the second shot went wide. Maybe that's why I was able to believe I'd blown a tire as I let momentum carry me off the edge of the road, rolling onto the uneven ground beyond the shoulder.

I finished steadying myself, dumped speed, and wrenched the bike to a stop twenty yards after I left the road. Panting, I kicked the stand down and unsealed my helmet before turning to stare at the carnage that had overwhelmed the road.

Rick's car was still at the front of the pack, but now it was lying stranded on its back, wheels spinning in the air. The tires on the right-hand side were nothing but shredded rubber stretched over bent steel. The equipment truck was on its side fifty or so yards behind him, smoke oozing from its shattered cabin.

There was no sign of the van.

Suddenly frantic, I fumbled my ear cuff from my pocket and shoved it onto my ear with enough force to leave a bruise that I wouldn't feel until later. "Shaun? Shaun? Pick up your goddamn *phone*, Shaun!"

"Georgia?" The connection was poor enough that his voice crackled in and out, but the relief was unmistakable; it would have been unmistakable even if the connection had been worse. He never called me by my full name unless he was angry, scared, or both. "Georgia, are you okay? Where are you?"

"Twenty yards off the road on the left-hand side, near some big rocks. I'm between the car and the equipment truck. There's smoke, Shaun, has anyone else tried to—"

"Don't make any more calls. I don't know if they can trace them. You stay *right there*, Georgia. Don't you fucking *dare* move!" The connection cut with a sharp, final click. In the distance, I heard tires squealing against the road.

Shaun had sounded panicked. Rick and Buffy were out of communication, the truck was on fire, my bike was down, and Shaun was panicking. That could only mean one thing: It was time to take cover.

Slamming my helmet back over my head, I ducked behind my bike and started surveying the surrounding hills. Short of a rocket launcher, there wasn't much that stood a viable chance of killing me in my body armor. Hurting me, yes, but killing me, not really.

There was nothing. No lights, no signs of motion; nothing.

"—ia? Come in, Georgia?"

"Rick?" I nodded to the right, confirming the connection. "Rick, is that you? Are you okay? Are you hurt?"

"I'm fine. Air bag stopped me from hitting the roof." He coughed. "Chest's a little banged up, and Lois is pissed as hell, but otherwise, we're okay. You?"

"Didn't dump the bike. I'm fine. Any word from Buffy?"

There was a pause. Finally, he said, "No. I was hoping she'd called you."

"Did you try to call her?"

"No word."

"Damn. Rick, what *happened*?"

"You mean you don't *know*?" He sounded genuinely surprised. "Georgia, somebody shot out my damn tires."

"Shot? What do you *mean*, sh—" Shaun came blasting around the curve of the road and off the pavement, moving so fast that our hydraulically balanced and weighted van nearly rocked onto two tires. "Shaun's here. We'll be right there to get you. Georgia out."

"Clear." The connection clicked off.

I pulled my helmet back off and climbed to my feet, waving my hands in the air. Shaun spotted the motion and turned the van toward my location, screeching to a stop beside me. The doors unlocked, and Shaun was throwing himself out of the driver's-side door, his heels slipping on the gravel-covered ground as he ran over to throw his arms around me. I let him crush me against his chest, taking a deep breath.

"You okay?" he asked, not letting go.

"You didn't get a blood test before coming over here."

"Don't need one. If you were infected, I'd know," Shaun said, and let me go. "I repeat, you okay?"

"I'm okay." I climbed in the open van door, sliding over to settle in the passenger seat. Shaun got in behind me. "You okay?"

"Better now," Shaun said, turning the engine back

on and slamming his foot down on the gas. The van leapt forward into a wide curve, rocketing toward Rick's car. "You hear the shots?"

"Bike was too loud. How many?"

"Eight. Two for each of us." He glanced at me. For a brief moment, I saw the raw worry in his eyes. "If they'd nailed both your tires . . ."

"I'd be dead." I leaned forward to open the glove compartment and pull out the .45 I keep there. Suddenly, being outside without a gun in my hand didn't seem like a good idea. "If whoever did this had done their damn homework, you'd be dead, too, so let's not dwell. Word from Buffy?"

"None."

"Great." I pulled back the slide, checking the chamber. Satisfied by my bullet count, I let the slide rack back into place. "So, is this enough excitement for you?"

"Maybe a bit much," he said. For once in his life, he sounded like he meant it.

It was true, though. If our attackers had done their homework, Shaun wouldn't have been driving; he'd have been dying. Normal tires blow when they take a bullet. Even armor plating won't prevent that. But some vehicles are too damn valuable to lose just because you lose a tire, and most vehicles in that class are the sort likely to draw heavy gunfire. So scientists developed a type of tire that doesn't give a damn about gunshots. They're called run flats: You put a bullet in them, and they keep on rolling. I might have skipped them—I did skip them on my bike, where they made the ride unbearably choppy—but Shaun insisted. He bought a new set every year.

For the first time since we got the van, it didn't seem like a waste of money.

Shaun focused on driving, and I focused on trying to page Buffy and Chuck, using every band and communications device we had. We knew communications weren't being jammed; at least some of my messages should have made it through. There were no replies on any channel. I'd been terrified. That's when I started to get numb.

Shaun pulled up next to Rick's car. "Think there's still a shooter out there?"

"Doubtful." I slid the gun into my pocket. "This was a targeted operation. They only took out *our* cars. If they'd been sticking around to make sure they killed us, you'd have kept taking bullets. And I made a damn good target when I first stopped my bike."

"Hope you're right," said Shaun, and opened his door.

Rick watched our approach through the car window, waving his arms to show that he was still alive. He was half-pinned by the air bag and blood was dripping into his hair from a small cut on his forehead, but other than that he looked fine. Lois and her carrier were strapped into the seat next to his. I didn't want to be the one to let that cat out of the box.

I knocked on the glass, calling, "Rick? Can you open the door?" Despite the urgency of the situation, I couldn't help but be impressed by the structural integrity of his little car. It had to have rolled at least once before coming to a stop on its roof, and yet it wasn't showing any dents: just scratches and a crack in the passenger-side window. The folks at VW really knew what they were doing.

"I think so!" he called back. "Can you get me out?"

Mirthlessly, I echoed, "I think so!"

"Not the most encouraging answer," he said, and twisted in the seat, movements constrained by seat belt and air bag, until he could kick the door. On his second kick, I grabbed the handle and pulled. I didn't have to pull that hard; despite the car's inverted position and the beating it had taken, the door swung open easily, leaving Rick's foot dangling in the air. He pulled it back into the car, saying, "Now what?"

"Now I get your belt, and you get ready to fall." I leaned into the car.

"Hurry up, George," said Shaun. "I don't like this."

"No one does," I said, and unsnapped Rick's belt. Gravity took over from there, sending Rick thumping against the roof of the car.

"Thanks," he said, reaching over to unhook Lois's carrier before climbing out. The cat hissed and snarled inside the box, expressing her displeasure. Straightening, Rick eyed his car. "How are we supposed to flip that back over?"

"Triple A is our friend," I said. "Get in the van. We need to check on Buffy."

Paling, Rick nodded and climbed in. Shaun and I were only a few feet behind him. I noted without surprise that Shaun had his own pistol—substantially larger than my emergencies-only .45—with specially modified ammo that did enough damage to human or posthuman tissue that it was illegal without a disturbing number of licenses, all of which Shaun obtained before he turned sixteen—out and at the ready. He wasn't buying my glib assurances of our safety. That was fine. Neither was I.

Shaun took my assumption of the driver's seat with just as little surprise and didn't bother fastening his belt as I slammed the gas pedal down, sending the van racing across the hard-packed ground between us and the still-smoking equipment truck. The truck wasn't likely to burst into flames; that only happens in the movies, which is almost a pity, given the number of zombies that arise from automotive accidents every year. Buffy and Chuck could die from smoke inhalation if we dawdled . . . assuming they weren't dead already.

Rick braced himself against the seat. "Has there been any word from Buffy?"

"Not since the truck went down," Shaun said.

"Why the hell didn't you go for her first?"

"Simple," I said, steering around a chunk of rubber torn from the truck's tires. "We knew you were alive, and we might need the backup."

Rick didn't say anything after that until we pulled up alongside the equipment truck. Shaun reached between the seats and pulled out a double-barreled shotgun which he passed to Rick. "What am I supposed to do with this?" Rick demanded.

"You see anything moving that isn't us, Chuck, or Buffy, you shoot," Shaun said. "Don't bother checking to see if it's dead. It'll be dead after you hit it."

"And if I hit emergency personnel?"

"We're stranded, and we've been the victims of a malicious attack in possible zombie territory," I said, stopping the engine and opening my door. "Cite *Johnston's*, and you'll get a medal instead of a manslaughter conviction." Manuel Johnston was a truck driver with several DUIs on his record, but when he gunned down a dozen zombies in highway patrolmen's uniforms outside Birmingham, Alabama, he became a national hero. Since Johnston, it's been legal to shoot people for no crime more defined than existing in rural hazard zones. We usually curse his name, since the precedent he set has gotten a lot of good journalists killed. Under the circumstances, he was a savior. "Shaun and I have the truck. You've got point."

"Got it," said Rick, grimly, and climbed out the van's side door as Shaun and I got out and moved toward the still-smoking truck.

It was obvious that the equipment truck had taken the worst of the beatings. Lacking the maneuverability of my bike, the armor of Rick's car, or the paranoia-fueled unstoppability of our van, it had taken two bullets to the front left tire and completely lost control. The cabin was half-smashed when the truck went over. The smoke had thinned without clearing, and that lowered visibility as we started toward the cab.

"Buffy?" I called. "Buffy, are you there?"

A piercing scream was the only answer, followed by a pause, a second scream, and silence. Zombies can scream. They just generally don't.

"Buffy? Answer me!" I ran the rest of the way to the truck and grabbed the handle of the nearer door, wrenching it as hard as I could. I barely noticed removing a layer of skin from my palms in the process. It didn't matter; the door was mashed in when the truck fell, and it wasn't budging. I tried again, yanking even harder, and felt it shudder on its hinges. "Shaun! Help me over here!"

"George, we have to make sure we're covering the area in case of—"

"Rick can do the goddamn covering! Help me while there's still a chance that she's alive!"

Shaun lowered his pistol, cramming it into the waistband of his pants and moving to put his hands over mine. Together, we counted, "One, two, *three*," and yanked. My shoulders strained until it felt like I would dislocate something. The door groaned and swung open, creaking along the groove of the broken frame. Buffy tumbled out onto the glass-sprinkled pavement, coughing hard.

That cough was reassuring. Zombies breathe, but they don't cough; the tissue of their throats is already so irritated by infection that they ignore little things like smoke inhalation and caustic chemical burns, right up until they render the body unable to function.

"Buffy!" I dropped to my knees next to her, feeling glass crunch through the reinforced denim of my jeans; I'd have to check for slivers before I put them on again. I put my hand against her back, trying to reassure her. "Honey, it's okay, you're okay. Just breathe, sweetheart, and we'll get you away from here. Come on, honey, breathe."

"Georgia . . ."

Shaun's voice was strained enough that he sounded almost sick. I looked up, my hand still flat against Buffy's back. "What—"

Shaun gestured for silence, attention fixed on the interior of the truck's cab. His right hand was moving with glacial slowness to the gun shoved into the belt of his jeans. Whatever he was looking at was outside my range of vision, and so I stood, leaving Buffy coughing on the ground as I reached up to remove my sunglasses. The smoke wouldn't irritate my eyes more than they already were, and I'd see better without them.

At first there seemed to be nothing but motion inside the cab of the truck. It was slow and irregular, like someone trying to swim through hardening cement. Then my pupils dilated that extra quarter-centimeter, my virus-enhanced vision compensating for the sudden change in light levels, and I realized what I was looking at.

"Oh," I said, softly. "Crap."

"Yeah," Shaun agreed. "Crap."

Buffy fell out of the cab when we opened the door; Buffy hadn't been wearing her seat belt. Buffy never wore her seat belt. She liked to ride cross-legged in her seat, and seat belts prevented that. Chuck, on the other hand, was a law-abiding citizen who obeyed traffic regulations. He fastened his seat belt every time he got into a moving vehicle. He'd fastened it before the convoy pulled out that morning. He was still wearing it now that he was too far gone to remember how to work the clasp, or even what a clasp was. His hands moved against the air in useless clawing motions as his mouth chomped mindlessly, stimulated by the presence of fresh meat.

There was blood around his mouth. Blood around his mouth, and blood on the seat belt, and blood on the seat where Buffy had been sitting.

"Cause of death?" I asked, as analytically as I could.

"Impact trauma," said Shaun. The creature that had been Chuck hissed at him, opening its mouth and beginning to moan. Unconcerned, Shaun raised his pistol and fired. The bullet hit the zombie square between the eyes, and it stopped trying to reach us, going limp as the message of its second, final death was transmitted throughout the body. Continuing as if he'd never paused, Shaun said, "It must have been instantaneous. Chuck was a small guy. Amplification would have been over in minutes."

"Source of the blood?"

Shaun looked toward me, and then back to Buffy, who was still down on her knees in the broken glass, hugging herself and coughing. "He didn't have time to bleed."

I stayed where I was for a seemingly endless moment, staring into the cab of the truck. Chuck remained slumped and unmoving. I wanted to find something, anything, I could use to explain the blood away. A scalp wound, maybe, or a nosebleed that started when he hit his head and didn't stop until he reanimated. There was nothing. Just one small, sad body, and bloodstains on the passenger seat that didn't match to any visible wounds.

I turned to Buffy, numbly unsurprised to see that Shaun had his pistol out. My feet crunched on the glass as I walked over to her. "Buffy? Can you hear me?"

"I'm dead, not deaf," she said, and lifted her head. Tears had left clean trails through the soot staining her cheeks. "I hear you just fine. Hi, Georgia. Is everyone all right? Is . . . is Chuck . . . ?"

"Chuck's resting now," I said, crouching down. "Shaun, radio Rick. Tell him to come back here, and to bring a field kit."

"George—"

"*Do it.*" I kept my eyes on Buffy and felt, rather

than saw, Shaun's angry stare. I was too close to her. Her body weight was too low, and I was too close; if she was undergoing amplification, I might not be able to move back fast enough. And I didn't care. "Buffy, are you hurt at all? There's some blood we can't identify. I need you to show me if you're hurt."

Buffy smiled. It was a small, utterly resigned expression, one that turned wry as she rolled up her right sleeve and turned her arm toward me, showing the place where a chunk had been bitten out of her forearm. Bone showed through the red. "You mean like this? I must've hit my head on the roof when the truck rolled, because I woke up when Chuck bit me."

The bleeding was already starting to slow. Rapid coagulation of blood; one of the first, classic signs of the Kellis-Amberlee virus going into amplification. I swallowed, saying in a soft, sickened tone, "That would probably account for it."

"I heard the gunshot, you know. If Chuck's 'resting,' it's the sort of rest you don't get better from." Buffy rolled her sleeve primly back down. "You should shoot me now. Take care of things while they can still be tidy."

"Rick's on his way with the field kit," said Shaun, stepping up next to me. He had his gun trained on Buffy the whole way. "She's right, you know."

"He'd just turned when he bit her. There's a chance his saliva hadn't gone live yet," I said, glancing at him over my shoulder. I was lying, to no one more than to myself, but he'd let me. Just for a few minutes, he'd let me. "We wait for the test."

"I was never any good at tests," said Buffy. She shifted on the ground, pulling her knees up against her chest in an unconsciously childlike gesture. "I always failed them in school. Hi, Shaun. Sorry about this."

"Not your fault," he said. His tone was gruff; anyone who didn't know him as well as I do might not have realized how upset he was. "You're taking this pretty well. Considering, y'know. The circumstances."

"Not much we can do about it now, is there?" Her tone was light, but her eyes were beginning to brim with tears. One escaped, running down the channel already cleaned by its peers. "I'm not happy about this. But I'm not going to take it out on you. I have faith that God will reward me for my forbearance."

"I hope you're right," I said, softly. The Catholic church declared all victims of zombie attack martyrs fifteen years ago, to deal with the messy little issue of last rites; it's hard to conduct them when death is fast, unexpected, and filled with teeth.

"I've got the kit!" shouted Rick, jogging up to the three of us. He had the shotgun tucked underneath his arm and a standard blood testing kit in his left hand. He came to a stop as he spotted Buffy, paling. "Please, please, tell me this isn't for you, Buffy."

"Sorry," she said and held up her hands. "Toss it here."

Eyes gone wide in his bloodless face, he tossed her the kit. She caught it with ease, sliding her right hand, the one nearest the bite, into the kit's opening. Then she closed her eyes, not watching the lights as they cycled green to red, green to red.

"You need to read my notes," she said, in a voice so tightly controlled as to be a model of reasonableness and calm. "They're stored on the server under my private directory. Log-in ID is the one I use for my poetry uploads, password is 'February dash four dash twenty-nine,' capital 'F' in 'February.' I don't have time to explain everything, so just read them."

February 4, 2029, was the day the United States government finally acknowledged that Alaska was too well-suited to the undead and would never be able to come below a Level 2 hazard zone. As that made it illegal for anyone without a very special and difficult to obtain license to even *enter* Alaska, much less live there, that was the day they began evacuating the last of the state's residents. Including Buffy's family. Like a lot of the displaced, they never got over losing Alaska.

"You're going to be fine," I said, watching the lights. They were still cycling, still measuring the viral payload of her blood, but the cycle was becoming irregular, hanging on red for six seconds before flashing back to green. The test results were being confirmed, and they were not in Buffy's favor.

"You're too attached to the truth, Georgia," she said. Her voice was serene, at peace with itself. "It makes you a crappy liar." The tears were falling faster now. "I swear I had no idea they were going to do those things. No idea at all. If I'd known, I would never have agreed to it. You have to believe me, I wouldn't have."

The lights had settled on a steady red, as damning as any doctor's report. The viral load Buffy picked up from Chuck's saliva might have been small, but it had been enough. That wasn't the only thing making me go cold. I stood, stepping back next to Shaun, and pulled the gun from my belt. "You wouldn't have agreed to what?"

"They said the country was drifting away from God. They said that we were losing sight of His desires for the nation, and that was why things are the way they are now. And I believed them."

"They who, Buffy?"

"They didn't give me a name. They just said they could make sure things went the way they needed to go. The way they *had* to go for this country to be great again. All I had to do was let them access our databases and follow the Ryman campaign."

Voice gone suddenly hard, Rick said, "When did you figure out what they were using that information to do, Buffy? Before or after Eakly?"

"After!" she said, opening her eyes and turning a plaintive look his way. "After, I *swear* it was after. It wasn't until the ranch that I realized . . . I realized . . ."

My hand shook, sending my aim wavering as I realized what she was saying and what it meant. "Oh, my God. With access to our databases, they'd known exactly where the senator was going to be, what sort of security he'd have, what times we had booked for any given location—"

"It gets worse," said Shaun. His own voice was flat. "She had our databases cued to the senator's databases. Didn't you, Buffy?"

"It seemed practical at the time, and Chuck said it wouldn't hurt anything as long as we stayed out of the more sensitive areas. It made things easier . . ."

"Lots of things," I said. "Like knowing when the ranch would be most vulnerable. You cut them off, didn't you? Told them you wouldn't be giving them anything else."

"How did you know?" She closed her eyes again, shuddering.

"Because they'd have no other reason to try to kill us all." I glanced toward Rick and Shaun. "We stopped being useful. So Buffy's 'friends' tried to take us out."

"My notes," said Buffy, with an air of desperation in her tone. Her tears were stopping. Another classic sign. The virus doesn't like to give moisture away. "You have to read my notes. They'll tell you everything I knew. I didn't know their names, but there are time stamps, there are IPs, you can try to . . . try to . . ."

"How could you do this, Buffy?" demanded Shaun. "How could you possibly have done this? To the senator? To *us*? People have *died*, for God's sake!"

"And I'm one of them. It's time to shoot me. Please."

"Buffy—"

"That's not my name," she said, and opened her eyes. Her pupils had dilated until they were as large as mine. She turned those unnaturally dark eyes toward me, shaking her head. "I don't remember my name. But that isn't it."

Shaun started to swing his pistol into place. I raised my hand, stopping him. "I hired her," I said, quietly. "It's my job to fire her."

I stepped forward, putting my left hand over my right to steady my grip on the gun. Buffy continued looking up at me, her expression calm. "I'm sorry," I said.

"It's not your fault," she replied.

"Your name is Georgette Marie Meissonier," I said, and pulled the trigger.

She fell without another sound. Shaun put his arms around my shoulders, and we stood there, frozen in the night.

Nothing would ever be the same.

BOOK IV

Postcards
from the Wall

Alive or dead, the truth won't rest. My name is Georgia Mason, and I am begging you: Rise up while you can.

—GEORGIA MASON

If you asked me now "Was it worth it? Were the things you got, the things you wanted?" I'd tell you "no," because there isn't any other answer. So I guess it's a good thing that nobody's ever going to ask. They never ask the things that really matter.

—SHAUN MASON

It is the unfortunate duty of the management of After the End Times to announce that the maintainer of this blog, Georgette Marie "Buffy" Meissonier, passed away this past Saturday night, April 17, 2040, at approximately eight-fifteen P.M. Buffy was involved in an automotive accident that led, tragically, to her being bitten by her boyfriend, Charles Wong, who had died and re-awakened only a few moments previously.

Please do not mistake the professional tone of this memo for a lack of compassion or mourning on the part of the staff here at After the End Times. Rather, take it for what it is, a sign of our respect and dismay over her sudden loss.

Buffy's family has been notified, and her entry has been transmitted to the Wall. Her blog and its archives will be maintained in her honor for the lifetime of this site.

Buffy, you will be missed.

—A message from Georgia Mason,
originally published in *By the Sounding Sea*,
the blog of Buffy Meissonier, April 18, 2040

Eighteen

My aim has never been as good as Shaun's, but it didn't matter at close range: Head shots get a lot easier when there's no real distance between you and your target. Even so, I kept my gun raised for several minutes, as much waiting to feel something as waiting for her to move. She was part of my team, part of our inner circle, and she was gone. Shouldn't I have felt *something*? But there was nothing beyond a vague sense of loss and a much stronger sense of onrushing dread.

The sound of Rick retching snapped me out of my fugue. I leaned back against Shaun's arm, sliding my sunglasses back on and feeling their familiar weight settle against my face before I lowered my gun and turned toward the other surviving member of our team. "Rick, what's your status?" He made more retching noises. I nodded. "About what I figured. Shaun, head for the van and get three more field kits."

"And you'll be doing what, exactly, as I leave you

alone in the middle of nowhere with the dead things and Captain Vomit?"

I unzipped the pocket of my jacket and pulled out my PDA, holding it up. "I'll be standing here, keeping an eye on Captain Vomit and calling for help. We'll need to provide clean test results before they'll approach us with anything more useful than bullets. We're going to need a full biohazard squad out here; we have two corpses, we have a contaminated truck, we have Buffy's blood on the ground—"

Shaun froze, going white as he looked from the slivers of glass embedded in the knees of my jeans to my hands, which were red and raw from where the door handle had stripped the skin from my palms. "And we need clean test results," he said, in a voice that bordered on numb.

"Exactly," I said. He looked scared. I distantly wished I could find it in me to be scared, but I couldn't. It wasn't making it past that damned numbness. "Go."

"Going," he said, and wheeled, breaking into a run as he headed for the van.

Rick was still on his hands and knees making soft retching sounds, but the actual vomiting had stopped. I moved to stand beside him, attempting to comfort with my presence as I tapped in an emergency channel call on my PDA. Opening a broad emergency channel while standing near a state highway would broadcast my message to every police scanner, hospital hazmat department, and federal agency within the receiving range. If there was help to be had, we'd have it.

"This is Georgia Carolyn Mason, license number

ABF dash one-seven-five-eight-nine-three, currently located between mile markers seventy-seven and seventy-eight on southbound Interstate 55 with a hazard zone upgrade for the vicinity and a priority-A distress call. Status is stable, awaiting test results on surviving party members. Request acknowledgment."

The reply was immediate. "This is the Memphis CDC. A biohazard team is being dispatched to your location. Please explain your presence in the hazard zone."

It isn't technically illegal to drive the federally maintained highways—people still have to get from place to place—but it's unusual unless you're a trucker, and even they have to file routes stating exactly where they expect to be at each step along the way. Caravans are held to many of the same restrictions. When the rulings first went into effect, some people complained that the government was limiting personal freedom, but they quieted when it was pointed out, rather harshly, that this wasn't as much a matter of tracking the movements of individuals as it was a matter of charting the mobility of potential outbreaks. Most people shut up as soon as "we just want to know where the zombies are going to be" came into the equation.

"Route registry forty-seven dash A, designation Ryman/Tate equipment caravan, registered drivers present at the scene are Georgia Carolyn Mason, Class M license; Shaun Phillip Mason, Class A license; Richard Cousins, Class C license; Charles Li Wong, Class A license. Registered passengers Georgette Marie Meissonier, Class C license. Purpose of trip registered as movement of heavy equipment from Parrish, Wisconsin, to Houston, Texas. Registered duration, four days, allowing for reasonable rest stops and sleeping periods for the available drivers. Two of our trucks are still on the road; I'm not sure of their status. If you give me your network key, I can transmit our precise route."

The man's tone was gentler when he spoke again; my information had been fed into his computer and was checking out clean. "That won't be necessary, Ms. Mason. Why are y'all calling for a hazard team?"

"Someone shot out the tires on three of our vehicles. We're down a car, with possible injuries to the driver. The rear equipment truck flipped. The driver, Charles Wong, was killed in the impact and reanimated before we were able to reach the vehicle. He infected his passenger, Georgette Meissonier. Her test results are recorded in a standard field test unit, manufacturer Sony, model number V dash fifteen dash eleven dash A, and were registered via wireless upload with the CDC mainframe at the time of confirmation. Due to the possibility of inaccurate positive with that model number, we did not take immediate action but maintained a safe distance until Ms. Meissonier began to experience pupil dilation and memory loss. Once her infection was confirmed, she was put down honorably." There was the grief and outrage, at last, beginning to chip away at the edges of my numbness. "We have hot blood in the cab of the truck and on the ground outside the truck, as well as two hot corpses in need of removal and disposal."

"The team will not approach until preliminary test

results for the surviving members of your party have been uploaded, and they will not offer direct physical assistance until you've been tested again on the CDC field units they provide," the man cautioned, some of the warmth leeching from his tone. Two bodies and a lot of hot blood on the road outside Memphis could spell an outbreak much larger than our little team. We both knew it. Now we had to contain it.

"Understood." My PDA started beeping, signaling an incoming call. "Sir, may I ask, what is your name?"

"Joseph Wynne, Ms. Mason. Stand tight; our team will be there soon."

"Thank you, Joe," I said.

"God be with you," he said. The line clicked off.

Shifting my PDA to my other hand, I pressed the Receive button. "Georgia." Shaun was running toward me, the field kits clutched against his chest. I raised my free hand, and he lobbed one at me. It was more than a simple game of catch; there are a hundred small tests and checks for infection that don't depend on medical science. If he could throw, and I could catch, the odds were better that we were both clean. I saw him relax when I caught the kit, even though he didn't slow down.

Senator Ryman's voice came through the receiver, made sharp and tight by panic: "Georgia, what's this I'm getting on the scanner about an accident? Is everyone all right out there?"

"Senator." I nodded to Shaun. He put Rick's testing kit down next to him, and the two of us popped the lids off our respective kits in comforting unison. Routine is the most reassuring thing there is. "I'm afraid I have to answer in the negative, sir, but the CDC is dispatching a biohazard team to our location. Once we have an all-clear, we're going to need a fresh truck and a team to move the equipment." I hesitated before adding, "We're also going to need a new driver. Rick doesn't have his Class A license, and I don't want to leave my bike behind."

There was a long pause, during which I tucked my PDA between my shoulder and my ear, freeing my hand, and mouthed a silent "one, two" at Shaun. On two, we both rammed our forefingers down on the unit the other held. The prick of the needle puncturing my thumb made me wince, nearly dislodging the PDA.

Finally, while the lights were blinking red to green and back again, the senator said, "Georgia . . . is Chuck . . . ?"

I closed my eyes, blocking those ever-hateful lights, and said, "I'm sorry, Senator."

He paused again. "Georgia . . ."

"Yes, Senator?"

"Buffy. Wasn't she . . ."

"I'm afraid that when the truck rolled, we were unable to save either of the occupants."

"Oh, Christ, Georgia, I'm sorry."

"So am I, sir; so am I. Can you arrange for another truck and driver to be sent to our location, and alert the rest of the convoy that we're being unavoidably delayed? We're just outside Memphis. You should be able to pull us up on the team GPS."

"I'll have someone on the way inside the next ten minutes." The third pause was longer than the other two, and when he spoke again, he sounded more exhausted than I'd ever heard him, even after we received the news of Rebecca's death. "Georgia, have the rest of you . . . have you . . ."

"The tests are running now. If anything changes, we'll call you."

"Thank you. I suppose I should let you get to it."

"That would be best."

"God save you, Georgia Mason," he said, and ended the call before I could say good-bye.

Lowering the PDA, I opened my eyes, looking to Shaun's face and avoiding the lights entirely. "He's sending help," I said.

"Good," he replied. "We're not infected."

I allowed myself to glance down to the field kits, whose lights had settled on a steady green. I took a single shallow breath, followed by another deeper one, and nodded. "Better." Turning, I looked at Rick. "Rick, we need a blood test."

"What?" He raised his head, eyes wide and blank.

"A blood test. The field kit is next to you. The biohazard team won't approach until we're either checked out clean or dead." I pulled my finger free, feeling the antiseptic tingle in the pinprick wound, and shook my hand briskly before depressing the signal button at the base of the kit. That would activate the built-in wireless transmitter, uploading the results into the CDC mainframe. A manual upload is only necessary in the event of a negative; the CDC doesn't care, under normal circumstances, about the fact that someone *isn't* about to turn into a zombie. Buffy's results uploaded themselves the second the lights settled on red. Once you've tested positive, the

CDC knows. Disabling the upload functionality of a blood testing unit is a federal offense.

Shaun mirrored my actions. He held out his hand and I passed him his test kit, which he dropped into one of the plastic bags he pulled from his belt. My test kit went into a separate bag, which he handed to me. Again in semi-unison, we pressed down the pressure seals, leaving our respective thumbprints on the corners of our bags. If they were tampered with in any way, the seals would turn scarlet and the kits inside would become worse than useless; they would become suspect.

"I . . . I'm not sure I can," said Rick, swallowing. "Buffy . . ."

"Buffy's dead, and so is Chuck. We need to know if you're clean." I handed the bag back to Shaun and moved to crouch next to Rick, picking up his test unit and popping off the plastic cover to reveal the pressure pad and needle inside. "Come on. You know the drill. It's just a little pinprick."

"What if the lights go red?"

"Then we'll sit with you until the CDC gets here; they have better units than we do, and they're on their way," I said, keeping my voice as reasonable as I could. I felt like crying. I didn't dare. Rick looked like he was barely holding himself together; if I started to cry, his control might shatter. "Unless you actually start to convert, we'll take no actions."

"If the lights go red, you'll take action immediately," he said, and his voice was suddenly cold, devoid of hesitation. "I want that bullet in my brain before I know what's going on."

"Rick—"

He leaned forward, jamming his thumb down on the needle's point. "I'm not upset that you shot her, Georgia. I'm upset that she had to go that far before you could." He tilted his face upward, looking to Shaun, then to me. "My son converted before he died. Please do me the great kindness of letting me die while I remember his name."

"Of course," I said and straightened, stepping back to my customary place beside Shaun. He raised his right hand, placing it against the middle of my back, while his left hand moved to rest, ever so lightly, on the holster of his pistol. If we lost a second teammate today, the bullet wouldn't be mine. Sometimes you have to spread the guilt around.

"I didn't know you had a kid, Ricky-boy," said Shaun, his tone almost jovial. "What else haven't you been telling us?"

"I wear women's underwear," Rick said. Then, very slightly, he smiled. "I'll show you his picture sometime. He just . . . he's the reason I left print media. Too many people there remembered him, and too many of them had known his mother. Too many people looked at me differently after I lost them. I still loved the news. But I didn't want to *be* the news. So I found another way to get the story out there."

The lights were flashing, red to green to red. "What was your son's name, Rick?" I asked.

"Ethan," Rick said, his smile growing more sincere and coloring with sorrow. "Ethan Patrick Cousins, after my father and his mother's grandfather. Her name was Lisa. His mother, I mean. Lisa Cousins. She was beautiful." He closed his eyes. "He had her smile."

The lights stopped flashing.

"We'll remember their names for you, if it ever comes to that," I said, "but it won't be today. You're clean, Rick."

"Clean?" He opened his eyes, looking at the test kit like it was some alien thing he'd never seen before. Then, slowly, he removed his finger from the needle and pressed the transmission button. "Clean."

"Which is a damn good thing because there was no way I was taking care of your mangy cat," said Shaun.

"He's right," I said, moving to offer a hand to Rick, to help him off the ground. "Shaun would have tossed her out the window at the first truck stop we passed."

"Now, George, don't be silly," chided Shaun. "I would've waited for one that had a 'Beware of Dog' sign. It wouldn't do for Lois to not have any *friends*."

Rick and I exchanged a startled look before we burst out laughing. I started to cry at the same time, and pulled Rick to his feet before slinging my arms around his shoulders and using him to steady myself. Shaun walked over and put his arms around the both of us, joining our laughter and smashing his face into my hair to hide his own tears. I knew they were there; Rick didn't need to. Some secrets don't need to be shared.

We stayed that way until the sound of tires alerted us to the approach of the biohazard convoy. Hastily, we pulled apart, trying to get ourselves into something that approached composure; Rick wiped his face with one hand, while Shaun dried his cheeks and I raked my fingers through my hair before shoving my sunglasses up the bridge of my nose. Looking to Shaun, I nodded and started toward the sound of the approaching vehicles, carrying my bagged test in one hand, digging my license beacon out with the other.

The convoy stopped about twenty yards away from the forerunning vehicle; my poor, abandoned motorcycle. The Memphis CDC didn't play around. They'd sent a full unit: two troop carriers with their standard Jeep-style frames surrounded by steel-reinforced clear plastic armor, a white medical van nearly twice the size of ours, and, most ominously, two of the vast armored trucks media pundits call "fire trucks." They were huge, painted safety orange with red biohazard signs blazoned on all sides, and their hoses didn't squirt water; instead, they delivered a nasty high-octane variant on napalm mixed with a concentrated form of insecticide. Once a fire truck sprays something down, it's sterile. The soil would be dead for decades, and anything that happened to be in the radius and alive when the trucks came wouldn't be breathing afterward, but the area would be clean.

One of the men in the foremost troop carrier raised a microphone as we approached, and the loudspeaker at the front of the car blared, "Put down your testing units and step back. Clean units will be put in their place. Do not approach personnel. Failure to comply with instructions will result in termination."

The headlights of the convoy were almost blinding, even through my sunglasses. I raised the hand with my license to shield my eyes, and squinted at the troop carrier. "Joe? Is that you?"

"Got it in one, darlin'," the voice replied, less formally. "Just go ahead and set those units on down, if you'd be so kind?"

"I'm leaving my license beacon with the test," I called. "It includes important medical data." If these people made me take my glasses off, the glare from their headlights would probably blind me.

A new voice, female and substantially more clinical, came over the loudspeaker. "We know about your retinal condition, Ms. Mason. Please comply with instructions."

"We're complying, jeez!" shouted Shaun, dropping his bagged testing unit and putting his license beacon on top. I bent to put mine down, somewhat more gently, and Rick did the same. The three of us then started backing away.

We made it about twenty feet before Joe's voice came over the speaker again, saying, "That's far enough, darlin'. You three hold tight, now." The door of the medical van opened and three technicians in biohazard containment suits emerged. I could hear the chugging of their positive pressure unit as it cycled the air, keeping outside particles from entering their sterile zone.

Moving with the sort of grace that implied hundreds, if not thousands, of hours spent in the bulky suits, the technicians walked over to collect our test kits and beacons, putting three sealed kits in their place. With this accomplished, they retreated, and Joe's voice called, "Please approach, open the testing units, and stay where you are until you've checked out clean."

"It's like playing Simon Says," muttered Shaun as we started forward.

"Where I grew up, Simon didn't usually have a truck full of napalm pointed at you," said Rick.

"Pansy," said Shaun.

The testing units left by the CDC technicians were Apple XH-229s, only slightly less advanced than the top of the line. Shaun whistled low under his breath.

"Wow. We really are a threat."

"Something like that," I said. I picked up the first kit and broke the seals with my thumbnail before removing the plastic lid. It was designed to cover my whole hand, all the way to the base of my wrist. There were at least fifteen visible points of contact. Grimacing, I rolled my sleeve up and slid my hand inside.

The mist of antiseptic across my skinned palm was deceptively soothing, a feeling that lasted only a second before needles drove themselves into my already damaged flesh, starting to sift through my blood looking for active viral bodies. The lights began to cycle, moving from red to yellow to green as the more advanced medical processes kicked in.

I was so intent on the lights and what they could mean about my future that I didn't hear the footsteps behind me over the drone of the positive pressure units, or feel the hypo until it was pressed against my neck. A wash of cold flowed over me, and I fell.

The last thing I saw was a row of lights, settling on a steady green. Then my eyes closed, and I didn't see anything at all.

*   *   *

———————

. . . the question I have been asked most frequently since my transition from the traditional news media to the online world is "Why?" Why would I want to give up an established career to strike out into a new field, one where my experience would not only be laughed at, but would actually work against me? Why would any sane man—and most people regard me as a sane man—want to do something like that?

For the most part, I've replied with the pretty, expected lies: I wanted a challenge, I wanted to test myself, and I believe in telling the truth and telling the news. Only that last part is true, because I *do* believe in telling the truth. And that's what I'm doing today.

I married young. Her name was Lisa. She was smart, she was beautiful, and, above all, she was as crazy in love with me as I was with her. We were still in college on our wedding day. I was going to be a journalist, and she was going to be a teacher—a career path that got put on hold when, three days after graduation, the pregnancy test came up positive. That was a test we passed, and gladly. It was the only test we passed.

Our son, Ethan Patrick Cousins, was born on April 5, 2028. He weighed eight pounds, six ounces. And routine testing of his bodily fluids and vital signs revealed a system crawling with the Kellis-Amberlee virus. His mother had condemned him without ever knowing it; further tests showed that the virus had set up camp in her ovaries, reproducing there without infecting her or changing her life in any way. Our son was not so lucky.

I was fortunate. I had nine good years with my son, despite the precautions and quarantines his condition entailed. He loved baseball. On his last Christmas, he wrote to Santa Claus and asked for a cure, so "Mommy and Daddy won't be sad anymore." He underwent spontaneous viral amplification two months and six days after his ninth birthday. Posthumous examination of his corpse displayed a final body weight of sixty-two pounds, six ounces. Lisa took her own life. And me? I found a new career.

One where I'm still allowed to tell the truth.

**—From *Another Point of True*,
the blog of Richard Cousins, April 21, 2040**

Nineteen

I woke in a white bed in a white room, wearing white cotton pajamas, with the cloying white smell of bleach in my nose. I sat up with a gasp, screwing my eyes shut in an automatic attempt to keep them from being burned by the overhead lights before I realized that I'd opened my eyes while I was lying on my back. I looked directly into the lights, and it hadn't hurt at all. A lack of sensitivity to pain is one of the many warning signs of early Kellis-Amberlee amplification. Was that why the CDC decided to attack us? Was I in some sort of fucked-up research facility? Rumors always abound, after all, and some of them just might be true.

Cautious now, I reached up to touch my face. My fingers found a thin band of plastic resting above my eyes, balanced to put next to no pressure on either the bridge of my nose or the sides of my head. I knew what it was when I felt it; they've been using polarized UV-blocker strips for hospital treatment of retinal KA for about fifteen years now. They're expensive as hell—just one can add five hundred dollars or more to your bill, even after insurance, and they're fragile, to boot—but they filter light better and less noticeably than any other treatment mechanism we've found so far. I relaxed. I wasn't amplifying. I was just a CDC kidnap victim.

It says something about the situation that I was able to find this reassuring.

I began studying the room. It was empty, except for me, the white bed with its white sheets and white duvet and white pillowcases, a white bedside table with foam-padded edges that rendered it effectively useless as a weapon, and a large tinted "mirror" that took up most of the wall next to the door. I squinted at the glass, looking into the sterile hallway beyond. There was no one watching my room. That spoke well for my continued nonzombie status. They'd have had guards out there if I was infected, assuming they had some reason not to have just shot me already.

If it hadn't been for my ocular condition, that "mirror" would have seemed like the real thing, allowing me the illusion of privacy while letting any attending physicians watch me from a distance. The days of beeping monitors and bulky machines are over; everything is streamlined now, all micromesh sensors and carefully concealed wireless monitors. It's as much for the protection of the doctors as it is for the comfort of the patients. After all, every reason to go into the room with someone who might go into viral amplification at any moment is another reason to stop practicing medicine and go into a safer profession. Like journalism.

Not that journalism seemed particularly safe at the moment. I closed my eyes. Buffy was right there waiting for me, looking up with virus-dark eyes as the infection took hold and the essential core of her dissolved. I got the feeling she always would be there. For the rest of my life, she'd be waiting.

Kellis-Amberlee is a fact of existence. You live, you die, and then you come back to life, get up, and shamble around trying to eat your former friends and loved ones. That's the way it is for everyone. Given what my parents do and what happened to their son, it might seem like it's had a huge impact on my family, but the fact is, all that happened before Shaun and I were old enough to understand. The virus is background noise to us. If it hadn't existed, Shaun and I would have found something else to do with our spare time, something that didn't involve poking zombies with sticks. Until Chuck and Buffy, it had never actually taken anyone away from me. It touched people I cared about. It killed acquaintances, like the security guards we lost in Oklahoma, or Rebecca Ryman, who I knew from pictures, if not from actual meetings. But it never touched *me*. Not until Memphis.

I opened my eyes. All the brooding in the world wasn't going to bring Buffy and Chuck back, and it didn't change the facts of the situation: The Memphis CDC had, for whatever reason, drugged us and transported us to a holding facility. I didn't have my clothes, my weapons, or any of my recording equipment. My ears were bare; they'd taken my short-range cellular devices along with everything else. Even my sunglasses were gone, replaced by a UV blocker that, while doubtless more effective, left me feeling naked.

My mother once told me that no woman is naked when she comes equipped with a bad mood and a steady glare. Fixing that fact at the forefront of my mind, I walked over to the room's single door and tried the knob.

It was unlocked.

That wasn't necessarily good.

The hallway was as sterile as the room where I woke up, all white walls, white floors, and stark white overhead lighting. More of those large faux-mirrors were spaced every ten feet, lining both sides of the corridor. I was in the isolation wing. That was even less reassuring than the unlocked door. Pushing the UV blocker up the bridge of my nose in a gesture that was deeply reassuring if not strictly functional, I started down the hall.

Rick was in the third room on the left, lying atop his bedcovers in white cotton pajamas identical to mine. The CDC isn't big on gender stereotyping. I knocked on the "window" to warn him that I was coming before opening the door and stepping inside.

"Do they actually have room service in this place? Because I'd just about die for a can of Coke right about now. Reanimation strictly optional."

"Georgia!" Rick sat up, relief and delight warring for control over his features. "Thank God! When I woke up in here alone, I was afraid—"

"What, that you were the last one left? Sorry, guy, but you don't get promoted that easily." I leaned against the door frame, assessing him. He wasn't visibly injured. That was good. If we needed to exit in a hurry, maybe he could keep up. "I am, in fact, immortal when annoyed."

"Wow."

"Wow?"

"You'll never die." He paused and raised his right hand, making vague gestures toward his eyes. "Georgia, you're not—"

"It's all right." I tapped the band. "UV-blocking plastic. The latest thing. Technically better than my sunglasses, even if everything is a little bright right now."

"Oh," he said. "Your eyes are brown."

"Well, yeah."

He shrugged. "I never knew."

"Life is an education." Keeping my tone as light as possible, I asked, "So were you just waiting for me? Have you seen Shaun?"

"No—like I said before, I woke up alone. I haven't seen anyone since the CDC Mickeyed us. Any idea what the hell is going on here?"

"I'm thinking it's more like they roofied us, and right now, I'm marginally more interested in finding my brother."

He gave me a speculative look. "You're more interested in your brother than in figuring out the truth?"

"Shaun's the *only* thing that concerns me more than the truth does."

"He's not here right now."

"Which is why we're going to find him." I stepped back into the hall. "Come on."

To his credit, Rick rose without argument. "They didn't lock the doors. That means they don't think we're infectious."

"That, or it means we're already in the middle of an outbreak, and they've sealed this whole wing."

"Aren't you just a little ray of happy sunshine?"

I slanted a tight smile in his direction. "I always have been."

"I understand your brother a little bit more with every day that passes."

"I'm choosing to ignore that remark." The hall was empty, stretching in both directions with no distinguishing features either way. I frowned. "Know anything about isolation ward layouts?"

"Yes."

His answer was surprisingly firm. I glanced toward him, eyebrows raised in silent question. He shrugged.

"Lisa and I spent a lot of time in places like this."

"Right," I said, after an uncomfortable pause. "Which way?"

"CDC iso wards all follow the same basic layout. We go left."

That made sense. Zombies don't learn, and if there's a chance your personnel are uninfected, you want them to know which way to run. It would also serve as a herding mechanism; those that had already amplified but were hoping for a way out would charge straight into the air lock, where a positive blood test would buy them a bullet to the brain.

Rick started walking. I hurried to keep up, and he glanced at me.

"I'm sure Shaun's fine."

"Mmm."

"If he'd amplified, we'd be seeing signs of the outbreak. Or at least smelling fresher disinfectant."

"Mmm."

"I'd like to take this opportunity to say, off the

record, that your eyes are much more attractive when you don't hide them behind those freaky-ass contact lenses. Blue really doesn't suit you."

I gave him a sidelong look.

Rick smiled. "You didn't go 'mmm' at me that time."

"Sorry. I get a little anxious when I don't know where Shaun is."

"Georgia, if this is 'a little anxious,' I never want to see you when you're actually uptight."

I shot him another sidelong look. "You're awfully relaxed."

"No," he said, in a measured tone, "I'm in shock. See, the difference is that if I were relaxed, I wouldn't be walking along, waiting for the reality of Buffy being dead to hit me like a brick to the side of the head."

"Oh."

This time, his smile was small and tight and held not a trace of humor. "Ethan taught me about CDC isolation. Lisa taught me about shock."

I didn't know what to say to that. We walked through the white halls, our white-clad reflections flickering like ghosts in the tinted-glass "windows" until something new appeared up ahead: a steel-barred door with an intercom and a blood testing unit set into the wall next to it.

"Friendly," I said, as we approached.

"The intercom connects to the duty station, and the test unit has an automatic upload function," said Rick.

"Friendly *and* efficient," I amended. I stopped in front of the door and pressed the button for the intercom. "Hello?"

Shaun's voice answered immediately, full of the

rampant cheer only I was likely to recognize as his way of masking grief and fear. "George! You decided to rejoin the world of the living!"

Something in the center of my chest unclenched and I could breathe again. "Good to see you haven't decided to leave it," I said. "Next time, leave me a damn note or something."

"Afraid that's my fault, Ms. Mason," said a deeper, Southern-accented voice. "We try not to leave anything that could serve for a weapon in the rooms. That includes paper. You understand the necessity."

I frowned. "Joe?"

"That's right, and I'm pretty properly glad to see you're both all right."

Both? Rick hadn't said a word since I activated the intercom. I turned and scanned the edge of the ceiling until I found a small discolored patch, off-cream against the white of the tile. Looking directly into it, finger still on the intercom button, I said, "You must have been real popular with the girls in high school. They love Peeping Toms."

"Hey, don't rag on the man, George. This way I get to see your adorable pajamas. You look like Frosty the Snowman. If he were on the rag, I mean."

"Frosty's going to be kicking your ass in a minute," I said. "Can someone tell me what the hell is going on here, before I get seriously pissed?"

"Door won't unlock without a blood test, George," said Shaun.

"Of course it won't." Turning, I slapped my hand down on the reader panel, barely even flinching as the needles bit into my skin. For every needle I felt, there were five more I didn't. The thicker needles on CDC kits are more for psychological reassurance than anything else—people don't believe they've been tested unless they feel the sting. Most of the information the CDC needs comes from hypos so small they're essentially acupuncture needles, sliding in and out without leaving marks.

A light over the door flashed on, going almost immediately from red to green, and the locks disengaged with a loud "click." I removed my hand from the panel.

"I assume alarms go off if Rick tries to follow right through?"

"Got it in one. Head into the air lock, let the door shut, and he can follow you."

"Right." I gave Rick a quick nod, which he returned, and opened the door and stepped through.

If the hallways seemed featureless, the air lock they fed into was antiseptic. The walls were so white that the stark light they reflected was enough to make my eyes ache, even through the UV-blocking strip. Half squinting, I shuffled to the middle of the room.

The intercom crackled, and Joe's voice said, "Stop there, Ms. Mason."

"Close eyes, hold breath?"

"Exactly," he said, with faint amusement in his tone. "It's always a pleasure to work with someone who knows the drill."

"I'm not really in a 'pleasure' place," I said. "Maybe after I have some pants on." Standing around and grousing wasn't going to get me to my clothes, or my brother, any faster. Closing my eyes, I removed the UV blocker, took a deep breath, and held it.

The smell of bleach and disinfecting agents filled

the room as a cool mist drifted down from the vents in the ceiling, blanketing me. I forced myself to keep holding my breath, counting backward from twenty. I'd reached seventeen when the fans kicked on and the mist pulled away, sucked into drains in the floor. It would be pulled into channels of superheated air, baked until any traces of infection that had managed to survive the chemical bath were burned away, and then pumped into an incinerator, where it would be destroyed. The CDC does a lot of things, but it doesn't fuck around with sterilization.

"You can open your eyes now, Ms. Mason."

Sliding the UV blocker back into place, I opened my eyes and proceeded to the door on the air lock's far side. The light above it was green, and when I touched the handle, it swung open without resistance. I continued on.

The duty station was one of those hybrid beasts that have become so common in the medical profession over the past twenty years: half nurse's station and medical triage, half guard point, with alarm buttons posted at several spots around the walls and a large gun cabinet next to the watercooler. A good medical duty station can provide an island of safety for the uninfected, even as an outbreak rages on all sides. If your air locks don't fail and you have enough ammo, you can hold out for days. One duty station in Atlanta did exactly that— four nurses, three doctors, and five security personnel kept themselves and eighteen patients alive for almost a week before the CDC was able to fight through the outbreak raging through the neighborhoods around the hospital and get them safely out. They made a movie about that incident.

Shaun, who had his own clothes on, the bastard, was sitting atop the counter with a cup of coffee in his hands. A man I didn't recognize was standing nearby, wearing a white doctor's coat over his clothes, and Senator Ryman was beside him, looking more anxious than the other two combined. Nurses and CDC techs moved past the station, talking among themselves like extras in a movie background—they completed the setting, but they weren't part of it, any more than the walls were.

The senator was the first to acknowledge my arrival. He straightened, relief radiating through his expression, and moved toward me, catching me in a tight hug before I had a chance to register what he was planning to do. I made a soft "*oof*" noise as the air was shoved out of my lungs, but he just squeezed tighter, seeming unfazed by the fact that my arms remained down by my sides. This was a hug for his comfort, not mine.

"Don't think she can breathe over there, chief," drawled Shaun. "Pretty sure she hasn't kicked the oxygen habit just yet."

The door opened and closed again behind me, and Rick said, sounding surprised, "Why is Senator Ryman trying to crush Georgia?"

"Post-traumatic shock," said Shaun. "He thinks he's a boa constrictor."

"You kids can laugh," said the senator, finally letting go. Relieved, I stepped back before he could decide to do it again. "You scared me to death."

"We scared ourselves pretty badly, too, Senator," I said, continuing my retreat until I was next to Shaun. He put his hand on my shoulder, squeezing.

There was a world of relief in that simple gesture. I leaned into his hand, looking toward the stranger. "Joe, I presume?"

"Dr. Joseph Wynne, Memphis CDC," he said and walked over to extend his hand in my direction. I took it. His grip was solid without being crushing. "I can't begin to say how glad I am to speak with you face-to-face."

"Glad to still be in the shape to speak," I said. Pleasantries accomplished, I frowned. "Now, can someone fill me in on why I was standing next to a highway, doing my civic duty, and suddenly woke up in a CDC iso ward? Also, if I could get hooked up with my clothes, that'd be awesome. I feel kind of naked here, and that's weird when there's a United States senator in the room."

"That's a funny story, actually," said Shaun.

Releasing Joe's hand, I craned my head around to eye my brother. "Define 'funny.'"

Shaun picked up a bundle from the counter on the other side of him and passed it to me. My clothes and a plastic bag containing my gun and all my jewelry. As I hugged the bundle to my chest, he said, with all apparent sincerity, "Someone called the CDC two minutes before you did and told them that we'd all been killed in the accident."

For a moment, all I could do was stare at him. Then, swiveling my head around to direct the stare to Joe and Senator Ryman, I demanded, "Is this true?"

Looking distinctly uncomfortable now, Joe said, "Well, darlin', we have to react to every call we get . . ."

"You had test results from us. You knew we weren't dead."

"Those types of test results can be falsified," Joe said. "We did the best we could."

I nodded grudgingly. Under the strict interpretation of the law, the CDC would have been within its rights to come into the valley, shoot us, sterilize the surrounding area, and deal with our remains. The fact that it took us alive for extensive testing was unusual, because it represented an unnecessary risk on its part—no one would have questioned it if the CDC had killed us.

"What made you take us alive?" I asked.

Joe smiled. "Ain't many people who can make a call that drastic to the CDC and sound that calm about it, Ms. Mason. I wanted to meet anyone who could do that."

"Our parents taught us well," I said. Raising the bundle of clothes and gear, I asked, "Is there a place where I could get dressed?"

"Kelly!" Turning, Joe flagged down a passing woman in a doctor's coat. She was fresh-faced and wide-eyed; she couldn't have been any older than Buffy, and her long blonde hair, clipped back with a barrette, created the illusion of resemblance. A knot formed in my throat.

Joe gestured from the woman to me. "Georgia Mason, Dr. Kelly Connolly. Dr. Connolly, if you could please show Ms. Mason to a changing room?"

Shaun slid off the counter. "C'mon, Rick. I'll show you the men's room."

"Much obliged," said Rick, snagging his own clothes from the counter.

"Certainly, Dr. Wynne," said Kelly. "Ms. Mason, if you'd come this way?"

"Sure," I said, and followed her.

We walked down a short hallway, this one painted a warm yellow, and Kelly opened a door leading into a small locker room. "The nurses change here," she said.

"Thanks," I said. Putting my hand on the knob, I glanced to her. "I can find my own way back."

"All right," she said. Hesitating, she looked at me. I looked back. Finally, she said, "I read your site. Every day. I used to follow you on Bridge Supporters, before you managed to schism off."

I raised an eyebrow. "Really? To what do I owe the honor?"

She reddened. "Your last name," she said, sounding abashed. "I did a report in medical school on human-to-animal transmission of the Kellis-Amberlee amplification trigger. I found you when I was looking for information on your . . . your brother. I stayed for the writing."

"Ah," I said. She seemed about to say something more. I waited, watching her.

Her blush deepened. "I just wanted to take this opportunity to say that I'm sorry."

I frowned. "About . . . ?"

"Buffy?"

It felt like all the blood in my veins had turned to ice. Careful to keep breathing, I asked, "How did you know about that?"

She blinked, surprise unconcealed as she said, "I saw the notice that she'd been added to the Wall."

"The Wall?" I said. "But how would they know to . . . oh, Jesus. The cameras."

"Ms. Mason? Georgia? Are you all right?"

"Huh?" At some point, I'd looked away from her. I looked back, shaking my head. "I just . . . I didn't realize she'd already be on the Wall. Thank you. Your condolences are appreciated." I turned and walked into the changing room without waiting for her to respond, closing the door behind me. Let her think I was rude. I'm a journalist. Journalists are supposed to be rude, right? It's part of the mystique.

Thoughts chased themselves through my head like leaves tumbling in the wind as I stripped off my CDC-issue pajamas and began getting my own clothes on. It took longer than normal because I had to pause every step along the way to get the appropriate recording devices, cameras, and wireless receivers into their assigned pockets. If I didn't, I wouldn't be able to find anything for weeks.

Buffy's death was on the Wall. I should have known it would be, since her family would have been notified, which meant there would have been an obituary, but somehow, knowing that simple fact—that she'd joined all the other victims of this endless plague on the Wall—made her death all the more impossible to deny. More, it reminded me of one crucial fact: We were connected to the rest of the world, even when we were isolated. The cameras were always rolling. And right now, that was what concerned me.

I slid my sunglasses into place, removing the UV blocker as I shoved them up the bridge of my nose. They made me feel less naked than anything else. Reaching up, I tapped my ear cuff. "Mahir," I said.

Several seconds later, Mahir's sleep-muddled voice came over the line, saying, "This had better be good."

"You realize your accent gets thicker when you're tired."

"Georgia?"

"Got it."

"Georgia!"

"Still got it."

"You're alive!"

"Barely, and we're in CDC custody, so I need to make this fast," I said. Mahir, being the good lieutenant that he is, shut up immediately. "I need you to download the footage from the external cameras on the van and my bike, check to make sure it's complete, and then wipe the originals."

"I'm doing this because . . . ?"

"I'll explain later." When I wasn't making the call from inside a government installation, where all communications were likely to be monitored. "Can you do it?"

"Of course. Right away."

"Thanks, Mahir."

"Oh, and Georgia? I'm very grateful that you're still alive."

I smiled. "So am I, Mahir. Get the footage and get some sleep." I tapped my ear cuff, cutting off the call.

Adjusting the collar on my jacket, I schooled my face back toward neutrality and left the changing room, heading for the duty station. The cameras. How could I have forgotten about them, even for a few minutes?

We keep the external cameras recording constantly. Sometimes we've found things when we've gone back to do review, like the time Shaun was able to use some shots of a totally normal highway median to track a pack of zombies hunting near the Colma border. Depending on the angle the shooter was working from, we might be able to use the latest footage to find a murderer. Assuming, of course, that whoever it was hadn't already been able to get to our hard drives, and that Buffy hadn't told any of her "friends" about our filming habits.

I was starting to feel like a conspiracy theorist. But that was all right because this was starting to feel very much like a conspiracy.

Rick had less equipment than I did; he and Shaun were back at the duty station when I arrived, and Rick had acquired a mug of coffee from somewhere. I started to give it a longing look, and stopped as Shaun handed me a can of Coke, still cold enough to have condensation beading on the sides.

"Truly, you are a God among men," I said.

"Now I'm a God, but tomorrow, when you have to stop me from playing with dead things again, you'll be right back to calling me an idiot, won't you?" Shaun said.

"Yup." I lifted the can, cracked the tab, and took a long drink before exhaling. "CDC has decent taste in soda."

"We try," said Joe.

That was the opening I needed. Lowering the can, I turned toward him, secure behind my sunglasses. "You received a call reporting us dead?"

"Time stamp puts it at two minutes before your call came in. The report flashed my screen while I was talking to you."

That explained his request for detailed credentials. "Did you get a name? Or better, a number?"

"Afraid not, on either," Joe said.

Shaun broke in: "It was an anonymous tip made from a disposable mobile phone."

"So the number's in their records—"

"But it doesn't mean anything."

"Cute." I continued watching Joe. "Dr. Wynne—"

"Joe, please. A girl comes back from the other side of 'legally dead,' she gets to call me by my Christian name." My surprise must have shown because he chuckled without amusement, saying, "The CDC gets a call that says you're virus-positive, you're dead until we confirm it's a hoax. It's a standard legal and safety precaution."

I stared at him. "Because it's not like anyone would hoax the CDC."

"No one should be, and believe me, Ms. Mason, when we find the people responsible, they'll be learning that lesson right well." Joe's smile drew down into a scowl. An understandable one: Most of the people who go to work for the CDC do it out of a genuine desire to better the human condition. If anyone's going to find a cure for Kellis-Amberlee, it's almost certainly going to be the Centers for Disease Control, with its near-global approval ratings and even more extensive pocketbooks. Young idealists fight tooth and nail over CDC postings, and only the best ever get them. That means the CDC employs a lot of very proud people, ones who don't take things that besmirch the honor of the institution sitting down.

"I'd be willing to bet that whoever made that call was also responsible for shooting out our tires," I said.

"Well, Ms. Mason—"

"Georgia, please."

"Well, Georgia, it seems like a bit of a sucker bet, and I don't customarily take those. It isn't often someone tries to pull a fast one on the CDC, and a fast one that happens to center on a convoy that's been attacked by snipers, well . . ."

"Do we have any ballistics on the gun the shooter used?"

Joe's expression turned remote. "I'm afraid that's classified."

I glanced at the senator. His own expression was equally distant, his eyes fixed on some point beyond our heads.

"Senator?"

"I'm sorry, Georgia. Doctor Wynne is right; information relating directly to the police investigation of this matter is classified."

I looked at him, grateful for the way my sunglasses concealed the bulk of my expression. Only Shaun was likely to realize how upset I was. "You mean it's classified from the media."

"Now, Georgia—"

"Are you seriously telling me that if I were some random Joe Public, you'd answer my questions, but because I work for a news site, you won't?" His silence was all the answer I needed. "God*dammit*, Peter. We are *dying* for you, and you won't tell us what kind of bullets they're using for the job? Why, because being reporters means we automatically have no sense of discretion? Is that it? We're going to run right out and cause a public panic, because, gee, no one's going to suspect a cover-up when one of our own gets dead and we don't say anything but 'Death sucks'!" I started stepping toward him and stopped as Rick and Shaun each grabbed me by an arm. "Screw you," I spat, not bothering to fight their hold. "I thought you were better than this."

Senator Ryman looked at me, shaking his head in open bewilderment. "She's dead, Georgia. Buffy's dead. Chuck's dead. You *should* be dead, all of you, dead and sanitized, not here and alive, shouting at me for not wanting you to rush right back out and keep getting yourselves killed! Georgia, I'm not keeping this from you because you're a reporter. I'm keeping it from you because I'd rather you didn't die."

"With all due respect, Senator, I think that's a decision you have to let us make for ourselves." I shook my arm free of Shaun's grasp. As soon as Shaun released me, Rick did the same. We looked at Senator Ryman together, waiting for his answer.

The senator glanced away. "I don't want your deaths on my conscience, Georgia. Or on my campaign."

"Well, then, Senator, I guess we'll just have to do our best not to die," I said.

He turned back to us. His expression was bleak. It was the face of a man who'd spent his life chasing a dream and was only now beginning to realize how much it might cost to get it.

"I'll have the reports sent to you," he said. "Our plane leaves in an hour. If you'll excuse me." It wasn't a question, and he didn't wait for an answer. He just turned and walked away.

. . . first time I met Buffy. Man, I didn't even know I was meeting her, y'know? It was one of those types of things. Me and George, we knew we needed a Fictional if we wanted to get hired at one of the *good* sites because you can't just log in and be like "Yo, we're two-thirds of a triple threat, give us our virtual desks." We needed a wedge, something to make us complete. And that was Buffy. We just didn't know it yet.

They do these online job fair things in the blogging community, like Craigslist gone even more super-specialized. Georgia and I flagged our need for a Fictional at the next fair, opened a virtual booth, and waited. We were about to give up when we got a chat request from somebody who IDed herself as "B.Meissonier" and said she didn't have any field experience but she was willing to learn. We talked for thirteen hours straight. We hired her that night.

Buffy Meissonier was the funniest woman I knew. She loved computers, poetry, and being the kind of geek who fixes your PDA before you know it's broken. She liked old TV and new movies, and she listened to all kinds of music, even the stuff that sounds like static and church bells. She played guitar really badly, but she meant every note.

There are people who are going to say she was a traitor. I'll probably be one of them. That doesn't change the fact that she was my friend. For a long time, before she did anything wrong, she was my friend, and I was with her when she died, and I'm going to miss her. That's what matters. She was my friend.

Buffy, I hope they have computers and cheesy television and music and people laughing where you are now. I hope you're happy, on the other side of the Wall.

We miss you.

—From *Hail to the King*,
the blog of Shaun Mason, April 21, 2040

Twenty

The senator and his security team came from Houston to Memphis via the Houston CDC's private plane. Every CDC installation has one fueled and ready at all times. Not because there could be an evacuation—any outbreak large enough to require evacuating an entire CDC installation would leave a distinct lack of uninfected people to actually *evacuate*—but for the transfer of specialists, patients, and, yes, politicians and other such notables from one location to another in a quick, efficient, and, above all, discreet manner. It wouldn't do to set off a public panic because someone had seen, say, the world's leading specialist in Kellis-Amberlee-related reservoir conditions being flown into a populated area. The nation is constantly poised on the edge of a riot, and the CDC is very aware of how easy it would be to be the match that starts the fire.

The last time I was on a CDC plane and conscious of the experience, I was nine and on my way to visit Dr. William Crowell. Dr. Crowell was that "world's leading specialist" I mentioned before, and he thought he might've found a cure for retinal KA. My parents, ever eager to do stupid shit in the name of a good story, flew me to Atlanta to let him test his treatment on me. His cure proved as artificial as his toupee and his "light therapy" left me seeing spots for a month, but I got to ride in an airplane and have an adventure without Shaun. For my nine-year-old self, that was almost enough.

They give you more snacks when you're nine. Also, airplane captains may be willing to let cute little girls in dark glasses hang out in the cabin, but they're not as understanding of adult journalists who just want to get away from their traveling companions. When you added the fact that the senator wouldn't look me in the eye, while Shaun spent the entire flight trying to take his seat apart with a screwdriver swiped from one of the guards, it's no surprise that I was happy as hell to touch down at our destination, even though landing came barely an hour after taking off.

My relief was partially fueled by the fact that CDC regulations forbade the use of wireless devices while in flight, and I hadn't heard from Mahir before we left Memphis. I was switching things on before they even opened the cabin doors. Mail alerts began sounding immediately. I had more than five hundred pending mail messages, and none were the message I wanted.

Six more guards were waiting on the runway, including Steve, who held a wicker cat carrier in one hand. Rick let out a wordless exclamation and pushed past Shaun to snatch the carrier, starting to make cooing noises at the wide-eyed, brush-tailed Lois.

"Cat didn't die," I said, adjusting my sunglasses.

Shaun shook his head. "Man needs a girlfriend."

"Hush. This is a touching reunion."

"I stand by my statement." Shaun tilted his head back, looking up at Steve. "You brought the man his cat."

Looking amused, the enormous security nodded. "I did."

"So where's *my* present?"

"Will the location of your van do?"

"I think so." Shaun glanced to me. "George?"

"I was planning on holding out for a million dollars, but as long as my bike's included in the deal, I guess I can let you off easy. This time." I flashed a thin smile. "Hey, Steve."

"Good to see you breathing, Georgia."

"It's good to be breathing, Steve."

Robert Channing—who got elevated from "chief aide" to "Chief of Staff" as soon as it became apparent that the campaign might have a genuine shot at the White House—pushed past the substantially larger guards, arrowing in on Senator Ryman like a hunting dog going for the kill. "Senator! We have twenty minutes to get halfway across the city, and you *can't* be late or Tate's going to take the stage alone." His tone implied that this would be a horror beyond all reckoning.

"And we can't have that, now, can we?" Senator Ryman grimaced, shooting an apologetic glance our way. "I'm sorry, but . . ."

"The job comes first," I said. "Rick, give me the cat."

Looking alarmed, Rick hugged the carrier to his chest. Lois yowled. "Why?"

"Because despite recent events and rampant stupidity, we're still reporters, assuming we're still allowed to be." I slanted a sidelong glance at the senator. He met my eyes and nodded. Turning back to Rick, I said, "You're going with the senator to cover whatever sort of appearance this is supposed to be—"

"Speaking to the Daughters of the American Revolution," said Robert.

"Right, whatever," I said, waving a hand to indicate my lack of interest in the specifics. "Rick, you're going to attend whatever sort of appearance this is supposed to be, and you're going to find something interesting to say about it. We're going to go check the equipment and see what sort of dive we're supposed to be camping out at."

Rick nodded with obvious regret, holding the carrier out to me. I almost felt bad taking it from him. Only almost. I needed to talk to my brother, and loath as I was to admit it, I needed to do that talking alone. Rick and Buffy had a past; Buffy betrayed us; Rick was still in the equation. If we were going to keep working with the illustrious Mr. Cousins, we had to decide to do it together, and without Rick participating in the discussion. And if we weren't, we needed to have all our ducks in a row before we invited him to seek employment elsewhere.

Sounding affronted, Robert said, "You're staying at the Plaza with the rest of us. It's five stars, all the latest in amenities, and fully licensed security. Senator, I'm sorry, but there isn't any more time to stand around and chat. Come on, please." Not pausing to allow any further discussion, he grabbed the senator by the arm and began steering him toward the waiting car. Rick followed, along with all but two of the security guards.

Steve was one of the guards remaining behind. The other was a Hispanic man I didn't recognize but whose sunglasses were dark enough to either be prescription strength or render him effectively blind. He would have seemed tall next to anyone else; next to Steve, he looked like a normal human.

Shifting Lois's carrier to my left hand, I looked toward Steve. "Babysitters?"

"Bodyguards," Steve replied, without levity. "You folks came close to dying out there on the road. We'd like to see to it that you don't do it again."

"So we don't do any long-distance driving."

"Not good enough."

Shaun stepped up beside me. "Are you planning to stop us from doing our jobs?"

"No. Just to keep an eye on you while you do them."

I could feel Shaun starting to bristle. Being an Irwin means frequently taking stupid chances for the amusement of the cameras. A good Irwin can make going to the corner store for a candy bar and a Coke look death defying and suicidal. The idea of trying to post reports with a security guard looking over his shoulder was probably about as appealing to Shaun as the idea of censorship was to me. I put a hand on his arm.

"So you're saying our jobs have become *so* dangerous that we need to be protected not from the hazards of the living dead, but from the hazards presented by our fellow man?" I asked.

"Not exactly how I would've put it, but you're in the neighborhood," said Steve.

Shaun relaxed grudgingly. "I guess it'll sound good in the headlines," he said, his tone implying that it wouldn't do anything of the kind.

At least he was mollified. Leaving my hand on Shaun's arm, I swung my head around until I was facing the second agent, not depending on my questionable peripheral vision. "I'm Georgia Mason; this is my brother, Shaun Mason. You would be . . . ?"

"Andres Rodriguez, ma'am," he replied. His tone was level. "Do I pass muster?"

"That's a question for the grand jury. You can, however, take us to our hotel now." Lois yowled. I amended: "*Right* now. I think someone's getting cranky."

"The cat isn't the only one," Shaun said.

"Behave," I said. Keeping the hand that wasn't holding the carrier on his arm, we turned and followed the agents to the car.

Steve and Andres took the front, leaving us with the back seat. A sheet of soundproof safety glass cut us off from our bodyguards, turning them into vaguely imposing silhouettes that might as well have been in another car. It was a small blessing, even if I couldn't quite bring myself to relax. I didn't trust it. I didn't feel like I really trusted anything anymore.

Shaun opened his mouth when the engine started, but I shook my head, gesturing toward the overhead light. He quieted. Without Buffy and her tiny armada of clever devices, we had no way of knowing whether the car was bugged. It turned out that even with Buffy we'd had no real way of knowing whether the car was bugged, since she'd sold us out, but at least we'd *believed* we could protect our privacy.

Brow furrowed, Shaun mouthed "Hotel?" I nodded. Once we were in our own space with our own things, we could sweep for bugs and set up an EMP field. After that, we could talk in something resembling security—and we needed to talk. We needed to talk about a lot of things.

The drive from the CDC airstrip to the hotel took approximately twenty minutes. It would have taken longer, but Steve took advantage of the priority override available to government officials and law enforcement, turning on the car's beacon and sliding us straight into the fast side of the carpool lane. The tollbooths flashed green as soon as we came into receiving range. Electronic pay passes have led to a general speed-up, but nothing moves your average driver as fast as knowing that someone else is picking up the ticket for his commute. We must have provided a free pass for dozens of commuters. That almost made up for the fact that we were cutting ahead of them during the beginning rush hour, when five minutes can make the difference between "home at a reasonable hour" and "late for dinner."

Lois yowled the whole way, while Shaun made a vague, disinterested show of trying to pick the lock on his side of the car. My brother's good with locks; the car's security was better. He'd made no progress by the time we pulled off the freeway and turned toward the hotel, and he put away his lock picks with a silent expression of disgust.

The Downtown Houston Plaza was one of those huge, intentionally imposing buildings built just after the Rising, when they still hadn't figured out how to walk the fine architectural line between "elegance" and "security." It looked like a prison coated in pink stucco and gingerbread icing. Palm trees were planted around the exterior, where they utterly failed to blunt the building's harsh angles. There were no windows at ground level, and the windows higher up the building were the dull matte of steel-reinforced security glass. The infected could batter on them for years without breaking through. Assuming they somehow made the intellectual leap necessary to figure out how to use a ladder.

Shaun eyed the building as we circled. It wasn't until the car pulled off at the parking garage entrance that he offered his professional opinion: "Death trap."

"Many of the early 'zombie-proof' buildings were." I adjusted my sunglasses. The garage doors creaked open as Steve waved a white plastic fob in front of the sensors, and we drove on into relative darkness. "What makes this one so deadly?"

"All that froufrou crap on the front of the building—"

"You mean the trim?"

"Right, the trim. It's supposed to be ornamental, right? Doesn't matter. I bet it would bear my weight. So if I get infected but I haven't converted, I can use the trim to climb the building looking for shelter. There are plenty of handholds. So I can get to the roof. And if this place followed the standard floor plan for the time period, there's a helicopter pad up there, and multiple doors connecting it to the interior, so any survivors could use it to evacuate during an outbreak." Shaun shook his head. "Run for the roof, it's covered in the people who ran there before you. And they're not looking for a rescue. They're looking for a snack."

"Charming," I said. The car pulled into a parking space and the engine cut off. "I guess we're here."

The front driver's-side door opened. Steve emerged, heading across the garage floor to the air lock. I tried my own door, but it was still locked; the safety latches hadn't disengaged.

"The hell—? Shaun, try your door."

He did, and scowled. "It's locked."

The car intercom clicked on. Andres's voice, distorted by the speakers, said, "Ms. Mason, Mr. Mason, if you could be patient for a moment. My colleague is going to pass through the air lock and will wait for you on the other side. The lock on the right will be disengaged as soon as he's tested clean, and Ms. Mason will be permitted to proceed. Once Ms. Mason has passed through the air lock, Mr. Mason will be permitted to go."

Shaun groaned. "Oh, you have *got* to be kidding me."

The intercom clicked again. "Standard safety precautions."

"You can take those safety precautions and shove 'em sideways up your—" Shaun began, pleasantly. I put a hand on his arm. He stopped.

"Mr. Rodriguez, it looks like Steve's made it through," I said, keeping my voice level. "If you'd unlock my door now, please?"

"Very well." My door unlocked. "Mr. Mason, please

remain seated. Ms. Mason, please proceed toward the—hey! What are you doing? You can't do that!"

Ignoring the shouts from the intercom, Shaun finished sliding out of the car, blowing a kiss back toward the agitated shape of Andres before slamming the door and following me to the air lock. True to expectations, Andres remained seated, mouth moving as he swore at us through the glass.

"Nobody who cares that much about security is going to come out into the open with a possible infection," I said, taking Shaun's hand in my left, swinging Lois's carrier in my right. She yowled, punctuating the statement. "We're dangerous."

"Man thought he could make us do this separately," said Shaun. Taking the still-yowling Lois from me, he slid the carrier into the luggage hatch. The sensors would record the fact that the box contained a living thing, but they would also record its weight. Lois was too small for amplification and would slide straight through. "Man's an idiot."

"No, he's an amateur," I said, moving into position in front of the blood testing panel. I raised my right hand. Shaun stepped into position next to me and raised his left. "One . . ."

"Two."

We pressed our palms flat.

Steve was waiting on the other side of the air lock, shaking his head. "You probably just scared Agent Rodriguez out of a year of his life," he scolded, without conviction.

"Given that Agent Rodriguez just annoyed me out of a year of *my* life, I'd say we're even," I said, retrieving Lois from the luggage bin. "Do we need to wait on him, or can you show us to our rooms?"

"And our van," Shaun said. "You promised me our van."

"Your van is in the parking garage, along with Georgia's bike," Steve said. Fishing two small plastic rectangles out of his jacket pocket, he passed them to us. "Shaun, you're in room two-fourteen. Georgia, you're in room two-seventeen."

We exchanged a look. "Those don't sound adjoining," I said.

"Originally, you were going to be sharing a room with Ms. Meissonier, Georgia, while Shaun and Mr. Cousins shared a room down the hall," Steve said. "It seemed best to let you keep your privacy, given recent . . . events."

"Right." Shaun handed his key back to Steve. "I'll just stalk along with George until you can get me my own key. Rick and Lois can have some valuable alone time to re-bond after their separation." As if on cue, Lois yowled.

Steve's eyebrows arched upward. "You two would rather share a room?"

His expression was a familiar one. We've been seeing it from teachers, friends, colleagues, and hotel concierges since we hit puberty. It's the "you'd rather share a room with your opposite-gender sibling than sleep alone?" face, and it never fails to irritate me. Social norms can bite me. If I need to have someone guarding my back when the living dead show up to make my life more interesting than I want it to be, I want that someone to be Shaun. He's a light sleeper, and I know he can aim.

"Yes," I said, firmly. "We two would rather share a room."

For a moment, Steve looked like he might argue. Then he shrugged, dismissing it as none of his business, and said, "I'll have them send up a second key and get your luggage moved. Georgia, all your things and the equipment that you had marked as vital are already in your room."

That meant they'd been searched—standard security—but I didn't particularly care. I make it a rule never to keep sensitive data unencrypted where other people might get at it. If Senator Ryman's security detail wanted to waste their time looking for answers in my underpants, they could be my guests. "Excellent. We'll just head for our room, then, if you don't mind? Assuming you don't feel the need to accompany us."

"I'm going to trust the two of you not to get yourselves killed between here and the elevator," said Steve.

"Thanks for the vote of confidence," I said. Shaun snapped a salute and we walked away, Lois still yowling, to follow the wall-mounted signs leading us to the elevators in the lobby.

The hotel was old enough that the elevators still ran up and down in fixed shafts. It would have been an interesting novelty if I hadn't been so wired and exhausted. As it was, I stared at the mirrors on the walls, trying to ignore my growing headache and the increasingly fevered pitch of Lois's complaints. She wanted out of the box, and she wanted out *now*. I understood the sentiment.

Our hotel room was as old as the elevator, with hideous wallpaper striped in yellow, green, and brown, and a steel-reinforced window looking out over the central courtyard. Sunlight reflecting off the pool three floors down turned the water into a giant flare of light, shining directly through our window. I whimpered involuntarily, whipping my face around and squeezing my eyes shut. Shaun shoved past me to close the blackout curtains, and I stumbled blind into the room, letting the door swing closed.

The lights were off, and when Shaun got the curtains fastened the room was plunged into blessed darkness. He walked back across the room, putting a hand on my elbow. "It's safe now," he said. "The beds are this way."

"That was a rotten trick," I complained, and let him guide me.

"But funny."

"Not funny."

"I'm laughing."

"I know where you're planning to sleep tonight."

"And yet somehow, still funny." He stopped walking, pushing down on my shoulder as he took the cat carrier out of my hands. "Sit. I'll get things set up."

"Don't forget the EMP screen," I said, settling on the bed and flopping backward. The mattress was younger than the décor. I bounced. "And get the servers up."

"I *have* done this before," said Shaun. The amusement was evident in his tone, but it wasn't enough to conceal the concern. "You look like hell."

"You can tell that with the lights off?"

"You looked like hell before the evil day star punched you in the face. Now you look like hell in a darkened room. Easier on the eyes, no less hellish."

"Why didn't you say anything before?"

"We were surrounded by people, and you were getting your bitchy-and-thwarted on. It didn't seem appropriate." Rattling noises marked his passage across the room, followed by a thump and the sound of a lightbulb being unscrewed. "I'm swapping the bulbs in the bedside lights."

"Thanks."

"No worries. You're more pleasant when you haven't got a migraine."

"In that case, toss me my big painkillers when you're done with that?"

There was a pause. "You actually want them?"

"I'm going to need them after we talk." I take a lot of generic drugs for the headaches my eyes give me. That's not the same thing as my "big painkillers," a nasty narcotic mix of ergot alkaloid, codeine, caffeine, and a few less-pronounceable chemical agents. They kill the pain. They also kill all higher brain functions for at least six hours after I've taken them. I avoid drugging myself whenever possible, because I don't usually have the time to waste, but I was getting the feeling this might be the last "free" time we were going to have for a while. If spending it drugged out of my mind meant I had the stamina to handle the rest, well, I've done worse in my pursuit of the truth.

"Georgia—"

"Don't argue."

"I was just going to say that there's time for a nap before we talk, if you want it, and painkillers after that. The Daughters of the American Revolution always talk for hours."

"No, there isn't. We ran out of time when someone decided we'd outlived our usefulness. Time is now officially something we don't have. Hit the lights as soon as you're ready."

"Right," said Shaun. There was a click. The room brightened before I heard him move away again. "Servers need to initialize, and I'll turn on the screens. Your computer's on the desk if you want to get it hooked up."

"Got it." My headache screamed when I opened my eyes. I ignored it. The lower-wattage bulbs Shaun put in were bearable, if not exactly pleasant; I could deal. Sitting up, I bent forward to open the cat carrier, which was still sitting on the floor near the base of the bed. Lois was out in a flash, vanishing into the bathroom.

I rose and walked over to take a seat at my desk, where I started connecting cables. I was moving gingerly, to upset my head as little as possible, and that slowed me down; I was only halfway done when Shaun called, "Clear." I put down the plug I'd been holding, and the air filled with an electrical buzz that made all the hair on my arms stand on end.

"You'd better have that set low enough not to fry anything," I said, going back to work.

"What do you take me for, an amateur?" Shaun was trying to sound affronted. I wasn't buying it. It's easy to slip when you're setting up a privacy screen— that's part of why I'm not fond of using them. They also make my teeth itch. "It'll short out anything around the perimeter, but as long as you don't get any closer to the walls, you'll be fine."

"If you're wrong, you owe me dinner."

"If I'm right, you owe me dessert."

"Deal." I swiveled in my chair. Shaun was sitting on the bed, leaning back on his hands in a pose of such sheer relaxation that it had to be forced. Skipping the preamble, I said, "Buffy sold us out, and someone tried to kill us."

"I got that."

"Did you get the part where, legally, we were dead as soon as the CDC got the call saying we were infected?"

"I did." Shaun frowned. "I'm surprised they didn't come in shooting."

"Call that the last of our luck," I said. "The way I see it, they weren't just gunning for Buffy. If they were, they wouldn't have bothered calling the CDC after they saw her truck go down. Horrible accident, very tragic, but there's no need to do that sort of mopping up."

"Makes sense," Shaun said and flopped over backward. "So what do we do? Pack our things and go running home?"

"That might not work, since presumably we already know something that's worth killing us for."

"Or Buffy knew something worth killing us for."

"Whoever's behind this has already proven that it's the same thing. I can't imagine we've got two conspiracies running in parallel. That means whoever had our tires shot out was also responsible for the ranch."

"And for Eakly," said Shaun. "Don't you dare forget Eakly."

"I wouldn't," I said. "I can't."

"I dream about Eakly." The statement was almost offhanded, but there was a depth of hurt to it that surprised even me, and I usually know what Shaun's thinking. "They never saw it coming. They never had a chance."

"So leaving isn't an option."

"Leaving never was."

"What are we going to do about Rick?"

"Keep him on, of course."

Raising my eyebrows, I leaned forward to rest my elbows on my knees. "There was no hesitation there. Why not?"

"Don't be an idiot." Shaun sat up, falling into a posture that was the natural mirror image of my own. "Buffy got bit, right?"

"Right."

"Buffy was dying—that's not right. Buffy was *dead*, and she knew it. She told us what she'd done and how to find out more about it, right? Rick was there, and she didn't finger him for a snitch. She was sorry for what she'd done, George. She didn't mean for anyone to die. So why would she've gone and left us with a cuckoo in our birdhouse?"

"What if she didn't know?"

"What if?" Shaun shook his head. "They tried to kill Rick, too. If his car was a little less reinforced, or if he'd hit at a slightly different angle, he'd have been a goner. There's no way to stage that. And the call to the CDC said we were all toast, not just the two of us. So what if Buffy didn't know? Rick's not a moron. He'd have said something by now."

"So you say he stays."

"I say we can't afford to lose anyone else. And I also say that with Buffy gone, I'm an equal partner in this enterprise, so get up."

I blinked. "What?"

"Get up." Shaun stood and pointed to the bed. "You're going to take a nap, and you're going to do it right now."

"I can't nap. I'm waiting for Mahir to call me back."

"He can talk to your voice mail."

"No. He can't."

"Georgia—"

"Just wait."

"No." Shaun's voice was firm. "I'll get the rest of the equipment set up, I'll get the servers running, and I'll check your caller ID every time your phone rings. If Mahir calls, I'll wake you, without consideration for the fact that you're going to work yourself to death. I'm agreeing to that, but I'm also making an executive decision, and my decision is that you, Georgia Carolyn Mason, are going to bed. If you do not like this decision, you may appeal to the court of me hitting you in the back of the head as soon as you turn around."

"Can I have my painkillers?"

"You can have two pills and a pillow," Shaun said. "When you wake up, the world will be a magical wonderland of candy canes, unicorns, and fully assembled servers. And Rick stays. Deal?"

"Deal." I stood, stepping out of my shoes before sitting back down on the bed. "Bastard."

"Close your eyes." I did. Shaun removed my sunglasses, pressing two small round objects into my hand. "Swallow those and you can have these back when you wake up."

"That's dirty pool," I complained, popping the pills into my mouth. They dissolved almost instantly, leaving the bitter taste of codeine behind. I wobbled and let myself fall sideways, eyes still closed. "Dirty pool player."

"That's me." Shaun kissed my forehead. "Rest, George. It'll be better when you wake up."

"No, it won't," I said, resigning myself to the inevitable. "It'll just be later. Later isn't better. Later is just when we have less time."

"Sleep," said Shaun.

So I did.

This is the truth: We are a nation accustomed to being afraid. If I'm being honest, not just with you but with myself, it's not just the nation, and it's not just something we've grown used to. It's the world, and it's an addiction. People crave fear. Fear justifies everything. Fear makes it okay to have surrendered freedom after freedom, until our every move is tracked and recorded in a dozen databases the average man will never have access to. Fear creates, defines, and shapes our world, and without it, most of us would have no idea what to do with ourselves.

Our ancestors dreamed of a world without boundaries, while we dream new boundaries to put around our homes, our children, and ourselves. We limit our potential day after day in the name of a safety that we refuse to ever achieve. We took a world that was huge with possibility, and we made it as small as we could.

Feeling safe yet?

—From *Images May Disturb You*,
the blog of Georgia Mason, April 6, 2040

Twenty-one

I awoke to the sound of Rick and Shaun arguing quietly, undercut by the comforting static buzz of servers and computers; true to his word, Shaun had managed to get the network up and running while I slept. I stretched experimentally and was pleased to discover that my head neither hurt nor felt like it was stuffed with medicated cotton wool. I'd live. I'd pay for it later—my headaches come from minor damage to the optical nerves, and the more I use artificial stimulants to ignore it, the more likely it becomes that the damage will be permanent—but I'd live.

"—telling you, we're letting her sleep until she wakes up. Work on your report."

"It's the Daughters of the American Revolution. They haven't said anything new *since* the American Revolution."

"So it should be an easy report."

"Asshole."

"Hey, man, I just want you to do your job and let my sister get some sleep. Is that so wrong?"

"Right now? Yes."

"Pet your cat and finish your report." Shaun sounded exhausted. I wondered how long I'd been asleep, lost in my dreamless, drug-induced wonderland while he wrangled the servers and waited for Mahir to call.

I must have sighed because I heard footsteps. The mattress bowed as Shaun leaned against the edge, asking, anxiously, "George? Did you want something?"

Another eight hours of sleep, replacement eyes, and Buffy back from the dead. Since I wasn't likely to get any of the things I really wanted, I sighed and answered, "My sunglasses?" My voice was dry and scratchy. I turned my face toward Shaun, my eyes still closed and eyebrows raised in silent punctuation to the question.

He touched my hand with the tips of his fingers before he pressed my sunglasses against my palm, saying, "You've been out for about ten hours. I've tried Mahir three times, but there's been no response. Becks says she spoke to him after we did, when she had to request a delete and re-upload of some of her journal files, but that's the last time stamp anybody has."

Becks . . . ? Oh, Rebecca Atherton, the Newsie he stole from me after things went wrong in Eakly. I slipped my sunglasses on and opened my eyes, taking a moment to orient myself before sitting up. Getting my eyes to focus took a little longer. Shaun put a hand on my knee, steadying me, and I covered it with my own, turning my still blurry eyes toward the distant glow of the computers against the far wall. There was a patch of blobby darkness there that looked out of place against the green, and I nodded to it, saying, "Hey, Rick."

"Hey, Georgia," the blob replied. "Feeling any better?"

"I'm half-blind, and it feels like a flock of seagulls crapped inside my head, but it doesn't hurt, so I guess I'll live." I squeezed Shaun's hand. "How was the DAR meeting?"

"Boring."

"Good. At least something in this world can be counted on to stay dull." My eyes were starting to work. The blob had a head now. "You planning on sticking around, or do we need to post your job opening, too?"

Rick paused. "Shaun said you'd already discussed it."

"The two of us, yes. The three of us? Not so much." I shrugged. "I figured you should get a say. You plan to stick around? We're not doing so well on the survival figures, I'm afraid. One out of four sort of sucks."

"I'd rather take my chances with you than anyplace else I can think of, if it's all the same."

I raised my eyebrows high enough that they crested above the tops of my sunglasses. "Oh? What's the logic behind that?"

"I know I haven't known you or your brother for long, and you don't have much reason to trust me; what I'm about to say probably won't help with that. But Buffy was a friend of mine for years. She was a good person, and she never meant to hurt anyone, but if I don't stay with this team long enough to make sure you remember that, one day the news is going to get out, and she's going to be remembered not as a great writer and a good friend, but as the cause of the Eakly Massacre and the cat's paw behind the death of Rebecca Ryman. The best she'll be able to hope for is 'traitor.' And I won't have that." I could hear the frown in his voice. "I'm staying because I have to. You can try to make me leave if you want to, but it's not going to be fun for any of us."

"I wouldn't dream of it." Giving Shaun's hand a final squeeze, I stood and walked over to sit down at my computer. This close up, my screen was a little fuzzy, but it was nothing I couldn't handle. "If you feel that strongly about staying, you stay. We're glad to have you." My screen blinked at me, prompting for a password. I entered it. Shaun could get me online, but that didn't mean he could access my files. Starting to type, I asked, "What's our general status?"

"Buffy's death hit the newswires five minutes after it happened," said Shaun, moving back to his own machine. "But that's not the fun part." He paused, portentously, until I glared at him. He's good at detecting glares, even through dark glasses. "You want the fun part?"

"Yes, Shaun," I said. "I've been asleep for ten hours, and I want the fun part."

"Fine. Here's the fun part: Our deaths hit the wires at the same time."

My eyes widened. *"What?"*

"We were all reported dead," Shaun said. "Half the news sites had the story before anyone could contradict it, and half of them are still listing you as deceased."

I looked to Rick, who nodded.

"Whoever called the CDC made sure the call was

'accidentally' made on a channel that several local news sites monitor for gossip," he said. "We all got listed as dead before we even made it to Memphis. They printed a retraction about Shaun when he posted to complain about the CDC coffee, and about half the sites did the same for me when I threw up the DAR blurb." He quirked a smile. "I'm not interesting enough to spread as quickly as a *Mason*."

"And me?" I asked, too annoyed not to.

"Still dead," said Rick. "They've got some great conspiracy theories going, too, about Shaun and me concealing your death until we can prove you weren't doing something forbidden by your licensing."

"Thus invalidating my life insurance," I said, putting a hand over my face. "Is there any more good news?"

"Only Buffy made it to the Wall," Shaun said. "She's the only one whose death has actually appeared in the public CDC database."

I bit back a groan. "How many people think we faked our own deaths to up ratings?"

"A lot," Shaun said, voice going grim. "On the plus side, if we'd really been doing that, it would've worked. We gained another three points of market share while people waited for the grisly details to pop up."

"And have they?"

"On us? No. On Buffy? Yeah. It's all over the place. Somebody broke into our main camera upload and—"

"I get the picture. I'll get our official report up tonight so we can put these damn hoax rumors to rest and let people know I'm still breathing. Buffy deserves better than to have her death tarred with some publicity stunt we didn't pull."

"How official is this official report going to be?" asked Rick.

"You mean, 'am I going to include the call the CDC got?'" I asked. He nodded. So did I. "Yes, I am."

"Is that—"

"Wise? Safe? A good idea? No, on all three counts, but I'm going to do it anyway." I pulled up my e-mail and started scanning the list of senders, looking for Mahir's name. "Somebody who's depending on secrecy wants us out of the way. So screw 'em. We're taking that secrecy away."

"And when they start shooting?"

"Who says they've stopped?" Even with Buffy's astonishingly well-constructed filters, the amount of spam that had managed to get through was daunting. I began deleting. "That reminds me. We need to hire a new head for the Fictionals."

Rick shot me a sharp look. "Doesn't that seem a little abrupt? Buffy just died."

"Buffy's death was abrupt; this is necessary. The Fictionals aren't like the Newsies or the Irwins. They won't keep working just because they don't know how to hold still. They need management, or it turns into a million works in progress and nothing that actually *progresses*. Unless we want to start getting angry letters from people wanting to know where the next installment of some fifty-part serial romance is, we need a new division head."

Shaun blinked. "Buffy didn't name anyone?"

"Buffy thought she was immortal. Talk to Magdalene; even if she won't do it, she can probably suggest somebody who will." Suddenly tired again, I set my spam purge to run on auto and minimized the window, pulling up the staff LW&T directory. That archive contained a current copy of the last will and testament of every employee currently on the After the End Times payroll, including details on the dispensation of their intellectual property. Properly filed and witnessed wills are legally required for all businesses whose normal routine brings them into contact with federally established hazard zones, the infected, or members of the working press. Journalists: as dangerous as zombies under modern American law. According to the directory time stamps, Buffy's file hadn't been updated since we left California.

I entered my password to open the file. Both Shaun and I possess the legal authority to access all files stored on our servers, just in case of situations like this. The document flashed open. It was a read-only copy of the actual document, which was being held, according to the header information, by the Meissonier family lawyer back in Berkeley. For our purposes, it was more than sufficient.

Shaun slid out of his chair and stepped up behind me, resting a hand on my shoulder. Buffy left the bulk of her personal possessions to her family, her written works and literary estate to the site as a whole, and her nonfiction—which is to say, her personal files— to Shaun and me. We had the right to use her data however we saw fit. There was no mention of a successor, but that didn't matter because that last rider told me everything we needed to know.

"Son of a bitch," I muttered. "She knew she was going to die over this. And she knew she was doing the wrong thing, even if she didn't want to admit it to herself. She *knew*."

"How can you say that?" asked Rick.

Shaun answered for me, saying, "She left us her personal files. Why would she do that if she didn't know we'd need something that's in them? Maybe she felt like she had to do this, but that doesn't mean she managed to convince herself that it was right. George . . ."

"Rick, I need you to find a new head for the Fictionals." I hit Print and closed the file. "That's your assignment for right now. Well, that and the DAR report. Shaun, I'm going to need to do a news report on what happened, but—"

"But the bulk of it's an Irwin thing. Got it." Shaun squeezed my shoulder before returning to his own machine. "What about Buffy's files? The server she told us to access?"

"I'd really like that camera footage Mahir has; I was hoping to get that out of the way first. But yeah, the files. I'll head over there now."

"George—"

"Just be quiet while I deal with this," I said, almost more curtly than I'd meant to, and began to type.

After the End Times maintains two file servers for employee use. One, the so-called "public" server, is open to uploads and downloads by every blogger we employ, as well as every blogger even remotely affiliated with the site. If you do any work for us at all, we open an account for you on the public server, and those accounts are rarely revoked unless there's active abuse. There's just no point, especially since we have a tendency to reuse freelancers. Why burn goodwill on a server purge? More important, why waste time by forcing your IT person to set up the same accounts more than once? When we're a little bigger—if we live that long—we'll need to reconsider that policy, but it's served us well so far.

The private server is a lot more locked down. There are presently seven people whose accounts include access to that server, and one of them is dead. Me, Mahir, and Rick from the Newsies; Buffy and Magdalene from the Fictionals; Shaun and Becks from the Irwins. That's where we keep the important things, from private financial records to stories about the campaign that still need to have their facts verified. That server is as hack-proof as it can be because one unverified story leaked under my byline would be enough to seriously cripple, if not kill, the news section of our site.

The news is serious business. If you're not willing to treat it that way, you shouldn't be anywhere near it.

I opened an FTP window and fed in the address for our secure server. When it prompted me for a user name and password, I typed in *soundingsea*, followed by the password *February-4-29*. Shaun and Rick abandoned their workstations and moved to stand behind me, watching as the screen flickered once, twice, and then rolled as a video player seized control of my machine. Tapping the Escape key did nothing to stop the program from opening, and so I settled back in my seat, comforted by the presence of my team. We weren't much, and we were dwindling by the day, but the three of us were all that we had left.

The screen stopped rolling as the much-beloved face of Buffy Meissonier became clear. She was seated cross-legged on the counter of our van, wearing her patchwork vest and a tattered broomstick skirt. I recognized that outfit; she'd been wearing it the day we left Oklahoma City, when we'd barely been speaking to one another. She'd wanted us to give it up. Hindsight is twenty-twenty, they say. Well, it was a little late now, but at least I understood why she'd wanted so badly to make us all head home. She'd been trying, in her misguided way, to save our lives.

Looking into the camera, Buffy smiled. "Hey," she said. Her voice and expression combined to paint the picture of a woman tired beyond all reckoning, so worn through that she was no longer sure she could be patched back together again. "I guess you guys are watching this. Schrödinger's video recording—if you can see it, it's too late for you to tell me what the picture quality is like. Isn't that always the way? It's my masterpiece, and I'll never see the reactions. I guess that means I won't have to live with the reviews, either. I should get down to business, though, because if you're watching this, you probably don't have much time left to waste.

"My name is Georgette Marie Meissonier, license number delta-bravo-echo-eight-four-one-two-zero-seven. I am of sound mind and body, and I am making this recording to testify that I have willingly and knowingly participated in a campaign to defraud the American public, beginning with my business partners, Shaun Phillip Mason and Georgia Carolyn Mason. As a part of this campaign, I have fed news reports and private feeds to third parties, with the understanding that they would use this information to undercut the presidential campaign of Senator Peter Ryman, and planted recording devices in private spaces, with the understanding that the material thus collected would be used to further undermine the campaign."

On the screen, Buffy paused to take a deep breath, looking suddenly very young behind her exhaustion. "I didn't know. I knew that what I was doing was wrong, and that I'd never work in the news again, but I didn't know anyone was going to get hurt. I didn't know until the ranch, and by then, I was in too deep to find a way out again. I'm sorry. That doesn't bring back the dead, but it's the truth, because I didn't want anyone to get hurt. I thought I was doing the right thing. I thought that when this was over, we'd be a stronger nation because of what I'd done." A tear escaped her left eye, running down her cheek. It would have seemed overly theatrical if I hadn't known Buffy as well as I did—knowing her, it wasn't theatrical *enough*. She was really crying. "I see them when I dream. I close my eyes, and they're all there. Everyone who died in Eakly. Everyone who died at the ranch. It was my fault, and I'm so afraid we got this job because someone who could manipulate the numbers knew I was for sale, if you offered the right price. I'm so sorry. I didn't mean it. I didn't mean any of it.

"If I knew who I'd been sold to, I'd tell you, but I don't. I went out of my way to never know, because if I'd known . . . I think, if I'd known, I would have realized it was wrong." Buffy looked away from the camera, wiping her eyes. "I got in too deep. I couldn't get back out. And you won't let us go home. Georgia, why can't we go home?" She turned back toward the lens, both eyes brimming with tears. "I don't want to die. I don't want you to see this. Please. Can't we just go *home*?"

"God, Buffy, I'm sorry," I whispered. My words dropped into the silence that followed her plea like rocks into a wishing well, with as little effect.

On the screen, Buffy took a deep breath and held it before letting it slowly out. "You're going to see this," she said, lips tugging up into a small and bitter smile. "You have to see it. Or you'll never know the truth. By triggering this file, you've mailed a video to my parents telling them how sorry I am, and how much I loved what I did. When it closes, you'll have access to my private directory, including a file named 'Confession.' It's locked and time stamped. If you don't open it, it'll be admissible in court. I didn't trust everything to the servers. I think I know better than anyone else right now just how dangerous it is to trust people. You have something of mine that no one else has. Look there. You'll find everything I've got, including the access codes for all those listening devices. Good luck. Avenge me if you can. And I'm sorry."

Buffy paused, smiling for real this time, and added, "This—being here, with you, following this campaign—really was what I wanted. Not all of it, maybe, but I'm glad I came. So thank you. And good luck." The picture winked out.

The three of us stayed frozen in our silent tableau for several minutes. A sniffle from behind my left shoulder told me Rick was crying. Not for the first time, I damned Kellis-Amberlee for taking that simple human comfort away from me.

"What did she mean, something we have that no one else does?" Shaun asked, putting his hand on my right shoulder. "All her luggage was in the truck."

"But we have her laptop," I said. Pushing my chair back from the desk, I rose, turning to face them. "Get me a tool kit and her computer."

Never steal another reporter's story; never take the last of another reporter's ammo; never mess with another reporter's computer. Those are the rules, unless you work for a tabloid, where they replace "never" with "always" . . . but once you're dead, you're meat, and all bets are off. I had to keep telling myself that as I used a screwdriver to work the bottom panel off Buffy's laptop. Shaun and Rick stood nearby, watching. We'd already scanned the machine itself and found nothing—literally nothing. She wiped the drives at some point, probably before we left on the drive that killed her. When it came to paranoia, Buffy was world class. She'd had good reason to be, after Eakly.

It was somehow anticlimactic when the laptop's bottom panel came free, tearing the tape stretched between it and the battery case and dropping a data stick into my hand. I held it up, showing it to the two of them. "The plot thickens," I said. "Shaun, Becks used to be a Newsie. How's she with computers?"

"Not as good as Buffy—"

"No one's as good as Buffy."

"But she's good."

"Good enough?"

"Only one way to find out." He held out his hand. I gave him the data stick without a moment's hesitation. The day I couldn't trust Shaun, it was over. Simple as that.

"Get her online and get her going through these files. Buffy said there were time stamps and IPs. We need to see what they can give us." I stood. "Rick, get back on that report."

"What are you going to do?"

"Rouse Mahir," I said, moving back to my machine. The chair was still warm; things were moving faster than they seemed. "I don't care what it takes. We need to get a copy of whatever's on that disk stored off-site, and I think 'London' qualifies."

"Georgia?" Rick's tone was soft. I glanced toward him. He hadn't moved back to his own machine; he was just standing there, looking at me.

"What?"

"Are we going to survive this?"

"Probably not. You want out?"

"No." He shook his head. "I just wanted to know whether you realized that."

"I do," I said. "Now get to work."

Both nodding, Rick and Shaun did exactly that.

For all that Mahir seemed to be out, or asleep—or, God forbid, if this was somehow even bigger than it looked, already dead—his machine address still registered on the network. I tapped it in along with my priority code, activating a personalized screamer. If he did *anything* online he'd start getting loud, intrusive pings demanding that he contact me immediately. Screamers are generally viewed as extremely poor form outside of emergencies. As far as I was concerned, this qualified as an emergency.

Satisfied that I'd done everything I could be reasonably expected to do in order to find my second, I bowed my head, set my fingers to the keys, and went to work.

There's something deeply reassuring about doing

a factual report. You have every bit of information you need at your fingertips waiting to be smoothed out and turned into something that makes sense. Take the facts, take the faces, take the facets of the truth, polish them until they gleam, and put them on paper—or, in my case, put them in pixels—as an exercise for the reader. I set my feed for a live page-by-page, with a license confirmation on the upload. Anyone who really thought this was some sort of cover-up for my death could report the site to the licensing committee for abuse of my number, and that would cancel the rumors faster than anything else I could do. It'd make good news, too.

The e-mail started coming in as soon as my first page was uploaded. Most of it was positive, congratulating me on my survival and assuring me that my readers had known all along that I'd get out alive. A few letters were less friendly, including one I tagged for upload with the op-ed piece I was planning to write; it said Shaun and I deserved to die at the hands of the living dead, since sinners like us were about as ethically advanced. It would fit perfectly with the reality of how Buffy had been bought.

Page six had just gone up when Shaun called, "Becks says she's cross-checking the IPs now. Most of them look to be scrambled."

"Meaning?"

"Meaning she can't follow them."

Damn. "How about the time stamps?"

"They prove it wasn't any of us, or the senator, but not too much other than that. Just going by the times, it could even be Mrs. Ryman."

Double damn. "Got any good news for me?"

Shaun looked up from his screen, grinning. "How does access codes on all Buffy's bugs sound?"

"Like good news," I said. I would have said more, but my computer beeped, flashing an urgent message light at the bottom of the screen. I double-clicked the prompt.

Mahir's face appeared in a video window, his hair unkempt and his eyes wild as he demanded, "What's going on? What's wrong?"

"You weren't answering your phone!" I said, embarrassed even as the words left my mouth. He was on the other side of the world; there was no way this situation could hold the same urgency for him.

"The local Fictionals were holding a wake and poetry reading in Buffy's honor." He brushed his hair out of his face. "I attended to report on it, and I'm afraid I had a bit too much to drink." Now he sounded sheepish. "I fell asleep as soon as I got home."

"That explains how you slept through the screamer," I said. Twisting in my seat, I asked, "Shaun, we have a local copy of those files?"

"In the local group directory," he confirmed.

"Good." I turned back to my computer. "Mahir, I'm going to upload some files to your directory. I want you to save them locally. Make at least two physical copies. I recommend storing one of them off-site."

"Should I delete them from the server once I've finished reading?"

His tone was light, attempting to joke with me. Mine wasn't light at all. "Yes. That would be a good idea. If you can pull the rest of your files long enough to reformat your sector, that wouldn't be a bad idea, either."

"Georgia . . ." He hesitated. "Is there something I should be aware of?"

I bit back the urge to start laughing. Buffy was dead; we'd been reported dead to the CDC; someone had tried to use us to undermine the United States government. There was a *lot* going on that he needed to be aware of. "Please," I said, "download the files, read them, and give me your honest opinion."

"You want my *honest* opinion?" His expression was filled with naked concern. "Get out of that country, Georgia. Come here before something happens that you can't bounce back from."

"England wouldn't want me."

"We'd find a way."

"Entertaining as political exile might be, Shaun would go crazy if I forced him to move, and I wouldn't go without him." Impulsively, I removed my sunglasses and offered Mahir's image a smile. "I'm sorry I may never get to meet you."

Mahir looked alarmed. "Don't talk that way."

"Just read the files. Tell me how to talk after you do that."

"All right," he said. "Be safe."

"I'll try." I tapped the keys to start the upload and his image winked out, replaced by a status bar.

"Georgia?"

Shaun's voice; the wrong name. I turned toward him, a cold spot forming in my stomach as I registered the fact that he hadn't called me "George." "What?"

"Becks has one of the bugs online."

"And?"

"And I think you ought to hear this." Reaching over, he pulled his headset jack out of the speakers.

The crackle and hiss of a live transmission promptly blared into the room, seeming all the louder in the sudden silence. Even Lois, crouched next to Rick's monitor, was silent and still, her ears slicked back and her eyes stretched wide.

"—hear me?" Tate's voice was almost impossibly loud, amplified by the bug's internal pickups and Shaun's speakers. "We are going to solve this problem, and we're going to solve it now, before things get any worse."

Another voice, this one indistinguishable. Shaun caught my eye and nodded. He'd have Becks running it through a filter as soon as we finished listening, trying to clean it up enough to determine the speaker. That was all we could really do.

"And I'm telling you, they're getting too close. With the Meissonier girl gone, we can't steer them anymore. There's no telling how many of those damn bugs she planted around the offices. I told you we couldn't trust a spook."

I caught my breath as Rick started swearing under his. Only Shaun was completely silent, his lips pressed into a tight line. Unaware that he was being listened to, Tate continued: "I'm in her little boyfriend's portable office. If there was any spot she wouldn't bug, it'd be the one where she was doing her own share of the sinning."

"He really didn't know her very well," Rick said, in a bitter, distant tone.

"Neither did we," Shaun replied.

"I don't care how you take the rest of them out," Tate barked. "Just do it. If the CDC couldn't finish them off, we'll find another way. Understand me?

Do it!" There was a slam, as if a receiver was being thrust rudely into its cradle, followed by the sound of footsteps. The hiss continued for a few more seconds, then cut off as suddenly as it had started.

"They only cut and save when there's sound being received," said Shaun needlessly. We all knew how Buffy's saver bugs worked. Plant them and they'd press anything they heard to file, going dormant to save their batteries when the space around them was silent. She must not have been listening to her files. Just saving and transmitting them, serene in her own certainty that her side was the right one.

"Tate," snarled Rick. "That *fuck*."

"Tate," I said. My eyes were burning. Finally sliding my sunglasses back into place, I looked from one to the other. "We have to see the senator."

"Can we trust him not to be a part of this?" Shaun asked.

I hesitated. "How good is Becks?"

"Not that good."

"Fine." I swiveled back to my screen. "Screamers on everyone. Get the whole team online. I don't care *where* they are, I want them here."

"Georgia . . . ?" said Rick, uncertainly.

I shook my head, already beginning to type. "Shut up, sit down, and get started. We have work to do."

*　　*　　*

———————

Every life has a watershed moment, an instant when you realize you're about to make a choice that will define everything else you ever do, and that if you choose wrong, there may not be that many things left to choose. Sometimes the wrong choice is the only one that lets you face the end with dignity, grace, and the awareness that you're doing the right thing.

I'm not sure we can recognize those moments until they've passed us. Was mine the day I decided to become a reporter? The day my brother and I logged onto a job fair and met a girl who called herself "Buffy"? The day we decided to try for the "plum assignment" of staff bloggers to the Ryman campaign?

Or was it the day we realized this might be the last thing we ever did . . . and decided not to care?

My name is Georgia Mason. My brother calls me George.

Welcome to my watershed.

—From *Images May Disturb You*,
the blog of Georgia Mason, April 8, 2040

Twenty-two

It took two hours and seventeen minutes to gather every blogger, associate blogger, administrative employee, system administrator, and facilities coordinator employed by After the End Times together in one hastily opened virtual conference room. Our conferencing system has eleven rooms, and the eleventh had never been successfully hacked, but Buffy "built" them all. The code was hers, and I didn't feel like we could trust it anymore. We would have invited the volunteer moderators—leaving them out didn't seem right—but we didn't have a way of contacting them without using unsecured channels. And that was the last thing I was willing to do just now.

With Becks, Alaric, and Dave—who was finally back from Alaska, having acquired several hundred hours of footage, and a minor case of frostbite—working in tandem, we almost had a functional replacement for Buffy. Alaric and Dave did most of the heavy lifting of setting up the room, freeing Becks to keep trying to sift through Buffy's data. There was a lot to sort through.

The atmosphere started out jovial, if tinged with unavoidable melancholy. Buffy was dead; we weren't, and every person who logged on seemed to feel the need to comment on both facts, congratulating us on our survival even as they mourned for her. The Fictionals were taking it the hardest. No surprise there, although I was pleased to see Magdalene stepping up to comfort the ones who seemed the most distraught. No fewer than four of the network connections we were getting off the Fictionals were coming from her house—Fictionals tend to be the most social and the most paranoid of the bloggers you're likely to encounter, but Maggie, with her sprawling old farmhouse with the military-grade security system, has a talent for getting them to set the second aside in favor of the first. She could've been an alpha at her own site, if she'd wanted it, but what she'd wanted was to work with Buffy. That wasn't an option anymore. I tapped an IM to Rick, reminding him to ask her about taking the department; if she was handling the mourning period this well, she'd definitely be an asset.

The grumbling started about an hour in, when the congratulatory celebration of our survival died down and it became apparent both that there were people online but working on some sort of secret project, and that we weren't planning to tell *anyone* what was going on until *everyone* arrived. No exceptions, no allowances. Not this time.

The last person to log on was a Canadian Fictional named Andrea, mumbling something about hockey games and cold-weather romances as her connection finished rolling and her picture stabilized. I wasn't really paying attention by that point. That wasn't why we were here.

"Is everyone's connection stable and secure?" I asked. Tapping out a predetermined sequence of characters on my keyboard caused the borders of the dozens of tiny video windows to flash yellow. "If the answer is yes, please input the security code now appearing at the bottom of your screen. If the answer is no, hit Enter. We will be terminating this conference immediately if we can't confirm security."

The grumbling slowed. People had been relieved to see us when we first called them, confused as I refused to let them off the line, and finally annoyed by our group refusal to tell them what was going on. Add draconian security measures and it became clear that something was up. One by one, the borders of the video windows representing our staff flashed white and then green as their security status was confirmed. Shaun's window was the last to change states; we'd agreed on that beforehand. He would close the loop.

"Excellent." I picked up my PDA, which had been cued to my e-mail client since the conference began, and tapped Send. "Please check your e-mail. You'll find your termination notice, along with a receipt confirming that your final paycheck has been deposited to your bank account. Due to California's at-will status and the fact that you're all employed under hazard restrictions, I'm afraid we're not required to give you any notice. Sorry about that."

The conference exploded as everyone started

talking at once, voices overlapping into a senseless barrage of sound. Almost everyone. Mahir, Becks, Alaric, and Dave stayed silent, all of them having ascertained from the process of getting the conference online that something huge was going on.

Shaun, Rick, and I sat quietly, waiting for the furor to die down. It took a while. The Irwins shouted the loudest, while the Newsies shouted the least; they knew me well enough to know that if I was supporting a grand gesture—and this *was* a grand gesture—there had to be a reason. They trusted me enough to wait and see what it was. Good team. I hired well.

I set my PDA aside when the shouting began to quiet, saying, "None of you work for us. None of you have any legal ties to keep you here. If you choose to log off at any point during the next five minutes, I'll see to it that you have a letter of recommendation stating that your value as a journalist is entirely beyond measure. You'll never have this easy a time finding another job in your life because I'll pull strings to get you hired, I'll make sure you're settled, and then I'll write you off. This is the all-or-nothing moment, folks: Walk away now if you want to walk, but if you do, you're walking for keeps."

There was a long silence, broken when Andrea asked, "Can you tell us why you're doing this?"

"Buffy's dead, and now we're fired," interjected Alaric. "You don't think these things might be connected?"

"I just—"

"Not very well, you didn't."

"Do me a favor, dears, and shut up so our former boss can speak?" Magdalene sighed. "You're giving me a headache."

"Thank you, Maggie." I looked around my screen, studying each video window in turn. "Andrea, the answer to why we're doing this is a simple one: We don't want any of you to feel obligated to stay with this site any longer than you already have. I'm sure you've all heard about the call the CDC received, reporting our deaths?" Murmurs of agreement. "It was received before we placed the call to tell *them* we were still alive. Someone shot out our tires, there was no one else on the road, and yet somebody told the CDC that we'd been killed."

"Do you have time stamps on that?" asked Alaric, suddenly alert.

"We do," I confirmed, nodding to Shaun, who began to type. Alaric glanced away from his video transmitter, signaling the arrival of the appropriate files, and quieted. "Buffy didn't die in an accident; Buffy was murdered, and her killers thought they'd killed us too. There's a lot more going on, but that's the important part right now: Buffy was *murdered*. Her *murderers* would have been happy to do the same to the three of us, and that means I can't put it past them to do the same to any of you. This is your chance to make a graceful exit before I tell you why they want us all dead." I tapped my PDA again. "If you check your e-mail, you'll see an offer of new employment—everyone but you, Magdalene, and you, Mahir. We need to talk to you off-line." From Magdalene's nod, it was apparent that she'd been expecting that request, or something similar. Mahir just looked floored. I'd been anticipating both responses. "Again, if you want to refuse, that's fine. You will have five minutes to make your decision. If you haven't decided within that time, I'll disconnect you from this conference. Should you choose to leave this organization, you will have twelve hours to remove your personal files from our servers. At the end of that time, your access will be revoked and you'll need to contact a member of the senior staff to obtain anything you haven't downloaded."

I paused, giving the others a chance to speak. No one said a word. "All right. Please review your contracts. If you accept, enter the security code listed under the space for your license number. If you do not accept, it's been a pleasure working with you. I wish you all the best in your future endeavors."

More silence followed this announcement as people opened and read their new employment agreements. Nothing had really changed from their original contracts; they got the same number of shares and the same percentages of the various merchandising lines, and they were expected to hold to the same deadlines and levels of journalistic conduct. In another way, everything had changed from their original contracts because when those contracts were signed, nobody was trying to kill us. We weren't offering hazard pay or guaranteed ratings. We were just offering a lot of danger, and the only real reward was the chance to be a part of telling a truth that was bigger than any of us on our own.

Andrea was again the first to speak, saying, "I . . . I'm sorry, Georgia. Shaun. I just . . . I was here because Buffy asked me to come. I never wanted to deal with this sort of thing. I can't."

"It's all right, Ace," said Shaun, soothingly. He's

always been good with this sort of thing. That makes one of us. "Thank you for all your hard work."

"I'm sorry I couldn't stay longer," said Andrea. "I . . . good luck, all of you." Wiping her cheeks with the back of her hand, she looked away from her webcam just before the picture blinked off, leaving a black rectangle on the corner of my screen.

That was the pebble that kicked off the avalanche. Screen borders started blinking white as people agreed to their new contracts; video windows started blacking as people mumbled their apologies and logged off. Some of the answers we got weren't a surprise. I knew Alaric and Becks would stay. Shaun had given me the same reassurance about Dave. With Buffy gone, there was no one to vouch for the Fictionals, but it seemed likely that we'd lose at least half of them. What I wasn't expecting was how many of my Newsies would be making their apologies along with them.

Luis put it best. "It's not that I don't think you're doing the right thing. I know you. You're doing the only thing you *can*. But people are going to get hurt, and I can't afford to be one of them. I have a family. I'm sorry." And then he was gone, disconnected like half the Fictionals and most of the administrative staff.

We were left with less than half of our original connections when the disconnections stopped, and the only windows not outlined in white were those belonging to Magdalene and Mahir. I looked to the window that held my anxious, former second-in-command and said, "I'll call you when this is over," before tapping out the code to close the connection. "Magdalene, you can stay, if you understand that you're not currently employed by this site."

"I'm assuming you're about to go over the current risk situation, and that you're not hiring me right away because my contract needs review, since you want me to do Buffy's job," said Magdalene, matter-of-factly. "Sound right?"

"Sounds exactly right," said Rick.

"I'll stay. It's my problem as much as it is yours, and my department's going to need me to know what's going on."

"Thank you," I said. I meant it. She'd never really replace Buffy, but her response told me that she was willing to try. "Rick, transmit the files."

"Done."

"Everyone, please check your mail. You'll find an attachment detailing what we currently know, including that whoever ordered Buffy's death was highly placed in the current government. Tate is involved. This information isn't just sensitive; it's potentially enough to get any one of us killed. Read it, transfer it to off-line storage, and wipe your mail. Whether you're involved with our ongoing efforts to find out what's going on is going to be up to you, but if we're convicted of, say, treason against the United States government, all of you have just placed your asses on the line. Welcome to our party." I stood. "Shaun and Rick will be remaining to answer any questions you may have; Shaun speaks for the Irwins, and Rick, as my new second, will be speaking for the Newsies. Thank you for coming. Now, if you'll excuse me, I need to make a phone call." Ignoring their protests, I walked into the bathroom, turning off the interior lights before closing the door behind me.

While Dave and Alaric were cobbling together a new conference room, Shaun and I had been isolating the bathroom in its own frequency screen, creating an envelope that could only be broken by transmissions made on a very specific set of bandwidths. Most of my equipment was as good as dead on the other side of that door, which was exactly how I wanted it to be. If I had that much trouble dialing out, the rest of the world was going to have one hell of a time dialing in.

Even with the screen's keys coded into my PDA, it took almost five minutes to establish a connection with Mahir's phone. His first words were delivered in a sharp, wounded tone: "What the hell was that about? Have I given you some reason to doubt my dedication to this site? Have I ever done anything other than precisely what you asked of me? Because I'm not feeling terribly valued at the moment, *Miss* Mason."

"Hello to you, too, Mahir," I said, leaning against the bathroom sink and removing my sunglasses. The glow from my PDA was enough for me to see by. It wasn't enough to relieve my headache, but it was a start. "You *are* terribly valued. That's why I fired you."

There was a long pause as he tried to sort through that sentence. Finally, he admitted, "I'm afraid I'm not following you."

"Look. There's every chance in the world that things are going to go wrong." I wished that I was lying to him. I've never wanted to be a liar so badly in my life. "We're playing in an arena we're not equipped for, and there's nobody we can call who has the tools we need to *get* equipped for it. We're either going to find what we're looking for, or we're going to go down in flames."

"What does that have to do with firing me? You seem happy to take everyone else down with you. What robs me of my right to a seat on the *Titanic*?"

"The fact that I need you to be receiving the signals in the Coast Guard tower."

There was a pause. Then: "I'm listening."

"If this goes as badly as it has the potential to go—if it goes *all the way* wrong—we could wind up dead, and everyone who works for the site could wind up charged with treason against the United States government. If whoever's behind all this can somehow turn it from *their* plot into *our* plot, that means every employee of After the End Times is in a position to be charged with terrorist involvement in the use of live-state Kellis-Amberlee to bring about human viral amplification."

". . . oh, my God," said Mahir, sounding horrified. "I hadn't considered that."

"I didn't think you had," I said, grimly.

The Raskin-Watts ruling of 2026 didn't impact just America. How could any country, however opposed to the United States government it might be, afford to look like it was soft on the matter of the infected? It couldn't. Every industrialized nation in the world with an extradition treaty had stepped forward by the end of 2027 to state that any individual found guilty of using or conspiring to use Kellis-Amberlee as a weapon would be turned over to the government of the affected nation or nations in order to stand trial. Being outside the boundaries of a country no longer protected you from that country's laws, if you were foolish enough to cross the one line everyone had agreed to draw in the sand.

The United States doesn't apply the death penalty to many crimes these days. Terrorism remains an exception to this particular rule. Use Kellis-Amberlee as a weapon and die. That plain. That simple. That universal.

"Georgia, I appreciate the thought, I truly do, but I don't think sparing me is going to save the rest of you."

"It's not intended to," I said.

"Well, then, what *is* it intended to do?"

"It's intended to give you time to download everything off the server, burn it to disk, and run for Ireland," I said. Ireland has never had an extradition treaty with the United States. It still doesn't. "If you can get across the border, you can probably lie low for years."

"And do what? Hope they forget that I'm an international terrorist?"

"Make sure the world finds out the truth."

The pause this time was even longer. When Mahir spoke again, his voice was quiet and very distant. "I'm not sure whether I should be flattered that you trust me this much, or disturbed that you've just informed me that my life is your contingency plan."

"Does that mean you won't do it?"

"Are you mad? Of course I'll do it. I'd have done it if you'd asked me upfront, and if you'd asked me in a month. It's the only way." He hesitated before adding, wistfully, "I just wish I were better with the notion of you doing this unsupported. Rick's a good fellow, but I've not worked with him long enough to feel like I'm leaving you in competent hands."

"What he can't manage, Shaun will," I said. "I'm going to cut off your official server access at midnight. I'll be mirroring all our findings on the old server address. You remember the old server?" The "old server" was a box we rented from Talking Points when we were all part of Bridge Supporters. We'd used it to back up our files when we were on the road, since Bridge Supporters wouldn't post anything that hadn't been through full validation and didn't store anything uploaded by a beta blogger for more than twenty-four hours. We hadn't used it since well before the campaign trail began, and almost no one outside the clerical staff at Talking Points knew I still had the lease. It wasn't entirely secure, but it wasn't ours, either. Mahir could access it without leaving a trail that would prove he was still a part of our group.

"I do," he said. "I suppose I shouldn't call you after this."

"Not a good idea. I'll contact you when I can."

"Right." He chuckled. "Cloak and dagger, that's us."

"Welcome to journalism."

"Indeed. I do wish I'd met you in the flesh, Georgia Mason. I truly do. It's been an honor and a privilege working with you."

"You may still get the chance, Mahir; I'm not ready to count us out yet." I slid my sunglasses back on. "Be good, be careful, and be alert. Your name is still connected to After the End Times. I can't change that."

"I wouldn't want you to. You do the same, won't you?"

"I'll try. Good night, Mahir."

"Good night, Georgia . . . and good luck."

The click of the call disconnecting sounded more final than it had any right to. Snapping my phone closed, I straightened, sighed, and reached for the door. It was time to get back to my team.

We had an awful lot of work to do.

———

It is with regret but without shame that I must announce my resignation from this site. We part, not over differences of politics or religion, but merely over a desire to explore different things. I wish the Masons the best in their future projects, and I look forward to seeing what they will accomplish.

I am sure it will be something spectacular.

—From *Fish and Clips*,
the blog of Mahir Gowda, April 9, 2040

Twenty-three

Six weeks is a long time in the news, even when you're not working on a big project. Following a political campaign is a big project, one that's capable of taking up the resources of an entire team of dedicated bloggers. Training a new division head is also a big project. The Fictionals tend to require the least amount of hand-holding, being largely content to sit around, tell each other stories, and look surprised when other people want to read them, but the person in charge of keeping them on-task needs to be more focused than the rest of the breed. There were contracts to sign and review, permissions to change, files to transfer, and a thousand little administrative things to handle that none of us wanted to deal with. Not with Buffy's blood still fresh in our minds.

Buffy caused her share of problems during those six weeks. Maybe she was gone, but she was still very much a part of the team—and not a productive one. Becks spent the bulk of her time hunting through our code and communications feeds looking for bugs and back doors. I'd clearly never realized how paranoid Buffy really was, because the number of confirmed recording devices hidden *internally* was over three digits, and Becks was still finding feeds for wireless listening devices hidden in just about every office, public gathering place, and conference center we'd been to since this whole thing started. "If she'd wanted to go CIA, she could have owned the place," Shaun muttered on the day Becks confirmed that there were still bugs running in Eakly.

"But would they have put up with her fixation on sappy purple poetry?"

"Guess not."

Alaric and Dave followed Becks through our systems, rebuilding the mess she made as she rooted out Buffy's worms. Together they were almost up to the task of remaking the things Buffy had built alone, although it was starting to wear on them; they'd signed on as journalists, not computer technicians. "Hire new field systems maintainer" was near the top of my to-do list, right under "uncover massive political conspiracy," "avenge Buffy's death," and "don't die."

And even with all of this going on, we still had a job to do. Multiple jobs, really. Not only did we need to keep following the Ryman-Tate Campaign—which continued to gather steam, now buoyed by not one, not two, but *three* major tragedies, earning us a lot of extra news cycles in the traditional media outlets, as well as online—we needed to keep our beta bloggers on-task and updating the rest of the site. The news marches on, whether you're walking wounded or not. That's one of the beautiful things about the news. It's also one of the most frustrating.

Two weeks in Houston. Two weeks of sending Rick on every assignment we could get away with sending him on, while Shaun and I locked ourselves in our hotel room and planned for a war we'd never signed up for, against an adversary we'd never volunteered to fight. Whose side was Ryman on? I was guessing he wasn't a part of Tate's plan; no sane man would sacrifice his daughter like that. Then again, Shaun and I were adopted to satisfy the Masons' desire to prove the zombie war had been won by the living, and they've never stopped us from walking into the jaws of death—if anything, they've encouraged it, living for the ratings, because when they lost Phil, the ratings were all they had. So who are we to judge the sanity of parents? We sat up until almost dawn every night, working through the darkness, making plans, making contingencies for those plans, looking for a way out of a maze we didn't see before we were already lost inside it.

Shaun pretended he didn't know I wasn't sleeping, and I pretended not to hear him punching the bathroom walls. Caffeine pills and surgical tape; that's what I'll always think of when I think of Houston. Caffeine pills and surgical tape.

I tried to talk to Ryman twice; he tried to talk to me three times. None of our attempts synchronized. I couldn't trust him when I didn't know whether or not he was working with Tate; he couldn't understand why we'd pulled away, or why we were overworked and snarly with exhaustion. Even Shaun was visibly withdrawn. He'd stopped going out in the field with Steve and the boys when he didn't need to file reports, and while he was still meeting his contracted duties, he wasn't doing it with anything like the flair and enthusiasm Ryman had come to expect from him. From all of us. There wasn't anything we could do about it. Until we knew if we could trust him, we couldn't tell him what was going on—what we suspected, what we knew, anything. And until we told him what was going on, we couldn't be sure we could trust him. It was a Möbius strip of a problem, endlessly twisting back on itself, and I couldn't see a way out of it. So we pushed him away and hoped he'd understand the reasons when things were over.

After Houston, it was time to get back on the road, rolling across the country like nothing had ever gone wrong. Not nothing; Chuck was gone, replaced by a pale-faced drone who scuttled around doing his job and avoiding anything that resembled socialization. Our security detail tripled while we were moving, and Shaun was no longer allowed to ride out unescorted. He took an almost malicious glee in forcing his babysitters to follow him into the nastiest, most dangerous terrain he could find, and some of the footage he got out of it has frankly been amazing. The Irwin community has been buzzing about putting him up for a Golden Steve-o award this year, and I'll be surprised if he doesn't win.

We spent a month glad-handing our way across the western half of the country while the other candidates stayed in the air and the major cities, assuming major metro areas would have better anti-infection measures. Tell that to San Diego. The devil-may-care approach was winning Ryman big percentage points, enough to keep him in the news even as the media flurry kicked up by this latest tragedy died down. "Man of the People Keeps the World Grounded"— human interest gold. A few outlets made the requisite noises about how Ryman's insistence on an old-fashioned campaign had dogged him with tragedy from the beginning, but the facts of Rebecca and Buffy's deaths were enough to pretty much silence them. Maybe you could blame the senator for Eakly if you reached, but you couldn't blame him for terrorist action or assassination attempts. America is the land of the free and the home of the paranoid, and yet, blessedly, we haven't fallen that far. Yet.

Six weeks after Memphis, we were overworked, overtired, and about to hit the crowds in one of the country's toughest, most essential markets: Sacramento, California.

You'd think Shaun and I would be excited about a stop in our state's capital, being California kids bred and raised. You'd be wrong. California is essentially a bunch of smaller states held together by political connections, water rights, and the stubborn refusal of any segment to cede the cash-cow name "California" to any of the others. The California secessionist movement has been around since before the Rising—not the state quitting the country, but the various parts of the state quitting each other. Sacramento has no love for the Bay Area. We get the good weather, the good press, and the big tourism dollars, and they? They get the state government and a lot of hard to defend farmland. To say that there's a little resentment there is to understate the case just a little. Whatever fellow-feeling Sacramento had for the rest of the state died when it stopped hosting the annual state fair and started hosting the annual "everybody hide in their houses and pray they don't die"-a-thon in its place.

The air was hot and so dry it seemed to suck the moisture out of my throat as we stepped out of the Sacramento Airport and onto the partitioned-off loading zone where we'd be meeting the senator's convoy. It was late afternoon, and the sun was bright enough to stab at my eyes through the lenses of my sunglasses. I staggered, catching myself on Rick's shoulder. He shot me a questioning glance. Silent, I shook my head. We were all feeling the strain, Shaun as much as any of us, and if Rick said anything, Shaun would spend the rest of the afternoon fussing over me. There was too much to do for me to let him do that.

Senator Ryman had flown in the day before, along with Governor Tate and most of the senior staff. We were supposed to be right behind them, flying commercial air rather than via private jet; unfortunately, a medical emergency grounded our plane in Denver, forcing us to wait on the tarmac with a hundred terrified passengers to see whether our aircraft was about to be declared a closed quarantine zone. I'll admit, for a few guilty moments, I was almost hoping it would be. At least then we'd be able to get some sleep before heading back to our home state. I was really starting to worry about Shaun. It had gotten to where he only went to bed when I *put* him there.

A familiar black car pulled up to the curb, and the door opened to reveal Steve, implacable and hulking as ever. "Miss Mason," he said, with a nod in my direction.

One corner of my mouth curled upward. "Nice to see you, too, Steve. What's our plan for the afternoon?"

"I'm your escort to the Assembly Center. The convoy leaves for the hall in ninety minutes."

"That doesn't leave much time." I grimaced, grabbing a suitcase in each hand as Steve got out of the car and moved to start hoisting our equipment. Senator Ryman was giving a keynote speech to the California Republicans, and it promised to be the sort of evening that resulted in lots of sound bites, accidental quotes, and competitive reporting. We all needed to be on our game. I'd been hoping to manage it with more rest and less caffeine, but you can't always get what you want. "Thanks for coming to meet us."

"Of course." A second car pulled up behind the first, Carlos getting out and joining in the collection of luggage. Our keepers—the unfortunate Andres and a blank-faced woman named Heidi, who I suspected had only been assigned to accompany us because my eyes meant I would have to go for a private security screening, and they didn't want "private" to mean "away from our guards"—joined him, first in moving the luggage, then in his car. I suppose a night at the airport with the three of us had rather soured them on our company.

"Ready?" asked Steve.

"Ready," Shaun confirmed, and we piled into the car, where blessed air conditioning washed over us. Steve glanced in the rearview mirror to be sure we were wearing our seat belts before turning on the flashers and pulling away from the curb.

I raised an eyebrow, and Shaun, taking his cue like a pro, asked, "We expecting trouble, sport?"

"There are a great many politicians in town," Steve said.

I knew what that meant: It meant Senator Ryman was concerned that whoever had been responsible for the attacks on his campaign was here in the city and would try to take care of unfinished business. They only got Buffy on their first try, after all. I forced the jet of fury rising in my chest down, refusing to let myself get riled. He didn't know the snake was in his camp; he didn't know it was Tate he needed to be watching out for. So why the *fuck* did he let us fly commercial?

Shaun put his hand on my arm, seeing my sudden tension. "Easy," he murmured.

"Hard," I said, and subsided.

In the carrier Rick was clutching, Lois yowled. I knew exactly how she felt.

Our diminutive convoy cut through the airport traffic in a bubble of open space created by the flashers, heading for the outskirts of town. Once, Sacramento was known for hosting the state fair, along with various rodeos, horse shows, and other large outdoor gatherings. After the Rising made those impractical, the city found itself missing a lot of vital revenue and it started looking for another way to make money. Several local taxes, a few private donations, and several major security contracts later, the fairgrounds reopened, given new life as the Sacramento Secure Assembly Center. Open-air, with standing structures and mobile home hookups for traveling convoys, a four-star hotel, a conference center . . . and the country's largest outdoor space certified as safe for public assembly. If you wanted to see a candidate speak outside, looking heroic and all-American against a blue summer sky, you did it in Sacramento. Presidencies were *made* there; no matter what your politics were or how clean a campaign you ran, it all came down to how the people reacted when they saw your silhouette against that sky.

According to the itinerary, Senator Ryman and Governor Tate were going to be spending the next seven days in Sacramento, giving speeches, meeting the press, and getting endorsements from California's political leaders. Not just the Republicans. My notes indicated that several prominent Democrats and Independents would be coming to have their pictures taken with the man many were beginning to suspect would be our next president. Assuming the scandal when we outed Tate didn't kill his career, of course.

"Jesus," said Rick, whistling as the fence around the Center came into view. "You people don't do anything small, do you?"

"Welcome to California," I said, rolling up my sleeves. Shaun was doing the same. Rick glanced at us, wincing, and I smiled. "Don't worry. They'll leave you a little bit."

After four blood tests and a call to the CDC databases to confirm that my retinal KA was legitimately registered and not a recent affliction, we were permitted to move into the Center. From here, blood tests would be required if we wished to enter a standing structure or leave the grounds; we'd also be subject to random testing by the Center's staff, which could happen as often as twice an hour or as rarely as once a week. Shaun made a game of pointing out the security cameras and motion detectors as we drove toward the spot assigned to the convoy.

"Start moving like a dead thing and they'll be on you in less than a minute," he said, with some satisfaction.

"Please tell me you're not speaking from experience," Rick said.

"I'm smarter than that." Shaun tried to sound affronted. He failed.

"Someone else got there first," I said. "How long did he get in state prison?"

"Two years, but it was for science," said Shaun.

"Uh-huh," I said. I might have gone on, but the car was turning, pulling down a narrow drive whose signpost identified it as "Convoy Parking #11." I sat up straighter, resettling my sunglasses. "We're here."

"Thank God," said Rick.

The Sacramento sun hadn't gotten any cooler during our drive. I shed my jacket and grabbed my laptop bag, scanning the assembled vehicles and trailers until I spotted my objective. A slow smile spread across my face.

"Van sweet van," murmured Shaun.

"Exactly." I started walking, trusting the security detail to bring the rest of our things. Our vehicles and the majority of our equipment were already in place.

"In a hurry?" Rick asked, trotting to catch up with me. Shaun gave him a look. He ignored it.

"I want to see if the boys have made any progress," I said, pressing my palm against the pressure pad on the van door. Needles bit into my hand. The door unloaded a few seconds later. Looking back over my shoulder, I asked, "Steve, which trailer are we?"

"The one on the far left with your name over the door. Mr. Cousins is in the trailer next to it," Steve said. "I assume you're anxious to get to work?"

"Yes, actually—crap." I paused, dismayed. "The keynote speech."

"I've got it," said Shaun. I must have looked stunned, because he shrugged. "I can wear a monkey suit and take notes like a Newsie. They'll never know the difference, and I bet the invite just says 'Mason.' Steve?"

"Yes . . ." said Steve, looking perplexed.

"It's settled. C'mon, Rick. Let's let George get some work done." My brother grabbed the startled Newsie by the arm and hauled him away. Steve smirked and followed, leaving me standing at the entrance to the van, wondering what had just happened. Then, not being one to look a bit of gift productivity in the mouth, I stepped inside.

We removed a few vital system components before letting them ship the van, like the backup drives, our files, and—most important—the data sticks that would unlock the servers. I made my way around the interior, taking my time as I brought each system up and online, ending with the perimeter cameras. There was a certain feeling of homecoming as the screens Buffy had worked so long to get installed began flickering on, showing rotating camera views of the outside. Nothing was happening. That's the way I like it. Once everything was stable, I flipped on the security systems. They would generate enough static to block any outside surveillance less sophisticated than the CIA's, and if we were being monitored by the CIA, we'd have been dead already. Sitting down at my console, I opened a chat window.

Most online networking is done via message boards—totally text, not quite real-time—or streaming video these days. Very few people remember the old chat relays that used to dominate the Internet. That's good. That means that if both sides of the chat are on servers you control, you can fly so far under the radar that you're essentially invisible.

Luck was with me. Dave was waiting when I connected.

What's the story? I typed. My words appeared white against the black command window.

Georgia? Confirm.

Password is 'tintinnabulation.'

Confirmed. Have you checked your e-mail?

Not yet. We just got in.

Log off. Go read. I don't want to waste your time with a reframe.

I paused, staring at those stark white words for a long moment before I typed, *How bad?*

Bad enough. Go.

I went.

Reading the files Dave and Alaric provided took the better part of an hour. Getting myself to stop hyperventilating took another twenty minutes. When my lungs stopped burning and I was sure I could control myself, I shut down my laptop, returned it to its case, and rose. I needed to get myself dressed; it was time to crash a party.

I always knew I wanted to be a journalist. When I was a kid, I thought they were the next best thing to superheroes. They told the truth. They helped people. I wouldn't find out about the other things journalists did—the lies and espionage and back-stabbing and bribes—for years, and by that point, it was too late. The news was in my blood. Like every junkie in the world, I needed my next hit too badly to give it up.

I've wanted nothing but the news and the truth and to make the world a better place since I was a little girl, and I never regretted it for a minute. Not until now. Because this is bigger than me, and it's bigger than Shaun, and God, I'm scared. And I'm still a junkie. I still can't walk away.

—From *Postcards from the Wall*,
the unpublished files of Georgia Mason, June 19, 2040

Twenty-four

Unfortunately for my need to hurry, the instructions regarding the senator's keynote speech and the dinner party to follow were clear: Formal attire was required for all attendees, even media representatives. Maybe especially media representatives—after all, everyone *else* paid fifteen hundred dollars for the privilege of eating rubber chicken and rubbing elbows with Senator Ryman, while we were getting in on that damned "freedom of the press" loophole. If they shut us out, we'd be free to start playing dirty. If they let us in, cosseted us, petted us, and put us in our places, they could maintain the semblance of control. Maybe it's never stopped a real scandal from growing legs, but it's done a lot to keep the little ones under the table where they belong.

The campaign staff had been careful with our luggage, placing mine and Shaun's on our respective sides of the trailer we'd be living in for the duration of the Sacramento stop. That was, sadly, before Shaun tore through like a hurricane, looking for his own formalwear. My suitcases were buried beneath a thick layer of Shaun's clothing, weaponry, paperwork, and other general debris. Locating them took the better part of ten minutes, and determining which case contained my own formalwear took another five. I cursed Shaun the whole time. It kept me distracted.

Men's formal attire is sensible: pants, suit coats, cummerbunds. Even ties can be useful, since they work as makeshift tourniquets or garrotes. Women's formal attire, on the other hand, hasn't changed since the Rising; it still seems designed to get the people wearing it killed at the first possible opportunity. Screw that. My dress was custom-made. The skirt is breakaway, the bodice is fitted to allow me to carry a recorder and a gun, and there's a pocket concealed at the waist for extra ammo. Even with all those alterations, it's the most confining garment I own, and the situations that call for me to wear it almost invariably require hose and heels. At least modern pantyhose are made with a polymer weave that's virtually puncture proof.

I'd wear the heels. I'd wear the hose. I'd even wear a layer of tinted lip gloss, since that would make it look like I'd applied makeup for the occasion. There was no way I was going to put my contacts in for what was, essentially, a snatch-and-grab to get me to the senator and my team, convince them I had news, and get them back to the compound. Still swearing, I yanked the shawl that went with the dress out of the side pocket of my garment bag, clipped my ID badge to the right side of my chest, and went storming back out of the trailer, heading for the motor pool.

Steve was on duty, standing at a relaxed sort of attention as he monitored the radio channels for security or vehicular needs. He straightened when he saw me coming, chin bobbing downward as he took in the way that I was dressed. It was impossible to see his eyes behind his sunglasses, but he took no pains to disguise the motion of his head, which rose again as he studied the tailoring of my dress, the shawl around my shoulders, and finally, with a quirk of one eyebrow, my sunglasses.

"Going somewhere?" he asked.

"I was planning on doing a little gate-crashing," I said. "Give a girl a ride?"

"Didn't you send your brother in your place?"

"Something came up. It's important that I get over there."

Steve studied me for a moment, his expression implacable. I looked back at him, keeping my own expression just as composed. We both had a lot of practice, but I was the one who had more to lose if I slipped up. It was Steve who gave in, nodding marginally before he said, "This got something to do with Eakly, Georgia?"

His partner died there. We knew there was a conspiracy. How likely was it that we'd still be alive if our security detail was a part of it? There might be listening devices. There was nothing I could do about that, and we were in the end game. It was time to go all-in. "This has everything to do with Eakly, and with the ranch, and with why Chuck and Buffy died. Please. I need you to get me to that dinner."

Steve remained still for a moment more, mulling over what I'd said. He was a big man, and people often assume big men must be slow. I never assumed that about Steve, and I didn't assume it now. He was getting his first real look at a situation my team and I had been living with for months, and it took some getting used to. When he did start to move, he moved quickly and with no hesitation. "Mike, Heidi, you cover this gate. Anybody radios for me, you say I'm in the can and I'll radio back when I'm done. Tell them I had franks and beans for dinner, if you think it'll keep them from asking more."

Heidi tittered, a high, nervous sound entirely out of keeping with her professional exterior. Mike frowned, expression betraying a slow confusion. "Yeah, we can do that," he said. "But why . . . ?"

"We hired you after the ranch, so I'm not going to smack you for asking that question. There's reasons." Steve glanced at me. "I'm guessing that if it was safe to give those reasons in a place as open as this one, they'd have already been given."

I nodded. I wouldn't have said as much as I had if he hadn't invoked the specter of Eakly first, but I wasn't going to lie to the man when I was asking for his help. Even if I thought I could pull it off, which I didn't, it would have been wrong.

"Just do it, Mike," said Heidi, aiming an elbow at the unfortunate Mike's side. He bore the blow stoically, only allowing a slight grunt to escape. Heidi withdrew her elbow. "We got it, Steve. Watch the gate, monitor the radio, don't tell anybody you're gone."

"Good. Miss Mason? This way." Steve turned, his legs eating ground with frightening efficiency as he led me to one of the motor pool's smaller vehicles. It was a modified Jeep with a hard black exterior that made it look like nothing so much as a strange new type of beetle. He produced the keys from one pocket and hit a button; the doors unlocked with a beep. "You'll forgive me if I don't open the door for you."

"Of course," I said. In a two-person vehicle this new, there would be blood test units built into the door handles to prevent some unfortunate driver from ending up sealed in an enclosed space with one of the infected. Chivalry wasn't dead. Chivalry just wanted to be certain I wasn't a zombie before I got into the car.

Even when concerned enough to abandon his post—and that's what he was doing, given that he hadn't radioed our whereabouts to base—Steve remained a careful, cautious driver. He sped down the roads back toward town at precisely the speed limit, without turning the flashers on. They would have attracted too much attention, especially from any members of our own camp who might start to wonder what he was doing out there. Our departure from the compound had been recorded, but those records were legally secured, save in the instance of an outbreak causing privacy laws to be suspended.

The hall where Senator Ryman's keynote speech and the associated dinner party were being hosted was downtown, in one of the areas that was rebuilt after the Rising. Shaun and I did a series of articles on the "bad" parts of Sacramento a few years ago, taking cameras past the cordons and into the areas that were never reapproved for human habitation. Burnt-out husks of buildings stare out on cracking asphalt, the biohazard tape still gleaming across their doors and windows. In the white marble and clean chrome paradise of the government assembly hall, you'd never know that side of Sacramento existed. Not unless you'd been there.

It took three blood tests to reach the foyer. The first was at the entrance to the underground parking garage, where valets in plastic gloves brought the test panels, clearly expecting us to allow the polite fiction that there weren't guards with automatic weapons flanking the booth. Those men stood there like statues, sending goose bumps marching across my arms. It wasn't the security; it was how blatantly it was displayed. No one would argue if they gunned us down. I had my recorders running, but without a security schematic, I couldn't afford to transmit across what might be compromised airspace, and without Buffy, I didn't have a security schematic I could trust. We needed her so badly. We always had.

Steve stayed behind in the garage, standing silent guard over the car; without my press pass and invitation, he'd never make it into the party without making a scene, and we didn't want to do that. Not yet. I was pretty sure there were a lot of scenes in my future. Assuming the senator listened long enough that we could keep on *having* a future.

It took a second blood test to get out of the garage and into the elevator. The third blood test came as a bit of a surprise; it was required to get *out* of the elevator. How they expected me to have been exposed to the virus during the ten seconds I'd spent between floors was a mystery to me, but they wouldn't have spent the money on a testing unit if it hadn't happened at least once. The elevator doors didn't open until the light over the door went green, and I spared a moment to wonder what happened when more than one person took the elevator at a time. Then I stepped out into the foyer and into a world that had never known the Rising.

The mystery of the extensive security was solved in an instant, because this huge, lavishly appointed room looked like it was lifted straight from the pre-infection world. No one carried visible weapons or wore protective gear. A few folks had the clear plastic strips over their eyes that signaled the presence of retinal Kellis-Amberlee, but that was it. The place even had picture windows, for God's sake. It took careful scrutiny to see that they were holograms, looking out over an image of a city too perfect to be real. Maybe that's how it was once, but I doubt it; corruption's been with us a lot longer than the living dead.

Even without visible weapons, there was security. A man with a portable bar-code scanner in one hand stopped me not two steps out of the elevator. "Name?"

"Georgia Mason, After the End Times. I'm with the Ryman campaign." I unclipped my badge, handing it over. He swiped it through his scanner and passed it back, frowning at the display. "You should have me on your list."

"According to this, Shaun Mason has already checked in with those credentials."

"If you'll check your list of associated journalists, you'll see that we're *both* registered as being attached to the Ryman campaign." I didn't bother trying to win him over with my scintillating wit.

He had the look of a natural bureaucrat, and that sort of person almost never yields from the stated outline of their job.

"Please wait while I access the list." He made a seemingly careless gesture with one hand. Only seemingly careless; I could see four people in the crowd who were now looking in our direction, and none of them was holding a drink or laughing. If four of the guards on duty were being that blatant, the math of professional security meant there were four more who weren't.

The scanning unit beeped as it connected to the wireless network and queried the files available on the press corps cleared for entrance. Eventually, it stopped beeping, and the officious little man's frown deepened.

"Your credentials are in order," he said, sounding as if the very fact that I hadn't lied was inconveniencing him. "You may proceed."

"Thank you." The watchers had melted into the crowd now that they were sure I wasn't gate-crashing. I clipped the badge back to my chest, putting several feet between myself and the man with the scanner before reaching up to tap my ear cuff. "Shaun," I muttered, quietly.

There was a pause, the transmitter beeping to signal that it was making a connection. Then Shaun's voice, close by and startled: "Hey, George. I figured you'd be neck-deep in site reviews by now. What gives?"

"Remember the punch line I forgot yesterday?" I asked, scanning the crowd as I moved toward what I presumed was the entrance to the main dining hall. "The *really* funny one?"

Shaun's surprise faded, replaced by wariness. "Yeah, I remember that one. Did you figure out the rest of the joke?"

"Uh-huh, I did. Some friends of mine found it on-line. Where are you?"

"We're at the podium. Senator Ryman's shaking hands. What's the punch line?"

"It'll be funnier if I tell you in person. How do I get to the podium?"

"Straight through the big doors and head for the back of the hall."

"Got it. Georgia out." I tapped the ear cuff, killing the connection, and walked on.

Shaun and Rick were a few feet to the left of the crowd of people the senator was glad-handing his way through. They'd paid for the privilege of meeting the man being predicted as our next president, and they were by God going to meet him, even if it was only for the few seconds it took to shake a hand and share a smile. On those few seconds are presidencies made. Here, behind the believable "safety" of a double-checked guest list and that guest list's triple-checked infection status, old-school politicians felt free to revert to their old habits, pressing the flesh like it had never gone out of style. You could tell the ones who were genuinely young from the ones who'd had all the plastic surgery and regenerative treatments money could buy, because the young ones were the ones looking nauseated by all the human contact around them. They hadn't grown up in this political culture. They just had to live with it until they became the old men at the top of the hill.

The senator didn't look uncomfortable at all. The

man was in his element, all toothy smiles and bits of practical wisdom sliced down to sound-bite size in case one of the nearby reporters was broadcasting on an open band. He'd known to do that sort of thing long before we joined his campaign, but having a constant press entourage had forced him to master the art. He was good. Given enough time, he'd be great.

Shaun was watching for my arrival, his shoulders set at the angle that meant he was tenser than hell and trying to hide it. They relaxed slightly as he saw me cutting through the crowd, and he nodded for me to approach. I shook my head, mouthing 'Where's Tate?'

Holding up a finger to signal me to quiet, Shaun pulled out his PDA and scrawled a message with the attached stylus. My watch beeped a second later, the message *other side o/room w/investors what's going on?????* scrolling across the screen. The message *I need to talk to Sen. Ryman w/o Tate hearing* would have taken too long to type on the tiny foldout keypad. I deleted the message and kept walking.

"Georgia," Rick greeted as I drew close. He was holding a flute of what appeared to be champagne, if you didn't pay too much attention to the bubbles. Sparkling cider: another trick of working the crowd. If people think you're getting as drunk as they are, they forget to be careful around you.

"Rick," I said, with a nod. Shaun was shooting me a concerned look, and failing in his efforts to hide it. I put a hand on his arm. "Nice tux."

"They call me Bond," he said, gravely.

"Figured they might." I looked toward the senator.

"Gonna need to wade in there. I wish I had a cattle prod."

"Are we going to find out what the situation is any time soon, or are we supposed to follow you blindly?" asked Shaun. "I ask because it determines whether I'm hitting you in the head sometime in the next eight seconds. Very vital information."

"It's a little hard to explain here," I said. "Unless you know who's broadcasting locally?"

Shaun groaned, attracting startled glances from several bystanders. A plastic smile snapping instantly into place, he said, "Jeez, George, that was a *terrible* joke."

"I didn't say it was a *good* punch line, just that I'd remembered it," I said, stepping a little closer. Pitching my voice so low it verged on inaudible, I said, "Dave and Alaric had their big breakthrough. They followed the money."

"Where'd it go?" Shaun was even better at this than I was. His lips didn't even seem to move.

" 'Where'd it *come* from?' would be a better question. It *went* to Tate. It *came* from the tobacco companies, and from some people they haven't traced yet."

"We knew it was Tate."

"The IPs they're pulling are from D.C. . . . and Atlanta."

There's only one organization in Atlanta important enough to bring me running the way I had, especially when we'd already known at least a part of the conspiracy. Shaun's eyes widened, need for secrecy eclipsed by sudden shock. If the CDC had been infiltrated . . .

"They don't know for sure?"

"They're trying, but the security is good, and they've nearly been caught twice."

Shaun sighed. That *was* audible, and I elbowed him in the side for it. He shook his head. "Sorry. I just wish Buffy were here."

"So do I." Palming a data stick, I slipped it into his pocket. To an observer, it would have looked like I was going for his wallet. Let them call security. It's not like there'd be anything for them to find. "That's a copy of everything. There are six more. Steve doesn't know he has one."

"Got it," said Shaun. Always back up your data, and scatter it as far as you can. I can't count the number of journalists who have forgotten that basic rule, and some have never recovered from the stories they lost. If we lost this one, getting discredited was going to be the least of our worries. "Off-site?"

"Multiple places. I don't know them all; the guys did their own backups."

"Good."

Rick had been observing our semi-audible conversation without comment. He raised his eyebrows as it stopped, and I shook my head. He took the refusal with good grace, sipping from his glass of "champagne" and continuing to scan the crowd. There were a few people who seemed to be holding the bulk of his interest. Some were politicians, while others were people I recognized from the campaign. I glanced to Rick, who nodded toward Tate. Got it. These were people whose loyalties he thought he knew, and thought belonged to our resident governor. Who just happened to be the man most likely to have caused the deaths of an awful lot of innocent people, as well as being responsible for the corruption and death of one of our own.

None of those people was standing close enough to hear our conversation unless one of them had listening devices planted on or around the senator. If I was going to risk anything, I needed to do it now. "I'm going in," I murmured to Shaun, and began working my way through the crowd surrounding Senator Ryman.

I'll give the flesh-pressers this: They didn't give ground easy, not even as I was none too gently elbowing my way into their midst. A lady old enough to have been my grandmother drove the heel of her left shoe down on the top of my foot with a degree of force that would have been impressive in a younger woman. Fortunately, even my dress shoes are made of reinforced polymer. Even so, I bit my tongue to keep myself from swearing out loud. Casual assault might be A-okay with security, but I was reasonably sure shouting "cock-sucking bitch" wouldn't be.

After a lot of shoving and several painful kicks to my shins and ankles, I found myself to the right of the senator, who was busy having his hand pumped up and down by a barrel-chested octogenarian whose eyes burned with the revolutionary fervor one only ever seems to see in those who discovered either religion or politics at a very young age. Neither man seemed to have registered the fact that I was there. I was neither the assaulting nor the assaulted, which left me on the outside of their present closed equation.

The handshaker showed no signs of stopping. If anything, his pumps were increasing in vigor as he started hitting his stride. I weighed the potential danger of octogenarian assault against waiting for him to tire, and settled on action as the better part of valor. Smoothly as I could, I moved to place my hand on Senator Ryman's free arm and said, in a sugar-sweetened tone, "Senator, if I could have a moment of your time, I'd be most appreciative."

The senator jumped. His assailant looked daggers at me, which moved up the scale to full-sized swords as the senator turned and flashed his best magazine-cover smile my way. "Of course, Miss Mason," he said. He deftly twitched his fingers free of the handshaker, saying, "If you wouldn't mind excusing me, Council-man Plant, I need to confer with a member of my press pool. Everyone, I'll be right back with you."

Fighting into the throng had taken almost five minutes. Getting out of it required nothing but the senator's hand at the small of my back, propelling me along as we made our way to the clear space to the left of the dais. "Not that I mind the save, Geor-gia, since I was starting to worry about the structural integrity of my wrist, but what are you doing here?" asked Senator Ryman, his voice pitched low. "Last I checked, you'd stayed at the Center, which is why your brother's been here annoying the staff and eat-ing all the shrimp canapés all evening."

"I *did* stay at the Center," I said. "Senator, I don't know if you're aware of this, but—" Someone shouted congratulations to the senator, who answered it with a grin and a broad thumbs-up. It was a perfect photo-op moment, and I snapped the shot with my watch's built-in camera before I even thought about what I was doing. Instincts. Clearing my throat, I tried again. "Buffy was working for someone who wanted to keep tabs on your campaign."

"You've told me this before," he said, more briskly. I recognized the impatience in his eyes from dozens of media briefings. "It's all some big shadow conspiracy looking to bring me down. What I don't understand is why this is suddenly so pressing that you need to rush over here and risk making a scene on what might be one of the most important political evenings of my life. There are a great many movers and shakers here tonight, Georgia—a *great* many. These are the men who could hand me California, as you'd know, if you'd bothered to read the briefing papers and attend my speech." *If you'd bothered to do your job*, said his subtext, so clearly that it might as well have been spoken aloud. I'd let him down. My reporting, which he'd come to depend on as one of the tools of his campaign—the objective reporter, won over by his politics and his rhetoric—was supposed to have been there, and it wasn't.

The senator had heard my excuses with increasing frequency in the time since Buffy's death, and it was clear that he was getting tired of them. More than tired; he was getting frustrated with them, and by extension, with me.

Talking faster now, in an effort to keep him from shutting me out before I could finish, I said, "Senator, I've had two of my people running traces for weeks now on every bit of data we could find. They've been following the money. That's what it always comes back to—the money. And they've managed to find—"

"We'll talk about this later, Georgia."

"But Senator Ryman, we—"

"I *said* we'd talk about this later." He was frowning now, his stiff, political smile, the one he used during debates, or when chastising recalcitrant interns. "This is neither the time nor the place for this discussion."

"Senator, we have proof Tate was involved in what happened to Buffy." The senator froze. Finally sensing that he might listen, I pressed my case. "We've had audio for a while, but my team found the payments. We found the contacts. Buffy wasn't the start. Eakly was the start. Eakly and the ranch—"

"No."

The word was soft but implacable. I stopped dead, run up against the side of that refusal like I'd just slammed into a wall. After a frozen moment, I tried again, saying, "Senator Ryman, please, if you'd just—"

"Georgia, this is not the time, and it's not the place, especially if those are the accusations you've come here to make." His face was cold. I'd never seen him look that cold toward anyone who wasn't a political rival. "David Tate and I may not have always seen eye to eye on this campaign trail, and God knows, I've always known there was no love lost between the two of you, but I'm not going to stand here and listen to you say these things about a man who spoke at my daughter's funeral. I can't have that."

"Senator, that man was just as responsible for your daughter's death as if he'd infected her himself."

Senator Ryman's shoulders tensed, and his hand actually rose several inches before he forced it down. He wanted to hit me; that truth was written so clear across his face that even Shaun could have seen it. He wanted to, but he wouldn't. Not here, not in front of all these witnesses.

"It's time for you to go, Georgia."

"Senator—"

"If the three of you aren't off the premises in the next fifteen minutes, you'll be spending tonight in the Sacramento County jailhouse, as I'll have had your press clearance pulled." His tone was calm, even reasonable, but there was no kindness in it, and kindness was the thing I was most accustomed to hearing from him. "When I get back to the Center, I'll come by your trailer, and you'll show me every scrap of proof you think you have."

"And then?" I asked, despite my own better judgment. I needed to know how seriously he was willing to take this.

"And then, if I believe you, I'll back you up when we call for the federal authorities, because what you're saying, Georgia, what you're *accusing* is terrorism, and if that accusation gets made without absolute proof behind it, well, there's more than one man's career it could destroy."

He was right. If it got out that the Ryman campaign had been harboring a man who'd use Kellis-Amberlee as a weapon—hell, that a man who'd use Kellis-Amberlee as a weapon was actually *on the ticket*—it would ruin him. His political enemies would never let the scandal die. Some of them would probably say he'd supported Tate's actions, even to the point of killing Rebecca, for the votes it bought him.

"If you don't believe me?" I asked, shaping the words with lips that had gone numb.

"If I don't believe you, you're all on the next bus to Berkeley, and we're parting ways before the sun comes up," the senator said and turned his back on me, all smiles as he shifted his attention to the crowd. "Congresswoman!" he said, joviality coming back into his voice as if he'd flipped a switch. "You're looking lovely tonight—is that your wife? Well, Mrs. Lancer, it surely is a pleasure to finally have the opportunity to meet you in the flesh, after seeing you in so many of those Christmas card photos—"

And then he was moving away, leaving me standing alone in the middle of the crowd, the important people of this little modern Babylon pressing all around me as they struggled for a moment of his attention, my colleagues standing not ten feet away, waiting to hear what I'd accomplished.

The truth had never felt like it was further away, or harder to make sense of. And I had never in my life felt like I was more lost, or more alone.

———

We were eleven when I first understood that we weren't immortal. I always knew the Masons had a biological son named Phillip. Our folks didn't talk about him much, but he came up every time someone mentioned Mason's Law. It's funny, but I sort of hero-worshipped him when I was a kid, because people remembered him. I never really considered the fact that they remembered him for dying.

George and I were hunting for our Christmas presents when she found the box. It was in the closet in Mom's office, and we'd probably overlooked it a thousand times before, but it caught George's eye that day for some reason, and she hauled it out, and we looked inside. That was the day I met my brother.

The box was full of photographs we'd never seen,

pictures of a laughing little boy in a world where he'd never been forced to worry about the things we lived with every day. Phillip riding a pony at the state fair. Phillip playing in the sand on a beach with no fences in sight. Phillip with his long-haired, short-sleeved, laughing mother, who didn't look anything like our mother, who wore her hair short and her sleeves long enough to hide the body armor, whose holster dug into my side when she kissed me good night. He had a smile that said he'd never been afraid of anything, and I hated him a little, because his parents were so much happier than mine.

We never talked about that day. We put the pictures back in the closet, and we never found our Christmas presents, either. But that was the day I realized . . . if Phillip, this happy, innocent kid, could die, so could we. Someday, we'd be cardboard boxes at the back of somebody's closet, and there wasn't a thing we could do about it. George knew it, too; maybe she even knew it before I did. We were all we had, and we could die. It's hard to live knowing something like that. We've done the best we could.

No one gets to ask us for anything more. Not now, not ever. When history looks our way—stupid, blind history, that judges everything and never gives a shit what we paid to get it—it better remember that no one had a right to ask us for this. No one.

—From *Hail to the King*,
the blog of Shaun Mason, June 19, 2040

Twenty-five

Georgia, what just happened?"

"George? You okay?"

Both of them sounded so concerned it left me wanting to scream. I settled for grabbing a flute of champagne from a passing server, draining it in one convulsive gulp, and snapping, "We have to go. Now."

That just redoubled their concern. Rick's eyes went wide, while Shaun's narrowed, accompanied by a sudden frown. "How pissed is he?" he asked.

"He's pulling our press passes in fifteen minutes."

Shaun whistled. "Nice. Even for you, that's impressive. What'd you do, suggest that his wife was having an affair with the librarian?"

"It was the tutor, that was the Mayor of Oakland's wife, and I was right," I said, starting to stalk for the exit. True to form, they followed. "I didn't say anything about Emily."

"Excuse me, but does one of you mind telling me what's going on?" interjected Rick, putting on a burst of speed to get in front of me. "Georgia just got us kicked out of a major political event, Senator Ryman's clearly pissed, and Tate's glaring. I'm missing something. I don't like that."

I went cold. "Tate's glaring at us?"

"If looks could kill—"

"We'd be joining Rebecca Ryman. I'll fill you in once we're in the car."

Rick hesitated, licking his lower lip as he registered the anxiety in my tone. "Georgia?"

"I'm serious," I said, and sped up, going as fast as I could manage without starting to a run. Shaun took the cue from me, linking one arm through mine and using his longer legs to give me a little extra speed. Rick hurried along behind us, holding his questions until we got outside. Bless him for that much, anyway.

It took only one blood test to get back to the car. Since everyone on the banquet level was assumed clean after the checks they'd endured to get there, the elevator came at the press of a button, no needles involved until we wanted to exit. Like a roach motel— the infected could check in, but they couldn't check out. My earlier curiosity about what would happen if more than one person took the elevator at the same time was answered as the interior sensors refused to let the doors open until the system detected three different, noninfected blood samples. Someone who unwittingly boarded the elevator with a person undergoing viral amplification would just die in there. Nice.

Steve was still next to the car, arms folded across his chest. He straightened when he saw the three of us come marching out of the elevator but he restrained his curiosity better than Rick had, waiting until we were reaching for the doors before he asked, "Well?"

"Threatened to yank our press passes," I said.

"Nice," said Steve, raising his eyebrows. "He pressing charges?"

"No, that'll probably come after tonight's episode of 'meet the press.'" I climbed into the back seat.

Shaun did the same on the opposite side of the car, commenting, "She means 'beat the press,' don'cha, George?"

"Possibly," I said.

"*Now* will you tell me what's going on?" asked Rick, getting into the front passenger seat and twisting around to face us.

"It's simple, really," I said, sagging into the seat. Shaun already had his arm in place to support me, offering as much comfort as he could. "Dave and Alaric followed the money and proved that Governor Tate was behind the attacks on Eakly and the ranch. Also, PS, the CDC is potentially involved, which isn't going to make me sleep any easier tonight, thanks. The senator wasn't thrilled with the idea that his running mate might be the goddamn devil, so he's asked us to go back to the Center to prepare our notes while he decides whether or not to fire our asses."

There was a long silence as the other three people in the car attempted to absorb what I'd just said. Surprisingly, it was Steve who spoke first, in a low rumble closer to a growl than a normal conversational tone. "Are you *sure*?" he asked.

"We have proof," I said, closing my eyes and leaning into Shaun's arm. "People have been funneling him money, and he's been funneling it on to the sort of folks who think weaponizing Kellis-Amberlee is a good thing. Some of that money's been coming from

Atlanta. Some of it's been coming from the big tobacco companies. And a lot of people have died, presumably so that nice ol' Governor Tate can be Vice
President of the United States of America. At least,
until the president-elect has some sort of tragic accident and he has to step into the position."

"Georgia . . ." Rick sounded almost awed, overwhelmed with the possibilities. "If we know this for
sure—Georgia, this is a really big deal. This is . . . Are
we allowed to know this and not just report it to the
FBI, or the CDC, or *somebody*? This is *terrorism*."

"I don't know, Rick; you're the one who worked
in print media. Why don't you try telling me for a
change?"

"Even in cases of suspected terrorism, a journalist
can protect his or her sources as long as they aren't
actually sheltering the suspect." Rick hesitated.
"We're not, are we? Sheltering him?"

"Pardon me for breaking in, Mr. Cousins, but if
Miss Mason's proof is as good as she seems to think,
it doesn't matter whether she plans on sheltering him
or not. My partner died in Eakly." Steve's tone was
normal now, almost casual. Somehow that was even
more disturbing. "Tyrone was a good man. He deserved better. Man who started that outbreak, well.
That man *doesn't* deserve better."

"Don't worry about it," I said. "I have no intention
of sheltering him. I'll talk it over with the senator,
and if he wants to throw us off the campaign, he's
welcome to. I'll mail our files to every open-source
blog, newspaper, and politician in the country while
we're on the road for home."

"This is crap," Shaun said, withdrawing his arm.

"Right," I agreed.

"Absolute fucking crap."

"No argument."

"I want to punch somebody right about now."

"Not it," Rick said.

"I punch back," Steve said. A note of amusement crept into his voice, making him sound a little less likely to explode. That was good. Not that I'd object to seeing Tate get the crap kicked out of him—I just didn't want to see Steve go to federal prison over it when the FBI would be just as happy to do the honors. Hell, after they had Tate in custody, and considering what had happened in Eakly, they might be willing to let Steve have his licks. Just as long as they got theirs first.

"Just have patience; this is all going to be over soon," I said. "One way or another, I guess we're finishing things tonight."

"Let's pick one way, okay?" said Shaun. "I don't like another."

"That's okay," I said. "Neither do I."

We finished the drive in silence, pulling through the Center gates and enduring the barrage of blood tests that followed with as much grace as we could muster. Three of us were exhausted, scared, and angry; Steve was just angry, and I almost envied him. Anger's easier to run on than exhaustion. It doesn't strip your gears as badly. Less than two hours after convincing him to abandon his post for my fool's errand, Steve drove back into the motor pool, his car heavier by two journalists and a whole lot of free-floating worry.

"Don't say anything, please," I said, as we climbed

out of the car. "I'm meeting with the senator tonight, when he gets back from his dinner. After that—"

"After that, I guess what needs doing is going to be clear one way or the other," said Steve. "Don't worry. I wouldn't have gone into security if I didn't know how to keep my mouth shut."

"Thanks."

"Don't mention it." Steve smiled, briefly. I smiled back.

"George, c'mon!" Shaun called, already a good four or five yards from the car. "I want to get out of this damn monkey suit!"

"Coming!" I shouted, muttering, "Jesus," before I turned to follow him back to the trailers.

Rick walked with us as far as the van; then he turned left, toward his trailer, while we turned right, toward ours. "He's a good guy," said Shaun, pressing his thumb against the lock on the trailer door. It clicked open, confirming Shaun's right to enter. "A little old-fashioned, but still a good guy. I'm glad we got the chance to work with him."

"You think he'll stay on after we all get home?" I started rummaging through the mass of clothing on the beds and floor, looking for the cotton shirt and jeans I'd been wearing earlier.

"He can write his own ticket after this campaign, but yeah, I think he may stick around." Shaun was already halfway out of his formal wear, shedding it with the ease of long practice. "He knows he can work with us."

"Good."

I was doing up the last of the buttons on my shirt when I heard the shouting. Shaun and I exchanged a wide-eyed, shocked look before we both went running for the trailer door. I made it out half a beat ahead of him, just in time to see a shell-shocked-looking Rick come staggering up the path with Lois cradled against his chest. I didn't have to be a veterinarian to know that something was horribly wrong with his cat. No living animal has a neck that bends that way or hangs that limply in its owner's arms.

"Rick . . . ?"

He stopped in his tracks, staring at me, the body of his cat still clutched against his chest. I ran the last fifteen feet between us, and Shaun ran close behind me. That was probably the part they didn't figure on: those fifteen feet.

Those fifteen stupid little feet saved our lives.

"What happened?" I asked, putting out a hand, as if there were a damn thing I could do. Seen this close, it was even more obvious that the cat had been dead for a while. Her eyes were open and glazed, staring blankly off at nothing.

"She was just . . . I got back to the trailer and I almost tripped on her." For the first time, I realized Rick was still wearing his formal clothes. He hadn't even had time to change. "She was just inside the doorway. I think . . . even after they hurt her, I think she tried to get away." Tears running down his cheeks. I'm not sure he was even aware of them. "I think she was trying to come and find me. She was just a *little* cat, Georgia. Why would anyone do this to such a *little* cat?"

Shaun stiffened. "She was inside? Are you *sure* this wasn't natural causes?"

"Since when do natural causes break your neck?"

asked Rick, in a tone that would have been reasonable if he hadn't been crying so hard.

"We should go to the van."

I frowned. "Shaun—?"

"I'm serious. We can talk about this in the van, but we should go there. Right now."

"Just let me get my gun," I said, and started to turn toward the trailer. Shaun grabbed my elbow, yanking me back. I stumbled.

The trailer exploded with a concussive bang, like an engine misfiring.

The first bang was followed by a second and larger bang, echoed in the distance as another trailer—probably Rick's—went up in a ball of blue-and-orange flame. Not that there was much time to make estimates about where the blast was coming from. Shaun still had my arm and he was running, dragging me in his wake as he rushed toward the van. Rick ran after us, clutching Lois's body to his chest, all of us bathed in the angry orange glare of the blast. Someone was trying to kill us. At this point, I didn't even have to wonder who. Tate knew we knew. There was no reason for him to play nice anymore.

Once he was sure I'd keep running, Shaun let go of me, dropping back as he tried to cover our retreat toward the van. I quashed the urge to worry about him, keeping my focus on the running. Shaun could take care of himself. I had to believe that or I'd never be able to believe anything else. Rick was running like a man in a dream, Lois bouncing limply in his arms with every step. And I just ran.

Something pricked my left biceps when we were about halfway to the van. I ignored it and kept going, more focused on getting to cover than on swatting at some mosquito with shit for timing. No one's ever been able to tell the insects of the world that they shouldn't interrupt the big dramatic moments, and so they keep on doing it. That's probably a good thing. If drama kept the bugs away, most people would never emotionally mature past the age of seventeen.

"Rick, get the doors!" shouted Shaun. He was hanging about five yards back, still moving fast. He had his .45 drawn, covering the area as we retreated. The sight of him was enough to make my heart beat faster and my throat get tight. I knew he was wearing Kevlar under his clothes, but Kevlar wouldn't save him from a headshot. Whoever blew up the trailers might be out there watching, and once they saw us scattering into the open, there was every chance they'd decide to finish what they'd started. And none of that mattered, because someone had to watch the rear, and someone had to open the van, and if we clustered together to make me feel better, neither of those things would happen, and we'd *all* die.

Knowing the realities of the situation didn't do a damn thing to make me feel better about leaving Shaun to twist in the wind. It just meant I understood that we didn't have a choice.

Rick put on a burst of speed, reaching the van a good twenty feet ahead of me. He finally seemed to realize he was carrying Lois because he dropped her body, reaching out to grab the handles of the rear doors and press his forefingers against the reader pads. There was a click as the onboard testing system ran his blood and prints, confirming he was both uninfected and an authorized driver before the locks released.

"Got it!" he yelled, and wrenched the doors open, motioning for us to get inside.

He didn't need to tell me twice. I sped up, breath aching in my chest as I raced to get out of the open. Shaun continued moving at the same pace, swinging his gun unhurriedly from side to side as he covered our retreat.

"Shaun, you idiot!" I yelled. "Get your ass in here! There's no one out there to save!"

He glanced over his shoulder, eyebrows rising in apparent surprise. Something in my expression must have told him that it wasn't worth arguing because he nodded and turned to run the rest of the way.

I didn't start really breathing again until he and Rick were both inside with the doors closed behind them. Shaun flipped the dead bolts on the rear doors, while Rick moved to do the same on the movable wall that shut the driver's cabin off from the rest of the vehicle. With those latches thrown, we were effectively cut off from the rest of the world. Nothing could get in, and unless we opened the locks, nothing could get out. Barring heavy explosives, we were as safe as it was possible to be.

I took a seat at the main console and brought up the security recordings for the last day. The scanner came up clean, showing no attempted break-ins or unauthorized contact with the van's exterior during that time. "Shaun, when was the last security sweep?"

"I ran one remotely while I was waiting for the senator's speech to finish."

"Good. That means we're clean." I leaned over

to turn on the exterior cameras—without them, we were flying blind and would have no way of knowing when help arrived—and froze.

"George?"

It was Shaun's voice, sounding distant and surprised. He'd seen me reach for the switches, and seen me stop; he just hadn't seen why. I didn't answer him. I was too busy staring.

"George, what's wrong?"

"I . . ." I began, and stopped, swallowing in an effort to clear the sudden dryness from my mouth. Forcing myself to start again, I said, "I think we may have a problem." Raising my right hand, I wrapped numb fingers around the hollow plastic dart projecting from my left biceps and pulled it free, turning to face the other two. Rick paled, seeing the red stain spreading through the fabric of my shirt. Shaun just stared at the dart, looking like he was seeing the end of the world.

In a very real and concrete way, there was an excellent chance that he was.

———————

If you want an easy job—if you want the sort of job where you never have to bury somebody who you care about—I recommend you pursue a career in whatever strikes your fancy . . . just so long as it isn't the news.

—From *Another Point of True*,
the blog of Richard Cousins, June 20, 2040

Twenty-six

Shaun broke the silence. "Please tell me that didn't break the skin," he said, almost pleading. "The blood came from something else, right George? Right?"

"We're going to need a biohazard bag." There was no fear in my voice. Really, there was nothing there at all. I sounded . . . empty, disconnected from everything around me. It was like my body and my voice existed in different universes, tethered by only the thinnest of threads. "Get one from the medical kit, put it on the counter, and step away. I don't want either of you touching this." Or me. I didn't want them touching *me* when there was a risk that I could infect them. I just couldn't say that. If I tried, I'd break down, and any chance of containing this would go right out the window.

"George—"

"We need a testing kit."

Rick's voice was surprisingly strong, considering the circumstances. Shaun and I turned to face him.

He was white-faced and shaking, but his voice was firm. "Shaun, I know you don't want to hear this, and if you want to hit me later, that's fine, but right now, we need a testing kit."

Storm clouds were gathering in Shaun's expression. He knew Rick was right; I could see it in his eyes and in the way he wasn't quite willing to look at me. If he hadn't known, he wouldn't have cared that Rick was calling for a blood test. But because he did, it was the last thing in the world he wanted. Well. Maybe not the *last* thing. Then again, it was starting to look like the last thing had already happened.

"He's right, Shaun." I placed the dart on the counter next to my keyboard. It was so small. How could something so small be the end of the world? I barely noticed when it hit me. I never thought it was possible to overlook your own death, but apparently it is. "Don't just grab a field box. Get the real kit. If we're going to do this, we're going to do it right." The XH-237 has never had a false result; it's one hundred percent accurate, as far as anyone can tell.

Shaun would never believe anything else. He was staring at me in open disbelief. He was denying this as hard as he could. So why wasn't I? "Georgia . . ." he began.

"If I'm overreacting, I'll buy a new one with my birthday money," I said, sagging backward in my chair. "Rick?"

"I'll get it, Georgia," he said, starting for the medical supplies.

I closed my eyes. "I'm not overreacting."

Almost too quiet for me to hear, Shaun whispered, "I know."

"I brought the bag," said Rick. I opened my eyes, turning toward his voice. He held up a Kevlar-reinforced biohazard bag. I nodded and he put the bag on the counter, before stepping away. We knew proper protocols. They'd been drilled into us for our entire lives. Until we knew I was clean, no one touched me . . . and I knew I wasn't clean.

Moving with exaggerated care, so both Shaun and Rick could see me every inch along the way, I reached for the bag and thumbed it open before picking up the dart. Dropping it into the bag, I activated the seal. It was a matter for the CDC now. Its people would break the seal after it was turned over to them, and what happened after that wasn't my concern. I wouldn't be around to see it.

I looked up once the bag was sealed and set aside. "Where's the test kit?" It felt like the muscles in my eyes were relaxing. It could be psychosomatic, but I didn't think so. The viral bodies responsible for the perpetual dilation of my pupils were moving on to greener pastures. Like the rest of my body.

"Here," said Shaun, holding it up. He stepped closer and knelt in front of me. He was only inches outside the federally defined "danger zone" for dealing with someone who might be amplifying. I shot him a sharp look, and he shook his head. "Don't start."

"I won't." I extended my left hand. If he wanted to administer the test himself, he had the right. Maybe it would make him believe the results.

"You could be wrong. You've been wrong before," Shaun said, sliding the testing kit over my hand. I flattened my palm until I felt the tendons stretch, and gave him the nod to clamp down the lid. He did, pinning my fingers in their wide, starfished position.

"I'm not wrong," I said. Dull pain lanced my hand as the needles—one for each finger, and five more set in a circle at the center of the palm—darted out, taking blood samples. The lights on the top of the unit began to flash, cycling from green to yellow, where they remained, blinking on and off, until one by one, they started settling into their final color.

Red. Every one of them. Red.

Tears prickled against my eyelids. It took me a moment to realize what they were, and then I had to resist the urge to blink them back. Kellis-Amberlee never let me cry before. It was damn well going to let me cry now. "Told you I was right," I said, trying to sound lighthearted. All I managed to sound was lost.

"Bet you're sorry," Shaun replied. I raised my head and met his shocked, staring eyes with my own.

We sat that way for several moments, looking at each other, waiting for an answer that wasn't going to come. It was Rick who spoke, voicing the one question we all wanted to ask and that none of us was quite prepared to answer.

"What do we do now?"

"Do?" Shaun frowned at him, looking utterly and honestly perplexed. That expression was enough to terrify me, because he looked like someone who didn't understand the idea that before too much longer, I was going to be making a concerted effort to eat him alive. "What do you mean, 'What do we do?'"

"I mean exactly what I said," Rick said. He shook his head, gesturing to me. "We can't just leave her like this. We have to—"

"No!"

The vehemence of Shaun's reply startled me. I turned toward him. *"No?"* I repeated. "Shaun, what the hell do you mean, 'no'? There isn't room for 'no.' 'No' is over."

"You don't know what you're saying."

"I know exactly what I'm saying." Rick was pale and shaking, beads of sweat standing out on his forehead. Poor guy. He didn't sign up for political assassinations when he decided to join the so-called "winning team." Despite that, he met my eyes without flinching and didn't try to avoid looking at me. He'd seen the virus before. It held no surprises for him. "You're the closest thing we've got to a virologist, Rick. How long do I have?"

"How much do you weigh?"

"One thirty-five, tops."

"I'd say forty-five minutes, under normal circumstances," he said, after a moment's consideration. "But these aren't normal circumstances."

"The run," I said.

He nodded. "The run."

Viral amplification depends on a lot of factors. Age, physical condition, body weight—how fast your blood is moving when you come into contact with the live virus. If someone gets bitten in their sleep without waking up, they may take the rest of the night to fully amplify, because they'll be calm enough that their body won't be helping the infection along. I, on the other hand, got hit with a viral payload a lot bigger than you'd find in a bite, and it happened while I was running for my life, heart pounding, adrenaline pushing my blood pressure through the roof. I'd cut my time in half. Maybe worse.

It was already getting harder to think; harder to focus; harder to *breathe*. I knew, intellectually, that my lungs weren't shutting down. It was just the virus enclosing the soft tissues of my brain and starting to disrupt normal neurological functions, making normally autonomic actions start intruding on the conscious mind. I've read the papers and the clinical studies. I knew what to expect. First comes the lack of focus, the lack of interest, the lack of capability to draw unrelated conclusions. Then comes hyperactivity as the circulatory system is pushed to overdrive. Then, when the virus reaches full saturation, the coup de grace: the death of the conscious mind. My body would continue to walk around, driven by raw instinct and the desires of the virus, but Georgia Carolyn Mason would be gone. Forever.

I was dead before the lights flashed red. I was dead the second the hypodermic hit my arm, and there was nothing anyone could do about it. But there was something I could do before I went.

Turning to Shaun, I nodded. There was a long pause—almost too long—before his expression calmed and he returned the gesture, looking more sure of himself, more *like* himself, despite the tears running down his cheeks.

"Rick?" he said.

Rick turned to him, shaking his head. "You can't beat this. There's no beating this. She's gone. You need to realize that. She's gone, and I'm sorry, but we have to—"

"Get me the medical kit from under the server

rack," Shaun said. I had to envy him the calmness in his voice. I couldn't have stayed that calm if he were the one undergoing explosive viral amplification. "The red one."

"What do you—"

"Do it!"

The words were barely out of his mouth before Rick was rushing to the front of the van, digging under the seat for the med kit. Mom packed it for us a million years ago, for use in absolute emergency. When she put it in my hands, she said she prayed we'd never have to use it. Sorry, Mom. Guess we let you down good this time. But hey, at least the ratings will be high.

I let out a long, shuddering sigh that somehow transformed into hysterical giggling. I bit my tongue before the giggles could turn to sobs. There wasn't time for that. There wasn't time for anything except the red box, and the things it held, and maybe—maybe, if I was lucky—one last article.

Rick came back to Shaun's side, holding the box at arm's length. His expression was cold. He didn't think Shaun would be able to do it. He didn't know him as well as he thought he did. I closed my eyes and leaned my head against the seat, suddenly tired.

"You can go now, Rick," I said. "Take my bike and the gray backup drive. Get as far away as you can, then hit a data station and upload everything to the site. Free space. No subscription required. Creative Commons licensing."

"What is it?" he asked, curiosity briefly overriding his determination to see me dead. Bless you, Rick. A journalist after my own heart, right up to the end.

"Everything I died for," I said. My eyes were starting to itch. I took my sunglasses off and threw them aside as I rubbed my eyes. "Files, bank records, everything. It's just everything. Now get out of here. You've done everything you can."

"Are you—"

"We're sure," said Shaun. I heard the box pop open and the distinctive snap of polyvinyl-Teflon gloves. They're nearly impossible to tear and so expensive that even the military only uses them under special circumstances. Shaun always insisted we carry a pair. Just one. Just in case. "Take my extra body armor. There's always a chance they're still shooting out there."

"Do you think they are?"

"Does it matter?"

"No. I guess it doesn't."

I listened as Rick moved around the van. He pulled Shaun's body armor out of the closet where it was stored and yanked it on over his clothes, snaps and zippers fastening with their quiet, distinctive sounds. It kept me distracted from the sounds that were coming from Shaun's direction, the sloshing, snapping sounds as he got the injector cartridges ready.

"Thanks, Rick," I said. "It's been one hell of a ride."

"I . . . right." I heard Rick's footsteps approach; the scrape of metal as he lifted the drive from beside my computer; then his retreat, until the door creaked open and he stopped, hesitating. "I . . . Georgia?"

"Yes, Rick?"

"I'm sorry."

I cracked my eyes open, allowing him a small, mirthless smile. For the first time that I could remember, the light didn't hurt. I was going into conversion. My body was losing the capacity to understand pain. "That's all right. So am I."

For a moment, he looked like he might say something else. Then his lips tightened and he nodded, before undoing the latches on the door. That was the last exit: When the van was locked again, it would detect infection and refuse to open for anyone inside.

"Shaun? Train's leaving," I said, quietly. "You want to jab and go?"

"And let you finish this without me?" He shook his head. "No way. Rick, you be careful out there."

Rick's shoulders tightened and he was gone, stepping out into the evening air. The door banged shut behind him.

Shaun sat down on the floor in front of me, the injector in his hands. It was a two-barrel array, ready to deliver a mixed payload of sedatives and my own hyper-activated white blood cells. Together, the mixture could slow conversion . . . for a while. Not for long, but if we were lucky, for long enough. Expression staying neutral, he said, "Give me your right arm."

I held it out.

Shaun pressed the twin needles to the thin skin at the bend of my elbow and a wash of coolness flowed into me as he pressed the plunger home.

"Thanks," I said, shivering.

"That's all we've got." He opened a biohazard bag and dropped the used injector into it before sealing the top. "You've got half an hour, tops. After that—"

"There's no guarantee I'll be lucid. I know." He rose, walking stiff-legged across to the biohazard bin and dropped the bag inside. I wanted to run after him, wrap my arms around him, and cry until there weren't any tears left in me, but I couldn't. I didn't dare. Even my tears would be infectious, and the sedatives he'd shot into my arm weren't going to work any miracles. Time was short.

I still had work to do.

I swung back to my monitor, trying to swallow away the dryness as I heard Shaun moving behind me, taking one of the spare revolvers out of the locker by the door and loading it, one careful cartridge at a time. What was it the reports said? The dryness of the mouth was one of the early signs of viral amplification, resulting from the crystal blocks of virus drawing away moisture and bringing on that lovely desiccated state that all the living dead seem to share? That seemed about right. It was getting harder to think about that sort of thing. Suddenly, it was all just a little too immediate.

My hands were still hovering above the keyboard while my mind struggled to find a beginning when I felt the barrel of the gun press against the base of my skull, cold and somehow soothing. Shaun wouldn't let me hurt anyone else. No matter what happened, he wouldn't let me hurt anyone else. Not even him. Not more than I already had.

"Shaun . . ."

"I'm here."

"I love you."

"I know, George. I love you, too. You and me. Always."

"I'm scared."

His lips brushed the top of my head as he bent forward and pressed them to my hair. I wanted to yell at him to get away from me, but I didn't. The barrel of the gun remained a cool, constant pressure on the back of my neck. When I turned, when I stopped being me, he would end it. He loved me enough to end it. Has any girl ever been luckier than I am?

"Shaun . . ."

"Shhh, Georgia," he said. "It's okay. Just write." And so I began. One last chance to roll the dice, tell the truth, and shame the devil. One last chance to make it all clear. What we fought for. What we died for. What we felt we had to do.

I never asked to be a hero. No one ever gave me the option to say I didn't want to, that I was sorry, but that they had the wrong girl. All I wanted to do was tell the truth and let people draw their own conclusions from there. I wanted people to think, and to know, and to understand. I just wanted to tell the truth. In the van that had carried us across a country, and through the last months of my life, with my brother standing ready to pull the trigger, my hands came down, and I wrote.

Was it worth it?

God, I hope so.

———————

RED FLAG DISTRIBUTION RED FLAG DISTRIBUTION RED
FLAG DISTRIBUTION

CREATIVE COMMONS LICENCE ALERT LEVEL ALPHA
SPREAD TO ALL NEWS SITES IMMEDIATELY

REPOST FREELY REPOST FREELY REPOST FREELY
FEED IS LIVE

My name is Georgia Mason. For the past several years,
I've been providing one of the world's many windows
into the news, chronicling current events and attempting, in my own small way, to offer context and perspec-
tive. I have always pursued the truth above all other
things, even when the truth came at the cost of my own
comfort and well-being. It seems, now, that I pursued
the truth even when it would mean my life, although I
was unaware of it at the time.

My name is Georgia Mason. According to the time
stamp on the field test unit (model XH-237, known for
reliability and, God help me, accuracy), I legally died
eleven minutes ago. But for now, at this moment, my
name is still Georgia Mason, and this is . . . I guess you
can call this my last postcard from the Wall. There are
some things you need to know, and we don't have much
time.

As I write this, my brother is standing behind me
with the barrel of a gun pressed against the back of my
neck, where a blast will sever the spinal cord with the
smallest possible spray radius. In my bloodstream, a

large dose of sedatives mixed with a serum based on my own immune system is running a race against the virus that is in the process of taking over my cells. My nose isn't clogged and I can swallow, but I feel lethargic, and it's hard to breathe. I tell you this so you'll understand that this isn't a hoax, this isn't some sophomoric attempt to increase ratings or site traffic. This is real. Everything I am about to tell you is the truth. Believe me, understand, and act, before it is too late.

If you're viewing this from the main page of After the End Times, you'll see a download link labeled "Campaign_Notes.zip" on the left-hand side of your screen. Possession of the documents behind that link may be considered treason by the government of the United States of America. Please. Click. Download. Read. Repost to any forum you can, any message board or photo-sharing site or blog that you can reach. The data contained in those files is as essential to our freedom and survival as the report of Dr. Matras proved to be during the Rising. I am not overstating the data's importance. There isn't enough time for that.

Neither is there enough time for me to repeat the facts that are already codified and ready for you to download. Let this suffice for all the things I cannot say, do not have the time to say, will never say, and wish I could: They are lying to us. They are willfully channeling research away from the pursuit of a cure for this disease, and they are doing it under the auspices of our own government. I don't know who "they" are. I didn't live long enough to find out. Governor Tate served their interests. So, I regret to say, did Georgette Meissonier, previously a part of this reporting site.

They want us to stay afraid.

They want us to stay controlled.

They want us to stay sick.

Please, don't let them do this to our world. I am begging you from the Wall, because it's all that's left for me to do. It's all I *can* do. Don't let them keep us frightened and hiding in our homes. Let us be what we were intended to be: human and free and able to make our own choices. Read what I have written, understand what they intend for us, for all of us, and decide to live.

They made a mistake in killing me because, alive or dead, the truth won't rest. My name is Georgia Mason, and I am begging you. Rise up while you can.

Mahir I'm so sorry.

Buffy I'm so sorry.

Rick I'm so sorry.

Shaun I'm sorry I'm sorry I'm sorry I didn't mean it I would take it all back if I could but I can't I cant I I I I I I I all fading words going cant do this cant Shaun please Shaun please I love you I love you I always you know I Shaun please cant hold on everything jfdh cant do this jhjnfbnnnn mmm have to my name my name is Shaun I love you Shaun please gngn please SHOOT ME SHAUN SHOOT ME N—

TERMINATE LIVE FEED
RED FLAG DISTRIBUTION RED FLAG DISTRIBUTION RED
FLAG DISTRIBUTION

REPOST FREELY

BOOK V
Burial Writes

I've spent my whole life imagining worlds other than the one that I was born in. Everybody does. The one world I never imagined was a world without a Georgia. So how come that's the world I have to live with?

—SHAUN MASON

I'm sorry.

—GEORGIA MASON

It is the sad duty of the management of After the End Times to announce the death of Georgia Carolyn Mason, the head of our Factual News Division, most commonly called "the Newsies," and one of the original founders of this site.

I've been trying to find the words for this announcement since I was asked to make it, some three hours ago. The request came with a promotion to which I never aspired, and a position made bitter by the knowledge of what it cost. I would sooner have my friend than all the promotions in the world. But that option is not open to me, or to any of those who will mourn for her.

Georgia Mason was my friend, and I will always regret that we never met in the flesh. She once told me she lived each day hoping and praying she would find the truth; that she was able to keep going through all life's petty disappointments because she knew that someday, the truth would set her free.

Good-bye, Georgia. May the truth be enough to bring you peace.

**—From *Fish and Clips*,
the blog of Mahir Gowda, June 20, 2040**

Twenty-seven

George's blood didn't all dry at the same rate.

Some of the smaller streaks dried almost immediately, staining the wall behind her ruined monitor. The gunshot collapsed the screen inward, safety-tempered glass holding its form as well as it could, even when the plastic casing shattered. It was like looking at some modern artist's reinterpretation of an old-school disco ball. "The party's in here, and we're just getting started." As long as you didn't mind the blood on the glass, that was. *I* minded the blood on the glass. I minded the blood on the glass a lot. I just didn't see a way to put it back where it belonged.

The bigger splashes were drying slow and sticky, the color maturing from bright red to a sober burgundy, where they seemed content to stay. That bothered me. I wanted the blood to dry, wanted it to settle in funeral colors and stop taunting me. I'm a good shot. I've been on firing ranges since I was seven years old, in the field—legally—since I was sixteen. Even if the virus still allowed her to feel pain, George didn't have *time* for pain. It was just the roar of the gun, and then she was slumping forward, face-first on her keyboard. That was the only real mercy. She landed face-first, so I didn't have to see what I'd . . . so I didn't have to see. She didn't have time to suffer. I just have to keep telling myself that, now, and tomorrow, and the next day, for as long as I can stay alive.

The sound of the gun fired inside the van would've been the loudest thing I'd ever heard if it hadn't been followed by the sound of George falling. That's the loudest thing I've ever heard. That's *always* going to be the loudest thing, no matter what else I hear. The sound of George, falling.

But I'm a good shot, and there was no shrapnel unless you wanted to count the aerosolized blood released when the bullet hit my . . . when I shot . . . not unless you counted the blood. I had to count the blood because it was enough to turn the entire damn van into a hot zone. If I was infected, I was infected—too late to worry about that kind of shit now—but that didn't mean I needed to make my chances worse. I moved as far away as I could and sat down with my back against the wall, the gun dangling loose against my left knee, to watch the blood dry, and to wait.

George turned the security cameras on before things got too . . . before it was too late to worry about that sort of stuff. I watched the Center's security forces rush around with the senator's men and some dudes I didn't recognize. Ryman wasn't the only candidate working Sacramento. There was no sign of Rick. Either he got dead or he got out of the quarantine zone before things went to hell. And things *had* gone to hell. I could spot at least three of the infected on every monitor, about half of them being gunned down by frantic guards who'd never dealt with a for-real-and-true zombie before. They were shooting stupid. They would have *known* they were shooting stupid if they'd paused to think for five seconds. You're not a sharpshooter, you don't go for the head, you go for the knees; a zombie that's been hobbled can't come at you as fast, and that leaves more time to aim. You're out of ammo, you leave the field. You don't reload where you stand unless there isn't any choice. When you're fighting a disease, you have to fight smarter than it does, or you may as well put down your weapons and surrender. Sometimes they just bite enough to infect if you don't put up a fight and if the pack's too small. You can avoid being eaten if you're willing to defect to the enemy's side.

Part of me wanted to get out there and help them, because it was clear they were pretty fucked without some sort of backup. Most of me wanted to stay where I was, watching the blood dry, watching the last signs of George slipping away forever.

My pocket buzzed. I slapped at it like it was a fly, fumbling out my phone and clicking it on. "Shaun."

"Shaun, it's Rick. Are you okay?"

It took me a moment to recognize the high, wavering sound in the van as my own distorted laughter. I clamped it down, clearing my throat before I said, "I don't think that word applies at this point. I'm alive, for now. If you're asking whether I'm infected, I don't know. I'm waiting until someone shows up to get me before I run a blood test. Seems a little pointless before that. Did you get out before the quarantine came down?"

"Barely. They were still reacting to the explosions when I got to Georgia's bike; they hadn't had time to do anything. I think they closed the gates right behind me. I—"

"Do me a favor. Don't tell me where you are." I let my head tilt back to touch the van's wall and discovered more blood I'd need to keep an eye on. This was on the ceiling. "I have no idea how tapped our phones are or who might be listening. I'm still in the van. Doors are probably locked anyway, since we confirmed an infection in here." The van's security system wasn't going to trust any attempt to open it from the inside, even if I registered uninfected. It would need an outside agent to free me. That or a rocket launcher, and even I don't pack *that* heavy for a little political rally.

Rick's reply was subdued. "I won't. I . . . I'm sorry, Shaun."

"Aren't we all?" I laughed again. This time the high, strangled sound seemed almost natural. "Tell me her last transmission got out. Tell me it's circulating now."

"That's why I called. Shaun, this is—it's insane. We're getting so many hits that it's swamped two of the servers. *Everyone* is downloading this; *everyone* is propagating it. Some folks started the usual 'it's a hoax' rumors, and Shaun, the *CDC* put out a press statement. *The CDC.*" He sounded awed. He damn well should. The CDC *never* puts out a statement with less than a week to prepare it. "They confirmed receipt of her test results with a time stamp and everything. This story doesn't just have legs—it has *wings*, and it's flying around the world."

"The name on the press release. It wasn't Wynne, was it?"

"Dr. Joseph Wynne."

"Guess our trip to Memphis did some good after all." The blood on the ceiling was more satisfying than the blood on the walls. It was thinner up there. It was drying so much faster.

"She didn't die for nothing. Her story—*our* story—it got out."

Suddenly, I was tired. So goddamn tired. "Sorry, Rick, but no. She died for nothing. No one should have died for this. You get away from here. Far as you can. Dump your phones, dump your transmitters, dump anything that could be used to bounce a signal, stick Georgia's bike in a garage, and don't call again until this is over."

"Shaun . . ."

"Don't argue." A bitter smile touched my lips. "I'm your boss now."

"Try not to die."

"I'll think about it."

I hung up and chucked my phone across the van, where it shattered against the wall with a satisfying crunch. Rick was out of the quarantine, and he was still running. Good. He was wrong—George damn well died for nothing—but he was also right. *She* would have thought this justified things. *She* would have said this was enough to pay for my being forced to put a bullet through her spine. Because she put the truth ahead of absolutely everything we ever had, and this had been the biggest truth of all.

"Happy now, George?" I asked the air.

The silence supplied her answer: *Ecstatic*.

The sound of beeping intruded on my contemplation of the bloody ceiling some ten minutes later. The fight outside was winding down. Bemused, I looked toward my shattered phone. Still broken. There were countless things in the van that could be beeping like that, about half of them on George's side. Hoping whatever it was happened to be voice activated, I said, "Answer."

One of the wall-mounted monitors rolled, the body of a dead security guard and the two infected feasting on his torso being replaced by the worried face of Mahir, my sister's longtime second and our secret weapon against government shut-down. Guess that cat didn't need to stay in the bag any longer. His eyes were wide and terrified, the whites showing all the way around, and his hair was disheveled, like he'd just gotten out of bed.

"Huh," I said, distantly pleased. "Guess it was voice activated after all. Hey, Mahir."

His focus shifted down, settling on where I sat against the wall. It wasn't possible for his eyes to get any wider, but they tried when he saw the gun in my hand. Still, his voice struggled to stay level as he said, with great and anxious seriousness, "Tell me this is a joke, Shaun. Please, tell me this is the most tasteless joke in a long history of tasteless jokes, and I will forgive you, happily, for having pulled it on me."

"Sorry, no can do," I said, closing my eyes rather than continuing to look at his worry-stricken face. Was this how it felt to be George? To have people looking at you, expecting you to have the answers about things that didn't involve shooting the thing that was about to chew your face off? Jesus, no wonder she was tired all the time. "The exact time and cause of death for Georgia Carolyn Mason has been registered with the Centers for Disease Control. You can access it in the public database. I understand there's been a statement confirming it. I'm gonna have to get that framed."

"Oh, dear God—"

"Pretty sure God's not here just now. Leave a message. Maybe He'll get back to you." It was nice, looking at the inside of my eyelids. Dark. Comfortable. Like all those hotel rooms I fixed up for her, because her eyes got hurt so easy . . .

"Shaun, where *are* you?" Horror was overwhelming the anxiety in his tone. He'd seen the van wall. He'd seen the gun. Mahir wasn't an idiot—he could never have worked for George if he'd been stupid— and he knew what my surroundings meant.

"I'm in the van." I nodded, still letting myself take comfort in the dark. I couldn't see his face. I couldn't see the blood drying on the walls. The dark was my *friend*. "George is here, too, but you can't really say hi just now. She's indisposed. Also, I blew her brains out all over the wall." The giggle escaped before I could bite it back, high and shrill in the confined air.

"Oh, my God." Now there was nothing *but* horror in his tone, wiping everything else away. "Have you activated your emergency beacon? Have you tested yourself? Shaun—"

"Not yet." I found myself beginning to get interested against my better judgment. "Do you think I should?"

"Don't you want to *live*, man?!"

"That's an interesting question." I opened my eyes and stood, testing my legs and finding them good. There was a moment of dizziness, but it passed. Mahir was watching me from the screen, his dark complexion gone pale with panic. "Do you think I should? I wasn't supposed to. George was supposed to. There's been a clerical error."

"Turn on your beacon, Shaun." His voice was firm now. "She wouldn't want it this way."

"Pretty sure she wouldn't want *any* of this. Especially not the part where she's dead. That would be the part she liked the least." My head was starting to clear as the shock faded, replaced by something cleaner and a lot more familiar: anger. I was furiously angry because it wasn't supposed to be this way; it was *never* supposed to be this way. Georgia would attend my funeral, give my eulogy, and I would never live in a world she wasn't a part of. We agreed on that when we were kids, and this . . . this was just plain wrong.

"Regardless, now that she's gone and you're not? She'd want you to make at least a small effort to stay that way."

"You Newsies. Always bringing the facts into things." I crossed the van, keeping my eyes away from the mess at my sister's terminal and the surrounding walls. The beacon—a button that would trigger a broadcast loop to let any local CDC or law enforcement agents know that someone in the van had been infected, and that someone else was alive—was a switch on the wall next to what had been Buffy's primary terminal, before she went and died on us.

First Buffy, now George. Two down, one to go,

and the more I forced myself out of the comfort of my shock, the more I realized that the story wasn't over. It didn't have an ending. George would have *hated* that.

"It is, as you might say, our job," Mahir said.

"Yeah, about that." I flipped the switch. A distant, steady beeping began, the beacon's signal being picked up and relayed by the illegal police scanner in the sealed-off front seat. "Who are you working for right now?"

"Ah . . . no one. I suppose I'm a free agent."

"Good, 'cause I want to hire you."

Mahir's surprise was entirely unfeigned as he demanded, *"What?"*

"This day can't be good for your blood pressure," I said, crossing to the weapons locker. The revolver wasn't going to cut it. For one thing, it was probably contaminated, and they'd take it away when they let me out of the van. For another, it lacked class. You can't go hunting United States governors with a generic revolver. It simply isn't done. "After the End Times has found itself with a sudden opening for a new Head of our Factual Reporting Department. I mean, I could hire Rick, but I don't think he's gonna have the guts for the job. He's one of nature's seconds. Besides, Georgia would've wanted me to give it to you." We'd never discussed it—the topic of her dying was so ludicrous that it never came up—but I was sure of what I was saying. She would've hired him if she had any say in the matter. She would've hired him, and she would've trusted him to take over the site if my death followed hers. So that was all right.

"I . . . I'm not sure what you . . ."

"Just say yes, Mahir. We have so many recorders running right now that you know a verbal contract will stand up in court, as long as I don't test positive when they come to let me out of here."

Mahir sighed, the sound seemingly summoned up from the very core of him. I glanced up from the process of loading bullets into Georgia's favorite .40, and saw him nod. "All right, Shaun. I accept."

"Good. Welcome back onboard." I've done my own hiring and firing from the start and I know what it takes to activate a new account or reactivate an old one. Leaning over the nearest blood-free keyboard, I called up an administrative panel and tapped in his user ID, followed by my own, my password, and my administrative override. "It'll take about ten minutes for your log-in to turn all the way back live." Just about as long as it had taken Georgia's typing to degrade. "Once you can get in, *get in*. I want you monitoring every inch of the site. Draft any-damn-body you can get your hands on—I don't care *what* department they belong to, you get them working the forums, watching the feeds, and making the goddamn news *go*. You need to hire people, you hire people. Until I come back, you're in charge. Your word is law."

"What's the goal here, Shaun?"

I looked toward the screen, teeth bared in a grin, and he recoiled. "We're not letting them kill my sister's story the way they killed her. She gets buried. It doesn't."

For a moment, it looked as if he might protest, but only for a moment. It passed as quickly as it had come, and he nodded. "I'll get on that. Are you about to do something foolish?"

"You could say that," I agreed. "Good night, Mahir."

"Good luck," he said, and the screen went black.

I had just finished loading Georgia's gun when the intercom buzzed. "Answer," I said, pulling down my Kevlar vest and slamming the weapons locker shut before starting to fasten the buckles around my chest.

"—there? I repeat: Shaun, are you in there?"

"Steve, my man!" I didn't have to feign my delight at the sound of his voice. "Dude, you're like a *cat*! How many lives you got, anyway?"

"Not as many as you," Steve replied, the rumble of his voice not quite hiding his concern. "Georgia in there with you, Shaun?"

"She is," I said, sliding a Taser into my pocket. It wouldn't stop someone who'd amplified all the way, but it would slow them down. The virus doesn't like to have the electrical current of its host messed with. "She's not really interested in talking, though, Steve-o, on account of the bullets I put through her spinal column. If you're not infected, and you'd be good enough to open the doors, I'd be greatly obliged."

"Did she bite, scratch, or come into contact with you in any way after exposure?"

They were routine questions. They'd never made me so angry in my life. "No, Steve, I'm afraid she didn't. No bites, no scratches, no hugs, not even a kiss good night before that Bible-thumping bastard's assassins sent my sister off to the great newsroom in the sky. If you've got a blood test unit and you'll open the doors, I'll prove it."

"You armed, Shaun?"

"You gonna leave me in here if I say yes? 'Cause I can lie."

The pause that followed was almost enough to make me think Steve had decided safe was better than sorry and was leaving me in the van to rot. That was a goal, sure, but not yet. The story wasn't done until the last of the loose ends were tied off, and one of those loose ends was slated to be George's honor guard. Finally, voice low, Steve said, "I haven't read her last entry all the way. I read enough. Stand back from the door and keep your hands where I can see them until you've tested out clean."

"Yes, sir," I said, and stepped backward.

The air that rushed in when the door opened was so fresh it almost hurt my lungs. The scents of blood and gunpowder were heavy, but not as heavy as they'd been inside the van. I took an involuntary step forward, toward the light, and stopped as a large dark blur raised what I could only assume was an arm and said, "Don't come any closer until I've moved away."

"You got it, Steve-o," I said. "You guys dealt with the little outbreak you had going out here? Sorry I didn't come to join your party. I was preoccupied."

"It's been contained, if not resolved, and I understand," said Steve, coming into focus as my eyes adjusted. He knelt, placed something on the ground, and retreated, allowing me to approach the object. As expected, it was a blood testing unit. Not the top of the line, but not the bottom, either; solidly middle of the road, enough to confirm or deny infection within an acceptable margin of error. "Acceptable." That's always seemed like such a funny word to use when you're talking about whether somebody lives or dies.

It weighed less than a pound. I broke the seal with my thumb, looking toward Steve as I did. "He doesn't walk away from this," I said.

"I promise," Steve replied.

Good enough for me. "Count of three," I said. "One . . ."

Inside my head, Georgia said, *Two . . .*

I slid my hand into the unit and pressed the relays down, watching as the lights started cycling through the available colors. Red-yellow-green, yellow-red-green. Every damn one of those lights danced between red and gold for a few seconds, long enough to make me sweat, before settling on a calm and steady green. *You're fine, son; just fine. Now go and be merry.*

"Merry" wasn't exactly in my plans. I held up the testing unit, letting Steve get a good long look. "This good enough?"

"It is," he said, and tossed me a biohazard bag. "What the hell happened, Shaun?"

"Just what George said. Some sick fucker killed Rick's cat and rigged our trailers to blow. When the blast didn't kill us, they hit George with one of those hypodermic darts like the one that triggered the outbreak at the Ryman place. Shit, I wish we'd been looking for the things back at Eakly. I bet we would've found one."

"I bet we would have, too," said Steve, watching as I dropped the testing unit into a biohazard bag. He was holding his sunglasses loosely in one hand, and his eyes were the eyes of a man who's looked into hell and found he couldn't cope with what he was seeing. I wouldn't have been willing to bet that my eyes were any better. "You got a plan from here?"

"Oh, the usual. Get a vehicle, head for whatever site they have the candidates under lockdown at—"

"Right where you left them," Steve interjected.

"Well, that's convenient. I know the security layout there. Anyway, head back to the candidates and have a chat with Governor Tate." I shrugged. "Maybe blow his brains out. I don't know. The plan is still in the formative stage."

"Need a ride?"

I grinned, the expression feeling foreign on my face. "I'd love one."

"Good. Because my boys and I—what's left of my boys—wouldn't like to see you get hurt just because you felt like being stupid and going it alone."

The ludicrousness of it all was enough to make me laugh. "Wait, you mean this was all I had to do to get myself a bigger security detail?"

"Guess so."

"Get your boys." The laughter faded as I looked at him. "It's time we got on the road."

———————

Sometimes we leave the connecting door between our rooms open all night. We'd still share a room if they'd let us, turn the other room into an office and have done with it. Because both of us hate to be alone, and both of us hate to have other people—people outside the country we've made together—around when we're defenseless. We're always defenseless when we're asleep.

We leave the connecting door open, and I wake up in

the night to the sound of him snoring, and I wonder how the hell I'm going to stay alive after he finally slips up. He'll die first, we both know it, but I don't know . . . I really don't know how long I'll stay alive without him. That's the part Shaun doesn't know. I don't intend to be an only child for long.

**—From *Postcards from the Wall*,
the unpublished files of Georgia Mason, June 19, 2040**

Twenty-eight

The outbreak was still going strong. The infected weren't actually everywhere; it just seemed that way, as they lurched and ran out of the shadows, following whatever weird radar signals the virus uses to tell the active hosts from the ones where the potential for infection is still just that, potential, sleeping and waiting for a wake-up. The scientists have been trying to figure out *that* little trick for twenty years, and as far as I know, they're no closer than they were the day Romero movies stopped being trashy horror and started being guides to staying alive. I should have been thrilled—it's not every day I get to walk through the center of an actual outbreak—but I was too busy being angry to really give a damn. Zombies didn't kill George. People did. Living, breathing, uninfected people.

I recognized a lot of faces among the infected. Interns from the campaign; a few security staffers, one long-faced man with thinning red hair who'd been traveling with us for about six weeks writing speeches for the senator. *No more speeches for you, buddy,* I thought, and put a bullet through the center of his forehead. He fell soundlessly, robbed of menace, and I turned away, nauseated.

"If I get out of this alive, I may need to look for another line of work."

"What's that?" asked Steve, between breathless radio calls to his surviving men. He was pulling them back to the motor pool. Several were moving slowly due to the need to herd less-well-armed survivors, going against the recommended survival strategies for an outbreak as they responded like human beings. You want to stay alive in a zombie swarm? You go alone or in a small group where everyone is of similar physical condition and weapons training. You never stop, you never hesitate, and you never show any mercy for the people that would slow you down. That's what the military says we should do, and if I ever meet anybody who listens to that particular set of commands, I may shoot them myself just to improve the gene pool. When you can help people stay alive, you help them. We're all we've got.

"Nothing," I said, with a shake of my head. "How're we looking for support?"

His mouth drew down in something between a wince and a scowl before he said, "Our last call from Andres came while I was on my way to get you. He was backed against a wall with half a dozen of the aides. I don't think we'll be seeing him again. Carlos and Heidi are at the motor pool; that zone's relatively clear. Mike . . . I haven't heard from Mike. Not Susan or Paolo, either. Everyone else is either on the way to meet with us or holding fast in a safe zone."

"Andres—crap, man, I'm sorry."

Steve shook his head. "I never was very good at partners." He turned and fired into the shadows at the side of a portable office. Something gurgled and fell. I gave him a sidelong look, and he actually smiled. "You thought we wore these sunglasses for our health?"

"I have *got* to get a pair of those."

We kept walking. What started as a pleasant, well-configured camp for visiting politicians had become a killing ground, full of cul-de-sacs and blind alleys that could hold almost anything. Complacency had long since destroyed the functionality of the layout. I couldn't blame them—there hadn't been an outbreak in Sacramento in years—but I didn't appreciate it, either. Luck was on our side: With the senator and most of his senior staff off the grounds for the keynote speech, we had fewer bodies to deal with than we might have otherwise. Our chances of survival had gotten better with every person who left the compound. "Just wish we hadn't come back," I muttered.

"What's that?" asked Steve.

I started to answer but was cut off as something hit me from behind, the momentum forcing me to the ground as hands clawed at my shoulders. Steve shouted. I was too occupied with trying to shake the zombie off to understand what he was saying. It was tearing at my back, trying to bite through the Kevlar. It would move up before too much longer, and my scalp was unprotected. The idea of having my brain literally eaten was really failing to appeal.

"Shaun!"

"Busy now!" I rolled to the left, ignoring the growls behind me as I struggled to get the Taser out of my belt. "Can you shoot it?"

"It's too close!"

"So get it off me before it figures out where to bite!" The Taser came free, almost falling into my hand. I twisted my arm as far behind me as I could, praying the thing wouldn't catch the unprotected flesh of my lower arm before the electricity could do its job. "Dammit, Steve, grab the fucking thing!"

Electricity spat and arced as the Taser made contact with the zombie's side. Luckily for me, it had been an intern, not a security guard; it wasn't wearing protective clothing. The thing screamed, sounding almost human as the viral bodies powering its actions became disoriented in the face of an electric current greater than their own. I hit it again, and Steve finally moved, grabbing the zombie and yanking it off. I rolled onto my back, reaching for Georgia's .40, and starting to fire almost as soon as I had it drawn. My first shot hit the zombie high in the shoulder, rocking it back. The second hit it in the forehead, and it went down.

My heart was pounding hard enough to echo in my ears, but my legs were steady as I scrambled back to my feet. Steve looked a lot more shaken. Sweat stood out on his forehead, and his complexion was several shades paler than it had been before I fell. I glanced around. Seeing that nothing else was about to rush me, I bent, picked up the Taser, and replaced both it and the gun in my belt. "You okay over there, Steve-o?"

"Did you get bit?" he demanded.

There was a predictable response. "Nope," I said, raising my hands to show the unbroken skin. "You can test me again when we hit the motor pool, okay? Right now, I think we should stop being out here, like, as soon as possible. That wasn't my favorite thing ever." I paused, and added, almost guiltily, "Besides, I didn't have a camera running." George would've kicked my ass for that, after she finished kicking my ass for getting that close to a live infection.

"You don't need the ratings," said Steve, and grabbed my arm, hauling me after him as he resumed moving, double-speed, toward the motor pool.

Maybe it was because Carlos and Heidi had access to an entire ammo shed, and maybe it was because the motor pool wasn't a popular hangout for the living, but the infected tapered off as we moved toward it, and we crossed the last ten feet to the fence without incident. Good thing; I was almost out of bullets, and I didn't feel like trusting myself to the Taser. The gate in the fence was closed, the electric locks engaged. Steve released my arm, reaching for the keypad, and a shot rang out over our heads, clearly aimed to warn, not wound. Small favors.

"Stop where you are!" shouted Carlos. I looked toward his voice and watched as he and Heidi stepped out from behind the shed, both bristling with weapons. I clucked my tongue disapprovingly. Sure, it *looked* good, but you can't intimidate a zombie, and they had so many things piled overlapping that they'd have trouble drawing much of anything when their primary guns ran out of bullets.

"Overkill," I muttered. "Amateurs."

"Stand down," barked Steve. "It's me and the Mason kid. He tested clean when I picked him up."

"Beg your pardon, sir, but how do we know you test clean *now*?" Heidi asked.

Smart girl. Maybe she could live. "You don't," I said, "but if you let us through the fence and keep us backed against it while you run blood tests, you'll have the opportunity to shoot before either of us can reach you."

She and Carlos exchanged a look. Carlos nodded. "All right," he said. "Step back from the gate."

We did as we were told, Steve giving me a thoughtful look as the gate slid open. "You're good at this."

"Top of my field," I said, and followed him into the motor pool.

Carlos chucked us blood testing units while Heidi reported on the status of the other units, still remaining at a safe distance. Susan was confirmed as infected; she'd been tagged by a political analyst as she was helping Mike evacuate a group of survivors to a rooftop. She stayed on the ground after she was bitten, shooting everything in sight before taking out the ladder and shooting herself. About the best ending you could hope for if you got infected in a combat zone. Mike was fine. So, surprisingly, was Paolo. There was still no word from Andres, and three more groups of security agents and survivors were expected to reach the motor pool at any time. Steve absorbed the news without changing his expression; he didn't even flinch when the needles on his testing unit bit into his hand. I flinched. After the number of blood tests I'd had recently, I was getting seriously tired of being punctured.

Heidi and Carlos relaxed when our tests flashed clean. "Sorry, sir," said Carlos, walking over with the biohazard bags. "We needed to be sure."

"Standard outbreak protocol," Steve said, dismissing the apology with a wave of his hand. "Keep holding this ground—"

"—while we break quarantine," I said, almost cheerfully. George snorted amusement in the back of my head. All for you, George. All for you. "Steve-o and I need to take a little trip. Loan us a car, give us some ammo, and open the gates?"

"Sir?" Heidi sounded uncertain; the idea of leaving a quarantine zone without military or CDC clearance is pretty much anathema to most people. It's just not done, ever. "What is he talking about?"

"One of the armored SUVs should do," said Steve. "Find the fastest one that's still on the grounds." Carlos and Heidi stared at him like he'd just gone into spontaneous amplification. "Move!" he barked, and they moved, scattering for the guard station where the keys to the parked vehicles were stored. Steve ignored their burst of activity, leading me to the weapons locker and keying open the lock. "Candy store is open."

"So all you have to do to break quarantine is shout 'move'?" I asked, beginning to load my pockets with ammunition. I considered grabbing a new gun, but dismissed the idea. Nothing but George's .40 was going to feel right in my hand. "Wow. Normally, I need a pair of wire cutters and some night-vision goggles."

"Gonna pretend you never said that."

"Probably for the best."

Carlos emerged from the guard station and tossed a set of keys to Steve, who caught them in an easy underhand. "We can unlock the rear gate, but once the central computer realizes the seal's been broken—"

"How long can we have?"

"Thirty seconds."

"That's long enough. You two hold your ground. Keep anyone who makes it here safe. Mason, you're with me."

"Yes *sir*!" I said, with a mocking salute. Steve shook his head and pressed the signal button on the key fob. One of the SUVs turned its lights on. Showtime.

Once we were inside, belts fastened and weapons secured, Steve started the engine and drove us to the gate. Carlos was already waiting, ready to hit the manual override. The manual exits exist in case of accidental or ineffective lockdown, to give the uninfected a chance to escape. They require a blood test and a retinal scan, and breaking quarantine without a damn good reason is a quick way to get yourself sent to prison for a long time. Carlos was risking a lot on Steve's order.

"That's what I call a chain of command," I said to myself, as the gate slid open.

"What's that?" asked Steve.

"Nothing. Just go."

We went.

The roads outside the Center were clear. That's standard for the time immediately following a confirmed outbreak in a noncongested area. The people inside the quarantine zone will survive or not without interference; it's all up to them the minute the fences come down. So the big health orgs and military intervention teams wait until the worst of it's had time to burn itself out before they head in. Let the infection peak. Ironically, that makes it *safer*, because it's trying to save the survivors that gets people killed. Once you know everyone around you is already dead, it gets easier to shoot without asking questions.

"How long since the quarantine went down?" I asked.

"Thirty-seven minutes."

Standard CDC response time says you leave a quarantine to cook for forty-five minutes before you go in. Given our proximity to the city, they wouldn't just be responding by air; they'd be sending in ground support to make sure nobody broke quarantine before they declared it safe. "Shit." With eight minutes between us and the end of the cooking time, we needed to get out of sight. "How good's the balance on this thing?"

"Pretty good. Why?"

"Quarantine. It's going to be forty-five minutes since the bell real soon here, and that means we're gonna have company. Now, I've got a way out, but only if you trust me. If you don't, we're probably gonna get the chance to tell some nice men why we're out here. Assuming they don't just shoot first."

"Kid, I'm already committed. Just tell me where to go."

"Take the next left turn."

Being a good Irwin is partially dependant on knowing as many ways to access an area as possible. That includes the location of handy things like, say, railroad trestle bridges across the American River.

See, they used to run trains through Sacramento, back when people traveled that way. The system's abandoned now, except for the automated cargo trains, but they run on a fixed schedule. I've had it memorized for years.

Steve started swearing once he realized where we were going, and he kept swearing as he pulled the SUV onto the tracks and floored the gas, trusting momentum and the structure of the trestle to keep us from plunging into the river. I grabbed the oh-shit handle with one hand and whooped, bracing the other hand on the dashboard. I couldn't help myself. Everything was going to hell, George was dead, and I was on my way to commit either treason or suicide, but who the hell cared? I was off-roading across a river in a government SUV. Sometimes, you just gotta kick back and enjoy what's going on around you.

We were halfway across the river when the first CDC copters passed overhead, zooming toward the Center. Three more followed close behind, in closed arrow formation. Fascinated, I leaned over and clicked on the radio, tuning it to the emergency band. "—repeat, this is not a drill. Remain in your homes. If you are on the road, remain in your vehicle until you have reached a safe location. If you have seen or had direct contact with infected individuals, contact local authorities immediately. Repeat, this is not a drill. Remain in—"

Steve turned the radio off. "Breaking quarantine is a federal offense, isn't it?"

"Only if they catch us." I settled back in my seat. "Doesn't bother me much, and they're not looking down."

"All right, then." He hit the gas again. The SUV rolled faster, hitting the end of the trestle and blazing onward toward the city. He glanced at me as we drove, saying, "I'm sorry about your sister. She was a good woman. She'll be missed."

"That's appreciated, Steve." The idea of looking at his face—it would be so earnest, if his words were anything to judge by, so anxious for understanding—made me tired all over again. There was nothing I could do now, nothing I could do until we got to the hall and to the man who had killed my sister. So I looked at my hands as I cleaned and reloaded Georgia's gun, and I was silent, and we drove on.

. . . but they were us, our children, our selves,
These shades who walk the cloistered dark,
With empty eyes and clasping hands,
And wander, isolate, alone, the space between
Forgiveness and the penitent's grave.

—From *Eakly, Oklahoma*,
originally published in *By the Sounding Sea*,
the blog of Buffy Meissonier, February 11, 2040

Twenty-nine

Quarantine procedures hit different social and economic classes in different ways, just like outbreaks. When Kellis-Amberlee breaks out in an urban area, it hits the inner cities and the business districts the hardest. That's where you have the largest number of people coming and going, experiencing the closest thing we have these days to casual contact. Interestingly, you tend to have more fatalities in the business districts. The slums may not have the same security features and weaponry, but they're mostly self-policing and fewer people try to conceal injuries when they know amplification isn't just going to cost them their coworkers; it's going to cost them their families. Inner cities and business districts turn into ghost towns when the quarantines come down. If you pass through while they're under quarantine, you can feel the inhabitants watching you, waiting for you to make a move.

Middle-class zones also tend to seal themselves off, but they're less blatantly aggressive about it;

windows too small or too high for a person to get in through can be left open, and not every glass door has a steel shield in front of it. You can enter those areas and still believe people live in them, even if those folks aren't exactly setting out the welcome mats. They'll kill you as quickly as anyone else will if you try to approach them. If you don't, they won't interfere.

The hall where they held the keynote speech was far enough from the Center that it wasn't technically in the quarantine zone. Street traffic was down to practically zero, but there were no retractable bars over the windows and no steel plating over the doors. Local businesses were open, even if there weren't any customers. I looked around as Steve pulled up to the first checkpoint, and I hated these people for being able to ignore what was going on outside their city. George was dead. Rick and Mahir said the whole world was mourning with me, but that didn't matter, because the man who did it—the man I intended to blame—wasn't even inconvenienced.

If the guard thought there was something odd about us arriving in a dusty, dented SUV over an hour after the Center went into lockdown, he didn't say anything. Our blood tests came back clean; that was what his job required him to give a damn about, and so he just waved us inside. I clenched my jaw so hard I almost tasted blood.

Calm down, counseled George. *It's not his fault. He didn't write the news.*

"Go for the writers," I muttered.

Steve shot me a look. "What's that?"

"Nothing."

We parked next to a press bus that had doubtless been loaded with reporters who were now thanking God for their timing, since being on assignment with a bunch of political bigwigs meant they weren't available to be sent out to report on the quarantine. Local Irwins would be flocking to the perimeter, getting footage of the CDC men as they locked and secured the site. I would've been with them not that long ago, and been happy about it. Now . . . I'd be just as happy if I never saw another outbreak. Somewhere between Eakly and George, I lost the heart for it.

Steve and I got into the elevator together. I glanced at him as he keyed in our floor, saying, "You don't have a press pass."

"Don't need one," he said. "The Center's under quarantine. By contract, I'm actually obligated to circumnavigate any security barricade between myself and the senator."

"Sneaky," I said, approvingly.

"Precisely."

The elevator opened on a sickeningly normal-looking party. Servers in starched uniforms circulated with trays of drinks and canapés. Politicians, their spouses, reporters, and members of the California elite milled around, chattering about shit that didn't mean a goddamn thing compared to George's blood drying on the wall. The only real difference was in their eyes. They knew about the quarantine—half of these people were staying at the Center, or worked there, or had a stake in its continued success—and they were terrified. But appearances have to be maintained, especially when you're looking at millions of dollars in lost city revenue because of an outbreak. So the party continued.

"Poe was right," I muttered. The man with the blood tests was waiting for us to check in. I slid my increasingly sore hand into the unit he held, watching lights run their cycle from red to yellow and finally to green. I wasn't infected. If being shut in a van with George's body didn't get me, nothing was going to. Infection would have been too easy a way out.

I yanked my hand free as soon as the lights went green, held up my press pass, and ducked into the crowd. Steve was right behind me. I dodged staff and guests, arrowing toward the room where I had last seen Senator Ryman. They wouldn't allow him to leave after the Center went into lockdown, and if he couldn't leave, he wouldn't have left the room where he had his surviving staff and supporters gathered. It just made sense.

People recoiled as I passed them, eyes going wide and suppressed fear surging to the front of their expressions. I paused, looking down at myself. Mud, powder burns, visible weapons—everything but blood. Somehow, I'd managed to avoid getting George's blood on me. That was a good thing, since she'd died infected and her blood would have made me a traveling hot zone, but still, it was almost a pity. At least then she would have seen the story find an ending.

"Shaun?"

Senator Ryman sounded astonished. I turned toward his voice and found him half standing. Emily was beside him, eyes wide, hands clapped over her mouth. Tate was on his other side. Unlike the

Rymans, the governor looked anything but relieved to see me. I could read the hatred in his eyes.

"Senator Ryman," I said, and finished my turn, walking to the table that looked like it held all the survivors of the Ryman campaign. Less than a dozen of us had been at this stupid speech; less than a dozen, from a caravan that had swelled to include more than sixty people. What kind of survival rate were we looking at? Fifty percent? Less? Almost certainly less. That's the nature of an outbreak, to kill what it doesn't conquer. "Mrs. Ryman." I smiled narrowly, the sort of expression that's always been more Georgia's purview than my own. "Governor."

"Oh, God, Shaun." Emily Ryman stood so fast she sent her chair toppling over as she threw her arms around me. "We heard the news. I'm so *sorry*."

"I shot her," I said conversationally, looking over Emily's shoulder to Senator Ryman and Governor Tate. "Pulled the trigger after she started to amplify. She was lucid until then. You can increase the duration of postinfection lucidity with sedatives and white blood cell boosters, and first-aid classes teach you to do that in the field. So you can get any messages they may have for their family or other loved ones."

"Shaun?" Emily pulled away, looking uncertain. She glanced over her shoulder at Governor Tate before looking back to me. "What's going on here?"

"How did you get out of the quarantine zone?" asked Tate. His voice was flat, verging on emotionless. He knew the score. He'd known it since I walked through the door. The bastard.

"A little luck, a little skill, a little applied journalism." Emily Ryman let me go entirely, taking a step backward, toward her husband. I kept my eyes on Tate. "Turns out most of the security staff liked my sister more than they ever liked you. Probably because George tried to *help* them, instead of using them to further her political ambitions. Once they knew what happened, they were happy to help."

"Shaun, what are you talking about?"

The confusion in Senator Ryman's voice was enough to distract me from Tate. I turned to blink at the man responsible for us being here in the first place, asking, "Haven't you seen Georgia's last report?"

"No, son, I haven't." His expression was drawn tight with concern. "Things have been a bit hectic. I haven't had a site feed since the outbreak bell rang."

"Then how did you—"

"The CDC puts out a statement, that tends to go around in a hurry." Senator Ryman closed his eyes, looking pained. "She was so damn *young*."

"Georgia was assassinated, Senator. Plastic dart full of live-state Kellis-Amberlee, shot straight into her arm. She never had a prayer. All because we figured out what was really going on." I swung my attention back to Tate and asked, more quietly, "Why Eakly, Governor? Why the ranch? And why, you fucker, why *Buffy*? I can actually understand trying to kill me and my sister, after everything else, but *why*?"

"Dave?" said Senator Ryman.

"This country needed someone to take real action for a change. Someone who was willing to do what needed to be done. Not just another politician preaching changes and keeping up the status quo." Tate met my eyes without flinching, looking almost calm. "We took some good steps toward God and safety after the Rising, but they've slowed in recent years. People are afraid to do the right thing. That's the key. Real fear's what motivates them to get past the fears that aren't important enough to matter. They needed to be reminded. They needed to remember what America stands for."

"Not sure I'd call terrorist use of Kellis-Amberlee a 'reminder.' Personally, I'd call it, y'know. Terrorism. Maybe a crime against humanity. Possibly both. I guess that's for the courts to decide." I drew Georgia's .40, and aimed it at Tate. The crowd went still, honed political instincts reacting to what had to look like an assassination attempt in the making. "Secure-channel voice activation, Shaun Phillip Mason, ABF-17894, password 'crikey.' Mahir, you there?"

My ear cuff beeped once. "Here, Shaun," said Mahir's voice, distorted by the encryption algorithms protecting the transmission. Secure channels are only good once, but, oh, how good they are. "What's the situation?"

"On Tate now. Start uploading everything you receive and download Georgia's last report directly to Senator Ryman. He needs to give it a glance." Governor Tate was glaring. I flashed him a smile. "I've been recording this whole time. But you knew that, didn't you? Smart guy like you. Smart enough to get around our security. To get around our *friends*."

"Miss Meissonier was a realist and a patriot who understood the trials facing this country," said Tate, tone as stiff as his shoulders. "She was proud to have the opportunity to serve."

"Miss Meissonier was a twenty-four-year-old journalist who wrote poetry for a living," I snapped.

"Miss Meissonier was our partner, and you had her killed because she wasn't useful anymore."

"David, is this true?" asked Emily, horror leeching the inflection from her voice. Senator Ryman had taken out his PDA and seemed to be growing older by the second as he stared at its screen. "Did you . . . Eakly? The ranch?" Fury twisted her features, and before either I or her husband could react, she was out of her chair, launching herself at Governor Tate. *"My daughter! That was my daughter, you bastard! Those were my parents! Burn in hell, you—"*

Tate grabbed her wrists, twisting her to the side and locking his arm around her neck. His left hand, which had been under the table since I arrived, came into view, holding another of those plastic syringes. Unaware, Emily Ryman continued to struggle.

The senator went pale. "Now, David, let's not do anything rash here—"

"I tried to send them home, Peter," said Tate. "I tried to get them off the campaign, out of harm's way, out of *my* way. Now look where they've brought us. Me, holding your pretty little wife, with just one outbreak left between us and a happy ending. I would have given you the election. I would have made you the greatest American president of the past hundred years, because together, we would have remade this nation."

"No election is worth this," Ryman said. "Emily, be still now, baby." Looking confused and betrayed, Emily stopped struggling. Ryman lifted his hands into view, palms upward. "What'll it take for you to release her? My wife's not a part of this."

"I'm afraid you're all a part of this now," Tate said,

with a small shake of his head. "No one's walking away. It's gone too far for that. Maybe if you'd disposed of the *journalists*," the word was almost spat, "it could have gone differently. But there's no use crying over spilled milk, now, is there?"

"Put down the syringe, Governor," I said, keeping the gun level. "Let her go."

"Shaun, the CDC is piggybacking our feed," said Mahir. "They're not stopping the transmission, but they're definitely listening in. Dave and Alaric are maintaining the integrity, but I don't know that we can stop it if they want to cut us off."

"Oh, they won't cut us off, will you, Dr. Wynne?" I asked. I was starting to feel a little light-headed. This was all moving so damn fast.

Keep it together, dummy, hissed George. *You think I want to be an only child?*

"I've got it, George," I muttered.

"What's that?" asked Mahir.

"Nothing. Dr. Wynne? You there?" If it was him, the CDC was with us. If it was anybody else . . .

There was a crackle as the CDC broke into our channel. "Here, Shaun," said the familiar southern drawl of Dr. Joseph Wynne. Mahir was swearing in the background. "Are you in any danger?"

"Well, Governor Tate's holding a syringe on Senator Ryman's wife, and since the last two syringes we've seen have been full of Kellis-Amberlee, I'm not betting this one's any different," I said. "I've got a gun on him, but I don't think I can shoot before he sticks her."

"We're on our way. Can you stall him?"

"Doing my best." I forced my attention back to

Governor Tate, who was watching me impassively. "Come on, Governor. You know this is over. Why not put that thing down and go out like a man instead of like a murderer? More of one than you already are, I mean."

"Not exactly diplomatic, there, Shaun," said Dr. Wynne in my ear.

"Doing the best I can," I said.

"Shaun, who are you talking to?" asked Senator Ryman. He looked edgy. Having a crazy dude holding a syringe of live virus on his wife probably had something to do with that.

"Dr. Joseph Wynne from the CDC," I said. "They're on the way."

"Thank God," breathed the senator.

"Want to put it down now, Governor?" I asked. "You know this is over."

Governor Tate hesitated, looking from me to the senator and finally to the horrified, receding crowd. Suddenly weary, he shook his head, and said, "You're fools, all of you. You could have saved this country. You could have brought moral fiber back to America." His grip on Emily slackened. She pulled herself free, diving into her husband's embrace. Senator Ryman closed his arms around her and rose, backing away. Governor Tate ignored them. "Your sister was a hack and a whore who would have fucked Kellis himself if she thought it would get her a story. She'll be forgotten in a week, when your fickle little audience of bottom-feeders moves on to something more recent. But they're going to remember me, Mason. They always remember the martyrs."

"We'll see," I said.

"No," he said. "We won't." In one fluid motion, he drove the syringe into his thigh and pressed the plunger home.

Emily Ryman screamed. Senator Ryman was shouting at the top of his lungs, ordering people to get back, to get to the elevators, behind secure doors, anything that would get them away from the man who'd just turned himself into a living outbreak. Still looking at me, Governor Tate started to laugh.

"Hey, George," I said, taking a few seconds to adjust my aim. There was no wind inside; that was a nice change. Less to compensate for. "Check this out."

The sound of her .40 going off was almost drowned out by the screams of the crowd. Governor Tate stopped laughing and looked, for an instant, almost comically surprised before he slumped onto the table, revealing the ruined mess that had replaced the back of his head. I kept the gun trained on him, waiting for signs of further movement. After several moments had passed without any, I shot him three more times anyway, just to be sure. It never hurts to be sure.

People were still screaming, pushing past each other as they rushed for the doors. Mahir and Dr. Wynne were trying to shout over each other on our open channel, both demanding status reports, demanding to know whether I was all right, whether the outbreak had been contained. They were giving me a headache. I reached up and removed my ear cuff, putting it on the table. Let them shout. I was done listening. I didn't need to listen anymore.

"See, George?" I whispered. When did I start crying? It didn't matter. Tate's blood looked just like George's. It was red and bright now, but it would start to dry soon, turning brown, turning old, turning into something the world could just forget. "I got him. I got him for you."

Good, she said.

Senator Ryman was shouting my name, but he was too far away to matter. Steve and Emily would never let him this close to a hot corpse. Until the CDC showed up, I could be alone. I liked that idea. Alone.

Taking two steps backward, I pulled out a chair and sat down at a table that would let me keep an eye on Tate. Just in case. There was a basket of breadsticks at the center, abandoned by fickle diners when the trouble started. I picked one up with my free hand and munched idly as I kept George's gun trained on Tate. He didn't move. Neither did I. When the CDC arrived to take command of the site fifteen minutes later, we were still waiting, Tate with his pool of slowly drying blood, me with my basket of breadsticks. They seized the site, sealed it, and ushered us all away to quarantine and testing. I kept my eye on him as long as I could, watching for some sign that it wasn't over, that the story wasn't done. He never moved, and George didn't say a word, leaving me alone in the echoing darkness of my mind.

Was it worth it, George? Well, was it? Tell me, if you can, because I swear to God, I just don't know.

I don't know anything anymore.

CODA:
Dying For You

The next person who says "I'm sorry" is going to get punched in the nose. Because "I'm sorry" doesn't do a damn thing except remind me that this can't be fixed. This is my world now. And I don't want it.

—SHAUN MASON

I love my brother. I love my job. I love the truth. So here's hoping no one ever makes me choose between them.

—GEORGIA MASON

Somebody once asked me if I believed in God. It was probably the windup to some major proselytizing, but it's a good question. Do I believe in God? That somebody made all this happen for a reason, that there's something waiting for us after we die? That there's a purpose to all this crap? I don't know. I'd like to be able to say "Yes, of course" almost as much as I'd like to be able to say "Absolutely not," but there's evidence on both sides of the fence. Good people die for nothing, little kids go hungry, corrupt men hold positions of power, and horrible diseases go uncured. And I got Shaun, maybe the only person who could make it seem worthwhile to me. I got Shaun.

So, is there a God? Sorry to dodge the question, but I just don't know.

**—From *Postcards from the Wall*,
the unpublished files of Georgia Mason, April 17, 2040**

Thirty

It took three months for the CDC to release Georgia's ashes. It would normally have taken longer, given the way she died. Lucky me, my sister died an international celebrity. That sort of thing gets you friends in high places. Even inside the CDC itself, which has been preoccupied with internal reviews as it tries to find the source of Tate's anonymous "donors." When Dr. Wynne went to his superiors and petitioned them for the right to let us have Georgia's ashes, they listened. Guess they didn't want to risk being our story of the week. No one does, these days. That'll fade with time—Mahir says we're losing percentages daily, as people move on to newer things—but we're always going to have a certain cachet after everything that went down. "After the End Times: So dedicated to telling you what you need to hear that they'll die to do it." I'd probably be a lot more disgusted by the whole thing if it weren't for the part where it let us bring George home.

Dr. Wynne brought the box containing her ashes

to me himself, accompanied by a fresh-faced, yellow-haired doctor I remembered from Memphis. Kelly Connolly. She's the one who gave me the pile of cards, handwritten by CDC employees from all over the country, and said they had three more as large from the WHO and USAMRIID. Her eyes were red, like she'd been crying. Buffy died, and we got accused of trying to hoax the world. George died, and that same world mourned with me. Maybe that should have been a comfort, but it wasn't. I didn't want the world to mourn. I just wanted George to come home.

She would have needed a forwarding address to find me. I came back from the campaign trail battered, exhausted, and ready to collapse, and discovered that home wasn't home anymore. My room was connected to George's room, and George wasn't there. I kept finding myself standing in her room, not sure how I got there, waiting for her to start yelling at me and tell me to knock first. She never did, and so I started packing my things. I wanted to get away from the ghosts. And I wanted to get away from the Masons.

George died, and the world mourned with me, sure. All the world but them. Oh, they did the right things in public, said the right things, made the right gestures. Dad did a series of articles on personal versus public responsibility and kept invoking the "heroic sacrifice" of his beloved adopted daughter, like that somehow made his platitudes more relevant. Guess it did, because it got him the highest ratings he'd had in years. George died a celebrity. Can't blame a man for capitalizing on that. Except for the part where I can. Oh, believe me, I can.

George and I've had our last wills and testaments

filed since before we were required to, and even though we both always assumed I'd go first, we both still filed with predeceasement clauses. If I went first, she got everything I had, including intellectual property, published and unpublished. If she went first, I got the same. We both had to die before anyone else had a shot at our estates, and even then, we didn't leave them to the Masons. We left them to Buffy, and, in the event that she hadn't survived whatever event managed to kill us both—since we always figured the only way we'd die together was something like the van breaking down in the middle of an outbreak—it all rolled to Mahir. Keep the site going. Keep the news in the right hands. The Masons haven't been in the chain of inheritance since we were sixteen. Only they didn't seem to have realized that because I hadn't been home for three days before they started harassing me to sign over George's unpublished files to them.

"It's what she would have wanted," Dad said, doing his best to look solemn and wise. "We can take care of things and leave you free to build a career of your own. She wouldn't have wanted you to put your life on hold to take care of what she left behind."

"You're one of the top Irwins in the world right now," Mom added. "You can write your own ticket. Whatever you want to do, you can do it. I bet you could even get a pass to visit Yosemite—"

"I know what she wanted," I said, and I left them sitting there at the kitchen table, not quite certain how they'd failed. I moved out the next morning. Two weeks couch-surfing with local bloggers who knew the score, and then I was in my own apartment. One bedroom, security controls so far out of date that the place would have been condemned if it hadn't been in such a well-certified hazard zone, and no ghosts or opportunistic parents waiting to ambush me in the halls. George followed me, of course, in the form of all her things, tucked into neat cardboard boxes by the movers that I'd hired . . . but she'd never been there while she was alive, and so sometimes, I was able to forget she wasn't there anymore. For minutes at a time, even, it seemed like the world was the way it was supposed to be.

Doctors Wynne and Connolly cut the delivery of George's ashes pretty close; they didn't bring them until the day before the funeral. I wouldn't have scheduled it at all, not until I had her back in hand and maybe had a little time to come to terms with things again, but circumstances didn't leave me much of a choice. It was the only day Senator Ryman could make it, and he'd asked that we hold the service when he could attend. I might still have put it off, except for the part where our team couldn't come out of the field if the senator—who was fighting, and apparently winning, an increasingly vicious battle for his political position—was still out there. Magdalene, Becks, and Alaric deserved their chance to say good-bye to George, too. Especially since they'd taken over where she and I, and Buffy, had to leave off.

Becks runs the Irwins now; I meant it when I said I didn't have the stomach for it anymore. Site administration is enough excitement for me, at least for right now. Mahir and Magdalene are doing fine with their departments. Ratings have actually gone up for the Fictionals. Magdalene is better at staying focused than Buffy ever was, even if she doesn't have a flair for technical things or espionage. And maybe that's good, too. We've been down that road before.

Mahir's flight from London landed at eleven the day of the funeral. I drove to the passenger collection zone at the edge of the airport's quarantine border, hoping I'd be able to pick him out of the crowd. I didn't really need to worry. His plane had been almost empty, and I would've known him anywhere, even if I hadn't been seeing him on video screens for years. He had the same empty confusion in his eyes that I saw in my mirror every morning, that odd sort of denial that only seems to come when the world decides to jump the rails without warning you first.

"Shaun," he said, and took my hand. "I'm so glad to finally meet you. I just wish it could have been under better circumstances."

"This is from George," I said, and pulled him into a hug. He didn't hesitate. He just hugged me back, and we stood there, crying on each other's shoulders, until airport security told us to clear out or be held in contempt of quarantine regulations. We left.

"What news?" Mahir asked, as we pulled onto the freeway. "I've been incommunicado for hours. Blasted flight."

"Mail from Rick—Senator Ryman's plane touched down about the same time yours did. They'll be meeting us at the funeral home. Emily couldn't make it, sends her regrets." I shook my head. "She sent a pie last week. An actual pie. That woman is so weird."

"How's Rick handling the transition?"

"He's taking it pretty well. I mean, he quit when the senator asked him to be the new VP candidate, and it doesn't seem to be driving him crazy. Who knows? Maybe they'll win. They're definitely bread and circuses enough for the general populace."

"American politics." Mahir shook his head. "Bloody bizarre."

"We work with what we've got."

"I suppose that's the way of the world." He hesitated, looking at me as I turned off the freeway and onto the surface streets. "I'm so sorry, Shaun. I just . . . There's nothing I can say that says how sorry I am. You know that, don't you?"

"I know you cared about her a lot," I said, shrugging. "She was your friend. You were hers. One of the best ones she ever had."

"She said that?" he asked, wonderingly.

"Actually, yeah. All the time."

Mahir wiped the back of his hand across his eyes. "I never even got to meet her, Shaun. It's just . . . it's so damned unfair."

"I know." I didn't bother wiping my own tears away. I stopped bothering weeks ago. Maybe if I let them fall they'd get around to stopping on their own. "It is what it is. Isn't that how these things always go? They are what they are. We just get to cope."

"I suppose that's true."

"At least she got her story." The parking lot of the funeral home was choked with cars. Packing the staff of multiple blog sites and a presidential campaign, as well as friends and family, into a single building will do that sort of thing. Their security must have been freaking out. The thought was enough to bring the ghost of a smile to my face, and the ghost of a chuckle from George in the back of my head.

Mahir glanced at me as I pulled into the last parking slot reserved in the "family" section of the lot. "I'm sorry, did I miss something? You're smiling."

"No," I said, unlocking the door. There'd be men with blood tests at the funeral home doors, and mourners waiting to tell me how sorry they were, to share their tears like I could understand them when I could barely understand my own. "You didn't miss anything at all, I guess. You got as much as I did." I climbed out of the car, Mahir still looking at me strangely. And then I stood there, waiting, until he followed me. "Come on. There's a whole bunch of people waiting for us."

"Shaun?"

"Yeah?"

"Was it worth it?"

No, whispered George, and, "No," I said. "But then again, when you get to the end, what really is?"

She told the truth as she saw it, and she died for it. I came along for the ride, and I lived. It wasn't worth it. But it was the truth, and it was what had to happen. I tried to hold onto that as we walked into the funeral home to say as many of our good-byes as we could. It wouldn't be all of them. It never could be. But it was going to have to be enough, for me, and for George, and for everyone. Because there wasn't going to be anything more.

"Hey, George," I whispered.

What?

"Check this out."

We stepped inside.

Acknowledgments

This is a book that truly could not have been written without the help of a dedicated and industrious team of editors, continuity checkers, and subject matter experts. From doctors and epidemiologists to people willing to attempt riding luggage carts over railroad trestles for the sake of research, there was as much field work as sit-down study. It was a group effort in many ways, and I owe an enormous debt of gratitude to all the people, named and unnamed, who helped me bring the world of *Feed* to life.

Rae Hanson and Sunil Patel were two of the first to join the proofing pool, providing valuable advice about technology, politics, the media, and the way the entertainment world would change after the zombies rose. (Rae also carved a jack-o-lantern with Shaun and Georgia riding the bike over a crowd of zombies. I have excellent friends.) Amanda and Steve Perry were my point people for everything having to do with wireless and cellular technology, and taught me a great deal about the miniaturization going on in the real world. Between them and Mike Whitaker, who did the majority of the technical design on Shaun and Georgia's van, I have much more accurate tech than I have any right to.

Matt Branstad was responsible for verifying the accuracy of my firearms design, and was invaluable when it came to finding new, exciting ways to kill zombies. Michelle and David McNeill-Coronado provided regional details on Sacramento (David actually suggested the railroad trestle), as well as providing active, engaging sounding boards for the political climate of the book.

Medical assistance was provided by Brooke Lunderville and Melissa Glasser, who rebuilt my medical technology from the ground up several times, while Debbie J. Gates helped out with the animal action. Alison Riley-Duncan, Rebecca Newman, Allison Hewett, Janet Maughan, Penelope Skrzynski, Phil Ames, Amanda Sanders, and Martha Hage were on tap for general proofreading and plot consultation; I couldn't have done this without them.

Finally, acknowledgment for forbearance must go to Kate Secor and Michelle Dockrey, who received the bulk of my "talking it out" during the writing process; to my agent, Diana Fox, who is never anything short of heroic; to my editor, DongWon Song, who understood the story from the first; and to Tara O'Shea and Chris Mangum, the incredible technical team behind www.MiraGrant.com. This book might have been written without them. It would not have been the same.

Rise up while you can.

extras

orbit

meet the author

Born and raised in California, **Mira Grant** has made a lifelong study of horror movies, horrible viruses, and the inevitable threat of the living dead. In college, she was voted Most Likely to Summon Something Horrible in the Cornfield, and was a founding member of the Horror Movie Sleep-Away Survival Camp, where her record for time survived in the Swamp Cannibals scenario remains unchallenged.

Mira lives in a crumbling farmhouse with an assortment of cats, horror movies, comics, and books about horrible diseases. When not writing, she splits her time between travel, auditing college virology courses, and watching more horror movies than is strictly good for you. Favorite vacation spots include Seattle, London, and a large haunted corn maze just outside of Huntsville, Alabama.

Mira sleeps with a machete under her bed, and highly suggests that you do the same. Find out more about the author at www.miragrant.com.

interview

Have you always known that you wanted to write novels?

I've always known that I wanted to be a writer—I was one of those kids writing six-page "books" in elementary school and harassing the other kids to buy them—but it was a long time before I realized that writers actually produce novels. I spent a long time viewing novels as these magical things that just sort of happened.

Once I figured out that people actually *create* novels, I absolutely knew that I wanted to be a novelist. I couldn't imagine anything better in the world.

How did the idea for Feed *develop?*

I love zombies and I love epidemiology, and my big problem with a lot of zombie fiction is that "Well, it was a disease" seems like an easy answer, but really isn't. So I started thinking about what sort of a disease you'd need to actually have a zombie apocalypse—and the thing about diseases is that they don't actually *want* to be slatewipers (diseases that wipe out the entire susceptible population) because doing that also destroys the disease itself. I started tinkering with my postzombie world, trying to figure out what it would take to rebuild society, what kinds of social structure would arise . . .

I'm also fascinated by the difference between terror and fear. Fear says, "Do not actually put your hand in the alligator," while terror says, "Avoid Florida entirely because alligators exist." I figured terror would be a huge component of the postzombie world. Everything arose from there.

What kind of research did you do while writing this novel?

Feed was a fantastic excuse for me to watch every zombie movie made in the last thirty years and call it serious research. It was an even better excuse for me to audit epidemiology courses and read books with titles like *Virus X*, *The Speckled Monster*, and *Return of the Black Death: The World's Greatest Serial Killer*. It was a good time.

I also did a lot of practical research. We "staged" several of the fight scenes, to confirm that our distances were accurate. I went to firing ranges and watched how people handled their firearms. I was unable to drive across the Sacramento River railway trestle, but believe me, the desire was there.

Are there any particular people, events, or places that you draw your inspiration from?

I draw inspiration from just about everything. Many of the locations in *Feed* are places that I've actually been, or adapted from places I've been. The Republican National Convention conference center, for example, was largely inspired by the crowds at the San Diego International Comic Convention. In terms of people, I read a lot about Hunter S. Thompson and Steve Irwin while I was working on the book, and I tried to embody some of their more iconic character traits in my lead characters.

Feed offers a distinctive take on a postapocalyptic zombified world by viewing it through the eyes of three young bloggers. Do you think blogs will ever overtake mainstream media—without the assistance of a zombie plague?

I think it's already happening. Newspapers are adapting and moving online, but much like how more and more people are looking to Jon Stewart and *The Daily Show* for their news, I think more and more online readers are looking to the blog community. Once you figure out the signal-to-noise ratio, it's a great way to get your news. I think what we're getting here in the real world is much more organic than the functions of blogger society in *Feed* because they were actually forced to organize, while here, the blog society is allowed to evolve.

At one point Georgia explains to the readers how the infrastructure of the blogging world is set up: Newsies, Stewarts, Irwins, and Fictionals. What kind of blogger do you think you'd be in their zombie-infested world?

I'd be a Fictional. A seemingly suicidal Fictional, given that I have a lot of Irwin tendencies—my first reaction to something horrible is usually "Ooo, let me see" and reaching for the stick—but I'd totally spend most of my time writing epic poetry about the movement of viral bodies.

Is there any particular scene in Feed *that you love?*

That's like asking me to pick my favorite zombie kitten! I have several favorites, but at the end of the day, I think I have to go with Georgia and Shaun in the van, after Rick leaves, and through her blog entry. I cried like a baby the day I wrote that. I actually hadn't realized how hard it would be until I had to do it.

Zombies aside, is there anything (fictional or otherwise) that sends you screaming in the other direction?

I can't stand leeches or slugs—anything without bones just creeps me out completely. Also, I can't take things being pulled out of people. That horror movie standard where the infected character starts pulling out their teeth or pulling off their fingernails? Yeah, that's where I go for popcorn. I freak out.

At the same time, if you have something horrific and decayed, I am so there.

Any interesting tidbit or teaser you can share about the next book in the Newsflesh series: Deadline*?*

Well, as you probably gathered from the end of *Feed*, Shaun's now the main narrator, and he's trying to cope with living in a world that doesn't have Georgia in it, which is something he just isn't equipped for. So he talks to her, and she talks back. Georgia is, in fact, still a main character because she's constantly advising Shaun and communicating with him—and if you tell him he can't talk to his dead sister, he'll hurt you.

Deadline is really focused on Shaun looking for revenge. He wants to know just how far the conspiracy goes because he wants to make absolutely everyone who was involved pay for taking her away from him. The After the End Times team isn't new, exactly— they were all in the first book—but they weren't in the field with the Ryman campaign, and they aren't entirely sure how to handle what's ahead of them.

Also, there are epileptic teacup bulldogs.

introducing

If you enjoyed FEED, look out for

DEADLINE

BOOK 2 OF THE NEWSFLESH TRILOGY

by Mira Grant

Sometimes you need the lies to stay alive.

—SHAUN MASON

Our story opens where countless stories have ended in the last twenty-seven years: with an idiot—in this case, Rebecca Atherton, the head of the After the End Times Irwins, three-time winner of the Golden Steve-o Award for valor in the face of the undead—deciding it would be a good idea to go out and poke a zombie with a stick to see what happens. Because, hey, there's always the chance that this time, maybe things will go differently. I know I always thought it would be different for me. George told me I was an idiot, but I had faith.

At least Becks was being smart about her stupidity and was using a crowbar to poke the zombie, which greatly improved her chances of survival. She'd managed to sink the clawed end under the zombie's collarbone, which made it a pretty effective defensive measure. It would eventually figure out that it couldn't move forward. When that happened, it would pull away, either yanking the crowbar out of her hands or dislocating its own collarbone, and then it would try coming at her from another angle. Given the intelligence of your average zombie, I figured she had about an hour before she really needed to be concerned. Plenty of time.

It was a thrilling scene. Woman versus zombie, locked in a visceral conflict that's basically ground into our cultural DNA by this point. And I didn't give a damn.

The guy standing next to her looked a whole lot less sanguine about the situation, maybe because he'd never been that close to a zombie in his life. The latest literature says we're supposed to call them "post-Kellis-Amberlee amplification manifestation syndrome humans," but fuck that. If they really wanted some fancy new term for "zombie" to catch on, they should have made it easy to shout at the top of your lungs, or at least made sure it formed a catchy acronym. They're zombies. They're brainless meat puppets controlled by a virus and driven by the endless need to spread their infection. All the fancy names in the world won't change that.

Anyway, Alaric had never been a field situation

kind of a guy. He was a natural Newsie, one of those people who is most comfortable when sitting somewhere far away from the action, talking about cause and motivation. Unfortunately for him, he'd finally decided that he wanted to go after some bigger stories, and that meant he needed to test for his Class-A journalism license. To get your Class-A, you have to prove that you can handle life in the field. Becks had been trying to help him for almost a week, and I was rapidly coming to believe that the kid was hopeless. He was destined for a life of sitting around the office compiling reports from people who had the balls to pass their exams.

You're being hard on him, Georgia chided.

"Don't really care," I replied, under my breath.

"Shaun?" Dave looked up from his screen, squinting as he turned in my direction. "Did you say something?"

"Not a thing." I shook my head, reaching for my half-empty Coke. "Five gets you ten he fails his practicals again."

"No bet," said Dave. "He's gonna pass this time."

I raised an eyebrow. "Why are you so sure?"

"Becks is out there with him. He wants to impress her."

"Does he now?" I returned my attention to the screen, more interested now. "Think she likes him back? It'd explain why she keeps wearing skirts to the office . . ."

"Maybe," said Dave, judiciously.

On the screen, Becks was trying to get Alaric to take the crowbar and have his own shot at holding off the zombie. No big deal, especially for someone as seasoned as Becks. At least, it wouldn't have been a big deal if there hadn't been six more infected lurching into view on the left-hand monitor. I flipped a switch to turn on the sound. Not a thing. They weren't moaning.

". . . the fuck?" I murmured. Flipping another switch to turn on the two-way intercom, I said, "Becks, check your perimeter."

"What are you talking about?" She turned to scan her surroundings, raising one hand to shield her eyes. "Our perimeter is—" Catching sight of the infected lurching closer by the second, she froze, eyes going wide. "Oh, *fuck* me."

"Maybe later," I said, standing. "Keep Alaric alive. I'm heading out to assist evac."

"Empty promises," she muttered, barely audible. "Alaric! Behind me, now!"

I heard him swearing in surprise, followed by the sharp report of Becks shooting their captive. Every infected within range would add to the intelligence of the pack. That meant that Becks and Alaric needed to cut the numbers by as much as possible. I didn't see her shoot; I was already heading for the door, grabbing my shotgun off the rack along the way.

Dave half-stood, asking, "Should I . . . ?"

"Negative. Stay here, get ready to drive like hell."

"Check," he said, scrambling from his seat toward the front of the van. I didn't really pay attention to that, either; I was busy kicking open the doors and stepping out into the blazing light of the afternoon.

When you're going to play with dead things, do it during the daylight if you possibly can. They don't see as well in bright light as humans do, and they don't hide as well when they don't have the shadows helping them. More important, the footage will be better. If you're gonna die, make sure you do it on camera.

The tracker on my wrist indicated that Becks and Alaric were two miles away. That's the federally mandated minimum distance between an intentional zombie encounter and a licensed traveling safe zone, such as our van. Not that the infected would avoid coming within two miles out of some sort of respect for the law; we just weren't allowed to lure them any closer than that. I did some quick mental math. If they'd already attracted a group of six, and the infected weren't moaning yet, that implied that there were enough zombies in the immediate vicinity to form a thinking pack. Not good.

"Right," I said, and swung myself into the driver's seat of Dave's Jeep. The keys were already in the ignition.

Unlike most field vehicles, Dave's Jeep has no armor to speak of, unless you count the run-flat tires and the titanium-reinforced frame. What it has is speed, and lots of it. The thing has been stripped down to the bare minimum, rebuilt, and stripped down again so many times now that I don't think there's a single piece that still conforms to factory standards. It offers about as much protection during an attack of the infected as a wet paper bag. A very fast wet paper bag. It's evac-only when we're in hostile territory. We haven't lost a man yet while we were using it.

Dropping my shotgun onto the passenger seat, I hit the gas.

After the Rising, large swaths of California were effectively abandoned for one reason or another. "Difficult to secure" was one; "hostile terrain giving the advantage to the enemy" was another. My personal favorite applied to the small, unincorporated community of Birds Landing in Solano County: "nobody cared enough to bother." They had a population of less than two hundred pre-Rising, and there were no survivors. When the federal government needed to appoint funds for cleanup and security, there was nobody to argue in favor of cleaning the place out. They still get the standard patrols, just because letting the zombies mob is in nobody's best interests, but for the most part, Birds Landing has been left to the dead.

It was the perfect place to run Alaric's last field trial, or should have been, anyway. Abandoned, isolated, close enough to Fairfield to allow for pretty easy evac if the need arose, but far enough away that we could still get some pretty decent footage. Not as dangerous as Santa Cruz, not as candy-ass as Bodega Bay. The ideal infected fishing hole. Only it seemed that the zombies thought so, too.

The roads were crap. Swearing softly but steadily to myself, I pressed the gas pedal farther down, getting the Jeep up to the highest speed that I was confident I could handle. The frame was shaking and jerking like it might fly apart at any second, and, almost unwillingly, I started to grin. I pushed the speed up a little farther. The shaking increased, and my grin widened.

Careful, cautioned George. *I don't want to be an only child.*

My grin died. "I already am," I said, and floored it.

My dead sister who only I can hear—and yes, I know I'm nuts, thanks for pointing out the obvious—isn't the only one who's been worried about me displaying suicidal tendencies since she passed away. "Passed away" is a polite, bloodless way of saying "was murdered," but it's better than trying to explain the situation every time she comes up in conversation. Yeah, I had a sister, and yeah, she died. Also yeah, I talk to her all the damn time, because as long as I'm only that crazy, I'll stay basically sane.

I stopped talking to her for almost a week once, on the advice of a crappy psychologist who said he could "help." By the fifth day, I wanted to eat a bullet for breakfast. That's one experiment that won't be repeated.

I gave up the bulk of my active field work when George died. I figured that might calm people down, but all it did was get them more worked up. I was Shaun Mason, Irwin to the president! I wasn't supposed to say, "Fuck this noise" and take over my Georgia's desk job! Only that was exactly what I did. Something about shooting my own sister in the spine just left me with a bad taste in my mouth when it comes to field work.

That didn't change the fact that I was licensed for support maneuvers. As long as I kept taking the yearly exams and passing my marksmanship tests, I could legally go out into the field any time I damn well wanted. I was close enough now that I could hear gunshots up ahead, accompanied by the sound of the zombies finally beginning to moan. The Jeep was already rattling so hard that I probably shouldn't try to make it go any faster.

I slammed my foot down as hard as I could.

The Jeep went faster.

I came screeching around the final bend in the road to find Becks and Alaric standing on top of someone's old abandoned tool shed, the two of them back to back at the center of the roof like the little figures on top of a wedding cake. The figures on wedding cakes aren't usually armed, however, and even when they are—it's amazing what you can order from a specialty bakery these days—they don't actually shoot. They also aren't customarily surrounded by a sea of zombies. The six I'd seen on the monitors had been quiet because they didn't need to call for reinforcements; the reinforcements were already there, and now a good thirty infected bodies stood between my people and the Jeep.

Becks had a pistol in each hand, making her look perversely like an illustration from some fucked-up pre-Rising horror/Western. *Showdown at the Decay Corral* or something. Her expression was one of intense and unflagging concentration, and every time she fired, a zombie went down. Automatically, I glanced at the dashboard, where the wireless tracker confirmed that all her cameras were still transmitting. Then I swore at myself, looking back toward the action.

George and I grew up with parents who wanted ratings more than they wanted children. It was a form of grief for them; their first son died, and so they stopped giving a damn about people. Lose people, they're gone forever. Lose your slot on the top ten and you could win it back. Numbers were safer.

I was starting to understand why they had made that decision. Because I woke up every day in a world that didn't have George in it anymore, and I looked in my mirror expecting to see Mom's eyes looking back at me.

That won't happen, you idiot, because I won't let it, said George. *Now get them out of there.*

"On it," I muttered, and reached for the shotgun.

Alaric was a lot less calm about his situation than Becks was. He had his rifle out and was taking shots at the teeming mass around them, but he wasn't having anything like her luck with his shots; he was firing three or four times just to take down a single zombie, and I saw a couple of his targets stagger back to their feet after he'd hit them. He wasn't aiming for the head properly, and I had no idea how much ammo he was carrying. Judging by the size of the mob around them, it was nowhere near enough.

Neither of them was wearing a face shield. That put grenades out, since aerosolized zombie will kill you just as sure as the clawing, biting kind. The Jeep wasn't equipped with any real defensive weapons of its own; they would have weighed it down. That left me with the shotgun, George's favorite .40, and the latest useful addition to my zombie-hunting arsenal, the extendable shock baton. The virus that controls their bodies doesn't appreciate electrical shocks. It won't kill a zombie, but it'll disorient the shit out of it, and sometimes that's enough.

The mob still hadn't noticed my arrival, being somewhat distracted by the presence of known meat. Attempting to lure them off wouldn't have done any good. Zombies aren't like sharks; they won't follow in a flock. Maybe a few would have followed me, but there was no way to guarantee I'd be able to handle them, and Becks and Alaric would still have been stranded. Recipe for disaster.

Not that what I was about to do was likely to be any better in the long run. Moving to a position about ten feet behind the mob, I pulled George's gun from its holster and fired until the cartridge was exhausted, barely pausing to aim between targets. My aim might still be good enough for the exams, but it was getting rusty in field situations; seventeen bullets, and only twelve zombies went down. Becks and Alaric looked up at the sound of gunshots, Alaric's eyes widening before he started to do a fascinating variant on the victory shuffle.

Becks was more subdued in her delight over my brainless cavalry charge. She just looked relieved.

There was no time to pay attention to my team members. My shots had alerted the zombies to the presence of fresh, less-elevated meat, and several outlying members of the mob were turning in my direction, starting to lurch, shuffle, or run toward me, depending on how long they'd been in the grips of full infection. Snapping another cartridge into the .40, I holstered it and raised the shotgun, aiming for the point of greatest density.

Fact about zombies that everyone knows: You have to aim for the head, since the virus that drives their bodies can repair or route around almost every other form of damage. This is very true.

Fact about zombies that almost no one knows, because you'd have to be a damn fool to take advantage of it: An injured zombie *does* slow down a bit, since you've just forced the relatively single-minded virus that controls the body to try its hand at double-tasking. What's more, the *right* kind of injury can make the difference between having time to reload and getting mowed down.

Bracing the shotgun against my shoulder, I emptied all three shots into the points of deepest concentration. A standard shotgun shell can blow a zombie's head clean off, if that's what you're going for. I wasn't firing standard shells.

Using live grenades when you have people on the ground is antisocial at best and grounds for a murder charge at worst. Shotgun grenade rounds, on the other hand, can be calibrated to have a much more focused charge, one that doesn't throw the resulting spray as high into the air. The wind still has to be with you, but as long as your people are more than eight feet away, you should be fine.

The shotgun went off with the usual sharp report, followed by several loud, wet bangs as the projectiles found their targets, fragmented into multiple slammer pieces, and exploded. Several zombies went down as shrapnel caught them in the head or spinal column. Others fell as their legs were blown out from under them. Those last didn't stay down; they started dragging themselves forward, the entire mob now moaning in earnest.

Say something witty now, moron, prompted George.

I reddened. I never used to need coaching from my sister on what it took to do my job. I dropped the now-useless shotgun and hit the general channel key on my watch, asking, "You guys mind if I join your party?"

Becks responded immediately, relief more evident in her voice than it had been in her face. Maybe she just wasn't as good at hiding it there. "What took you so long?"

"Oh, traffic. You know how it goes." The entire mob was moving toward me now, apparently deciding that meat on the hoof was more interesting than meat that wouldn't come out of its tree. I snapped the electric baton into its extended position, redrawing George's .40, and offered the oncoming infected a merry smile. "Hi. You want to party?"

Shaun . . . said George.

"Yeah, yeah, I know," I muttered, adding more loudly, "You guys get down from there and try to circle to the Jeep. Hit the horn once you're in. There's more ammo under the passenger seat."

"And you're going to do what, exactly?" asked Becks. She sounded sensibly wary. At least one of us was being sensible for a change.

"I'm going to earn my ratings," I said. Then the zombies were on top of me, and there was no more time for discussion. Quietly, I was glad.

There's a sort of art to fighting the infected. It was almost a good thing that this mob had started off so large; we were cutting down the numbers rapidly, since we had the ability to think tactically, but the survivors were still behaving like members of a pack. They wanted to eat, not infect. "They wanted to kill me" may not sound like much of an advantage—just trust me on this one. A zombie that's out to infect will spit at you if it can. It'll try to smear you with fluids. That gives it a lot more weapons. A zombie that wants to eat you is just going to come at you with its mouth, and that means it only has one viable avenue of attack. That evens the odds, just a little.

Just a little can be more than enough.

Using my baton, I swept a constant perimeter around myself, shocking any zombie that came into range and trusting the Kevlar in my jacket to keep my arm from getting tagged before I could pull it back. The electricity slowed them down enough for me to keep firing, and more important, it kept them from getting positions established behind me. I could track Becks and Alaric by the sound of gunshots, which came almost as regularly as my own. I was taking out two zombies for every three shots. Not the best odds in the world. Not the worst odds, either.

I was grinning as I backed toward the Jeep, letting the zombies think that they were herding me while I kept thinning out their ranks. I couldn't help it. Maybe facing possible death isn't supposed to make me happy, but years of training can't be shrugged off overnight, and I was an Irwin for a long time before I retired.

Aim, fire. Swing, zap. Aim, fire. It was almost like dancing, a series of utterly soothing, utterly predictable movements. I couldn't hear gunshots anymore; either Becks and Alaric had made it to the Jeep, or my brain had started filtering out the sounds of their combat as inconsequential. I had my own zombies to play with. They could deal with their own. Even George had fallen quiet for once, leaving me to move in a small bubble of almost perfect contentment. It didn't matter that my sister was dead, or that the assholes who'd ordered her killed were still out there somewhere, doing God knows what to God knows whom. I had zombies. I had bullets. Everything else was essentially just details.

"Shaun!"

The shout came from behind me, rather than from inside my head or over the intercom. I barely squashed the urge to turn toward it, which could have been fatal in the field. I put two bullets into the zombie that was lunging at me, and shouted back, "What?"

"We've made the Jeep! Can you retreat?"

Could I retreat? "Well, that's an interesting question, Becks!" I shouted. Aim, fire. Aim again. "Is there anything behind me?"

"Don't move!"

"I can do that!" I fired again. Another zombie went down. And hell opened up behind me. Not literally, but the sound of a belt-fed automatic shotgun can be very similar. Becks, it seemed, had found more than just ammo under the seat. Dave and I were going to need to have a long talk about making sure I knew what my assets were before we let me head into the field.

"Clear!"

"Great!" My throat was starting to ache from all the shouting. I surveyed the zombies remaining in front of me. None of them looked fresh enough to put up a real chase, and so I did exactly what you're not supposed to do in a field situation if you have any choice in the matter:

I took a chance.

Turning my back on the mob, I ran for the Jeep, whacking anything that looked likely to move with my electric baton. Becks was in the back, covering the area, while Alaric sat in the passenger seat, looking shell-shocked. Nothing grabbed me, and in just a few seconds, I was using the stripped-down frame to swing myself into the driver's seat.

Not bothering with the seat belt, I hit the gas, and we went roaring out of there, leaving the moaning remains of the Birds Landing zombie mob behind.